For all those who helped make
these books possible, especially
Anna Zahn
Betsy Mitchell
Lucy Autrey Wilson
and, of course, the man whose vision started it all,
George Lucas

STAR WARS

Volume 1

Heir To The Empire

The New York Times No. 1 bestseller

'They're back! An all-new space swashbuckler that's chock full of all the good stuff you've come to expect from a battle of good against evil'—*New York Daily News*

'All of our favourite characters (and androids) are still key players in the rebellion and are woven into an action-packed plot . . . Destined to be a bestseller'—*Associated Press*

Volume 2

Dark Force Rising

The Sunday Times bestseller

'Continues (Zahn's) remarkable extrapolation from George Lucas's trilogy'—*Chicago Sun-Times*

'Skilfully paced entertainment . . . Fans can expect Zahn's lively tale to spill over to the next and final instalment of his series'—*Publishers Weekly*

Also by Timothy Zahn

The Blackcollar
Cobra
Blackcollar: The Backlash Mission
Dead Man's Switch
Cascade Point
Cobra Bargain
Cobra Strike!
A Coming of Age
Dark Force Rising
Heir to the Empire
Spinneret
Time Bomb & Zahndry Others
Triplet
Warhorse

THE LAST COMMAND

STAR WARS®

VOLUME 3

TIMOTHY ZAHN

BANTAM BOOKS
TORONTO • NEW YORK • LONDON • SYDNEY • AUCKLAND

STAR WARS 3: THE LAST COMMAND

A BANTAM BOOK 0 553 40443 1

Originally published in Great Britain by Bantam Press,
a division of Transworld Publishers Ltd.

PRINTING HISTORY
Bantam Press edition published 1993
Bantam Books edition published 1994
Bantam edition reprinted 1994

Set in 10/11pt Times by
Kestrel Data, Exeter

Bantam Books are published by Transworld Publishers Ltd,
61–63 Uxbridge Road, Ealing, London W5 5SA,
in Australia by Transworld Publishers (Australia) Pty Ltd,
15–25 Helles Avenue, Moorebank, NSW 2170,
and in New Zealand by Transworld Publishers (NZ) Ltd,
3 William Pickering Drive, Albany, Auckland.

Printed and bound in Great Britain by
Cox & Wyman Ltd, Reading, Berks.

CHAPTER 1

Gliding through the blackness of deep space, the Imperial Star Destroyer *Chimaera* pointed its mighty arrowhead shape toward the dim star of its target system, three thousandths of a light-year away. And prepared itself for war.

'All systems show battle ready, Admiral,' the comm officer reported from the portside crew pit. 'The task force is beginning to check in.'

'Very good, Lieutenant,' Grand Admiral Thrawn nodded. 'Inform me when all have done so. Captain Pellaeon?'

'Sir?' Pellaeon said, searching his superior's face for the stress the Grand Admiral must be feeling. The stress he himself was certainly feeling. This was not just another tactical strike against the Rebellion, after all – not a minor shipping raid or even a complex but straightforward hit-and-fade against some insignificant planetary base. After nearly a month of frenzied preparations, Thrawn's master campaign for the Empire's final victory was about to be launched.

But if the Grand Admiral was feeling any tension, he was keeping it to himself. 'Begin the countdown,' he told Pellaeon, his voice as calm as if he were ordering dinner.

'Yes, sir,' Pellaeon said, turning back to the group of one-quarter-size holographic figures standing before him in the *Chimaera*'s aft bridge hologram pod. 'Gentlemen: launch marks. *Bellicose*: three minutes.'

'Acknowledged, *Chimaera*,' Captain Aban nodded, his proper military demeanor not quite masking his eagerness to take this war back to the Rebellion. 'Good hunting.'

The holo image sputtered and vanished as the *Bellicose* raised its deflector shields, cutting off long-range communications. Pellaeon shifted his attention to the next image in line. '*Relentless*: four point five minutes.'

'Acknowledged,' Captain Dorja said, cupping his right fist

in his left in an ancient Mirshaf gesture of victory as he, too, vanished from the hologram pod.

Pellaeon glanced at his data pad. '*Judicator*: six minutes.'

'We're ready, *Chimaera*,' Captain Brandei said, his voice soft. Soft, and just a little bit wrong . . .

Pellaeon frowned at him. Quarter-sized holos didn't show a lot of detail, but even so the expression on Brandei's face was easy to read. It was the expression of a man out for blood.

'This is war, Captain Brandei,' Thrawn said, coming up silently to Pellaeon's side. 'Not an opportunity for personal revenge.'

'I understand my duty, Admiral,' Brandei said stiffly.

Thrawn's blue-black eyebrows lifted slightly. 'Do you, Captain? Do you indeed?'

Slowly, reluctantly, some of the fire faded from Brandei's face. 'Yes, sir,' he muttered. 'My duty is to the Empire, and to you, and to the ships and crews under my command.'

'Very good,' Thrawn said. 'To the living, in other words. Not to the dead.'

Brandei was still glowering, but he gave a dutiful nod. 'Yes, sir.'

'Never forget that, Captain,' Thrawn warned him. 'The fortunes of war rise and fall, and you may be assured that the Rebellion will be repaid in full for their destruction of the *Peremptory* at the *Katana* fleet skirmish. But that repayment will occur in the context of our overall strategy. Not as an act of private vengeance.' His glowing red eyes narrowed slightly. 'Certainly not by any Fleet captain under my command. I trust I make myself clear.'

Brandei's cheek twitched. Pellaeon had never thought of the man as brilliant, but he was smart enough to recognize a threat when he heard one. 'Very clear, Admiral.'

'Good.' Thrawn eyed him a moment longer, then nodded. 'I believe you've been given your launch mark?'

'Yes, sir. *Judicator* out.'

Thrawn looked at Pellaeon. 'Continue, Captain,' he said, and turned away.

'Yes, sir.' Pellaeon looked at his data pad. '*Nemesis* . . .'

He finished the list without further incident. By the time the last holo image disappeared, the final check-in from their own task force was complete.

'The timetable appears to be running smoothly,' Thrawn said as Pellaeon returned to his command station. 'The *Stormhawk* reports that the guide freighters launched on time with tow cables functioning properly. And we've just intercepted a general emergency call from the Ando system.'

The *Bellicose* and its task force, right on schedule. 'Any response, sir?' Pellaeon asked.

'The Rebel base at Ord Pardron acknowledged,' Thrawn said. 'It should be interesting to see how much help they send.'

Pellaeon nodded. The Rebels had seen enough of Thrawn's tactics by now to expect Ando to be a feint, and to respond accordingly. But on the other hand, an attack force consisting of an Imperial Star Destroyer and eight *Katana* fleet Dreadnaughts was hardly something they could afford to dismiss out of hand, either.

Not that it really mattered. They would send a few ships to Ando to fight the *Bellicose*, and a few more to Filve to fight the *Judicator*, and a few more to Crondre to fight the *Nemesis*, and so on and so on. By the time the *Death's Head* hit the base itself, Ord Pardron would be down to a skeleton defense and screaming itself for all the reinforcements the Rebellion could scramble.

And that was where those reinforcements would go. Leaving the Empire's true target ripe for the picking.

Pellaeon looked out the forward viewport at the star of the Ukio system dead ahead, his throat tightening as he contemplated again the enormous conceit of this whole plan. With planetary shields able to hold off all but the most massive turbolaser and proton torpedo bombardment, conventional wisdom held that the only way to subdue a modern world was to put a fast-moving ground force down at the edges and send them overland to destroy the shield generators. Between the fire laid down by the ground force and the subsequent orbital assault, the target world was always badly damaged by the time it was finally taken. The alternative, landing hundreds of thousands of troops in a major ground campaign that could stretch into months or years, was no better. To capture a planet relatively undamaged but with shield generators still intact was considered an impossibility.

That bit of military wisdom would fall today. Along with Ukio itself.

'Intercepted distress signal from Filve, Admiral,' the comm officer reported. 'Ord Pardron again responding.'

'Good.' Thrawn consulted his chrono. 'Seven minutes, I think, and we'll be able to move.' His lips compressed, just noticeably. 'I suppose we'd better confirm that our exalted Jedi Master is ready to do his part.'

Pellaeon hid a grimace. Joruus C'baoth, insane clone of the long-dead Jedi Master Jorus C'baoth, who a month ago had proclaimed himself the true heir to the Empire. He didn't like talking to the man any more than Thrawn did; but he might as well volunteer. If he didn't, it would simply become an order. 'I'll go, sir,' he said, standing up.

'Thank you, Captain,' Thrawn said. As if Pellaeon would have had a choice.

He felt the mental summons the moment he stepped beyond the Force-protection of the ysalamiri scattered about the bridge on their nutrient frames. Master C'baoth, clearly, was impatient for the operation to begin. Preparing himself as best he could, fighting against C'baoth's casual mental pressure to hurry, Pellaeon made his way down to Thrawn's command room.

The chamber was brightly lit, in marked contrast to the subdued lighting the Grand Admiral usually preferred. 'Captain Pellaeon,' C'baoth called, beckoning to him from the double display ring in the center of the room. 'Come in. I've been waiting for you.'

'The rest of the operation has taken my full attention,' Pellaeon told him stiffly, trying to hide his distaste for the man. Knowing full well how futile such attempts were.

'Of course,' C'baoth smiled, a smile that showed more effectively than any words his amusement with Pellaeon's discomfort. 'No matter. I take it Grand Admiral Thrawn is finally ready?'

'Almost,' Pellaeon said. 'We want to clear out Ord Pardron as much as possible before we move.'

C'baoth snorted. 'You continue to assume the New Republic will dance to the Grand Admiral's tune.'

'They will,' Pellaeon said. 'The Grand Admiral has studied the enemy thoroughly.'

'He's studied their artwork,' C'baoth countered with another snort. 'That will be useful if the time ever comes when the New Republic has nothing but artists left to throw against us.'

A signal from the display ring saved Pellaeon from the need to reply. 'We're moving,' he told C'baoth, starting a mental countdown of the seventy-six seconds it would take to reach the Ukio system from their position and trying not to let C'baoth's words get under his skin. He didn't understand himself how Thrawn could so accurately learn the innermost secrets of a species from its artwork. But he'd seen that knowledge proved often enough to trust the Grand Admiral's instincts on such things. C'baoth hadn't.

But then, C'baoth wasn't really interested in an honest debate on the subject. For the past month, ever since declaring himself to be the true heir to the Emperor, C'baoth had been pressing this quiet war against Thrawn's credibility, implying that true insight came only through the Force. And, therefore, only through him.

Pellaeon himself didn't buy that argument. The Emperor had been deep into this Force thing, too, and he hadn't even been able to predict his own death at Endor. But the seeds of uncertainty C'baoth was trying to sow were nevertheless starting to take hold, particularly among the less experienced of Thrawn's officers.

Which was, for Pellaeon, just one more reason why this attack had to succeed. The outcome hinged as much on Thrawn's reading of the Ukian cultural ethos as it did on straight military tactics. On Thrawn's conviction that, at a basic psychological level, the Ukians were terrified of the impossible.

'He will not always be right,' C'baoth said into Pellaeon's musings.

Pellaeon bit down hard on the inside of his cheek, the skin of his back crawling at having had his thoughts so casually invaded. 'You don't have any concept of privacy, do you?' he growled.

'I am the Empire, Captain Pellaeon,' C'baoth said, his eyes glowing with a dark, fanatical fire. 'Your thoughts are a part of your service to me.'

'My service is to Grand Admiral Thrawn,' Pellaeon said stiffly.

C'baoth smiled. 'You may believe that if you wish. But to business – true Imperial business. When the battle here is over, Captain Pellaeon, I want a message sent to Wayland.'

'Announcing your imminent return, no doubt,' Pellaeon said sourly. C'baoth had been insisting for nearly a month now that he would soon be going back to his former home on Wayland, where he would take command of the cloning facility in the Emperor's old storehouse inside Mount Tantiss. So far, he'd been too busy trying to subvert Thrawn's position to do anything more than talk about it.

'Do not worry, Captain Pellaeon,' C'baoth said, all amused again. 'When the time is right, I will indeed return to Wayland. Which is why you will contact Wayland after this battle is over and order them to create a clone for me. A very special clone.'

Grand Admiral Thrawn will have to authorize that, were the words that came to mind. 'What kind do you want?' were the ones that inexplicably came out. Pellaeon blinked, running the memory over in his mind again. Yes, that was what he'd said, all right.

C'baoth smiled again at his silent confusion. 'I merely wish a servant,' he said. 'Someone who will be waiting there for me when I return. Formed from one of the Emperor's prize souvenirs – sample B-2332-54, I believe it was. You will, of course, impress upon the garrison commander there that this must be done in total secrecy.'

I will do nothing of the sort. 'Yes,' Pellaeon heard himself

14

say instead. The sound of the word shocked him; but certainly he didn't mean it. On the contrary, as soon as the battle was over he'd be reporting this little incident directly to Thrawn.

'You will also keep this conversation a private matter between ourselves,' C'baoth said lazily. 'Once you have obeyed, you will forget it even happened.'

'Of course,' Pellaeon nodded, just to shut him up. Yes, he'd report this to Thrawn, all right. The Grand Admiral would know what to do.

The countdown reached zero, and on the main wall display the planet Ukio appeared. 'We should put up a tactical display, Master C'baoth,' he said.

C'baoth waved a hand. 'As you wish.'

Pellaeon reached over the double display ring and touched the proper key, and in the center of the room the holographic tactical display appeared. The *Chimaera* was driving toward high orbit above the sunside equator; the ten *Katana* fleet Dreadnaughts of its task force were splitting up into outer and inner defense positions; and the *Stormhawk* was coming in as backstop from the night side. Other ships, mostly freighters and other commercial types, could be seen dropping through the brief gaps Ground Control was opening for them in Ukio's energy shield, a hazy blue shell surrounding the planet about fifty kilometers above the surface. Two of the blips flashed red: the guide freighters from the *Stormhawk*, looking as innocent as all the rest of the ships scurrying madly for cover. The freighters, and the four invisible companions they towed.

'Invisible only to those without eyes to see them,' C'baoth murmured.

'So now you can see the ships themselves, can you?' Pellaeon growled. 'How Jedi skills grow.'

He'd been hoping to irritate C'baoth a little – not much, just a little. But it was a futile effort. 'I can see the men inside your precious cloaking shields,' the Jedi Master said placidly. 'I can see their thoughts and guide their wills. What does the metal itself matter?'

Pellaeon felt his lip twist. 'I suppose there's a lot that doesn't matter to you,' he said.

15

From the corner of his eye he saw C'baoth smile. 'What doesn't matter to a Jedi Master does not matter to the universe.'

The freighters and cloaked cruisers were nearly to the shield now. 'They'll be dropping the tow cables as soon as they're inside the shield,' Pellaeon reminded C'baoth. 'Are you ready?'

The Jedi Master straightened up in his seat and closed his eyes to slits. 'I await the Grand Admiral's command,' he said sardonically.

For another second Pellaeon looked at the other's composed expression, a shiver running up through him. He could remember vividly the first time C'baoth had tried this kind of direct long-distance control. Could remember the pain that had been on C'baoth's face; the pinched look of concentration and agony as he struggled to hold the mental contacts.

Barely two months ago, Thrawn had confidently said that C'baoth would never be a threat to the Empire because he lacked the ability to focus and concentrate his Jedi power on a long-term basis. Somehow, between that time and now, C'baoth had obviously succeeded in learning the necessary control.

Which left C'baoth as a threat to the Empire. A very dangerous threat indeed.

The intercom beeped. 'Captain Pellaeon?'

Pellaeon reached over the display ring and touched the key, pushing away his fears about C'baoth as best he could. For the moment, at least, the Fleet needed C'baoth. Fortunately, perhaps, C'baoth also needed the Fleet. 'We're ready, Admiral,' he said.

'Stand by,' Thrawn said. 'Tow cables detaching now.'

'They are free,' C'baoth said. 'They are under power . . . moving now to their appointed positions.'

'Confirm that they're beneath the planetary shield,' Thrawn ordered.

For the first time a hint of the old strain crossed C'baoth's face. Hardly surprising; with the cloaking shield preventing the *Chimaera* from seeing the cruisers and at the same time blinding the cruisers' own sensors, the only way to know exactly where they were was for C'baoth to do a precise location check on the minds he was touching. 'All four ships are beneath the shield,' he said.

'Be absolutely certain, Jedi Master. If you're wrong—'

'I am not wrong, Grand Admiral Thrawn,' C'baoth cut him off harshly. 'I will do my part in this battle. Concern yourself with yours.'

For a moment the intercom was silent. Pellaeon winced, visualizing the Grand Admiral's expression. 'Very well, Jedi Master,' Thrawn said calmly. 'Prepare to do your part.'

There was the double click of an opening comm channel. 'This is the Imperial Star Destroyer *Chimaera*, calling the Overliege of Ukio,' Thrawn said. 'In the name of the Empire, I declare the Ukian system to be once again under the mandate of Imperial law and the protection of Imperial forces. You will lower your shields, recall all military units to their bases, and prepare for an orderly transfer of command.'

There was no response. 'I know you're receiving this message,' Thrawn continued. 'If you fail to respond, I will have to assume that you mean to resist the Empire's offer. In that event, I would have no choice but to open hostilities.'

Again, silence. 'They're sending another transmission,' Pellaeon heard the comm officer say. 'Sounds a little more panicked than the first one was.'

'I'm certain their third will be even more so,' Thrawn told him. 'Prepare for firing sequence one. Master C'baoth?'

'The cruisers are ready, Grand Admiral Thrawn,' C'baoth said. 'As am I.'

'Be sure that you are,' Thrawn said, quietly threatening. 'Unless the timing is absolutely perfect, this entire show will be worse than useless. Turbolaser battery three: stand by firing sequence one on my mark. Three . . . two . . . one . . . fire.'

On the tactical hologram a double lance of green fire angled out from the *Chimaera*'s turbolaser batteries toward the planet below. The blasts struck the hazy blue of the planetary shield, splashed slightly as their energy was defocused and reflected back into space—

17

And with the desired perfect timing the two cloaked cruisers hovering on repulsorlifts beneath the shield at those two points fired in turn, their turbolaser blasts sizzling through the atmosphere into two of Ukio's major air defense bases.

That was what Pellaeon saw. The Ukians, with no way of knowing about the cloaked cruisers, would have seen the *Chimaera* fire two devastating shots cleanly through an impenetrable planetary shield.

'Third transmission cut off right in the middle, sir,' the comm officer reported with a touch of dark humor. 'I think we surprised them.'

'Let's convince them it wasn't a fluke,' Thrawn said. 'Prepare firing sequence two. Master C'baoth?'

'The cruisers are ready.'

'Turbolaser battery two: stand by firing sequence two on my mark. Three . . . two . . . one . . . fire.'

Again the green fire lanced out, and again, with perfect timing, the cloaked cruisers created their illusion. 'Well done,' Thrawn said. 'Master C'baoth, move the cruisers into position for sequences three and four.'

'As you command, Grand Admiral Thrawn.'

Unconsciously, Pellaeon braced himself. Sequence four had two of the Ukians' thirty overlapping shield generators as its targets. Launching such an attack would mean that Thrawn had given up on his stated goal of taking Ukio with its planetary defenses intact.

'Imperial Star Destroyer *Chimaera*, this is Tol dosLla of the Ukian Overliege,' a slightly quavering voice came from the intercom speaker. 'We would ask you to cease your bombardment of Ukio while we discuss terms for surrender.'

'My terms are quite simple,' Thrawn said. 'You will begin by lowering your planetary shield and allowing my forces to land. They will be given control of the shield generators themselves and of all ground-to-space weaponry. All fighting vehicles larger than command speeders will be moved to designated military bases and turned over to Imperial control. Though you will, of course, be ultimately answerable to the Empire, your political and social systems will remain under your control. Provided your people behave themselves, of course.'

'And once these changes have been implemented?'

'Then you will be part of the Empire, with all the rights and duties that implies.'

'There will be no war-level tax levies?' dosLla asked suspiciously. 'No forced conscription of our young people?'

Pellaeon could imagine Thrawn's grim smile. No, the Empire would never need to bother with forced conscription again. Not with the Emperor's collection of Spaarti cloning cylinders in their hands.

'No, to your second question; a qualified no to your first,' Thrawn told the Ukian. 'As you are obviously aware, most Imperial worlds are currently under war-status taxation levels. However, there are exceptions, and it is likely that your share of the war effort will come directly from your extensive food production and processing facilities.'

There was a long pause from the other end. DosLla was no fool, Pellaeon realized – the Ukian knew full well what Thrawn had in mind for his world. First it would be direct Imperial control of the ground/space defenses, then direct control of the food distribution system, the processing facilities, and the vast farming and livestock grazing regions themselves; and in a very short time the entire planet would have become nothing more than a supply depot for the Imperial war machine.

But the alternative was for him to stand silently by and watch as his world was utterly and impossibly demolished before his eyes. And he knew that, too.

'We will lower the planetary shields, *Chimaera*, as a gesture of good faith,' dosLla said at last, his tone defiant but with a hint of defeat to it. 'But before the generators and ground/space weaponry can be turned over to Imperial forces we shall require certain guarantees regarding the safety of the Ukian people and our land.'

'Certainly,' Thrawn said, without any trace of the gloating that most Imperial commanders would have indulged in at this point. A small act of courtesy that, Pellaeon knew, was as precisely calculated as the rest of the attack had been. Permitting the Ukian leaders to surrender with their dignity intact would slow down the inevitable resistance to Imperial rule until it was too late. 'A representative will be on his way shortly to discuss the particulars with your government,' Thrawn continued. 'Meanwhile, I presume you have no objection to our forces taking up preliminary defense positions?'

A sigh, more felt than really heard. 'We have no objections, *Chimaera*,' dosLla said reluctantly. 'We are lowering the shield now.'

On the tactical display, the blue haze surrounding the planet faded away. 'Master C'baoth, have the cruisers move to polar positions,' Thrawn ordered. 'We don't want any of the drop ships blundering into them. General Covell, you may begin transporting your forces to the surface. Standard defensive positions around all targets.'

'Acknowledged, Admiral,' Covell's voice said, a little too dryly, and Pellaeon felt a tight smile twitch at his lip. It had only been two weeks since the top Fleet and army commanders had been let in on the secret of the Mount Tantiss cloning project, and Covell was one of those who still hadn't adjusted completely to the idea.

Though the fact that three of the companies he was about to lead down to the surface were composed entirely of clones might have had something to do with his skepticism.

On the tactical hologram the first waves of drop ships and TIE fighter escorts had exited the *Chimaera* and *Stormhawk*, fanning out toward their assigned targets. Clones in drop ships, about to carry out Imperial orders. As the clone crews in the cloaked cruisers had already done so well.

Pellaeon frowned, an odd and uncomfortable thought suddenly striking him. Had C'baoth been able to guide the cruisers so well because each of their thousand-man crews were composed of variants on just twenty or so different minds? Or – even more disturbing – could part of the Jedi Master's split-second control have been due to the fact that C'baoth was himself a clone?

And either way, did that mean that the Mount Tantiss project was playing directly into C'baoth's hands in his bid for power? Perhaps. One more question he would have to bring to Thrawn's attention.

Pellaeon looked down at C'baoth, belatedly remembering that in the Jedi Master's presence such thoughts were not his private property. But C'baoth wasn't looking at him, knowingly or otherwise. He was staring straight ahead, his eyes unfocused, the skin of his face taut. A faint smile just beginning to crease his lips. 'Master C'baoth?'

'They're there,' C'baoth whispered, his voice deep and husky. 'They're there,' he repeated, louder this time.

Pellaeon frowned back at the tactical hologram. 'Who's where?' he asked.

'They're at Filve,' C'baoth said. Abruptly, he looked up at Pellaeon, his eyes bright and insane. 'My Jedi are at Filve.'

'Master C'baoth, confirm that the cruisers have moved to polar positions,' Thrawn's voice came sharply. 'Then report on the feint battles—'

'My Jedi are at Filve,' C'baoth cut him off. 'What do I care about your battles?'

'C'baoth—'

With a wave of his hand, C'baoth shut off the intercom. 'Now, Leia Organa Solo,' he murmured softly, 'you are mine.'

The *Millennium Falcon* twisted hard to starboard as a TIE fighter shot past overhead, lasers blazing away madly as it tried unsuccessfully to track the freighter's maneuver. Clenching her teeth firmly against the movement, Leia Organa Solo watched as one of their escort X-wings blew the Imperial starfighter into a cloud of flaming dust. The sky spun around the *Falcon*'s canopy as the ship rolled back toward its original heading—

'Look out!' Threepio wailed from the seat behind Leia as another TIE fighter roared in toward them from the side. The warning was unnecessary; with deceptive ungainliness the *Falcon* was already corkscrewing back the other direction to bring its ventral quad laser battery to bear. Faintly audible even through the cockpit door, Leia heard the sound of a Wookiee battle roar, and the TIE fighter went the way of its late partner.

'Good shot, Chewie,' Han Solo called into the intercom as he got the *Falcon* leveled again. 'Wedge?'

'Still with you, *Falcon*,' Wedge Antilles' voice came promptly. 'We're clear for now, but there's another wave of TIE fighters on the way.'

'Yeah.' Han glanced at Leia. 'It's your call, sweetheart. You still want to try and reach ground?'

Threepio gave a little electronic gasp. 'Surely, Captain Solo, you aren't suggesting—'

'Put a choke valve on it, Goldenrod,' Han cut him off. 'Leia?'

Leia looked out the cockpit canopy at the Imperial Star Destroyer and eight Dreadnaughts arrayed against the beleaguered planet ahead. Clustering around it like mynocks around an unshielded power generator. It was to have been her last diplomatic mission before settling in to await the birth of her twins: a quick trip to calm a nervous Filvian government and demonstrate the New Republic's determination to protect the systems in this sector.

Some demonstration.

'There's no way we can make it through all that,' she told Han reluctantly. 'Even if we could, I doubt the Filvians would risk opening the shield to let us in. We'd better make a run for it.'

'Sounds good to me,' Han grunted. 'Wedge? We're pulling out. Stay with us.'

'Copy, *Falcon*,' Wedge said. 'You'll have to give us a few minutes to calculate the jump back.'

'Don't bother,' Han said, swiveling around in his seat to key in the nav computer. 'We'll feed you the numbers from here.'

'Copy. Rogue Squadron: screen formation.'

'You know, I'm starting to get tired of this,' Han told Leia, swiveling back to face front. 'I thought you said your Noghri pals were going to leave you alone.'

'This has nothing to do with the Noghri.' Leia shook her head, an odd half-felt tension stretching at her forehead. Was it her imagination, or were the Imperial ships surrounding Filve starting to break formation? 'This is Grand Admiral Thrawn playing with his new Dark Force Dreadnaughts.'

'Yeah,' Han agreed quietly, and Leia winced at the momentary flash of bitterness in his sense. Despite everyone's best efforts to persuade him otherwise, Han still considered it his own personal fault that Thrawn had gotten to the derelict *Katana* fleet ships – the so-called Dark Force – ahead of the New Republic. 'I wouldn't have thought he could get them reconditioned this fast,' Han added as he twisted the *Falcon*'s nose away from Filve and back toward deep space.

Leia swallowed. The strange tension was still there, like a distant malevolence pressing against the edges of her mind. 'Maybe he has enough Spaarti cylinders to clone some engineers and techs as well as soldiers.'

'That's sure a fun thought,' Han said; and through her tension Leia could sense his sudden change in mood as he tapped the comm switch. 'Wedge, take a look back at Filve and tell me if I'm seeing things.'

Over the comm, Leia could hear Wedge's thoughtful intake of air. 'You mean like the whole Imperial force breaking off their attack and coming after us?'

'Yeah. That.'

'Looks real enough to me,' Wedge said. 'Could be a good time to get out of here.'

'Yeah,' Han said slowly. 'Maybe.'

Leia frowned at her husband. There'd been something in his voice . . . 'Han?'

'The Filvians would've called for help before they put up their shield, right?' Han asked her, forehead furrowed with thought.

'Right,' Leia agreed cautiously.

'And the nearest New Republic base is Ord Pardron, right?'

'Right.'

'OK. Rogue Squadron, we're changing course to starboard. Stay with me.'

He keyed his board, and the Falcon started a sharp curve to the right. 'Watch it, *Falcon* – this is taking us back toward that TIE fighter group,' Wedge warned.

'We're not going that far,' Han assured him. 'Here's our vector.'

He straightened out the ship onto their new course heading and threw a look at the rear display. 'Good – they're still chasing us.'

Behind him, the nav computer beeped its notification that the jump coordinates were ready. 'Wedge, we've got your coordinates,' Leia said, reaching for the data transmission key.

'Hold it, *Falcon*,' Wedge cut her off. 'We've got company to starboard.'

Leia looked that direction, her throat tightening as she saw what Wedge meant. The approaching TIE fighters were coming up fast, and already were close enough to eavesdrop on any transmission the *Falcon* tried to make to its escort. Sending Wedge the jump coordinates now would be an open invitation for the Imperials to have a reception committee waiting at the other end.

'Perhaps I can be of assistance, Your Highness,' Threepio offered brightly. 'As you know, I am fluent in over six million forms of communication. I could transmit the coordinates to Commander Antilles in Boordist or Vaathkree trade language, for example—'

'And then you'd send them the translation?' Han put in dryly.

'Of course—' The droid broke off. 'Oh, dear,' he said, sounding embarrassed.

'Yeah, well, don't worry about it,' Han said. 'Wedge, you were at Xyquine two years ago, weren't you?'

'Yes. Ah. A Cracken Twist?'

'Right. On two: one, two.'

Outside the canopy, Leia caught a glimpse of the X-wings swinging into a complicated new escort formation around the *Falcon*. 'What does this buy us?' she asked.

'Our way out,' Han told her, checking the rear display again. 'Pull the coordinates, add a two to the second number

24

of each one, and then send the whole package to the X-wings.'

'I see,' Leia nodded her understanding as she got to work. Altering the second digit wouldn't change the appearance of their exit vector enough for the Imperials to catch on to the trick, but it would be more than enough to put any chase force a couple of light-years off target. 'Clever. And that little flight maneuver they did just now was just window dressing?'

'Right. Makes anyone watching think that's all there is to it. A little something Pash Cracken came up with at that fiasco off Xyquine.' Han glanced at the rear display again. 'I think we've got enough lead to outrun them,' he said. 'Let's try.'

'We're not jumping to lightspeed?' Leia frowned, an old and rather painful memory floating up from the back of her mind. That mad scramble away from Hoth, with Darth Vader's whole fleet breathing down their necks and a hyperdrive that turned out to be broken . . .

Han threw her a sideways look. 'Don't worry, sweetheart. The hyperdrive's working fine today.'

'Let's hope so,' Leia murmured.

'See, as long as they're chasing us they can't bother Filve,' Han went on. 'And the farther we draw them away, the longer the backup force'll have to get here from Ord Pardron.'

The brilliant green flash of a near miss cut off Leia's intended response. 'I think we've given them all the time we can,' she told Han. Within her, she could sense the turmoil coming from her unborn twins. 'Can we please get out of here?'

A second bolt spattered off the *Falcon*'s upper deflector shield. 'Yeah, I think you're right,' Han agreed. 'Wedge? You ready to leave this party?'

'Whenever you are, *Falcon*,' Wedge said. 'Go ahead – we'll follow when you're clear.'

'Right.' Reaching over, Han gripped the hyperdrive levers and pulled them gently back. Through the cockpit canopy the stars stretched themselves into starlines, and they were safe.

Leia took a deep breath, let it out slowly. Within her, she could still sense the twins' anxiety, and for a moment she turned her mind to the job of calming them down. It was a strange sensation, she'd often thought, touching minds that dealt in emotion and pure sensation instead of pictures and words. So different from the minds of Han and Luke and her other friends.

So different, too, from the distant mind that had been orchestrating that Imperial attack force.

Behind her, the door slid open and Chewbacca came into the cockpit. 'Good shooting, Chewie,' Han told the Wookiee as he heaved his massive bulk into the portside passenger seat beside Threepio. 'You have any more trouble with the horizontal control arm?'

Chewbacca rumbled a negative. His dark eyes studying Leia's face, he growled her a question. 'I'm all right,' Leia assured him, blinking back sudden and inexplicable tears. 'Really.'

She looked at Han, to find him frowning at her, too. 'You weren't worried, were you?' he asked. 'It was just an Imperial task force. Nothing to get excited about.'

She shook her head. 'It wasn't that, Han. There was something else back there. A kind of . . .' She shook her head again. 'I don't know.'

'Perhaps it was similar to your indisposition at Endor,' Threepio offered helpfully. 'You remember – when you collapsed while Chewbacca and I were repairing the—?'

Chewbacca rumbled a warning, and the droid abruptly shut up. But far too late. 'No – let him talk,' Han said, his sense going all protectively suspicious as he looked at Leia. 'What indisposition was this?'

'There wasn't anything to it, Han,' Leia assured him, reaching over to take his hand. 'On our first orbit around Endor we passed through the spot where the Death Star blew up. For a few seconds I could feel something like the Emperor's presence around me. That's all.'

'Oh, that's all,' Han said sarcastically, throwing a brief glare back at Chewbacca. 'A dead Emperor tries to make a grab for you, and you don't think it's worth mentioning?'

'Now you're being silly,' Leia chided. 'There was nothing

to worry about – it was over quickly, and there weren't any after-effects. Really. Anyway, what I felt back at Filve was completely different.'

'Glad to hear it,' Han said, not yet ready to let it go. 'Did you have any of the med people check you over or anything after you got back?'

'Well, there really wasn't any time before—'

'Fine. You do it as soon as we're back.'

Leia nodded with a quiet sigh. She knew that tone; and it wasn't something she could wholeheartedly argue against, anyway. 'All right. If I can find time.'

'You'll *make* time,' Han countered. 'Or I'll have Luke lock you in the med center when he gets back. I mean it, sweetheart.'

Leia squeezed his hand, feeling a similar squeeze on her heart as she did so. Luke, off alone in Imperial territory . . . but he was all right. He had to be. 'All right,' she told Han. 'I'll get checked out. I promise.'

'Good,' he said, his eyes searching her face. 'So what was it you felt back at Filve?'

'I don't know.' She hesitated. 'Maybe it was the same thing Luke felt on the *Katana*. You know – when the Imperials put that landing party of clones aboard.'

'Yeah,' Han agreed doubtfully. 'Maybe. Those Dread-naughts were awfully far away.'

'There were probably a lot more clones, though, too.'

'Yeah. Maybe,' Han said again. 'Well . . . I suppose Chewie and me'd better get to work on that ion flux stabilizer before it quits on us completely. Can you handle things up here OK, sweetheart?'

'I'm fine,' Leia assured him, just as glad to be leaving this line of conversation. 'You two go ahead.'

Because the other possibility was one she'd just as soon not think about right now. The Emperor, it had long been rumored, had had the ability to use the Force to exercise direct control over his military forces. If the Jedi Master Luke had confronted on Jomark had that same ability . . .

Reaching down, she caressed her belly and focused on the

27

pair of tiny minds within her. No, it was indeed not something she wanted to think about.

'I presume,' Thrawn said in that deadly calm voice of his, 'that you have some sort of explanation.'

Slowly, deliberately, C'baoth lifted his head from the command room's double display circle to look at the Grand Admiral. At the Grand Admiral and, with undisguised contempt, at the ysalamir on its nutrient frame slung across Thrawn's shoulders. 'Do you likewise have an explanation, Grand Admiral Thrawn?' he demanded.

'You broke off the diversionary attack on Filve,' Thrawn said, ignoring C'baoth's question. 'You then proceeded to send the entire task force on a dead-end chase.'

'And you, Grand Admiral Thrawn, have failed to bring my Jedi to me,' C'baoth countered. His voice, Pellaeon noticed uneasily, was slowly rising in both pitch and volume. 'You, your tame Noghri, your entire Empire – all of you have failed.'

Thrawn's glowing red eyes narrowed. 'Indeed? And was it also our failure that you were unable to hold on to Luke Skywalker after we delivered him to you on Jomark?'

'You did not deliver him to me, Grand Admiral Thrawn,' C'baoth insisted. 'I summoned him there through the Force—'

'It was Imperial Intelligence who planted the rumor that Jorus C'baoth had returned and been seen on Jomark,' Thrawn cut him off coldly. 'It was Imperial Transport who brought you there, Imperial Supply who arranged and provisioned that house for you, and Imperial Engineering who built the camouflaged island landing site for your use. The Empire did its part to get Skywalker into your hands. It was you who failed to keep him there.'

'No!' C'baoth snapped. 'Skywalker left Jomark because Mara Jade escaped from you and twisted his mind against me. And she will pay for that. You hear me? She shall pay.'

For a long moment Thrawn was silent. 'You threw the entire Filve task force against the *Millennium Falcon*,' he said at last, his voice under control again. 'Did you succeed in capturing Leia Organa Solo?'

'No,' C'baoth growled. 'But not because she didn't want to come to me. She does. Just as Skywalker does.'

Thrawn threw a glance at Pellaeon. 'She wants to come to you?' he asked.

C'baoth smiled. 'Very much,' he said, his voice unexpectedly losing all its anger. Becoming almost dreamy . . . 'She wants me to teach her children,' he continued, his eyes drifting around the command room. 'To instruct them in the ways of the Jedi. To create them in my own image. Because I am the master. The only one there is.'

He looked back at Thrawn. 'You must bring her to me, Grand Admiral Thrawn,' he said, his manner somewhere halfway between solemn and pleading. 'We must free her from her entrapment among those who fear her powers. They'll destroy her if we don't.'

'Of course we must,' Thrawn said soothingly. 'But you must leave that task to me. All I need is a little more time.'

C'baoth frowned with thought, his hand slipping up beneath his beard to finger the medallion hanging on its neck chain, and Pellaeon felt a shiver run up his back. No matter how many times he saw it happen, he would never get used to these sudden dips into the slippery twilight of clone madness. It had, he knew, been a universal problem with the early cloning experiments: a permanent mental and emotional instability, inversely scaled to the length of the duplicate's growth cycle. Few of the scientific papers on the subject had survived the Clone Wars era, but Pellaeon had come across one that had suggested that no clone grown to maturity in less than a year would be stable enough to survive outside of a totally controlled environment.

Given the destruction they'd unleashed on the galaxy, Pellaeon had always assumed that the clonemasters had eventually found at least a partial solution to the problem. Whether they had recognized the underlying cause of the madness was another question entirely.

It could very well be that Thrawn was the first to truly understand it.

'Very well, Grand Admiral Thrawn,' C'baoth said abruptly.

'You may have one final chance. But I warn you: it will be your last. After that, I will take the matter into my own hands.' Beneath the bushy eyebrows his eyes flashed. 'And I warn you further: if you cannot accomplish even so small a task, perhaps I will deem you unworthy to lead the military forces of my Empire.'

Thrawn's eyes glittered, but he merely inclined his head slightly. 'I accept your challenge, Master C'baoth.'

'Good.' Deli̇ erately, C'baoth resettled himself into his seat and closed his eyes. 'You may leave me now, Grand Admiral Thrawn. I wish to meditate, and to plan for the future of my Jedi.'

For a moment Thrawn stood silently, his glowing red eyes gazing unblinkingly at C'baoth. Then he shifted his gaze to Pellaeon. 'You'll accompany me to the bridge, Captain,' he said. 'I want you to oversee the defense arrangements for the Ukio system.'

'Yes, sir,' Pellaeon said, glad of any excuse to get away from C'baoth.

For a moment he paused, feeling a frown cross his face as he looked down at C'baoth. Had there been something he had wanted to bring to Thrawn's attention? He was almost certain there was. Something having to do with C'baoth, and clones, and the Mount Tantiss project . . .

But the thought wouldn't come, and with a mental shrug, he pushed the question aside. It would surely come to him in time.

Stepping around the display ring, he followed his commander from the room.

CHAPTER 2

It was called the Calius saj Leeloo, the City of Glowing Crystal of Berchest, and it had been one of the most spectacular wonders of the galaxy since the earliest days of the Old

Republic. The entire city was nothing more or less than a single gigantic crystal, created over the eons by saltile spray from the dark red-orange waters of the Leefari Sea that roiled up against the low bluff upon which it rested. The original city had been painstakingly sculpted from the crystal over decades by local Berchestian artisans, whose descendants continued to guide and nurture its slow growth.

At the height of the Old Republic Calius had been a major tourist attraction, its populace making a comfortable living from the millions of beings who flocked to the stunning beauty of the city and its surroundings. But the chaos of the Clone Wars and the subsequent rise of the Empire had taken a severe toll on such idle amusements, and Calius had been forced to turn to other means for its support.

Fortunately, the tourist trade had left a legacy of well-established trade routes between Berchest and most of the galaxy's major systems. The obvious solution was for the Berchestians to promote Calius as a trade center; and while the city was hardly to the level yet of Svivren or Ketaris, they had achieved a modest degree of success.

The only problem was that it was a trade center on the Imperial side of the line.

A squad of stormtroopers strode down the crowded street, their white armor taking on a colored tinge from the angular red-orange buildings around them. Taking a long step out of their way, Luke Skywalker pulled his hood a bit closer around his face. He could sense no particular alertness from the squad, but this deep into Imperial space there was no reason to take chances. The stormtroopers strode past without so much as a glance in his direction, and with a quiet sigh of relief Luke returned his attention to his contemplation of the city. Between the stormtroopers, the Imperial fleet crewers on layover between flights, and the smugglers poking around hoping to pick up jobs, the darkly businesslike sense of the city was in strange and pointed contrast to its serene beauty.

And somewhere in all that serene beauty was something far more dangerous than mere Imperial stormtroopers.

A group of clones.

Or so New Republic Intelligence thought. Painstakingly sifting through thousands of intercepted Imperial communiqués, they'd tentatively pinpointed Calius and the Berchest system as one of the transfer points in the new flood of human duplicates beginning to man the ships and troop carriers of Grand Admiral Thrawn's war machine.

That flood had to be stopped, and quickly. Which meant finding the location of the cloning tanks and destroying them. Which first meant backtracking the traffic pattern from a known transfer point. Which first meant confirming that clones were indeed coming through Calius.

A group of men dressed in the dulbands and robes of Svivreni traders came around a corner two blocks ahead, and as he had so many times in the past two days, Luke reached out toward them with the Force. One quick check was all it took: the traders did not have the strange aura he'd detected in the boarding party of clones that had attacked them aboard the *Katana*.

But even as he withdrew his consciousness, something else caught Luke's attention. Something he had almost missed amid the torrent of human and alien thoughts and sensations that swirled together around him like bits of colored glass in a sandstorm. A coolly calculating mind, one which Luke felt certain he'd encountered before but couldn't quite identify through the haze of mental noise between them.

And the owner of that mind was, in turn, fully aware of Luke's presence in Calius. And was watching him.

Luke grimaced. Alone in enemy territory, with his transport two kilometers away at the Calius landing field and his only weapon a lightsaber that would identify him the minute he drew it from his tunic, he was not exactly holding the high ground here.

But he had the Force . . . and he knew his follower was there. All in all, it gave him fair odds.

A couple of meters to his left was the entrance to the long arched tunnel of a pedestrian bridgeway. Turning down it, Luke stepped up his pace, trying to remember from his study of the city maps exactly where this particular bridge went.

Across the city's icy river, he decided, and up toward the taller and higher-class regions overlooking the sea itself. Behind him, he sensed his pursuer follow him into the bridgeway; and as Luke put distance between himself and the mental din of the crowded market regions behind him, he was finally able to identify the man.

It was not as bad as he'd feared. But potentially at least, it was bad enough. With a sigh, Luke stopped and waited. The bridgeway, with its gentle curve hiding both ends from view, was as good a place as any for a confrontation.

His pursuer came to the last part of the curve. Then, as if anticipating that his quarry would be waiting there, he stopped just out of sight. Luke extended his senses, caught the sound of a blaster being drawn – 'It's all right,' he called softly. 'We're alone. Come on out.'

There was a brief hesitation, and Luke caught the momentary flicker of surprise; and then, Talon Karrde stepped into sight.

'I see the universe hasn't run out of ways to surprise me,' the smuggler commented, inclining his head to Luke in an abbreviated bow as he slid his blaster back into its holster. 'From the way you were acting I thought you were probably a spy from the New Republic. But I have to admit you're the last person I would have expected them to send.'

Luke eyed him, trying hard to read the sense of the man. The last time he'd seen Karrde, just after the battle for the *Katana*, the other had emphasized that he and his smuggling group intended to remain neutral in this war. 'And what were you going to do after you knew for sure?'

'I hadn't planned on turning you in, if that's what you mean,' Karrde said, throwing a glance behind him down the bridgeway. 'If it's all the same to you, I'd like to move on. Berchestians don't normally hold extended conversations in bridgeways. And the tunnel can carry voices a surprising distance.'

And if there were an ambush waiting for them at the other end of the bridgeway? But if there were, Luke would know before they reached it. 'Fine with me,' he said, stepping to the side and gesturing Karrde forward.

The other favored him with a sardonic smile. 'You don't trust me, do you?' he said, brushing past Luke and heading down the bridgeway.

'Must be Han's influence,' Luke said apologetically, falling into step beside him. 'His, or yours. Or maybe Mara's.'

He caught the shift in Karrde's sense: a quick flash of concern that was as quickly buried again. 'Speaking of Mara, how is she?'

'Nearly recovered,' Luke assured him. 'The medics tell me that repairing that kind of light neural damage isn't difficult, just time-consuming.'

Karrde nodded, his eyes on the tunnel ahead. 'I appreciate you taking care of her,' he said, almost grudgingly. 'Our own medical facilities wouldn't have been up to the task.'

Luke waved the thanks away. 'It was the least we could do after the help you gave us at the *Katana*.'

'Perhaps.'

They reached the end of the bridgeway and stepped out into a street considerably less crowded than the one they'd left. Above and ahead of them, the three intricately carved government headquarter towers that faced the sea could be seen above the nearby buildings. Reaching out with the Force, Luke did a quick reading of the people passing by. Nothing. 'You heading anywhere in particular?' he asked Karrde.

The other shook his head. 'Wandering the city,' he said casually. 'You?'

'The same,' Luke said, trying to match the other's tone.

'And hoping to see a familiar face or two? Or three, or four, or five?'

So Karrde knew, or had guessed, why he was here. Somehow, that didn't really surprise him. 'If they're here to be seen, I'll find them,' he said. 'I don't suppose you have any information I could use?'

'I might,' Karrde said. 'Do you have enough money to pay for it?'

'Knowing your prices, probably not,' Luke said. 'But I could set you up a credit line when I get back.'

'*If* you get back,' Karrde countered. 'Considering how many

Imperial troops there are between you and safe territory, you're not what I would call a good investment risk at the moment.'

Luke cocked an eyebrow at him. 'As opposed to a smuggler at the top of the Empire's locate-and-detain list?' he asked pointedly.

Karrde smiled. 'As it happens, Calius is one of the few places in Imperial space where I'm perfectly safe. The Berchestian governor and I have known each other for several years. More to the point, there are certain items important to him which only I can supply.'

'Military items?'

'I'm not part of your war, Skywalker,' Karrde reminded him coolly. 'I'm neutral, and I intend to stay that way. I thought I'd made that clear to you and your sister when we last parted company.'

'Oh, it was clear enough,' Luke agreed. 'I just thought that events of the past month might have changed your mind.'

Karrde's expression didn't change, but Luke could detect the almost unwilling shift in his sense. 'I don't particularly like the idea of Grand Admiral Thrawn having access to a cloning facility,' he conceded. 'It has the long-term potential for shifting the balance of power in his favor, and that's something neither of us wants to see happen. But I think your side is rather overreacting to the situation.'

'I don't know how you can call it overreacting,' Luke said. 'The Empire has most of the two hundred Dreadnaughts of the *Katana* fleet, and now they've got an unlimited supply of clones to crew them with.'

' "Unlimited" is hardly the word I would use,' Karrde said. 'Clones can only be grown so quickly if you want them mentally stable enough to trust with your warships. One year minimum per clone, as I recall the old rule of thumb.'

A group of five Vaathkree passed by in front of them along a cross street. So far the Empire had been only cloning humans, but Luke checked them out anyway. Again, nothing. 'A year per clone, you say?'

'At the absolute minimum,' Karrde said. 'The pre-Clone Wars documents I've seen suggest three to five years would be a more appropriate period. Quicker than the standard human growth cycle, certainly, but hardly any reason for panic.'

Luke looked up at the carved towers, their sunlit red-orange in sharp contrast to the billowing white clouds rolling in from the sea behind them. 'What would you say if I told you the clones who attacked us on the *Katana* were grown in less than a year?'

Karrde shrugged. 'That depends on how much less.'

'The full cycle was fifteen to twenty days.'

Karrde stopped short. 'What?' he demanded, turning to stare at Luke.

'Fifteen to twenty days,' Luke repeated, stopping beside him.

For a long moment Karrde locked eyes with him. Then, slowly, he turned away and began walking again. 'That's impossible,' he said. 'There must be an error.'

'I can get you a copy of the studies.'

Karrde nodded thoughtfully, his eyes focused on nothing in particular. 'At least that explains Ukio.'

'Ukio?' Luke frowned.

Karrde glanced at him. 'That's right – you've probably been out of touch for a while. Two days ago the Imperials launched a multiple attack on targets in the Abrion and Dufilvian sectors. They severely damaged the military base at Ord Pardron and captured the Ukio system.'

Luke felt a hollow sensation in his stomach. Ukio was one of the top five producers of foodstuffs in the entire New Republic. The repercussions for Abrion sector alone—'How badly was Ukio damaged?'

'Apparently not at all,' Karrde said. 'My sources tell me it was taken with its shields and ground/space weaponry intact.'

The hollow feeling got a little bigger. 'I thought that was impossible to do.'

'A knack for doing the impossible was one of the things Grand Admirals were selected for,' Karrde said dryly. 'Details of the attack are still sketchy; it'll be interesting to see how he pulled it off.'

So Thrawn had the *Katana* Dreadnaughts; and he had clones to man them with; and now he had the ability to provide food for those clones. 'This isn't just the setup to another series of raids,' Luke said slowly. 'The Empire's getting ready to launch a major offensive.'

'It does begin to look that way,' Karrde agreed. 'Offhand, I'd say you have your work cut out for you.'

Luke studied him. Karrde's voice and face were as calm as ever, but the sense behind them wasn't nearly so certain any more. 'And none of this changes your mind?' he prompted the other.

'I'm not joining the New Republic, Skywalker,' Karrde said, shaking his head. 'For many reasons. Not the least being that I don't entirely trust certain elements in your government.'

'I think Fey'lya's been pretty well discredited—'

'I wasn't referring only to Fey'lya,' Karrde cut him off. 'You know as well as I do how fond the Mon Calamari have always been of smugglers. Now that Admiral Ackbar's been reinstated to his Council and Supreme Commander positions, all of us in the trade are going to have to start watching over our shoulders again.'

'Oh, come on,' Luke snorted. 'You don't think Ackbar's going to have time to worry about smugglers, do you?'

Karrde smiled wryly. 'Not really. But I'm not willing to risk my life on it, either.'

Stalemate. 'All right, then,' Luke said. 'Let's put it on a strictly business level. We need to know the Empire's movements and intentions, which is something you probably keep track of anyway. Can we buy that information from you?'

Karrde considered. 'That might be possible,' he said cautiously. 'But only if I have the final say on what I pass on to you. I won't have you turning my group into an unofficial arm of New Republic Intelligence.'

'Agreed,' Luke said. It was less than he might have hoped for, but it was better than nothing. 'I'll set up a credit line for you as soon as I get back.'

'Perhaps we should start with a straight information trade,'

Karrde said, looking around at the crystalline buildings. 'Tell me what started your people looking at Calius.'

'I'll do better than that,' Luke said. The distant touch on his mind was faint but unmistakable. 'How about if I confirm the clones are here?'

'Where?' Karrde asked sharply.

'Somewhere that way,' Luke said, pointing ahead and slightly to the right. 'Half a kilometer away, maybe – it's hard to tell.'

'Inside one of the Towers,' Karrde decided. 'Nice and secure and well hidden from prying eyes. I wonder if there's any way to get inside for a look.'

'Wait a minute – they're moving,' Luke said, frowning as he tried to hang on to the contact. 'Heading . . . almost toward us, but not quite.'

'Probably being taken to the landing field,' Karrde said. He glanced around, pointed to their right. 'They'll probably use Mavrille Street – two blocks that direction.'

Balancing speed with the need to remain inconspicuous, they covered the distance in three minutes. 'They'll probably use a cargo carrier or light transport,' Karrde said as they found a spot where they could watch the street without being run over by the pedestrian traffic along the edges of the vehicle way. 'Anything obviously military would attract attention.'

Luke nodded. Mavrille, he remembered from the maps, was one of the handful of streets in Calius that had been carved large enough for vehicles to use, with the result that the traffic was running pretty much fore to aft. 'I wish I had some macrobinoculars with me,' he commented.

'Trust me – you're conspicuous enough as it is,' Karrde countered as he craned his neck over the passing crowds. 'Any sign of them?'

'They're definitely coming this way,' Luke told him. He reached out with the Force, trying to sort out the clone sense from the sandstorm of other thoughts and minds surrounding him. 'I'd guess twenty to thirty of them.'

'A cargo carrier, then,' Karrde decided. 'There's one coming now – just behind that Trast speeder truck.'

'I see it.' Luke took a deep breath, calling on every bit of his Jedi skill. 'That's them,' he murmured, a shiver running up his back.

'All right,' Karrde said, his voice grim. 'Watch closely; they might have left one or more of the ventilation panels open.'

The cargo carrier made its way toward them on its repulsorlifts, coming abruptly to a halt a short block away as the driver of the speeder truck in front of it suddenly woke up to the fact that he'd reached his turn. Gingerly, the truck eased around the corner, blocking the whole traffic flow behind it.

'Wait here,' Karrde said, and dived into the stream of pedestrians heading that direction. Luke kept his eyes sweeping the area, alert for any sense that he or Karrde had been seen and recognized. If this whole setup was some kind of elaborate trap for offworld spies, now would be the obvious time to spring it.

The truck finally finished its turn, and the cargo carrier lumbered on. It passed Luke and continued down the street, disappearing within a few seconds around one of the red-orange buildings. Stepping back into the side street behind him, Luke waited; and a minute later Karrde had returned. 'Two of the vents were open, but I couldn't see enough to be sure,' he told Luke, breathing heavily. 'You?'

Luke shook his head. 'I couldn't see anything, either. But it was them. I'm sure of it.'

For a moment Karrde studied his face. Then, he gave a curt nod. 'All right. What now?'

'I'm going to see if I can get my ship offplanet ahead of them,' Luke said. 'If I can track their hyperspace vector, maybe we can figure out where they go from here.' He lifted his eyebrows. 'Though two ships working together could do a better track.'

Karrde smiled slightly. 'You'll forgive me if I decline the offer,' he said. 'Flying in tandem with a New Republic agent is not exactly what I would call maintaining neutrality.' He glanced over Luke's shoulder at the street behind him. 'At any rate, I think I'd prefer to try backtracking them from here. See if I can identify their point of origin.'

'Sounds good,' Luke nodded. 'I'd better get over to the landing field and get my ship prepped.'

'I'll be in touch,' Karrde promised. 'Make sure that credit line is a generous one.'

Standing at the uppermost window of Central Government Tower Number One, Governor Staffa lowered his macrobinoculars with a satisfied snort. 'That was him, all right, Fingal,' he said to the little man hovering at his side. 'No doubt about it. Luke Skywalker himself.'

'Do you suppose he saw the special transport?' Fingal asked, fingering his own macrobinoculars nervously.

'Well, of course he saw it,' Staffa growled. 'You think he was hanging around Mavrille Street for his health?'

'I only thought—'

'Don't think, Fingal,' Staffa cut him off. 'You aren't properly equipped for it.'

He sauntered to his desk, dropped the macrobinoculars into a drawer, and pulled up Grand Admiral Thrawn's directive on his data pad. It was a rather bizarre directive, in his private and strictly confidential opinion, more peculiar even than these mysterious troop transfers the Imperial High Command had been running through Calius of late. But one had no choice under the circumstances but to assume Thrawn knew what he was doing.

At any rate, it was on his own head – not Staffa's – if he didn't, and that was the important thing. 'I want you to send a message to the Imperial Star Destroyer *Chimaera*,' he told Fingal, lowering his bulk carefully into his chair and pushing the data pad across the desk. 'Coded as per the instructions here. Inform Grand Admiral Thrawn that Skywalker has been on Calius and that I have personally observed him near the special transport. Also as per the Grand Admiral's directive, he has been allowed to leave Berchest unhindered.'

'Yes, Governor,' Fingal said, making notes on his own data pad. If the little man saw anything unusual about letting a

Rebel spy walk freely through Imperial territory, he wasn't showing it. 'What about the other man, Governor? The one who was with Skywalker down there?'

Staffa pursed his lips. The price on Talon Karrde's head was up to nearly fifty thousand now – a great deal of money, even for a man with a planetary governor's salary and perks. He had always known that someday it would be in his best interests to terminate the quiet business relationship he had with Karrde. Perhaps that time had finally come.

No. No, not while war still raged through the galaxy. Later, perhaps, when victory was near and private supply lines could be made more reliable. But not now. 'The other man is of no importance,' he told Fingal. 'A special agent I sent to help smoke the Rebel spy into the open. Forget him. Go on – get that message coded and sent.'

'Yes, sir,' Fingal nodded, stepping toward the door.

The panel slid open – and for just a second, as Fingal stepped through, Staffa thought he saw an odd glint in the little man's eye. Some strange trick of the outer office light, of course. Next to his unbending loyalty for his governor, Fingal's most prominent and endearing attribute was his equally unbending lack of imagination.

Taking a deep breath, putting Fingal and Rebel spies and even Grand Admirals out of his mind, Staffa leaned back in his chair and began to consider how he would use the shipment that Karrde's people were even now unloading at the landing field.

CHAPTER 3

Slowly, as if climbing a long dark staircase, Mara Jade pulled herself out of a deep sleep. She opened her eyes, looked around the softly lit room, and wondered where in the galaxy she was.

It was a medical area – that much was obvious from the

41

biomonitors, the folded room dividers, and the other multi-position beds scattered around the one she was lying in. But it wasn't one of Karrde's facilities, at least not one she was familiar with.

But the layout itself was all too familiar. It was a standard Imperial recovery room.

For the moment she seemed to be alone, but she knew that wouldn't last. Silently, she rolled out of bed into a crouching position on the floor, taking a quick inventory of her physical condition as she did so. No aches or pains; no dizziness or obvious injuries. Slipping into the robe and bedshoes at the end of the bed, she padded silently to the door, preparing herself mentally to silence or disable whatever was out there. She waved at the door release, and as the panel slid open she leaped through into the recovery anteroom—

And came to a sudden, slightly disoriented halt.

'Oh, hi, Mara,' Ghent said distractedly, glancing up from the computer terminal he was hunched over before returning his attention to it. 'How're you feeling?'

'Not too bad,' Mara said, staring at the kid and sifting furiously through a set of hazy memories. Ghent – one of Karrde's employees and possibly the best slicer in the galaxy. And the fact that he was sitting at a terminal meant they weren't prisoners, unless their captor was so abysmally stupid that he didn't know better than to let a slicer get within spitting distance of a computer.

But hadn't she sent Ghent to the New Republic headquarters on Coruscant? Yes, she had. On Karrde's instructions, just before collecting some of his group together and leading them into that melee at the *Katana* fleet.

Where she'd run her Z-95 up against an Imperial Star Destroyer . . . and had had to eject . . . and had brilliantly arranged to fly her ejector seat straight through an ion cannon beam. Which had fried her survival equipment and set her drifting, lost forever, in interstellar space.

She looked around her. Apparently, forever hadn't lasted as long as she'd expected it to. 'Where are we?' she asked, though she had a pretty good idea now what the answer would be.

She was right. 'The old Imperial Palace on Coruscant,' Ghent told her, frowning a little. 'Medical wing. They had to do some reconstruction of your neural pathways. Don't you remember?'

'It's a little vague,' Mara admitted. But as the last cobwebs cleared from her brain, the rest of it was beginning to fall into place. Her ejector seat's ruined life-support system; and a strange, light-headed vagueness as she drifted off to sleep in the darkness. She'd probably suffered oxygen deprivation before they'd been able to locate her and get her to a ship.

No. Not *they: him*. There was only one person who could possibly have found a single crippled ejector seat in all the emptiness and battle debris out there. Luke Skywalker, the last of the Jedi Knights.

The man she was going to kill.

YOU WILL KILL LUKE SKYWALKER.

She took a step back to lean against the doorjamb, knees suddenly feeling weak as the Emperor's words echoed through her mind. She'd been here, on this world and in this building, when he'd died over Endor. Had watched through his mind as Luke Skywalker cut him down and brought her life crashing in ruins around her head.

'I see you're awake,' a new voice said.

Mara opened her eyes. The newcomer, a middle-aged woman in a duty medic's tunic, was marching briskly across the room toward her from a far door, an Emdee droid trailing in her wake. 'How are you feeling?'

'I'm fine,' Mara said, feeling a sudden urge to lash out at the other woman. These people – these enemies of the Empire – had no right to be here in the Emperor's palace . . .

She took a careful breath, fighting back the flash of emotion. The medic had stopped short, a professional frown on her face; Ghent, his cherished computers momentarily forgotten, had a puzzled look on his. 'Sorry,' she murmured. 'I guess I'm still a little disoriented.'

'Understandable,' the medic nodded. 'You've been lying in that bed for a month, after all.'

Mara stared at her. 'A *month*?'

'Well, most of a month,' the medic corrected herself. 'You also spent some time in a bacta tank. Don't worry – short-term memory problems are common during neural reconstructions, but they nearly always clear up after the treatment.'

'I understand,' Mara said mechanically. A month. She'd lost a whole month here. And in that time—

'We have a guest suite arranged for you upstairs whenever you feel ready to leave here,' the medic continued. 'Would you like me to see if it's ready?'

Mara focused on her. 'That would be fine,' she said.

The medic pulled out a comlink and thumbed it on; and as she began talking, Mara stepped past her to Ghent's side. 'What's been happening with the war during the last month?' she asked him.

'Oh, the Empire's been making the usual trouble,' Ghent said, waving toward the sky. 'They've got the folks here pretty stirred up, anyway. Ackbar and Madine and the rest have been running around like crazy. Trying to push 'em back or cut 'em off – something like that.'

And that was, Mara knew, about all she would get out of him on the subject of current events. Aside from a fascination with smuggler folklore, the only thing that really mattered to Ghent was slicing at computers.

She frowned, belatedly remembering why Karrde had ordered Ghent here in the first place. 'Wait a minute,' she said. 'Ackbar's back in command? You mean you've cleared him already?'

'Sure,' Ghent said. 'That suspicious bank deposit thing Councilor Fey'lya made such a fuss over was a complete fraud – the guys who did that electronic break-in at the bank planted it in his account at the same time. Probably Imperial Intelligence – it had their noseprints all over the programming. Oh, sure; I proved that two days after I got here.'

'I imagine they were pleased. So why are you still here?'

'Well . . .' For a moment Ghent seemed taken aback. 'No

one's come back to get me, for one thing.' His face brightened. 'Besides, there's this really neat encrypt code someone nearby is using to send information to the Empire. General Bel Iblis says the Imperials call it Delta Source, and that it's sending them stuff right out of the Palace.'

'And he asked you to slice it for them,' Mara nodded, feeling her lip twist. 'I don't suppose he offered to pay you or anything?'

'Well . . .' Ghent shrugged. 'Probably they did. I don't remember, really.'

The medic replaced her comlink in her belt. 'Your guide will be here momentarily,' she told Mara.

'Thank you,' Mara said, resisting the urge to tell the other that she probably knew the Imperial Palace better in her sleep than any guide they had could do in broad daylight. Co-operation and politeness – those were the keys to talking them out of a ship and getting her and Ghent out of this place and out of their war.

Behind the medic the door slid open, and a tall woman with pure white hair glided into the room. 'Hello, Mara,' she said, smiling gravely. 'My name is Winter, personal aide to Princess Leia Organa Solo. I'm glad to see you on your feet again.'

'I'm glad to be there,' Mara said, trying to keep her voice polite. Someone else associated with Skywalker. Just what she needed. 'I take it you're my guide?'

'Your guide, your assistant, and anything else you need for the next few days,' Winter said. 'Princess Leia asked me to look after you until she and Captain Solo return from Filve.'

'I don't need an assistant, and I don't need looking after,' Mara said. 'All I really need is a ship.'

'I've already started working on that,' Winter said. 'I'm hoping we'll be able to find something for you soon. In the meantime, may I show you to your suite?'

Mara hid a grimace. The usurpers of the New Republic, graciously offering her hospitality in what had once been her own home. 'That's very kind of you,' she said, trying not to sound sarcastic. 'You coming, Ghent?'

'You go on ahead,' Ghent said absently, gazing at the

computer display. 'I want to sit on this run for a while.'

'He'll be all right here,' Winter assured her. 'This way, please.'

They left the anteroom, and Winter led the way toward the rear of the Palace. 'Ghent has a suite right next to yours,' Winter commented as they walked, 'but I don't think he's been there more than twice in the past month. He set up temporary shop out there in the recovery anteroom where he could keep an eye on you.'

Mara had to smile at that. Ghent, who spent roughly 90 percent of his waking hours oblivious to the outside world, was not exactly what she would go looking for in either a nurse or a bodyguard. But it was the thought that counted. 'I appreciate you people taking care of me,' she told Winter.

'It's the least we could do to thank you for coming to our assistance at the *Katana* battle.'

'It was Karrde's idea,' Mara said shortly. 'Thank him, not me.'

'We did,' Winter said. 'But you risked your life, too, on our behalf. We won't forget that.'

Mara threw a sideways look at the white-haired woman. She had read the Emperor's files on the Rebellion's leaders, including Leia Organa, and the name Winter wasn't ringing any bells at all. 'How long have you been with Organa Solo?' she asked.

'I grew up with her in the royal court of Alderaan,' Winter said, a bittersweet smile touching her lips. 'We were friends in childhood, and when she began her first steps into galactic politics, her father assigned me to be her aide. I've been with her ever since.'

'I don't recall hearing about you during the height of the Rebellion,' Mara probed gently.

'I spent most of the war moving from planet to planet working with Supply and Procurement,' Winter told her. 'If my colleagues could get me into a warehouse or depot on some pretext, I could draw a map for them of where the items were that they wanted. It made the subsequent raids quicker and safer.'

Mara nodded as understanding came. 'So you were the one called Targeter. The one with the perfect memory.'

Winter's forehead creased slightly. 'Yes, that was one of my code names,' she said. 'I had many others over the years.'

'I see,' Mara said. She could remember a fair number of references in pre-Yavin Intelligence reports to the mysterious Rebel named Targeter, much of the politely heated discussion centering around his or her possible identity. She wondered if the data-pushers had ever even gotten close.

They'd reached the set of turbolifts at the rear of the Imperial Palace now, one of the major renovations the Emperor had made in the deliberately antiquated design of the building when he'd taken it over. The turbolifts saved a lot of walking up and down the sweeping staircases in the more public parts of the building . . . as well as masking certain other improvements the Emperor had made in the Palace. 'So what's the problem with getting me a ship?' Mara asked as Winter tapped the call plate.

'The problem is the Empire,' Winter said. 'They've launched a massive attack against us, and it's tied up basically everything we have available, from light freighter on up.'

Mara frowned. Massive attacks against superior forces didn't sound like Grand Admiral Thrawn at all. 'It's that bad?'

'It's bad enough,' Winter said. 'I don't know if you knew it, but they beat us to the *Katana* fleet. They'd already moved nearly a hundred and eighty of the Dreadnaughts by the time we arrived. Combined with their new bottomless source of crewers and soldiers, the balance of power has been badly shifted.'

Mara nodded, a sour taste in her mouth. Put that way, it *did* sound like Thrawn. 'Which means I nearly got myself killed for nothing.'

Winter smiled tightly. 'If it helps, so did a lot of other people.'

The turbolift car arrived. They stepped inside, and Winter keyed for the Palace's residential areas. 'Ghent mentioned that the Empire was making trouble,' Mara commented as the car began moving upward. 'I should have realized that anything that could penetrate that fog he walks around in had to be serious.'

' "Serious" is an understatement,' Winter said grimly. 'In the past five days we've effectively lost control of four sectors, and thirteen more are on the edge. The biggest loss was the food production facilities at Ukio. Somehow, they managed to take it with its defenses intact.'

Mara felt her lip twist. 'Someone asleep at the board?'

'Not according to the preliminary reports.' Winter hesitated. 'There are rumors that the Imperials used a new superweapon that was able to fire straight through the Ukians' planetary shield. We're still trying to check that out.'

Mara swallowed, visions of the old Death Star spec sheets floating up from her memory. A weapon like that in the hands of a strategist like Grand Admiral Thrawn . . .

She shook the thought away. This wasn't her war. Karrde had promised they would stay neutral in this thing. 'I suppose I'd better get in touch with Karrde, then,' she said. 'See if he can send someone to pick us up.'

'It would probably be faster than waiting for one of our ships to be free,' Winter agreed. 'He left a data card with the name of a contact you can send a message through. He said you'd know which encrypt code to use.'

The turbolift let them out on the President's Guests floor, one of the few sections of the Palace that the Emperor had left strictly alone during his reign. With its old-fashioned hinged doors and hand-carved exotic wood furnishings, walking around the floor was like stepping a thousand years into the past. The Emperor had generally reserved the suites here for those emissaries who had fond feelings for such bygone days, or for those who could be impressed by his carefully manufactured continuity with that era. 'Captain Karrde left some of your clothes and personal effects for you after the *Katana* battle,' Winter said, unlocking one of the carved doors and pushing it open. 'If he missed anything, let me know and I can probably supply it. Here's the data card I mentioned,' she added, pulling it from her tunic.

'Thank you,' Mara said, inhaling deeply as she took the

card. This particular suite was done largely in Fijisi wood from Cardooine; and as the delicate scent rose around her, her thoughts flashed back to the glittering days of grand Imperial power and majesty . . .

'Can I get you anything else?'

The memory faded. Winter was standing before her . . . and the glory days of the Empire were gone. 'No, I'm fine,' she said.

Winter nodded. 'If you want anything, just call the duty officer,' she said, gesturing to the desk. 'I'll be available later; right now, there's a Council meeting I need to sit in on.'

'Go ahead,' Mara said. 'And thank you.'

Winter smiled and left. Mara took another deep breath of Fijisi wood, and with an effort pushed the last of the lingering memories away. She was here, and it was now; and as the Emperor's instructors had so often drummed into her, the first item of business was to fit into her surroundings. And that meant not looking like an escapee from the medical wing.

Karrde had left a good assortment of clothing for her: a semi-formal gown, two outfits of a nondescript type that she could wear on the streets of a hundred worlds without looking out of place, and four of the no-nonsense tunic/jumpsuit outfits that she usually wore aboard ship. Choosing one of the latter, she got dressed, then began sorting through the other things Karrde had left. With any luck – and maybe a little foresight on Karrde's part—

There it was: the forearm holster for her tiny blaster. The blaster itself was missing, of course – the captain of the *Adamant* had taken it away from her, and the Imperials weren't likely to return it anytime soon. Looking for a duplicate in the New Republic's arsenals would probably be a waste of effort, as well, though she was tempted to ask Winter for one just to see the reaction.

Fortunately, there was another way.

Each residential floor of the Imperial Palace had an extensive library, and in each of those libraries was a multicard set entitled *The Complete History of Corvis Minor*. Given how unexceptional most of Corvis Minor's history had been, the odds of anyone actually pulling the set off the shelf were extremely slim. Which, given there were no actual data cards in the box, was just as well.

The blaster was a slightly different style from the one Mara had lost to the Imperials. But its power pack was still adequately charged, and it fit snugly into her forearm holster, and that was all that mattered. Now, whatever happened with either the war or New Republic infighting, she would at least have a fighting chance.

She paused, the false data card box in her hand, a stray question belatedly flicking through her mind. What had Winter meant by that reference to a bottomless source for crewers and soldiers? Had one or more of the New Republic's systems gone over to the Imperial side? Or could Thrawn have discovered a hitherto unknown colony world with a populace ripe for recruitment?

It was something she should probably ask about sometime. First, though, she needed to get a message encrypted and relayed out to Karrde's designated contact. The sooner she was out of this place, the better.

Replacing the empty data card set, the comforting weight of the blaster snugged up against her left arm, she headed back to her suite.

Thrawn raised his glowing red eyes from the putrid-looking alien artwork displayed on the double display ring surrounding his command chair. 'No,' he said. 'Completely out of the question.'

Slowly, deliberately, C'baoth turned back from the holographic Woostroid statue he'd been gazing at. 'No?' he repeated, his voice rumbling like an approaching thunderstorm. 'What do you mean, no?'

'The word is self-explanatory,' Thrawn said icily. 'The military logic should be, as well. We don't have the numbers for a frontal assault on Coruscant; neither have we the supply lines and bases necessary for a traditional siege. Any attack would be both useless and wasteful, and the Empire will therefore not launch one.'

C'baoth's face darkened. 'Have a care, Grand Admiral Thrawn,' he warned. 'I rule the Empire, not you.'

'Do you really?' Thrawn countered, reaching up behind him to stroke the ysalamir arched over his shoulder on its nutrient frame.

C'baoth drew himself up to his full height, eyes blazing with sudden fire. 'I rule the Empire!' he shouted, his voice echoing through the command room. 'You will obey me, or you will die!'

Carefully, Pellaeon eased a little deeper into the Force-empty bubble that surrounded Thrawn's ysalamir. At those times when he was in control of himself, C'baoth appeared more confident and in control than he ever had before; but at the same time these violent bursts of clone madness were becoming more frequent and more vicious. Like a system in a positive feedback loop, swinging farther from its core point with each oscillation until it ripped itself apart.

So far C'baoth hadn't killed anyone or destroyed anything. In Pellaeon's opinion it was just a matter of time before that changed.

Perhaps the same thought had occurred to Thrawn. 'If you kill me, you'll lose the war,' he reminded the Jedi Master. 'And if you lose the war, Leia Organa Solo and her twins will never be yours.'

C'baoth took a step toward Thrawn's command seat, eyes blazing even hotter – and then, abruptly, he seemed to shrink again to normal size. 'You would never speak that way to the Emperor,' he said, almost petulantly.

'On the contrary,' Thrawn told him. 'On no fewer than four occasions I told the Emperor that I would not waste his troops and ships attacking an enemy which I was not yet prepared to defeat.'

C'baoth snorted. 'Only fools spoke that way to the Emperor,' he sneered. 'Fools, or those tired of life.'

'The Emperor also thought that way,' Thrawn agreed. 'The first time I refused he called me a traitor and gave my attack force to someone else.' The Grand Admiral reached up again to stroke his ysalamir. 'After its destruction, he knew better than to ignore my recommendations.'

For a long minute C'baoth studied Thrawn's face, his own expression twitching back and forth as if the mind behind it was having trouble maintaining a grip on thought or emotion. 'You could repeat the Ukian fraud,' he suggested at last. 'That trick with cloaked cruisers and timed turbolaser blasts. I would help you.'

'That's most generous of you,' Thrawn said. 'Unfortunately, that, too, would be a waste of effort. The Rebel leaders on Coruscant wouldn't be as quick to surrender as Ukio's farmfolk were. No matter how accurate our timing, they'd eventually realize that the turbolaser blasts hitting the surface weren't the same as those fired by the *Chimaera*, and come to the proper conclusion.'

He gestured to the holographic statues filling the room. 'The people and leaders of Woostri, on the other hand, are a different matter entirely. Like the Ukians, they have a strong fear of the unknown and what they perceive to be the impossible. Equally important, they have a tendency to magnify rumors of menace far out of proportion. The cloaked cruiser stratagem should work quite well there.'

C'baoth's face was starting to redden again. 'Grand Admiral Thrawn—'

'But as to Organa Solo and her twins,' Thrawn cut him off smoothly, 'you can have them whenever you wish.'

The embryonic tantrum evaporated. 'What do you mean?' C'baoth demanded warily.

'I mean that attacking Coruscant and carrying off Organa Solo by brute force is impractical,' Thrawn said. 'Sending in a small group to kidnap her, on the other hand, is perfectly feasible. I've already ordered Intelligence to assemble a commando team for that purpose. It should be ready within the day.'

'A commando team.' C'baoth's lip twisted. 'Need I remind you how your Noghri have continually failed you in this matter?'

'I agree,' Thrawn said, an oddly grim note to his voice. 'Which is why the Noghri will not be involved.'

Pellaeon looked down at the Grand Admiral in surprise, then threw an involuntary glance at the door to the command room anteroom where Thrawn's bodyguard Rukh was waiting. Ever since the Lord Darth Vader had first duped the Noghri into their perpetual service to the Empire, the gullible gray-skinned aliens had insisted on putting their own personal honor on the line with each mission. Being pulled off an assignment, especially one this important, would be like a slap in the face to them. Or worse. 'Admiral?' he murmured. 'I'm not sure—'

'We'll discuss it later, Captain,' Thrawn said. 'For now, all I need to know is whether Master C'baoth is truly ready to receive his young Jedi.' One blue-black eyebrow lifted. 'Or whether he prefers simply discussing it.'

C'baoth smiled thinly. 'Am I to take that as a challenge, Grand Admiral Thrawn?'

'Take it any way you like,' Thrawn said. 'I merely point out that a wise tactician considers the cost of an operation before launching it. Organa Solo's twins are due to be born any day now, which means you would have two infants as well as Organa Solo herself to deal with. If you're not certain you can handle that, it would be best to postpone the operation.'

Pellaeon braced himself for another explosion of clone madness. But to his surprise, it didn't come. 'The only question, Grand Admiral Thrawn,' C'baoth said softly, 'is whether newborn infants will be too much for your Imperial commandos to handle.'

'Very well,' Thrawn nodded. 'Our rendezvous with the rest of the fleet will be in thirty minutes; you'll transfer to the *Death's Head* at that time to assist in their attack on Woostri. By the time you return to the *Chimaera*' – again the eyebrow lifted – 'we should have your Jedi for you.'

'Very well, Grand Admiral Thrawn,' C'baoth said. He drew himself up again, smoothing his long white beard away from his robe. 'But I warn you: if you fail me this time, you will not be pleased with the consequences.' Turning, he strode across the command room and through the door.

'It's always such a pleasure,' Thrawn commented under his breath as the door slid shut.

Pellaeon worked moisture into his mouth. 'Admiral, with all due respect—'

'You're worried about my having promised to get Organa Solo out of possibly the most secure place in Rebellion-held territory?' Thrawn said.

'Actually, sir, yes,' Pellaeon said. 'The Imperial Palace is supposed to be an impregnable fortress.'

'Yes, indeed,' Thrawn agreed. 'But it was the Emperor who made it that way . . . and as in most things, the Emperor kept a few small secrets about the Palace to himself. And to certain of his favorites.'

Pellaeon frowned down at him. Secrets . . . 'Such as a private way in and out?' he hazarded.

Thrawn smiled up at him. 'Precisely. And now that we can finally insure that Organa Solo will be staying put in the Palace for a while, it becomes profitable to try sending in a commando team.'

'But not a Noghri team.'

Thrawn lowered his eyes to the collection of holographic sculptures surrounding them. 'There's something wrong with the Noghri, Captain,' he said quietly. 'I don't yet know what it is, but I know it's there. I can sense it with every communication I have with the dynasts on Honoghr.'

Pellaeon thought back to that awkward scene a month ago, when that painfully apologetic envoy from the Noghri dynasts had come aboard with the news that the suspected traitor Khabarakh had escaped from their custody. So far, despite their best efforts, they'd been unable to recapture him. 'Perhaps they're still fidgeting over that Khabarakh thing,' he suggested.

'And well they should be,' Thrawn said coldly. 'But it's more than that. And until I find out how much more, the Noghri will remain under suspicion.'

He leaned forward, tapped two controls on his board. The holographic sculptures faded and were replaced by a tactical map of the current position of the major battle planes. 'But at the moment we have two more pressing matters to consider,' he continued, leaning back in his seat again. 'First, we have to divert our increasingly arrogant Jedi Master from this mistaken notion that he has the right to rule my Empire. Organa Solo and her twins are that diversion.'

Pellaeon thought about all the other attempts to capture Organa Solo. 'And if the team fails?'

'There are contingencies,' Thrawn assured him. 'Despite his power and even his unpredictability, Master C'baoth can still be manipulated.'

He gestured toward the tactical map. 'What's even more important right now, though, is that we insure the momentum of our battle plan. So far, the campaign is reasonably on schedule. The Rebellion has resisted more firmly than anticipated in the Farrfin and Dolomar sectors, but elsewhere the target systems have generally bowed to Imperial power.'

'I wouldn't consider any of the gains all that solid yet,' Pellaeon pointed out.

'Precisely,' Thrawn nodded. 'Each depends on our maintaining a strong and highly visible Imperial presence. And for that, it's vital that we maintain our supply of clones.'

He paused. Pellaeon looked at the tactical map, his mind racing as he searched for the response Thrawn was obviously waiting for him to come up with. The Spaarti cloning cylinders, hidden away for decades in the Emperor's private storehouse on Wayland, were about as safe as anything in the galaxy could be. Buried beneath a mountain, protected by an Imperial garrison, and surrounded by hostile locals, its very existence was unknown to anyone except the top Imperial commanders.

He froze. Top Imperial commanders; and perhaps – 'Mara Jade,' he said. 'She's convalescing on Coruscant. Would she have known about the storehouse?'

'That is indeed the question,' Thrawn agreed. 'There's a good chance she doesn't – I knew many of the Emperor's secrets, and it still took me a great deal of effort to find Wayland. But it's not a risk we can afford to take.'

Pellaeon nodded, suppressing a shiver. He'd been

wondering why the Grand Admiral had chosen an Intelligence squad for this mission. Unlike standard commando units, Intelligence units were trained in such nonmilitary methods as assassination . . . 'Will a single team be handling both missions, sir, or will you be sending in two?'

'One team should be adequate,' Thrawn said. 'The two objectives are well enough interlocked to make that reasonable. And neutralizing Jade does not necessarily mean killing her.'

Pellaeon frowned. But before he could ask what Thrawn had meant by that, the Grand Admiral touched his board and the tactical holo was replaced by a map of Orus sector. 'In the meantime, I think it's time to underline the importance of the Calius saj Leeloo for our enemies. Do we have a follow-up report yet from Governor Staffa?'

'Yes, sir,' Pellaeon said, pulling it up on his data pad. 'Skywalker left at the same time as the decoy shuttle, and is presumed to have followed its vector. If so, he'll reach the Poderis system in approximately thirty hours.'

'Excellent,' Thrawn said. 'He'll undoubtedly report in to Coruscant before he reaches Poderis. His subsequent disappearance should go a long way toward convincing them that they've found the conduit for our clone traffic.'

'Yes, sir,' Pellaeon said, keeping to himself his doubts as to their chances of actually causing Skywalker to disappear. Thrawn presumably knew what he was doing. 'One other thing, sir. There was a second follow-up to Staffa's original report, one that came in under an Intelligence encrypt code.'

'From his aide, Fingal,' Thrawn nodded. 'A man with Governor Staffa's casual loyalties practically begs us to assign him a quiet watchdog. Were there any discrepancies with the governor's report?'

'Just one, sir. The follow-up gave a complete description of Skywalker's contact, a man Staffa had indicated was one of his own agents. Fingal's description strongly suggests the man was, in fact, Talon Karrde.'

Thrawn exhaled thoughtfully. 'Indeed. Did Fingal suggest any explanation for Karrde's presence in Calius?'

'According to him, there are indications that Governor Staffa has had a private trade arrangement with Karrde for several years,' Pellaeon said. 'Fingal reports he was going to have the man picked up for questioning, but was unable to find a way to do so that wouldn't have alerted Skywalker.'

'Yes,' Thrawn murmured. 'Well . . . what's done is done. And if smuggling was all that was involved, there's no harm. Still, we can't have random smugglers buzzing around our deceptions and perhaps accidentally poking holes in them. And Karrde has already proved he can be a great deal of trouble.'

For a moment Thrawn gazed in silence at the Orus sector map. Then, he looked up at Pellaeon. 'But for now we have other matters to deal with. Prepare a course for the Poderis system, Captain; I want the *Chimaera* there within forty hours.' He smiled thinly. 'And signal the garrison commander that I expect him to have a proper reception prepared by the time we arrive. Perhaps in two or three days' time we'll have an unexpected gift to present to our beloved Jedi Master.'

'Yes, sir.' Pellaeon hesitated. 'Admiral . . . what happens if we get Organa Solo and her twins for C'baoth and he's able to turn them the way he thinks he can? We'd have four of them to deal with then instead of just one. Five, if we're able to capture Skywalker at Poderis.'

'There's no need for concern,' Thrawn said, shaking his head. 'Turning either Organa Solo or Skywalker would take C'baoth a great deal of time and effort. It would be even longer before the infants are old enough to be of any danger to us, no matter what he does to them. Long before any of that occurs' – Thrawn's eyes glittered – 'we'll have come to a suitable arrangement with our Jedi Master over the sharing of power in the Empire.'

Pellaeon swallowed. 'Understood, sir,' he managed.

'Good. Then you're dismissed, Captain. Return to the bridge.'

'Yes, sir.' Pellaeon turned and headed across the room, the muscles in his throat feeling tight. Yes, he understood, all right. Thrawn would come to an arrangement with C'baoth . . . or he would have the Jedi Master killed.

If he could. It was not, Pellaeon decided, a confrontation he would like to place any bets on.

Or, for that matter, be anywhere near when it happened.

CHAPTER 4

Poderis was one of that select group of worlds generally referred to in the listings as 'marginal': planets that had remained colonized not because of valuable resources or convenient location, but solely because of the stubborn spirit of its colonists. With a disorienting ten-hour rotational cycle, a lowland slough ecology that had effectively confined the colonists to a vast archipelago of tall mesas, and a nearly perpendicular axial tilt that created tremendous winds every spring and autumn, Poderis was not the sort of place wandering travelers generally bothered with. Its people were tough and independent, tolerant to visitors but with a long history of ignoring the politics of the outside galaxy.

All of which made it an ideal transfer point for the Empire's new clone traffic. And an ideal place for that same Empire to set a trap.

The man shadowing Luke was short and plain, the sort of person who would fade into the background almost anywhere he went. He was good at his job, too, with a skill that implied long experience in Imperial Intelligence. But that experience had naturally not extended to trailing Jedi Knights. Luke had sensed his presence almost as soon as the man had begun following him, and had been able to visually pick him out of the crowd a minute later.

Leaving only the problem of what to do about him.

'Artoo?' Luke called softly into the comlink he'd surreptitiously wedged into the neckband of his hooded robe. 'We've got company. Probably Imperials.'

There was a soft, worried trill from the comlink, followed by something that was obviously a question. 'There's nothing you can do,' Luke told him, taking a guess as to the content of the question and wishing Threepio was there to translate. He could generally pick up the gist of what Artoo was saying, but in a situation like this the gist might not be enough. 'Is there anyone poking around the freighter? Or around the landing field in general?'

Artoo chirped a definite negative. 'Well, they'll be there soon enough,' Luke warned him, pausing to look in a shop window. The tail, he noted, moved forward a few more steps before finding an excuse of his own to stop. A professional, indeed. 'Get as much of the preflight done as you can without attracting attention. We'll want to get off as soon as I get there.'

The droid warbled acknowledgement. Reaching to his neck, Luke shut off the comlink and gave the area a quick scan. The first priority was to lose the tail before the Imperials made any more overt moves against him. And to do that, he needed some kind of distraction . . .

Fifty meters ahead in the crowd was what looked to be his best opportunity: another man striding along the street in a robe of similar cut and color to Luke's. Cautiously picking up his pace, trying not to give the appearance of hurrying, Luke moved toward him.

The other robed figure continued to the T-junction ahead and turned the corner to his right. Luke picked up his pace a bit more, sensing as he did so his shadower's suspicion that he'd been spotted. Resisting the urge to break into a flat-out run, Luke strolled casually around the corner.

It was a street like most of the others he'd already seen in the city: wide, rock-paved, reasonably crowded, and lined on both sides with graystone buildings. Automatically, he reached out with the Force, scanning the area around him and as far ahead as he could sense—

And abruptly caught his breath. Directly ahead, still distant but clearly detectable, were small pockets of darkness where his Jedi senses could read absolutely nothing. As if the Force that carried the information to him had somehow ceased to exist . . . or was being blocked.

Which meant this was no ordinary ambush, for an ordinary New Republic spy. The Imperials knew he was here and had come to Poderis equipped with ysalamiri.

And unless he did something fast, they were going to take him.

He looked again at the buildings around him. Squat, two-story structures, for the most part, with textured facades and decorative roof parapets. Those to his immediate right were built in a single solid row; directly across the street to his left, the first building after the T-junction had a warped facade, leaving a narrow gap between it and its neighbor's. It wasn't much in the way of cover – and the distance itself was going to be a reach – but it was all he had. Hurrying across the street, half expecting the trap to be sprung before he got there, he slipped into the opening. Bending his knees, letting the Force flow into his muscles, he jumped.

He almost didn't make it. The parapet directly above him was angled and smooth, and for a second he seemed to hang in midair as his fingers scrabbled for a hold. Then, he found a grip, and with a surge of effort pulled himself up and over to lie flat along the rooftop.

Just in time. Even as he eased one eye over the edge of the parapet, he saw his tail come racing around the corner, all efforts at subtlety abandoned. Shoving aside those in his way, he said something inaudible into the comlink in his hand—

And from the cross street a block away, a row of white-armored stormtroopers stepped into view. Blaster rifles held high against their chests, the dark elongated shapes of ysalamiri slung on backpack nutrient frames across their shoulders, they cordoned off the end of the street.

It was a well-planned, well-executed net; and Luke had maybe three minutes to get across the roof and down before they realized their fish had slipped out of it. Easing back from the edge, he turned his head toward the other side of the roof.

The roof didn't have another side. Barely sixty centimeters from where he lay, the roof abruptly became a blank wall that angled steeply downward for perhaps a hundred meters, extending in both directions as far as Luke could see. Beyond its lower edge, there was nothing but the distant mists in the lowlands beneath the mesa.

He'd miscalculated, possibly fatally. Preoccupied with the man shadowing him, he'd completely missed the fact that his path had taken him to the outer edge of the mesa. The slanting wall beside him was one of the massive shield-barriers designed to deflect the planet's vicious seasonal winds harmlessly over the city.

Luke had escaped the Imperial net . . . only to discover that there was literally nowhere else for him to go.

'Great,' he muttered under his breath, easing back to the parapet and looking down into the street. More stormtroopers had joined the first squad now and were beginning to sift through the stunned crowd of people caught in the trap; behind them, two squads from the other direction of the T-junction had moved in to seal off the rear of the street. Luke's erstwhile shadow, a blaster now gripped his hand, was pushing his way through the crowd, making for the other robed figure Luke had noticed earlier.

The other robed figure . . .

Luke bit at his lip. It would be a rather unfriendly trick to play on a totally innocent bystander. But on the other hand, the Imperials obviously knew who they were looking for and just as obviously wanted him alive. Putting the man down there in deadly danger, he knew, would be unacceptable behavior for a Jedi. Luke could only hope that inconveniencing him wouldn't fall under the same heading.

Gritting his teeth, he reached out with the Force and plucked the blaster from the shadow's hand. Spinning it low over the heads of the crowd, he dropped it squarely into the other robed figure's hand.

The shadow shouted to the stormtroopers; but what had begun as a call of triumph quickly became a screech of warning. Focusing the Force with all the control he could manage, Luke turned the blaster back toward its former owner and fired.

Fired safely over the crowd, of course – there was no possible way for him to aim accurately enough to hit the

Imperial, even if he'd wanted to. But even a clean miss was enough to jolt the stormtroopers into action. The Imperials who'd been checking faces and IDs abandoned their task to push through the crowd toward the man in the robe, while those guarding the ends of the street hurried forward into backup positions.

It was, not surprisingly, too much for the man in the robe. Shaking away the blaster that had inexplicably become attached to his hand, he slipped past the frozen onlookers beside him and disappeared into a narrow alleyway.

Luke didn't wait to see any more. The minute anyone got a good look at the fleeing man's face, the diversion would be over, and he had to be off this roof and on his way to the landing field before that happened. Sidling to the edge of his narrow ledge, he looked down.

It didn't look promising. Built to withstand two-hundred-kilometer winds, it was perfectly smooth, with no protuberances that could get caught in eddy currents. Nor were there any windows, service doors, or other openings visible. That, at least, shouldn't be a problem; he could cut himself a makeshift doorway with his lightsaber if it came to that. The real question was how to get out of range of the Imperials' trap before they started hunting him in earnest.

He glanced back. And he had to do it fast. From the direction of the official landing area at the far end of the city, the distant specks of airspeeders had begun to appear over the squat city buildings.

He couldn't drop back down on the street side without attracting unwelcome attention. He couldn't crawl along the narrow upper edge of the shield-barrier, at least not fast enough to get out of sight before the airspeeders got here. Which left him only one direction. Down.

But not necessarily *straight* down . . .

He squinted into the sky. Poderis's sun was nearly to the horizon, moving almost visibly through its ten-hour circuit. Right now its light was shining straight into the eyes of the approaching airspeeder pilots, but within five minutes it would be completely below the horizon. Giving the searchers a clear view again, and leaving behind a dusk where a lightsaber blade would be instantly visible.

It was now or never.

Pulling his lightsaber from beneath his robe, Luke ignited it, making sure to keep the glowing green blade out of sight of the approaching airspeeders. Using the tip, he carefully made a shallow cut to the right and a few degrees down across the slanting shield-barrier. His robe was made of relatively flimsy material, and it took only a second to tear off the left sleeve and wrap it around the fingertips of his left hand. The padded fingers slipped easily into the groove he'd just made, with enough room to slide freely along it. Getting a firm grip, he set the tip of his lightsaber blade into the end of the groove and rolled off the ledge. Supported by his fingertips, the lightsaber held outstretched in his right hand carving out his path for him as he went, he slid swiftly across and down the shield-barrier.

It was at the same time exhilarating and terrifying. Memories flooded back: the wind whipping past him as he fell through the center core of the Cloud City of Bespin; hanging literally by his fingertips barely minutes later beneath the city; lying exhausted on the floor in the second Death Star, sensing through his pain the enraged helplessness of the Emperor as Vader hurled him to his death. Beneath his chest and legs, the smooth surface of the shield-barrier slid past, marking his rapid approach to the edge and the empty space beyond . . .

Lifting his head, blinking against the wind slapping into his face, he looked over his shoulder. The lethal edge was visible now, racing upward toward him at what felt like breakneck speed. Closer and closer it came . . . and then, at the last second, he changed the angle of his lightsaber. The downward path of his fingerguide shifted toward horizontal, and a few seconds later he slid smoothly to a halt.

For a moment he just hung there, dangling precariously by one hand as he caught his breath and got his heartbeat back under control. Above him, its edge catching the last rays of the setting sun, he could see the groove he'd just cut, angling up and to his left. Over a hundred meters to his left, he estimated. Hopefully, far enough to put him outside the Imperials' trap.

He'd find out soon enough.

Behind him, the sun dipped below the horizon, erasing the thin line of his passage. Moving carefully, trying not to dislodge his straining fingertips, he began to cut a hole through the shield-barrier.

'Report from the stormtrooper commander, Admiral,' Pellaeon called, grimacing as he read it off his comm display. 'Skywalker does not appear to be within the cordon.'

'I'm not surprised,' Thrawn said darkly, glowering at his displays. 'I've warned Intelligence repeatedly about underestimating the range of Skywalker's sensing abilities. Obviously, they didn't take me seriously.'

Pellaeon swallowed hard. 'Yes, sir. But we know he *was* there, and he couldn't have gotten very far. The stormtroopers have established a secondary cordon and begun a building-to-building search.'

Thrawn took a deep breath, then let it out. 'No,' he said, his voice even again. 'He didn't go into any of the buildings. Not Skywalker. That little diversion with the decoy and the blaster . . .' He looked at Pellaeon. 'Up, Captain. He went up onto the roof-tops.'

'The spotters are already sweeping that direction,' Pellaeon said. 'If he's up there, they'll spot him.'

'Good.' Thrawn tapped a switch on his command console, calling up a holographic map of that section of the mesa. 'What about the shield-barrier on the west edge of the cordon? Can it be climbed?'

'Our people here say no,' Pellaeon shook his head. 'Too smooth and too sharply angled, with no lip or other barrier at the bottom. If Skywalker went up that side of the street, he's still there. Or at the bottom of the mesa.'

'Perhaps,' Thrawn said. 'Assign one of the spotters to search that area anyway. What about Skywalker's ship?'

'Intelligence is still trying to identify which one is his,'

Pellaeon admitted. 'There's some problem with the records. We should have it in a few more minutes.'

'Minutes which we no longer have, thanks to their shadower's carelessness,' Thrawn bit out. 'He's to be demoted one grade.'

'Yes, sir,' Pellaeon said, logging the order. A rather severe punishment, but it could have been far worse. The late Lord Vader would have summarily strangled the man. 'The landing field itself is surrounded, of course.'

Thrawn rubbed his chin thoughtfully. 'A probable waste of time,' he said slowly. 'On the other hand . . .'

He turned his head to gaze out the viewport at the slowly rotating planet. 'Pull them off, Captain,' he ordered. 'All except the clone troopers. Leave those on guard near the likeliest possibilities for Skywalker's ship.'

Pellaeon blinked. 'Sir?'

Thrawn turned back to face him, a fresh glint in those glowing red eyes. 'The landing field cordon doesn't have nearly enough ysalamiri to stop a Jedi, Captain. So we won't bother trying. We'll let him get his ship into space, and take him with the *Chimaera*.'

'Yes, sir,' Pellaeon said, feeling his forehead furrow. 'But then . . .'

'Why leave the clones?' Thrawn finished for him. 'Because while Skywalker is valuable to us, the same is not true of his astromech droid.' He smiled slightly. 'Unless, of course, Skywalker's heroic efforts to escape Poderis convince it that this is indeed the main conduit for our clone traffic.'

'Ah,' Pellaeon said, finally understanding. 'In which case, we find a way to allow the droid to escape back to the Rebellion?'

'Exactly,' Thrawn gestured to Pellaeon's board. 'Orders, Captain.'

'Yes, sir.' Pellaeon turned back to his board, feeling a cautious stirring of excitement as he began issuing the Grand Admiral's commands. Maybe this time Skywalker would finally be theirs.

* * *

Artoo was jabbering nervously when Luke finally charged through the door of their small freighter and slapped the seal behind him. 'Everything ready to go?' he shouted over his shoulder to the droid as he hurried to the cockpit alcove.

Artoo trilled back an affirmative. Luke dropped into the pilot's seat, giving the instruments a quick once-over as he strapped himself in. 'OK,' he called back. 'Here we go.'

Throwing power to the repulsorlifts, Luke kicked the freighter clear of the ground, wrenching it hard to starboard. A pair of Skipray blastboats rose with him, moving into tandem pursuit formation as he headed for the edge of the mesa. 'Watch those Skiprays, Artoo,' Luke called, splitting his own attention between the rapidly approaching city's edge and the airspace above them. The fight with those clone troopers guarding the landing field had been intense, but it had been far too brief to be realistic. Either the Empire had left someone totally incompetent in charge, or they'd let him get to his ship on purpose. Carefully herding him into the real trap . . .

The edge of the mesa shot past beneath him. Luke threw a quick glance at the rear display to confirm that he was clear of the city, then punched in the main sublight drive.

The freighter shot skyward like a scalded mynock, leaving the pursuing Skiprays flatfooted in its wake. The official-sounding orders to halt that had been blaring from the board turned into a surprised yelp as Luke reached over and shut the comm off. 'Artoo? You all right back there?'

The droid chirped an affirmative, and a question scrolled across Luke's computer screen. 'They were clones, all right,' he confirmed grimly, an uncomfortable shiver running through him. The strange aura that seemed to surround the Empire's new duplicate humans was twice as eerie up close. 'I'll tell you something else, too,' he added to Artoo. 'The Imperials knew it was me they were chasing. Those stormtroopers were carrying ysalamiri on their backs.'

Artoo whistled thoughtfully, gave a questioning gurgle. 'Right – that whole Delta Source thing,' Luke agreed, reading the droid's comment. 'Leia told me that if we couldn't get the leak closed fast, she was going to recommend we move operations out of the Imperial Palace. Maybe even off Coruscant entirely.'

Though if Delta Source was a human or alien spy instead of some impossibly undetectable listening system in the Palace itself, moving anywhere would just be so much wasted effort. From Artoo's rather pointed silence, Luke guessed the droid was thinking that, too.

The distant horizon, barely visible as dark planet against dark but starlit sky, was starting to show a visible curvature now. 'Better start calculating our jump to lightspeed, Artoo,' he called over his shoulder. 'We're probably going to have to get out of here in a hurry.'

He got a confirming beep from the droid's position and turned his attention back to the horizon ahead. A whole fleet of Star Destroyers, he knew, could be lurking below that horizon, out of range of his instruments, waiting for him to get too far from any possible cover to launch their attack.

Out of range of his instruments, but perhaps not out of range of Jedi senses. Closing his eyes to slits, flooding his mind with calmness, he stretched out through the Force—

He got it an instant before Artoo's startled warning shrill shattered the air. An Imperial Star Destroyer all right; but not cutting across his path as Luke had expected. Instead, it was coming up from behind, in an atmosphere-top forced orbit that had allowed it to build up speed without sacrificing the advantages of planetary cover.

'Hang on!' Luke shouted, throwing emergency power to the drive. But it was a futile gesture, and both he and the Imperials knew it. The Star Destroyer was coming up fast, its tractor beams already activated and tracking him. Within a handful of seconds, whey were going to get him.

Or at least, they were going to get the freighter . . .

Luke hit his strap release, opening a disguised panel as he did so and touching the three switches hidden there. The first switch keyed in the limited autopilot; the second unlocked the aft proton torpedo launcher and started it firing blindly back toward the Star Destroyer.

The third activated the freighter's self-destruct.

His X-wing was wedged nose forward in the cargo area behind the cockpit alcove, looking for all the world like some strange metallic animal peering out of its burrow. Luke leaped to the open canopy, coming within an ace of cracking his head on the freighter's low ceiling in the process. Artoo, already snugged into the X-wing's droid socket, was jabbering softly to himself as he ran the starfighter's systems from standby to full ready. Even as Luke strapped in and pulled on his flight helmet, the droid signaled they were clear to fly.

'OK,' Luke told him, resting his left hand on the special switch that had been added to his control board. 'If this is going to work, we're going to have to time it just right. Be ready.'

Again he closed his eyes, letting the Force flow through his senses. Once before, on his first attempt to locate the Jedi Master C'baoth, he'd tangled like this with the Imperials – an X-wing against an Imperial Star Destroyer. That, too, had been a deliberate ambush, though he hadn't realized it until C'baoth's unholy alliance with the Empire had been laid bare. In that battle, skill and luck and the Force had saved him.

This time, if the specialists back at Coruscant had done their job right, the luck was already built in.

With his mind deeply into the Force, he sensed the locking of the tractor beam a half second before it actually occurred. His hand jabbed the switch; and even as the freighter jerked in the tractor beam's powerful grip, the front end blew apart into a cloud of metallic shards. An instant later, kicked forward by a deck-mounted blast-booster, the X-wing shot through the glittering debris. For a long, heart-stopping moment it seemed as though the tractor beam was going to be able to maintain its hold despite the obscuring particle fog. Then, all at once, the grip slackened and was gone.

'We're free!' Luke shouted back at Artoo, rolling the X-wing over and driving hard for deep space. 'I'm going evasive – hang on.'

He rolled the X-wing again, and as he did so a pair of brilliant green flashes shot past the transparisteel canopy. With their tractor beams outdistanced, the Imperials had apparently decided to settle for shooting him out of the sky. Another barrage of green flame scorched past, and there was a yelp from Artoo as something burned through the deflectors to slap against the X-wing's underside. Reaching out again to the Force, Luke let it guide his hands on the controls—

And then, almost without warning, it was time. Reaching to the hyperdrive lever, Luke pulled it back.

With a flicker of pseudomotion, the X-wing vanished into the safety of hyperspace, the *Chimaera*'s turbolaser batteries still firing uselessly for a second at where it had been. The batteries fell silent; and Pellaeon let out a long breath, afraid to look over at Thrawn's command station. It was the second time Skywalker had escaped from this kind of trap . . . and the last time he'd done so, a man had died for that failure.

The rest of the bridge crew hadn't forgotten that, either. In the brittle silence the faint rustling of cloth against seat material was clearly audible as Thrawn stood up. 'Well,' the Grand Admiral said, his voice strangely calm. 'One must give the Rebels full credit for ingenuity. I've seen that trick worked before, but not nearly so effectively.'

'Yes, sir,' Pellaeon said, trying without success to hide the strain in his voice.

Out of the corner of his eye he could see Thrawn looking at him. 'At ease, Captain,' the Grand Admiral said soothingly. 'Skywalker would have made an interesting package to present to Master C'baoth, but his escape is hardly cause for major concern. The primary objective of this exercise was to convince the Rebellion that they'd discovered the clone conduit. That objective has been achieved.'

The tightness in Pellaeon's chest began to dissipate. If the Grand Admiral wasn't angry about it . . .

'That does not mean, however,' Thrawn went on, 'that the actions of the *Chimaera*'s crew should be ignored. Come with me, Captain.'

Pellaeon got to his feet, the tightness returning. 'Yes, sir.'

Thrawn led the way to the aft stairway and descended to

the starboard crew pit. He walked past the crewers at their consoles, past the officers standing stiffly behind them, and came to a halt at the control station for the starboard tractor beams. 'Your name,' he said quietly to the young man standing at rigid attention there.

'Ensign Mithel,' the other said, his face pale but composed. The expression of a man facing his death.

'Tell me what happened, Ensign.'

Mithel swallowed. 'Sir, I had just established a positive lock on the freighter when it broke up into a cluster of trac-reflective particles. The targeting system tried to lock on all of them at once and went into a loop snarl.'

'And what did you do?'

'I – sir, I knew that if I waited for the particles to dissipate normally, the target starfighter would be out of range. So I tried to dissipate them myself by shifting the tractor beam into sheer-plane mode.'

'It didn't work.'

A quiet sigh slipped through Mithel's lips. 'No, sir. The target-lock system couldn't handle it. It froze up completely.'

'Yes.' Thrawn cocked his head slightly. 'You've had a few moments now to consider your actions, Ensign. Can you think of anything you should have done instead?'

The young man's lip twitched. 'No, sir. I'm sorry, but I can't. I don't remember anything in the manual that covers this kind of situation.'

Thrawn nodded. 'Correct,' he agreed. 'There isn't anything. Several methods have been suggested over the past few decades for counteracting the covert shroud gambit, none of which has ever been made practical. Yours was one of the more innovative attempts, particularly given how little time you had to come up with it. The fact that it failed does not in any way diminish that.'

A look of cautious disbelief was starting to edge into Mithel's face. 'Sir?'

'The Empire needs quick and creative minds, Ensign,' Thrawn said. 'You're hereby promoted to lieutenant . . . and your first assignment is to find a way to break a covert shroud.

After their success here, the Rebellion may try the gambit again.'

'Yes, sir,' Mithel breathed, the color starting to come back into his face. 'I – thank you, sir.'

'Congratulations, Lieutenant Mithel.' Thrawn nodded to him, then turned to Pellaeon. 'The bridge is yours, Captain. Resume our scheduled flight. I'll be in my command room if you require me.'

'Yes, sir,' Pellaeon managed.

And stood there beside the newly minted lieutenant, feeling the stunned awe pervading the bridge as he watched Thrawn leave. Yesterday, the *Chimaera*'s crew had trusted and respected the Grand Admiral. After today, they would be ready to die for him.

And for the first time in five years, Pellaeon finally knew in the deepest level of his being that the old Empire was gone. The new Empire, with Grand Admiral Thrawn at its head, had been born.

The X-wing hung suspended in the blackness of space, light-years away from any solid mass larger than a grain of dust. It was, Luke thought, almost like a replay of that other battle with a Star Destroyer, the one that had left him stranded in deep space and had ultimately led him to Talon Karrde and Mara Jade and the planet Myrkr.

Fortunately, appearance was the only thing they had in common. Mostly.

From the droid socket behind him came a nervous warble. 'Come on, Artoo, relax,' Luke soothed him. 'It's not that bad. We couldn't have made it anywhere near Coruscant without refueling anyway. We'll just have to do it a little sooner, that's all.'

The response was a sort of indignant grunt. 'I *am* taking you seriously, Artoo,' Luke said patiently, keying the listing on his nav display over to the droid. 'Look – here are all the places we can get to with half our primary power cells blown out. See?'

For a moment the droid seemed to mull over the list, and

Luke took the opportunity to give it another look himself. There were a lot of choices there, all right. The problem was that many of them wouldn't be especially healthy for a lone New Republic X-wing to show up at. Half were under direct Imperial control, and most of the others were either leaning that way or keeping their political options open.

Still, even on an Imperial-held world, there were sensor gaps a single starfighter could probably slip through. He could put down in some isolated place, make his way on foot to a spaceport, and buy some replacement fuel cells with the Imperial currency he still had left. Getting the cells back to the X-wing could be a bit of a problem, but nothing he and Artoo couldn't solve.

Artoo chirped a suggestion. 'Kessel's a possibility,' Luke agreed. 'I don't know, though – last I heard Moruth Doole was still in charge there, and Han's never really trusted him. I think we'd do better with Fwillsving, or even—'

He broke off as one of the planets on the list caught his eye. A planet Leia had programmed into his onboard nav system, almost as an afterthought, before he left on this mission.

Honoghr.

'I've got a better idea, Artoo,' Luke said slowly. 'Let's go visit the Noghri.'

There was a startled, disbelieving squawk from behind him. 'Oh, come on,' Luke admonished him. 'Leia and Chewie went there and got back all right, didn't they? And Threepio, too,' he added. 'You don't want Threepio saying you were afraid to go somewhere *he* wasn't afraid of, would you?'

Artoo grunted again. 'Doesn't matter whether or not he had a choice,' Luke said firmly. 'The point is that he went.'

The droid gave a mournful and rather resigned gurgle. 'That's the spirit,' Luke encouraged him, keying the nav computer to start the calculation to Honoghr. 'Leia's been wanting me to go visit them, anyway. This way we kill two dune lizards with one throw.'

Artoo gave a single discomfited gurgle and fell silent . . . and even Luke, who fully trusted Leia's judgement of the

Noghri, privately conceded that it was perhaps not the most comforting figure of speech he could have used.

CHAPTER 5

The battle data from the Woostri system scrolled to the bottom of the data pad and stopped. 'I still don't believe it,' Leia said, shaking her head as she laid the data pad back down on the table. 'If the Empire had a superweapon that could shoot through planetary shields, they'd be using it in every system they attacked. It has to be a trick or illusion of some kind.'

'I agree,' Mon Mothma said quietly. 'The question is, how do we convince the rest of the Council and the Assemblage of that? Not to mention the outer systems themselves?'

'We must solve the puzzle of what happened at Ukio and Woostri,' Admiral Ackbar said, his voice even more gravelly than usual. 'And we must solve it quickly.'

Leia picked up her data pad again, throwing a quick look across the table at Ackbar as she did so. The Mon Calamari's huge eyes seemed unusually heavy-lidded, his normal salmon color noticeably faded. He was tired, desperately so . . . and with the Empire's grand offensive still rolling toward them across the galaxy, he wasn't likely to be getting much rest anytime soon.

Neither were any of the rest of them, for that matter. 'We already know that Grand Admiral Thrawn has a talent for understanding the minds of his opponents,' she reminded the others. 'Could he have predicted how quickly both the Ukians and the Woostroids would be to surrender?'

'As opposed to, say, the Filvians?' Mon Mothma nodded slowly. 'Interesting point. That might indicate the illusion is one that can't be maintained for very long.'

'Or that the power requirements are exceedingly high,' Ackbar added. 'If the Empire has learned a method for focusing nonvisible energy against a shield, it could conceivably weaken a section long enough to fire a turbolaser blast through the opening. But such a thing would take a tremendous power output.'

'And should also show up as an energy stress on the shield,' Mon Mothma pointed out. 'None of our information suggests that was the case.'

'Our information may be wrong,' Ackbar retorted. He threw a brief glare at Councilor Borsk Fey'lya. 'Or it may have been manipulated by the Empire,' he added pointedly. 'Such things have happened before.'

Leia looked at Fey'lya, too, wondering if the thinly veiled insult to his people would finally drive the Bothan out of his self-imposed silence. But Fey'lya just sat there, his eyes on the table, his cream-colored fur motionless. Not speaking, not reacting, perhaps not even thinking.

Eventually, she supposed, he would regain his verbal courage and a measure of his old political strength. But for now, with his false denunciation of Ackbar still fresh in everyone's minds, he was in the middle of his species' version of penance.

Leia's stomach tightened in frustration. Once again, the Bothans' inflexible all-or-nothing approach to politics was running squarely counter to the New Republic's best interests. A few months earlier. Fey'lya's accusations against Ackbar had wasted valuable time and energy; now, when the Council needed every bit of insight and resourcefulness it could muster – including Fey'lya's – he was playing the silent martyr.

There were days – and long, dark nights – when Leia privately despaired of ever holding the New Republic together.

'You're right, of course, Admiral,' Mon Mothma said with a sigh. 'We need more information. And we need it quickly.'

'Talon Karrde's organization is still our best chance,' Leia said. 'They've got the contacts, both here and on the Imperial side. And from what Luke said in his last message, Karrde sounded interested.'

'We can't afford to wait on the convenience of a smuggler,' Ackbar growled, his mouth tendrils stiffening with distaste.

'What about General Bel Iblis? He was fighting alone against the Empire for several years.'

'The General has already turned his intelligence contacts over to us,' Mon Mothma said, a muscle in her cheek twitching. 'So far, we're still integrating them into our own system.'

'I wasn't referring to his contacts,' Ackbar said. 'I meant the General himself. Why isn't he here?'

Leia looked at Mon Mothma, her stomach tightening again. Garm Bel Iblis had been one of the early forces behind the consolidation of individual resistance units into the all-encompassing Rebel Alliance, and for years had formed a shadowy triad of leadership with Mon Mothma and Leia's own adoptive father, Bail Organa. But when Organa died with his people in the Death Star's attack on Alderaan – and as Mon Mothma began subsequently to draw more and more power to herself – Bel Iblis had left the Alliance and struck out on his own. Since then, he had continued his private war against the Empire . . . until, almost by accident, he had crossed paths with fellow Corellian Han Solo.

It was Han's urgent request that had brought Bel Iblis and his force of six Dreadnaughts to the New Republic's aid at the *Katana* battle. Mon Mothma, speaking words about burying past differences, had welcomed Bel Iblis back.

And had then turned around and sent him to bolster the defenses in the outer sectors of the New Republic. As far from Coruscant as he could possibly have gone.

Leia was not yet ready to ascribe vindictiveness to Mon Mothma's decision. But there were others in the New Republic hierarchy who remembered Bel Iblis and his tactical genius . . . and not all of them were quite so willing to give Mon Mothma the benefit of the doubt.

'The General's expertise is needed at the battlefront,' Mon Mothma said evenly.

'His expertise is also needed here,' Ackbar retorted; but Leia could hear the resignation in his voice. Ackbar himself had just returned from a tour of the Farrfin and Dolomar defenses, and would be leaving in the morning for Dantooine.

With the Imperial war machine on the move, the New Republic couldn't afford the luxury of burying their best line commanders away in ground-side offices.

'I understand your concerns,' Mon Mothma said, more gently. 'When we get the situation out there stabilized, I fully intend to bring General Bel Iblis back and put him in charge of tactical planning.'

If we get the situation stabilized, Leia amended silently, again feeling her stomach tighten. So far, the offensive was going uniformly the Empire's way—

The thought broke off in midstride, a sudden belated awareness flooding in on her. No – it wasn't her *stomach* that was tightening . . .

Ackbar was speaking again. 'Excuse me,' Leia cut him off, getting carefully to her feet. 'I'm sorry to interrupt, but I need to get down to Medical.'

Mon Mothma's eyes widened. 'The twins?'

Leia nodded. 'I think they're on their way.'

The walls and ceiling of the birth room were a warm tan color, with a superimposed series of shifting lights that had been synchronized with Leia's own brain wave patterns. Thoretically, it was supposed to help her relax and concentrate. As a practical matter, Leia had already decided that after ten hours of looking at it, the technique had pretty well lost its effectiveness.

Another contraction came, the hardest one yet. Automatically, Leia reached out with the Force, using the methods Luke had taught her to hold off the pain coming from protesting muscles. If nothing else, this whole birth process was giving her the chance to practice her Jedi techniques.

And not just those having to do with pain control. *It's all right*, she thought soothingly toward the small minds within her. *It's all right. Mother's here.*

It didn't really help. Caught in forces they couldn't comprehend, their tiny bodies being squeezed and pushed as they were driven slowly toward the unknown, their undeveloped minds were fluttering with fear.

Though to be perfectly fair, their father wasn't in much better shape.

'You all right?' Han asked for the umpteenth time since they'd come in here. He squeezed her hand a little more tightly, also for the umpteenth time, in sympathetic tension with her hunching shoulders.

'I'm still fine,' Leia assured him. Her shoulders relaxed as the contraction ended, and she gave his hand a squeeze in return. 'You don't look so good, though.'

Han made a face at her. 'It's past my bedtime,' he said dryly.

'That must be it,' Leia agreed. Han had been as nervous as a tauntaun on ball bearings ever since the labor started in earnest, but he was making a manly effort not to show it. More for her sake, Leia suspected, than for any damage such an admission might do to his image. 'Sorry.'

'Don't worry about it.' Han threw a look to the side, where the medic and two Emdee droids were hovering around the business end of the birth bed. 'Looks like we're getting close, sweetheart.'

'Count on it,' Leia agreed, the last word strangled off as another contraction took her attention. 'Oh . . .'

Han's anxiety level jumped another notch. 'You all right?'

Leia nodded, throat muscles momentarily too tight to speak through. 'Hold me, Han,' she breathed when she could talk again. 'Just hold me.'

'I'm right here,' he said quietly, sliding his free hand into a comfortable grip under her shoulder.

She hardly heard him. Deep within her, the small lives that she and Han had created were starting to move . . . and abruptly their fluttering fear had become full-blown terror.

Don't be afraid, she thought at them. *Don't be afraid. It'll be all right. I'm here. Soon, you'll be with me.*

She wasn't really expecting a reaction – the twins' minds were far too undeveloped to understand anything as abstract as words or the concept of future events. But she continued anyway, wrapping them and their fear as best she could in her love and peace and comfort. There was another contraction

– the inexorable movement toward the outside world continued—

And then, to Leia's everlasting joy, one of the tiny minds reached back to her, touching her in a way that neither twin had ever responded to her nonverbal caresses before. The rising fear slowed in its advance, and Leia had the sudden mental image of a baby's hand curled tightly around her finger. *Yes*, she told the infant. *I'm your mother, and I'm here.*

The tiny mind seemed to consider that. Leia continued her assurances, and the mind shifted a little away from her, as if the infant's attention had been drawn somewhere else. A good sign, she decided; if it was able to be distracted from what was happening to it—

And then, to her amazement, the second mind's panic also began to fade. The second mind, which to the best of her knowledge had not yet even noticed her presence . . .

Later, in retrospect, the whole thing would seem obvious, if not completely inevitable. But at that moment, the revelation was startling enough to send a shiver through the core of Leia's soul. The twins, growing together in the Force even as they'd grown together within her, had somehow become attuned to each other – attuned in a way and to a depth that Leia knew she herself would never entirely share.

It was, at the same time, one of the proudest and yet one of the most poignant moments of Leia's life. To get such a glimpse into the future – to see her children growing and strengthening themselves in the Force . . . and to know that there would be a part of their lives together that she would never share.

The contraction eased, the grand and bittersweet vision of the future fading into a small nugget of ache in a corner of her mind. An ache that was made all the worse by the private shame that, in all of that flood of selfish emotion, it hadn't even occurred to her that Han would be able to share even less of their lives than she would.

And suddenly, through the mental haze, a bright light seemed to explode in her eyes. Reflexively, she clutched harder at Han's hand. 'What—?'

'It's coming,' Han yelped, gripping back. 'First one's halfway out.'

Leia blinked, the half-imagined light vanishing as her mind fumbled free of her contact with her children. Her children, whose eyes had never had to deal with anything brighter than a dim, diffuse glow. 'Turn that light down,' she gasped. 'It's too bright. The children's eyes—'

'It's all right,' the medic assured her. 'Their eyes will adjust. All right: one last push.'

And then, seemingly without warning, the first part was suddenly over. 'Got one,' Han told her, his voice sounding strangely breathless. 'It's—' He craned his neck. 'It's our daughter.' He looked back at Leia, the tension in his face plastered over with the lopsided grin she knew so well. 'Jaina.'

Leia nodded. 'Jaina,' she repeated. Somehow, the names they'd decided on had never sounded quite the same as they did right now. 'What about Jacen?'

'Offhand, I'd say he's anxious to join his sister,' the medic said dryly. 'Get ready to push – he looks like he's trying to crawl out on his own. OK . . . *push.*'

Leia took a deep breath. Finally. After ten hours of labor – after nine months of pregnancy – the end was finally in sight.

No. Not the end. The beginning.

They laid the twins in her arms a few minutes later . . . and as she looked first at them and then up at Han, she felt a sense of utter peace settle over her. Out among the stars there might be a war going on; but for here, and for now, all was right with the universe.

'Watch it, Rogue Leader,' the voice of Rogue Ten snapped in Wedge's ear. 'You've picked up a tail.'

'Got it,' Wedge told him, cutting his X-wing hard over. The TIE interceptor shot past, spitting laser fire as he went, and attempted to match Wedge's maneuver. Blurring in barely half a second behind the Imperial, a pursuing X-wing blew him into a cloud of flaming dust.

'Thanks, Rogue Eight,' Wedge said, blowing a drop of

sweat from the tip of his nose and checking his scanners. Temporarily, at least, it looked like their little corner of the melee was in the clear. Putting his X-wing into a slow turn, he gave the overall battle scene a quick assessment.

It was worse than he'd feared. Worse, for that matter, than it had been even five minutes ago. Two more *Victory*-class Star Destroyers had appeared from hyperspace, dropping into mauling position at point-blank range from one of their three remaining Calamari Star Cruisers. And at the rate the Star Destroyers were pouring turbolaser fire into it – 'Rogue Squadron: change course to twenty-two mark eight,' he ordered, turning onto the intercept heading and wondering how in blazes the Imperials had managed this one. Making so precise a jump was difficult under ideal circumstances; to do so into the heat and confusion of a battle should have been well-nigh impossible. Just one more example of the Empire's incredible new talent for coordinating their forces.

There was a warning twitter from the astromech droid riding in the socket behind him: they were now registering too close to a large mass to jump to lightspeed. Wedge glanced around with a frown, finally spotted the Interdictor Cruiser hovering off in the distance, keeping well out of the main battle itself. Apparently, the Imperials didn't want any of the New Republic ships sneaking out of the party early.

Dead ahead, some of the Victory Star Destroyers' TIE fighters were sweeping up to meet them. 'Porkins' Formation,' Wedge ordered his team. 'Watch out for flankers. Star Cruiser *Orthavan*, this is Rogue Squadron; we're coming in.'

'Stay there, Rogue Leader,' a gravelly Mon Calamari voice said. 'We're too badly overmatched. You can't help us.'

Wedge gritted his teeth. The Mon Cal was probably right. 'We're going to try, anyway,' he told the other. The Advancing TIE fighters were almost in range now. 'Hang on.'

'Rogue Squadron, this is Bel Iblis,' a new voice cut in. 'Break off your attack. On my mark cut thirty degrees to portside.'

With an effort, Wedge suppressed the urge to say something that would probably have earned him a court-martial. On his list, as long as a ship was in one piece, there was still hope of saving it. Apparently, the great General Bel Iblis had decided otherwise. 'Copy, General,' he sighed. 'Rogue Squadron: stand by.'

'Rogue Squadron . . . mark.'

Obediently, reluctantly, Wedge swung his X-wing to the side. The TIE fighters shifted course to follow; seemed to suddenly get flustered—

And with a roar that carried clearly even through the tenuous gases of interplanetary space, an assault formation of A-wings shot through the space Rogue Squadron had just exited. The TIE fighters, already in motion to match the X-wings' maneuver, were caught flat-footed. Before they could get back into barricade position, the A-wings were past them, heading at full throttle for the embattled Star Cruiser. 'OK, Rogue Squadron,' Bel Iblis said. 'Your turn. Clear their backs for them.'

Wedge grinned tightly. He should have known better of Bel Iblis. 'Copy, General. Rogue Squadron: let's take them.'

'And then,' Bel Iblis added grimly, 'prepare to retreat.'

Wedge blinked, the grin fading. *Retreat?* Turning his X-wing toward the TIE fighters, he looked back at the main battle area.

A few minutes earlier, he'd realized the situation had looked bad. Now, it was on the edge of disaster. Bel Iblis's force was down to barely two-thirds of the fifteen capital ships he'd started with, with most of those huddled into a last-ditch bastion formation. Surrounding it, systematically battering at its defenses, were over twenty Star Destroyers and Dreadnaughts.

Wedge looked back at the approaching TIE fighters; and, beyond them, to the Interdictor Cruiser. The Interdictor Cruiser, whose gravity well projectors were keeping the beleaguered battle force from escaping to lightspeed . . .

And then they were on the TIE fighters, and there was no more time for thought. The battle was sharp, but short – the sudden appearance of the A-wings from Rogue Squadron's shadow had apparently thrown the TIE fighters just enough off stride. Three minutes, maybe four, and Rogue Squadron was again in the clear.

'What now, Rogue Leader?' Rogue Two asked as the squadron re-formed through the debris.

Mentally crossing his fingers, Wedge looked back at the *Orthavan*. If Bel Iblis's gamble hadn't worked . . .

It had. The A-wing slash had distracted the Victory Star Destroyers' attack just enough for the Star Cruiser to catch its breath and go back on the offensive. The *Orthavan* had both its extensive turbolaser and ion cannon batteries going, scrambling the Imperials' systems and pummeling away at their hulls. Even as Wedge watched, a geyser of superheated gas erupted from the midsection of the nearer Star Destroyer, sending the ship rotating ponderously away. Pulling under the derelict's hull, the Star Cruiser moved away from the battle and headed for the Interdictor Cruiser.

'Change course for the *Orthavan*,' Wedge ordered. 'They may need backup.'

The words were barely out of his mouth when, shooting in from lightspeed, a pair of Dreadnaughts suddenly appeared at the *Orthavan*'s flank. Wedge held his breath, but the Star Cruiser was already moving too fast for the Dreadnaughts to get more than a wild shot at it. It passed them without pausing; and as they turned to follow it, the A-wing squadron reenacted their earlier slash maneuver. Once again, the distraction's effectiveness was vastly out of proportion to the actual damage inflicted. By the time the starfighters broke off, the *Orthavan* was beyond any chance the Dreadnaughts might have to catch up.

And the Imperials knew it. Behind Wedge, the astromech droid beeped: the pseudogravity field was fading away as the distant Interdictor Cruiser shut down its gravity well projectors in preparation for its own escape to lightspeed.

The Interdictor Cruiser . . .

And belatedly the explanation struck him. He'd been wrong – those Victory Star Destroyers hadn't needed to rely on any half-mystical coordination technique to jump in so close to the Star Cruiser. All they'd had to do was fly in along a hyperspace vector supplied to them by the Interdictor Cruiser and wait until the edge of the gravity well cone yanked them back into normal space.

Wedge felt his lip twist. Overestimating the enemy's abilities, he'd been taught a long time ago, could be just as dangerous as underestimating them. It was a lesson he would have to start remembering.

'Interdictor gravfield is down,' Bel Iblis's voice came in his ear. 'All units: acknowledge and prepare to retreat on your marks.'

'Rogue Squadron: copy,' Wedge said, grimacing as he turned on to their preplanned escape vector and looked back at what was left of the main battle group. There was no doubt about it: they'd been beaten, and beaten badly, and about all Bel Iblis's legendary tactical skill had been able to do had been to keep the defeat from turning into a rout.

And the price was likely to be yet another system lost to the Empire.

'Rogue Squadron: go.'

'Copy,' Wedge sighed, and pulled back the hyperspace lever . . . and as the stars flared into starlines, a sobering thought occurred to him.

For the foreseeable future, at least, underestimating the Empire was not likely to be all that much of a problem.

CHAPTER 6

The starlines shrank back into stars, and the *Wild Karrde* was back in normal space. Straight ahead was the tiny white dwarf sun of the Chazwa system, not all that distinguishable from the bright background stars around it. Nearby and a little to one side, a mostly dark circle edged by a slender lighted crescent, was the planet Chazwa itself. Scattered around it in the darkness of space the exhaust glows of perhaps fifty ships could be seen, both incoming and outgoing. Most were freighters and bulk cruisers, taking advantage of Chazwa's central transshipment location. A few were clearly Imperial warships.

'Well, here we are,' Aves said conversationally from the co-pilot station. 'Incidentally, Karrde, I'd like to go on record as saying this is an insane idea.'

'Perhaps,' Karrde conceded, shifting course toward the planet and checking his displays. Good; the rest of the group had made it in all right. 'But if the Empire's clone transport route does indeed run through Orus sector, the Chazwa garrison should have records of the operation. Possibly even the origin point, if someone was careless.'

'I wasn't referring to the details of the raid,' Aves said. 'I meant that it was crazy for us to be getting involved in the first place. It's the New Republic's war, not ours – let them chase it down.'

'If I could trust them to do so, I would,' Karrde said, peering out the starboard viewport. Another freighter seemed to be sidling slowly in the *Wild Karrde*'s general direction. 'But I'm not sure they're up to the task.'

Aves grunted. 'I still don't buy Skywalker's numbers. Seems to me that if you could grow stable clones that fast, the old clonemasters would have done it.'

'Perhaps they did,' Karrde pointed out. 'I don't think any information on the cloning techniques of that era has survived. Everything I've ever seen has come from the much earlier prewar experiments.'

'Yeah, well . . .' Aves shook his head. 'I'd still rather sit the whole thing out.'

'We may discover we don't have a choice in the matter.' Karrde gestured to the freighter still moving up on them. 'We seem to have a caller. Would you pull up an ID on him?'

'Sure.' Aves threw a quick look at the freighter, than turned to his board. 'Not registering as any ship I've ever heard of. Wait a minute . . . yeah. Yeah, they've altered their ID – simple transponder overlay, looks like. Let's see if Ghent's magic decoded package can untangle it.'

Karrde nodded, the mention of Ghent's name sending his

thoughts flicking briefly across the galaxy to Coruscant and the two associates he'd left there under New Republic care. If the timetable their medical people had given him was correct, Mara should be about recovered by now. She should be trying to get in touch with him soon, and he made a mental note to check in with the contact pipeline as soon as they were finished here.

'Got it,' Aves said triumphantly. 'Well, well – I do believe it's an old friend of yours, Karrde. The *Kern's Pride*; the slightly less-than-honorable Samuel Tomas Gillespee, proprietor.'

'Is it, now,' Karrde said, eyeing the ship pacing them a hundred meters away. 'I suppose we'd better see what he wants.'

He keyed for a tight-beam transmission. 'This is Talon Karrde calling the *Kern's Pride*,' he said. 'Don't just sit there, Gillespee – say hello.'

'Hello, Karrde,' a familiar voice came back. 'You don't mind if I figure out who I'm talking to before I say hello, do you?'

'Not at all,' Karrde assured him. 'Nice little overlay on your ship ID, by the way.'

'Obviously could have been nicer,' Gillespee said dryly. 'We weren't even close to slicing yours yet. What are you doing here?'

'I was about to ask you the same thing,' Karrde said. 'I was under the impression you'd been planning to retire.'

'I did,' Gillespee said grimly. 'Out of the business for good, and thanks for everything. Bought myself a big chunk of land on a nice little out-of-the-way world where I could watch the trees grow and stay out of everything that smelled like trouble. Place called Ukio – ever hear of it?'

Beside Karrde, Aves shook his head and muttered something under his breath. 'I seem to remember hearing that name recently, yes,' Karrde conceded. 'Were you there for the Imperial attack?'

'I was there for the attack, the surrender, and all the occupation I could stomach,' Gillespee growled. 'Matter of fact, I had about as good a front-row seat to the bombardment as you could get. It was pretty spectacular, I'll tell you that.'

'It could be profitable as well,' Karrde said, thinking hard. As far as he knew, the New Republic still didn't have a handle on what exactly the Empire had done at Ukio. Hard data on the attack could be invaluable to their tactical people. As well as commanding a hefty fee for both witness and finder. 'I don't suppose you took any readings during the attack.'

'I've got a little from the bombardment part of it,' Gillespee said. 'The data card from my macrobinoculars. Why?'

'There's a good chance I can find you a buyer for it,' Karrde told him. 'It might compensate somewhat for your lost property.'

'I doubt your buyer's got that much to spend,' Gillespee sniffed. 'You wouldn't have believed it, Karrde – you really wouldn't. I mean, we're not talking Svivren here, but even Ukio should have taken them a little longer to overrun.'

'The Empire's had a lot of practice overrunning worlds,' Karrde reminded him. 'You're lucky you made it out at all.'

'You got that one right,' Gillespee agreed. 'Faughn and Rappapor popped me about half a jump ahead of the storm-troopers. And half a jump behind the workers they sent to turn my land into a crop farm. I'm telling you, that new clone system they've got going is really creepy.'

Karrde threw a look at Aves. 'How so?'

'What do you mean, how so?' Gillespee retorted. 'I don't happen to think people ought to come off an assembly line, thanks. And if they did, I sure as mynocks wouldn't put the Empire in charge of the factory. You should have seen the guys they had manning the roadblocks – put a shiver right straight through you.'

'I don't doubt it,' Karrde said. 'What are your plans after leaving Chazwa?'

'I don't hardly have any plans *before* I get there,' Gillespee countered sourly. 'I was hoping to get in touch with Brasck's old contact man here, see if they'd be interested in taking us on. Why, you got something better?'

'Possibly. We can start by sending that macrobinocular data

card on to my buyer, drawing payment for you against a credit line I have set up with him. After that, I have another project in mind which you might find both interesting—'

'We got company,' Aves cut him off. 'Two Imperial ships, heading this way. Looks like *Lancer*-class Frigates.'

'Uh-oh,' Gillespee muttered. 'Maybe we didn't get off Ukio as clean as I thought.'

'I think it more likely that we're their target,' Karrde said, feeling his lip twist as he keyed an evasion course into the helm. 'It's been nice talking to you, Gillespee. If you want to continue the conversation, meet me in eight days at the Trogan system – you know the place.'

'I can make it if you can,' Gillespee countered. 'If you can't, don't make it too easy for them.'

Karrde broke the contact. 'Hardly,' he murmured. 'All right; here we go. Nice and easy . . .'

He eased the *Wild Karrde* into a shallow portside drop, trying to make it look as if they were planning to cut past the planet itself and pick up a new hyperspace vector. 'Do I alert the others?' Aves asked.

'Not yet,' Karrde said, giving his displays a quick look and setting the nav computer to work calculating their jump to light-speed. 'I'd rather abort the mission and try again later than tangle with a pair of Lancers who were serious about fighting.'

'Yeah,' Aves said slowly. 'Karrde . . . they're not changing course.'

Karrde looked up. Aves was right: neither Lancer had so much as twitched. They were still heading on their original vector.

Straight for the *Kern's Pride*.

He looked at Aves, to find the other looking back at him. 'What do we do?' Aves asked.

Karrde looked back at the Imperial ships. The *Wild Karrde* was a long way from being helpless in a fight, and his people were some of the best. But with weaponry that had been designed to take out enemy starfighters, two Lancers would be better than an even match for the group he'd brought to Chazwa.

As he watched, the *Kern's Pride* suddenly made its move. Rolling into a sort of mutated drop-kick Koiogran maneuver, it took off at high speed at a sharp angle from its original course. The Lancers, not fooled a bit by the ploy, were right behind it.

Which left the *Wild Karrde* completely in the clear. They could continue on to Chazwa, hit the garrison records, and be out before the Lancers could make it back. Fast, clean, and certainly preferable as far as the New Republic was concerned.

But Gillespee was an old acquaintance . . . and on Karrde's scale, a fellow smuggler placed higher than any interstellar government he didn't belong to. 'Apparently, Gillespee didn't get off Ukio as cleanly as he thought,' he commented, bringing the *Wild Karrde* around and keying for intercom. 'Lachton, Chin, Corvis – fire up the turbolasers. We're going in.'

'What about the other ships?' Aves asked as he activated the deflector shields and punched up a tactical display.

'Let's get the Lancers' attention first,' Karrde said. The three men at the turbolasers signaled ready; taking a deep breath, he threw power to the drive.

The Lancers' commander wasn't anyone's fool. Even as the *Wild Karrde* drove toward them, one of the Imperial ships broke off its pursuit of the *Kern's Pride* and turned to confront this new threat. 'I think we've got their attention,' Aves said tightly. 'Can I call the others into the party yet?'

'Go ahead,' Karrde told him, keying his own comm for a tight beam to the *Kern's Pride*. 'Gillespee, this is Karrde.'

'Yeah, I see you,' Gillespee came back. 'What do you think you're doing?'

'Giving you a hand,' Karrde said. Ahead, the Lancer's twenty quad laser batteries opened up, raining green flashes down on the *Wild Karrde*. The turbolasers fired back, their three groups of fire looking rather pathetic in comparison. 'All right – we've got this one tied down. Better get out before that other one finds the range.'

'You've got *him* tied down?' Gillespee retorted. 'Look, Karrde—'

'I said get out,' Karrde cut him off sharply. 'We can't hold him for ever. Don't worry about me – I'm not exactly alone out here.'

'Here they come,' Aves said, and Karrde took a moment to glance into the rear display. They were coming, all right: fifteen freighters strong, all zeroing in on the suddenly outgunned Lancer.

From the comm came an amazed whistle. 'You weren't kidding, were you?' Gillespee commented.

'No, I wasn't,' Karrde said. 'Now get going, will you?'

Gillespee laughed out loud. 'I'll let you in on a little secret, Karrde. I'm not alone, either.'

And suddenly, barely visible through the haze of laser fire hammering at the *Wild Karrde*'s viewports, the exhaust glows of nearly twenty ships suddenly veered off their individual courses. Sweeping in like hungry Barabel, they converged on the second Lancer.

'So, Karrde,' Gillespee continued conversationally. 'At a guess, I'd say neither of us is going to get much business done at Chazwa this time around. What say we continue this conversation somewhere else? Say, in eight days?'

Karrde smiled. 'I'll look forward to it.'

He looked back at the Lancer, and his smile faded. Standard Lancer crew was 850; and from the capable way that one was holding off the rest of the ships, he would guess they were running with full complement. How many of them, he wondered, had been freshly created at Grand Admiral Thrawn's clone factory? 'By the way, Gillespee,' he added, 'if you happen to run into any of our colleagues on the way, you might want to invite them along. I think they'd be interested in what I have to say.'

'You got it, Karrde,' Gillespee grunted. 'See you in eight.'

Karrde switched off the comm. So that was it. Gillespee would broadcast the word to the other major smuggling groups; and knowing Gillespee, the open invitation would quickly transmute into something just short of a command appearance. They'd be at Trogan – all of them, or near enough.

Now all he had to figure out was what exactly he was going to say to them.

Grand Admiral Thrawn leaned back in his command chair. 'All right, gentlemen,' he said, his gaze flicking in turn to each of the fourteen men standing in a loose semicircle around his console. 'Are there any questions?'

The slightly rumpled-looking man at one end of the semicircle glanced at the others. 'No questions, Admiral,' he said, his precise military voice in sharp contrast to his civilian-sloppy appearance. 'What's our timetable?'

'Your freighter is being prepped now,' Thrawn told him. 'You'll leave as soon as it's ready. How soon do you expect to penetrate the Imperial Palace?'

'No sooner than six days from now, sir,' the rumpled man said. 'I'd like to hit one or two other ports before taking the ship in to Coruscant – their security will be easier to breach if we have a legitimate data trail they can backtrack. Unless you want it done sooner, of course.'

Thrawn's glowing eyes narrowed slightly, and Pellaeon could tell what he was thinking. Mara Jade, sitting there in the middle of Rebel headquarters. Perhaps at this very moment giving them the location of the Emperor's storehouse on Wayland . . . 'Timing is critical in this operation,' Thrawn told the commando leader. 'But speed alone is useless if you're compromised before even entering the Palace. You will be the man on the scene, Major Himron. I leave it to your judgment.'

The commando leader nodded. 'Yes, sir. Thank you, Admiral. We won't fail you.'

Thrawn smiled fractionally. 'I know you won't, Major. Dismissed.'

Silently, the fourteen men turned and filed out of the command room. 'You seemed surprised, Captain, at some of my instructions,' Thrawn commented as the door slid shut behind them.

'Yes, sir, I was,' Pellaeon admitted. 'It all made sense, of course,' he added hastily. 'I simply hadn't thought the operation out to that end point.'

'All end points must be prepared for,' Thrawn said, keying his board. The lights muted, and on the walls of the command room a sampling of holographic paintings and planics appeared. 'Mriss artwork,' he identified it for Pellaeon's benefit. 'One of the most curious examples of omission to be found anywhere in the civilized galaxy. Until they were contacted by the Tenth Alderaanian Expedition, not a single one of the dozens of Mriss cultures had ever developed any form of three-dimensional artwork.'

'Interesting,' Pellaeon said dutifully. 'Some flaw in their perceptual makeup?'

'Many of the experts still think so,' Thrawn said. 'It seems clear to me, though, that the oversight was actually a case of cultural blind spots combined with a very subtle but equally strong social harmonization. A combination of traits we'll be able to exploit.'

Pellaeon looked at the artwork, his stomach tightening. 'We're attacking Mrisst?'

'It's certainly ripe for the taking,' Thrawn pointed out. 'And a base there would give us the capability to launch attacks into the very heart of the Rebellion.'

'Except that the Rebellion must know that,' Pellaeon said carefully. If C'baoth's ongoing demands for an attack on Coruscant had finally gotten to the Grand Admiral . . . 'They'd launch a massive counterattack, sir, if we so much as made a move toward Mrisst.'

'Exactly,' Thrawn said, smiling with grim satisfaction. 'Which means that when we're finally ready to draw the Coruscant sector fleet into ambush, Mrisst will be the perfect lure to use. If they come out to meet us, we'll defeat them then and there. And if they somehow sense the trap and refuse to engage, we'll have our forward base. Either way, the Empire will triumph.'

He reached to his board again, and the holographic artwork faded into a tactical star map. 'But that battle is still in the future,' he said. 'For now, our prime goal is to build a force strong enough to ensure that ultimate victory. And to keep the Rebellion off balance while we do so.'

Pellaeon nodded. 'The assault on Ord Mantell should go a long way toward accomplishing that.'

'It will certainly create a degree of fear in the surrounding systems,' Thrawn agreed. 'As well as drawing away some of the Rebel pressure on our shipyard supply lines.'

'That would be helpful,' Pellaeon said with a scowl. 'The last report from Bilbringi said the shipyards there were running critically low on Tibanna gas, as well as hfredium and kammris.'

'I've already ordered the Bespin garrison to step up their Tibanna gas production,' Thrawn said, tapping his control board. 'As for the metals, Intelligence recently reported locating a convenient stockpile.'

The report came up, and Pellaeon leaned forward to read it. He got as far as the location listing – '*This* is Intelligence's idea of a convenient stockpile?'

'I take it you disagree?' Thrawn asked mildly.

Pellaeon looked at the report again, feeling a grimace settling in on his face. The Empire had hit Lando Calrissian's walking mining complex on the superhot planet Nkllon once before, back when they needed mole miners for Thrawn's assault on the Sluis Van shipyards. That other raid had cost the Empire over a million manhours, first in preparing the Star Destroyer *Judicator* for the intense heat at Nkllon's close-orbit distance from its sun, and then for repairing the damage afterward. 'I suppose that depends, sir,' he said, 'on how long we'll be losing the use of whichever Star Destroyer is detailed to the raid.'

'A valid question,' Thrawn agreed. 'Fortunately, there will be no need this time to tie up any Star Destroyers. Three of our new Dreadnaughts should be more than adequate to neutralize Nkllon's security.'

'But a Dreadnaught won't be able to – ah,' Pellaeon interrupted himself as he suddenly understood. 'It won't have to be big enough to survive in open sunlight. If they can take over one of the shieldships that fly freighters in and out of the inner system, a Dreadnaught would be small enough to stay behind its umbrella.'

'Exactly,' Thrawn nodded. 'And capturing one should pose no problem. For all their impressive size, shieldships are little more than shielding, coolant systems, and a small container ship's worth of power and crew. Six fully loaded assault shuttles should make quick work of it.'

Pellaeon nodded, still skimming the report. 'What happens if Calrissian sells his stockpiles before the assault force gets there?'

'He won't,' Thrawn assured him. 'The market price for metals has just begun to rise again; and men like Calrissian always wait for it to go just a little higher.'

Unless Calrissian was suddenly overcome with a swell of patriotic fervor toward his friends back in the New Republic hierarchy and decided to sell his metals at a reduced price. 'I'd still recommend, sir, that the attack be carried out as soon as possible.'

'Recommendation noted, Captain,' Thrawn said, smiling slightly. 'And, as it happens, already acted upon. The raid was launched ten minutes ago.'

Pellaeon smiled tightly. Some day, he decided, he'd learn not to try to second-guess the Grand Admiral. 'Yes, sir.'

Thrawn leaned back in his chair. 'Return to the bridge, Captain, and prepare to make the jump to lightspeed. Ord Mantell is waiting.'

CHAPTER 7

The beeping from his board prodded Luke out of his light doze. Blinking away the sleep, he gave the displays a quick scan. 'Artoo?' he called, stretching as best he could in the tight confines of the cockpit. 'We're just about there. Get ready.'

A nervous-sounding warble came in acknowledgement. 'Come on, Artoo, relax,' Luke urged the droid, settling his fingertips around the X-wing's hyperspace lever and letting the Force flow through him. Almost time . . . *now*. He pulled the lever back, and the starlines appeared and collapsed back into stars.

And there, directly ahead, was the Noghri home world of Honoghr.

Artoo gave a soft whistle. 'I know,' Luke agreed, feeling a little sick himself. Leia had told him what to expect; but even with that warning the sight of the world lying in the X-wing's path was a shock. Beneath the sparse white clouds floating over the surface, the entire planetary landmass was a flat, uniform brown. *Kholm*-grass, Leia had called it: the local Honoghran plants the Empire had genetically modified to perpetuate their systematic destruction of the planet's ecology. That deceit, combined with first Vader's and later Thrawn's carefully limited aid, had bought the Empire four decades of Noghri service. Even now, squads of Noghri Death Commandos were scattered around the galaxy, fighting and dying for those whose cold-blooded treachery and counterfeit compassion had turned them into slaves.

Artoo warbled something, and Luke broke his gaze away from the silent monument to Imperial ruthlessness. 'I don't know,' he admitted as the droid's question scrolled across his computer display. 'We'd have to get a team of environment and ecology specialists out here before we could tell. Doesn't look very hopeful, though, does it?'

The droid chirped – an electronic shrug that turned suddenly into a startled shrill. Luke's head jerked up, just as a small fast-attack patrol ship shot past overhead. 'I think they've spotted us,' he commented as casually as possible. 'Let's hope it's the Noghri and not an Imp—'

'Starfighter, identify yourself,' a deep, catlike voice mewed from the comm.

Luke keyed for transmission, reaching out with the Force toward the patrol ship that was now curving back into attack position. Even at this range he should have been able to sense a human pilot, which meant that it was indeed a Noghri out there. At least, he hoped so. 'This is Luke Skywalker,' he said. 'Son of the Lord Darth Vader, brother of Leia Organa Solo.'

For a long moment the comm was silent. 'Why have you come?'

Normal prudence, Luke knew, would have suggested that

he not bring up the matter of his power cells until he had a better idea of how matters stood politically with the Noghri leaders. But Leia had mentioned several times how impressed she'd been by the Noghri sense of honor and straightforward honesty. 'My ship's primary power cells have been damaged,' he told the other. 'I thought you might be able to help me.'

There was a soft hiss from the comm. 'You place us in great danger, son of Vader,' the Noghri said. 'Imperial ships come to Honoghr at random times. If you are sighted, all will suffer.'

'I understand,' Luke said, a small weight lifting from him. If the Noghri were worried about him being spotted by Imperials, at least they hadn't completely rejected Leia's invitation to rebel against the Empire. 'If you'd prefer, I'll leave.'

He held his breath as, behind him, Artoo moaned softly. If the Noghri took him up on his offer, it was questionable as to whether they'd be able to get anywhere else on the power they had left.

Apparently, the Noghri pilot was thinking along the same lines. 'The Lady Vader has already risked much on behalf of the Noghri,' he said. 'We cannot permit you to endanger your life. Follow me, son of Vader. I will bring you to what safety the Noghri can offer.'

According to Leia, there was only a single small area on Honoghr that had been made capable of supporting any plant life other than the Empire's bioengineered *kholm*-grass. Khabarakh and the maitrakh of the clan Kihm'bar had kept her, Chewbacca, and Threepio in one of the villages there, managing with skill and more than a little luck to hide her from prying Imperial eyes. Leia had included the location of the Clean Land along with the coordinates of the system itself . . . and as Luke followed the patrol ship down toward the surface of the planet, it quickly became apparent that they weren't going there.

'Where are we headed?' he asked the Noghri pilot as they dipped beneath a layer of clouds.

'To the future of our world,' the alien said.

'Ah,' Luke murmured under his breath. A double line of jagged cliffs could be seen ahead, looking a little like stylized dorsal ridges from a pair of Tatooine krayt dragons. 'Is your future in those mountains?' he suggested.

There was another soft hiss from the comm. 'As the Lady Vader, and the Lord Vader before her,' the Noghri said. 'You also read the souls of the Noghri.'

Luke shrugged. It hadn't been much more than a lucky guess, actually. 'Where do we go?'

'Others will show you,' the pilot said. 'For here I must leave you. Farewell, son of Vader. My family will long cherish the honor of this day.' The patrol ship cut sharply upward, heading back toward space—

And in perfect synchronization, two combat-equipped cloudcars rose from seemingly nowhere to settle into flanking positions. 'We greet you, son of Vader,' a new voice said from the comm. 'We are honored to guide you. Follow.'

One of the cloudcars moved ahead to take the point, the other dropping back to rearguard position. Luke stayed with the formation, trying to see just where they might be headed. As far as he could tell, the cliffs were as barren as the rest of the planet.

Artoo chirped, and a message scrolled across Luke's display. 'A river?' Luke asked, peering out his canopy. 'Where – oh, there it is. Emptying out from between the two cliff lines, right?'

The droid beeped an affirmative. It looked to be a pretty fast-moving river, too, Luke decided as they flew closer and he could see the numerous lines of white water indicating submerged rocks. Probably explained why the gorge between the two cliff lines was so sharp and deep.

They reached the end of the cliff lines a few minutes later. The lead cloudcar turned to portside, lifting smoothly over a set of foothills and disappearing around the side of one of the higher crags. Luke followed, smiling tightly as an old memory came to mind. *You're required to maneuver straight down this trench* . . . Guiding the X-wing around the foothills, he flew into the shadow of the cliffs themselves.

And into an entirely different world. Along the narrow banks of the river the ground was a solid mass of brilliant green.

Artoo whistled in startled amazement. 'They're plants,' Luke said, realizing only after the words were out of his mouth how ridiculous they sounded. Of course they were plants; but to find plants on Honoghr—

'It is the future of our world,' one of his escort said, and there was no mistaking the grim pride in his voice. 'The future which the Lady Vader gave us. Continue to follow, son of Vader. The landing area is still ahead.'

The landing area turned out to be a large, flat-topped boulder jutting partway into the swift-moving river about two kilometers along the gorge. With a cautious eye on the racing water beneath him, Luke eased the X-wing down. Fortunately, it was larger than it had looked from fifty meters up. The cloudcars waited until he had touched down, then swung around and headed back down the gorge. Shutting the X-wing's systems back to standby, Luke looked around.

The greenery, he saw now, was not as monochromatic as he'd first thought. There were at least four slightly different shades represented, intermingled in a pattern that was too consistent to be accidental. A pipe could be seen angling down into the river at one point, its other end disappearing up into the plant growth. Utilizing the pressure of the current, he decided, to bring water up over the bank for irrigation. A few meters downstream from the boulder, hidden from view by a rock overhang, he could see a small hutlike building. Two Noghri stood just outside its door: one with steely-gray skin, the other a much darker gray. Even as he watched, they started toward him.

'Looks like the reception committee,' Luke commented to Artoo, hitting the switch to pop his canopy. 'You stay put here. And I mean *stay put*. You fall in the water like you did that first trip to Dagobah and you'll be lucky if we can even find all the pieces.'

There was no need to give the order twice. Artoo warbled a nervous acknowledgement, then an equally nervous question. 'Yes, I'm sure they're friendly,' Luke assured him, pulling off his flight helmet and getting to his feet. 'Don't worry, I won't be going far.' Vaulting over the X-wing's side, he headed toward his hosts.

The two Noghri were already at the edge of the landing boulder, standing silently watching him. Luke grimaced to himself as he walked toward them, stretching out with the Force and wishing he were skilled enough to get some reading – any reading – on this species. 'In the name of the New Republic, I bring you greetings,' he said when he was close enough to be heard over the roar of the river. 'I'm Luke Skywalker. Son of the Lord Darth Vader, brother of Leia Organa Solo.' He held out his left hand, palm upward, as Leia had instructed him to do.

The older Noghri stepped forward and touched his snout to Luke's palm. The nostrils flattened themselves against his skin, and Luke had to fight to keep from twitching away from the tickling sensation. 'I greet you, son of Vader,' the alien said, releasing Luke's hand. In unison, both Noghri dropped to their knees, hands splaying out to the sides in the deference gesture Leia had described. 'I am Ovkhevam clan Bakh'tor. I serve the Noghri people here at the future of our world. You honor us with your presence.'

'I am honored by your hospitality,' Luke said as both aliens rose again to their feet. 'And your companion is . . . ?'

'I am Khabarakh clan Kihm'bar,' the younger Noghri said. 'The clan of Vader has now doubly honored me.'

'Khabarakh clan Kihm'bar,' Luke repeated, eyeing the young alien with new appreciation. So this was the young Noghri commando who had risked everything, first in bringing Leia to his people, then in protecting her from Grand Admiral Thrawn. 'For your service to my sister Leia I thank you. My family and I are in your debt.'

'The debt is not yours, son of Vader,' Ovkhevam said. 'The debt rather belongs to the Noghri people. The actions of Khabarakh clan Kihm'bar were only the first line of repayment.'

Luke nodded, not really sure of what to say to that. 'You called this place the future of your world?' he asked, hoping to change the subject.

'It is the future given to the Noghri people by the Lady Vader,' Ovkhevam said, waving his hands in a circular gesture that took in the entire valley. 'Here with her gift we cleansed the land of the Empire's poisoned plants. Here will someday be enough food to provide for all.'

'It's impressive,' Luke said, and meant it. Out in the open, all that greenery would have stood out against the background *kholm*-grass like a bantha at a Jawa family gathering. But here, with the twin cliff lines blocking the view from everywhere except more or less straight up, there was a good chance incoming Imperial ships would never even suspect its existence. The river supplied ample water, the lower latitude implied a slightly longer growing season than that at the Clean Land itself; and if worse came to worst, a number of properly placed explosives could dam the river or bring down part of the cliffs themselves, burying the evidence of their quiet rebellion against the Empire.

And the Noghri had had barely a month to plan, design, and build it all. No wonder Thrawn and Vader before him had found the Noghri to be such useful servants.

'It was the Lady Vader who made it possible,' Ovkhevam said. 'We have little to offer in the way of hospitality, son of Vader. But what we have is yours.'

'Thank you,' Luke nodded. 'But as your patrol ship pilot pointed out, my presence on Honoghr is a danger to you. If you can provide my ship with replacement power cells, I'll be on my way as quickly as I can. I would pay, of course.'

'We could accept no payment from the son of Vader,' Ovkhevam said, looking shocked at the very idea. 'It would be merely a single line of the debt owed by the Noghri people.'

'I understand,' Luke said stifling a sigh. They meant well, certainly, but all this guilt about their service to the Empire was going to have to stop. Races and beings far more sophisticated than they were had been equally taken in by the Emperor's deceits. 'I suppose the first step is to find out whether you have spares that'll fit my ship. How do we go about doing that?'

'It is already done,' Khabarakh said. 'The cloudcars will carry word of your need to the spaceport at Nystao. The power cells and technicians to install them will be here by nightfall.'

'Meanwhile, we offer you our hospitality,' Ovkhevam added, throwing a sideways look at Khabarakh. Perhaps feeling the younger Noghri should let his elder do the talking.

'I'd be honored,' Luke said. 'Lead the way.'

The hut under the cliff overhang was as small as it had looked from the landing boulder. Most of the available space was taken up by two narrow cots, a low table, and what appeared to be the food storage/preparation module from a small spaceship. But at least it was quieter than outside.

'This will be your home while you are on Honoghr,' Ovkhevam told him. 'Khabarakh and I will stand guard outside. To protect you with our lives.'

'That won't be necessary,' Luke assured them, looking around the room. Clearly, it had been set up for long-term occupancy. 'What do you two do here, if I may ask?'

'I am caretaker to this place,' Ovkhevam said. 'I walk the land, to see that the plants are growing properly. Khabarakh clan Kihm'bar—' He looked at the younger alien, and Luke got the distinct impression of a grim humor in the glance. 'Khabarakh clan Kihm'bar is a fugitive from the Noghri people. Even now we have many ships searching for him.'

'Of course,' Luke said dryly. With Grand Admiral Thrawn threatening to subject Khabarakh to a complete Imperial interrogation, it had been vital that the young commando 'escape' from custody and drop out of sight. It was equally vital that knowledge of the Empire's betrayal be passed on to the Noghri commando teams scattered around the galaxy. The two objectives dovetailed rather nicely.

'Do you require food?' Ovkhevam asked. 'Or rest?'

'I'm fine, thank you,' Luke said. 'I think the best thing

would probably be for me to go back to my ship and start pulling those power cells out.'

'May I assist?' Khabarakh asked.

'I'd appreciate that, yes,' Luke said. He didn't need any help, but the sooner the Noghri worked out this supposed debt of theirs, the better. 'Come on – tool kit's in the ship.'

'There is further word from Nystao,' Khabarakh said, moving invisibly through the darkness to where Luke sat with his back against the X-wing's landing skid. 'The captain of the Imperial ship has decided to complete minor repairs here. He expects the work to take two days.' He hesitated. 'To you, son of Vader, the dynasts express their apologies.'

'No apology necessary,' Luke assured him, looking up past the shadow of the starfighter's wing at the thin band of stars shining down amid the otherwise total blackness. So that was that. He was stuck here for two more days. 'I knew when I came here that this might happen. I'm just sorry I have to impose further on you.'

'Your presence is not an imposition.'

'I appreciate the hospitality.' Luke nodded toward the stars overhead. 'I take it there's still no indication they might have spotted my ship?'

'Would the son of Vader not know if that happened?' Khabarakh countered.

Luke smiled in the darkness. 'Even Jedi have limitations, Khabarakh. Distant danger is very hard to detect.'

And yet, he reminded himself silently, the Force was obviously still with him. That Strike Cruiser up there could easily have turned up at a far more awkward time – say, while the Noghri tech team had been in transit to or from the valley, or even while Luke himself was heading out to space. An alert captain could have picked up on either, and brought the whole thing crashing down right there.

There was a whisper of movement, felt rather than heard over the sound of the river, as Khabarakh sat down beside him. 'It is not enough, is it?' the Noghri asked quietly. 'This place. The dynasts call it our future. But it is not.'

101

Luke shook his head. 'No,' he had to admit. 'You've done a tremendous job with this place, and it'll certainly help you feed your people. But the future of Honoghr itself . . . I'm not an expert, Khabarakh. But from what I've seen here, I don't think Honoghr can be saved.'

The Noghri hissed between his needle teeth, the sound barely audible over the racing water below. 'You speak the thought of many of the Noghri people,' he said. 'Perhaps none really believe otherwise.'

'We can help you find a new home,' Luke promised. 'There are many worlds in the galaxy. We'll find you a place where you can begin again.'

Khabarakh hissed again. 'But it will not be Honoghr.'

Luke swallowed hard. 'No.'

For a minute neither spoke. Luke listened to the sounds of the river, his heart aching with sympathy for the Noghri. But what had been done to Honoghr was far beyond his power to change. The Jedi, indeed, had their limitations.

There was another ripple of air as Khabarakh climbed back to his feet. 'Are you hungry?' he asked Luke. 'If so, I can bring food.'

'Yes, thank you,' Luke said.

The Noghri left. Stifling a sigh, Luke shifted position against the landing skid. It was bad enough knowing there was a problem he was helpless to solve; to have to sit here for two days with the whole thing staring him accusingly in the face only made it worse.

He looked up at the thin trail of stars, wondering what Leia had thought of the whole situation. Had she, too, realized that Honoghr was too far gone to save? Or could she have had some idea of how to bring it back?

Or had she been too busy with the immediate concerns of survival to even think that far ahead?

He grimaced as another small pang of guilt tugged at him. Somewhere out there, on Coruscant, his sister was about to give birth to her twins. Might have already done so, for all he knew. Han was with her, of course, but he'd wanted to be there, too.

But if he couldn't be there in person . . .

Taking a deep breath, he allowed his body to relax. Once before, on Dagobah, he'd been able to reach out to the future. To see his friends, and the path they were on. Then, he'd had Yoda to guide him . . . but if he could find the proper pattern on his own, he might be able to catch a glimpse of his niece and nephew. Carefully, keeping his thoughts and will focused, he stretched out through the Force . . .

Leia was crouching in the darkness, her blaster and lightsaber in her hands, her heart racing with fear and determination. Behind her was Winter, holding tightly to two small lives, helpless and fragile. A voice – Han's – filled with anger and the same determination. Chewbacca was somewhere nearby – somewhere overhead, he thought – and Lando was with him. Before them were shadowy figures, their minds filled with menace and a cold and deadly purpose. A blaster fired – and another – a door burst open—

'Leia!' Luke blurted, his body jerking violently as the trance broke like a bubble, one final image flickering and vanishing into the Honoghr night. A faceless person, moving toward his sister and her children from behind the shadowy evil. A person edged with the power of the Force . . .

'What is it?' a Noghri voice snapped beside him.

Luke opened his eyes to find Khabarakh and Ovkhevam crouching in front of him, a small glow rod bathing their nightmare faces in dim light. 'I saw Leia,' he told them, hearing the trembling of reaction in his voice. 'She and her children were in danger.' He took a shuddering breath, purging the adrenaline from his body. 'I have to get back to Coruscant.'

Ovkhevam and Khabarakh exchanged glances. 'But if the danger is now . . . ?' Ovkhevam said.

'It wasn't now,' Luke shook his head. 'It was the future. I don't know how far ahead.'

Khabarakh touched Ovkhevam's shoulder, and for a minute the Noghri conversed quietly in their own language. *All right*, Luke told himself, running through the Jedi calming techniques. *All right*. Lando had been in the vision – he distinctly remembered seeing Lando there. But Lando, as far as he knew, was still out at his Nomad City mining operation on Nkllon. Which meant Luke still had time to get back to Coruscant before the attack on Leia could happen.

Or did it? Was the vision a true image of the future? Or could a change in events alter what he'd seen? *Difficult to see*, Master Yoda had said of Luke's vision on Dagobah. *Always in motion is the future.* And if someone of Yoda's depth of knowledge in the Force had been unable to sift through the uncertainties . . .

'If you wish it, son of Vader, the commandos will seize the Imperial ship,' Ovkhevam said. 'If its people were destroyed quickly, there would be no word from it that would point blame at the Noghri.'

'I can't let you do that,' Luke shook his head. 'It's too dangerous. There's no way to guarantee they wouldn't get a message off.'

Ovkhevam drew himself up. 'If the Lady Vader is in danger, the Noghri people are willing to take that risk.'

Luke looked up at them, an odd sensation rippling through him. Those nightmare Noghri faces hadn't changed; but in the space of a heartbeat, Luke's perception of them had. No longer were they just another abstract set of alien features. Suddenly, they had become the faces of friends.

'The last time I had a vision like this, I rushed off without thinking to try and help,' he told them quietly. 'Not only didn't I help them any, but I also nearly cost them their own chance at escape.' He looked down at his artificial right hand. Feeling again the ghostly memory of Vader's lightsaber slicing through his wrist . . . 'And lost other things, too.'

He looked back up at them. 'I won't make that same mistake again. Not with the lives of the Noghri people at stake. I'll wait until the Imperial ship is gone.'

Khabarakh reached out to gently touch his shoulder. 'Do not be concerned for their safety, son of Vader,' he said. 'The Lady Vader will not easily be defeated. Not with the Wookiee Chewbacca at her side.'

Luke looked up at the stars overhead. No, with Han and

Chewie and the whole of Palace security beside her, Leia should be able to handle any normal intruders.

But there was that final unformed image. The person who he'd sensed drawing on the Force . . .

On Jomark, the Jedi Master C'baoth had made it abundantly clear that he wanted Leia and her children. Could he want them badly enough to personally go to Coruscant for them?

'They will prevail,' Khabarakh repeated.

With an effort, Luke nodded. 'I know,' he said, trying to sound like he meant it. There was no sense in all of them worrying.

The last of the fires were out, the last of the microfractures sealed, the last of the injured taken to sick bay . . . and with an odd mixture of resignation and cold-blooded fury, Lando Calrissian gazed out his private command room window and knew that it was over. Cloud City on Bespin; and now Nomad City on Nkllon. For the second time, the Empire had taken something he'd worked to create – had worked and sweated and connived to build – and had turned it into ashes.

From his desk console came a beep. Stepping over to it, he leaned down and touched the comm switch. 'Calrissian,' he said, wiping his other hand across his forehead.

'Sir, this is Bagitt in Engine Central,' a tired voice came. 'The last drive motivator just went.'

Lando grimaced; but after all the damage those TIE fighters had inflicted on his walking mining operation, it didn't exactly come as a surprise. 'Any chance of fixing enough of them to get us moving again?' he asked.

'Not without a frigate's worth of spare parts,' Bagitt said. 'Sorry, sir, but there are just too many things broken or fused.'

'Understood. In that case, you'd better have your people concentrate on keeping life support going.'

'Yes, sir. Uh . . . sir, there's a rumor going around that we've lost all long-range communications.'

'It's only temporary,' Lando assured him. 'We've got people working on it right now. And enough spare parts to build two new transmitters.'

'Yes, sir,' Bagitt said, sounding a shade less discouraged. 'Well . . . I guess I'll get over to life support.'

'Keep me informed,' Lando told him.

Switching off the comm, he walked back to the window. Twenty days, they had; just twenty days before Nkllon's slow rotation took them from the center of the night side across into full sunlight. At which point it wouldn't much matter whether or not the drive motivators, communication gear, or even life support were working. When the sun began its slow crawl up the horizon over there, everyone still left in Nomad City would be on their way to a very fast and very warm death.

Twenty days.

Lando gazed out the viewport at the night sky, letting his eyes flick across the constellation patterns he'd dreamed up in his occasional idle moments. If they could get the long-range transmitter fixed in the next day or so, they should be able to call Coruscant for help. No matter what the Imperial attack force might have done to the shieldships at the outer system depot, the New Republic's spaceship techs ought to be able to get one of them flying again, at least well enough for one last trip into the inner system. It would be tight, but with any luck at all—

Abruptly, his train of thought broke off. There, just shy of directly overhead, the brilliant star of an approaching shield-ship had appeared.

Reflexively, he took a step toward his desk to sound battle stations. If that was the Imperials again, come to finish the job . . .

He stopped. No. If it was the Imperials, then that was that. He had no more fighters left to send against them, and no defenses remaining on Nomad City itself. There was no point in stirring up the rest of his people for nothing.

And then, from the desk came the screeching static of a comm override signal. 'Nomad City, this is General Bel Iblis,' a well-remembered voice boomed out. 'Can anyone hear me?'

Lando dived for the desk. 'This is Lando Calrissian, General,' he said, striving for as much nonchalance as he could muster. 'Is that you out there?'

'That's us,' Bel Iblis acknowledged. 'We were out at Qat Chrystac when we picked up your distress signal. I'm sorry we couldn't get here in time.'

'So am I,' Lando said. 'What's it look like at the shieldship depot?'

'Afraid it's something of a mess,' Bel Iblis said. 'These shieldships of yours are too big to easily destroy, but the Imperials took a crack at it just the same. At the moment this one seems to be the only one in any shape to fly.'

'Well, it's all pretty academic, anyway,' Lando said. 'Nomad City is done for.'

'No way to get it moving again?'

'Not in the twenty days we've got before the dawn line catches up with us,' Lando told him. 'We might be able to dig it underground deep enough to last out a trip around the day side, but we'd need heavy equipment that we haven't got.'

'Maybe we can pull it off Nkllon entirely and take it to the outer system for repairs,' Bel Iblis suggested. 'An Assault Frigate and a couple of heavy lifters should do the trick if we can get another shieldship flying.'

'And can convince Admiral Ackbar to divert an Assault Frigate from the battle planes,' Lando reminded him.

'Point,' Bel Iblis admitted. 'I suppose I should hear the rest of the bad news. What did the Empire get?'

Lando sighed. 'Everything,' he said. 'All our stockpiles. Hfredium, kammris, dolovite – you name it. If we mined it, they got it.'

'How much in all?'

'About four months' worth. A little over three million at current market prices.'

For a moment Bel Iblis was silent. 'I didn't realize this place was that productive. Makes it all the more imperative that we persuade Coruscant to help get you up and running again. How many people do you have down there?'

'Just under five thousand,' Lando told him. 'Some of them are in pretty bad shape, though.

'I've had plenty of experience moving injured people,' Bel

Iblis said grimly. 'Don't worry, we'll get them aboard. I'd like you to detail a group to stay behind and get the shieldships operational. We'll transport everyone else to Qat Chrystac. Be as good a place as any for you to transmit a formal request for assistance to Coruscant.'

'I didn't think there *were* any good places to transmit requests from,' Lando growled.

'They've got a lot on their minds back there,' Bel Iblis agreed. 'For what it's worth, I'd say you've got a better-than-average chance that yours won't get lost in the shuffle.'

Lando chewed at his lip. 'So let's skip the shuffle entirely. Take me to Coruscant and let me talk to them in person.'

'That'll cost you an extra five days in travel time,' Bel Iblis pointed out. 'Can you afford it?'

'Better five days spent that way than sitting around Qat Chrystac wondering if my transmission has even gotten out of the communications center yet,' Lando countered. 'Figure five days to Coruscant, another day or two to talk Leia into reassigning a ship and lifters, and then ten more to get them here and finish the job.'

'Seventeen days. Cuts it pretty close.'

'I don't have any better ideas. What do you say?'

Bel Iblis snorted gently. 'Well, I'd been planning to head over to Coruscant soon anyway. Might as well be now.'

'Thank you, General,' Lando said.

'No problem. Better start getting your people ready – we'll be launching our shuttles as soon as we're in the planetary umbra.'

'Right. See you soon.'

Lando switched off the comm. It was a long shot, all right – he knew that much going in. But realistically, it was the only shot he had. And besides, even if they turned him down flat, a trip to Coruscant right now wouldn't be such a bad idea. He'd get to see Leia and Han and the brand-new twins, maybe even run into Luke or Wedge.

He glanced out the viewport, his lip twisting. And on Coruscant, at least he wouldn't have to worry about Imperial attacks.

Keying the intercom, he began issuing the evacuation orders.

CHAPTER 8

Jacen had fallen asleep midway through his dinner, but Jaina was still going at it. Lying on her side, Leia shifted position as much as she could on the bed without pulling out of her daughter's reach and picked up her data pad again. By her own slightly fuzzy count, she'd tried at least four times to get through this page. 'Fifth time's the charm,' she commented wryly to Jaina, stroking her daughter's head with her free hand.

Jaina, with more immediate things on her mind, didn't respond. For a moment Leia gazed down at her daughter, a fresh surge of wonder rippling upward through her weariness. Those tiny hands that flailed gently and randomly against her body; the skullcap of short black hairs covering her head; that small face with its wonderfully earnest expression of infant concentration as she worked at eating. A brand-new life, so fragile and yet so remarkably resilient.

And she and Han had created it. Had created both of them.

Across the room, the door from the living areas of their suite opened. 'Hi, sweetheart,' Han called quietly. 'Everything all right?'

'Fine,' she murmured back. 'We're just having another dinner.'

'They eat like starving Wookiees,' Han said, crossing to the bed and giving the situation a quick scan. 'Jacen done already?'

'Just wanted a snack, I guess,' Leia said, craning her neck to look at the sleeping baby lying on the bed behind her. 'He'll probably want the second course in an hour or so.'

'I wish they'd get together on scheduling,' Han said, sitting carefully down on the side of the bed and easing the tip of his forefinger into Jacen's palm. The tiny hand curled reflexively around his finger, and Leia looked up at her husband in time to see his familiar lopsided grin. 'He's going to be a strong one.'

'You should feel the grip at this end,' Leia told him, looking back at Jaina. 'Is Lando still downstairs?'

'Yeah, he and Bel Iblis are still talking to Admiral Drayson,' Han said, reaching over to rest his free hand on Leia's shoulder. The warmth felt good through her thin dressing gown. Almost as good as the warmth of his thoughts against her mind. 'Still trying to convince him to divert a couple of ships to Nkllon.'

'How does it look?'

Han wiggled his finger gently in Jacen's grip, clucking softly at his sleeping son. 'Not too good,' he admitted. 'We're not going to get Nomad City off the ground without something the size of an Assault Frigate. Drayson isn't exactly eager to pull anything that big off the line.'

'Did you point out how much we need the metals Lando's been mining there?'

'I mentioned it. He wasn't impressed.'

'You have to know how to talk to Drayson.' Leia looked down at Jaina. She was still going at it, but her eyes were beginning to drift closed. 'Maybe when Jaina's asleep I can go downstairs and give Lando a hand.'

'Right,' Han said dryly. 'No offense, sweetheart, but falling asleep on the table's not going to impress anyone.'

Leia made a face at him. 'I'm not *that* tired, thank you. And I'm certainly getting as much sleep as you are.'

'Not even close,' Han said, shifting his hand from Leia's shoulder to stroke Jaina's cheek. 'I get to doze in the middle of those late-night feedings.'

'You shouldn't be waking up for them at all,' Leia said. 'Winter or I could get the babies out of their crib just as well as you can.'

'Nice,' Han said in mock indignation. 'You know, you thought I was pretty handy to have around before the kids showed up. Now you don't need me any more, huh? Just go ahead and toss me aside.'

'Of course I need you,' Leia soothed him. 'As long as most of the droids are out on defense duty and there are two babies who have to be changed, you'll always have a place here.'

'Oh, great,' Han growled. 'I think I'd rather get tossed aside.'

'It's way too late for that,' Leia assured him, stroking his hand and turning serious again. 'I know you want to help, Han, and I really do appreciate it. I just feel guilty.'

'Well, don't,' Han told her, taking her hand and squeezing it. 'We old-time smugglers are used to strange hours, remember.' He glanced over at the door to Winter's room. 'Winter gone to bed already?'

'No, she hasn't come back up yet,' Leia said, stretching her mind toward the room. As near as she could tell, it was indeed empty. 'She's got some project of her own going downstairs – I don't know what.'

'I do,' Han said, his sense turning thoughtful. 'She's been down to the library sifting through the old Alliance archives.'

Leia craned her neck to study his face. 'Trouble?'

'I don't know,' Han said slowly. 'Winter doesn't talk much about what she's thinking. Not to me, anyway. But she's worried about something.'

Beyond the door, Leia caught the flicker of another presence. 'She's back,' she told Han. 'I'll see if I can get her to tell me about it.'

'Good luck,' Han grunted, giving Leia's hand one last squeeze and standing up. 'I guess I'll go back downstairs. See if I can help Lando sweet-talk Drayson a little.'

'The two of you ought to get him into a sabacc game,' Leia suggested. 'Play for ships, like you and Lando did with the *Falcon*. Maybe you can win an Assault Frigate.'

'What, playing against Drayson?' Han said with a snort. 'Thanks, hon, but Lando and I wouldn't know what to do with a fleet of our own. I'll see you later.'

'OK. I love you, Han.'

He gave her another lopsided smile. 'I know,' he said, and left. With a sigh, Leia adjusted her shoulder against the pillow and half turned toward Winter's room. 'Winter?' she called softly.

111

There was a short pause; then the door swung quietly open. 'Yes, Your Highness?' Winter asked, stepping into the room.

'I'd like to talk to you for a minute, if it's convenient,' Leia said.

'Of course,' Winter said, gliding forward in that wonderfully graceful way of hers that Leia had always envied. 'I think Jacen's asleep. Shall I put him in the crib?'

'Please,' Leia nodded. 'Han tells me you've been doing some research in the old Alliance archives.'

Winter's face didn't change, but Leia could sense the subtle change in her sense and body language. 'Yes.'

'May I ask why?'

Carefully, Winter lifted Jacen from the bed and carried him toward the crib. 'I think I may have discovered an Imperial agent in the Palace,' she said. 'I was trying to confirm that.'

Leia felt the hairs on the back of her neck stand up. 'Who is it?'

'I'd really rather not make any accusations before I have more information,' Winter said. 'I could easily be wrong.'

'I appreciate your scruples,' Leia said. 'But if you have an idea about this Delta Source information leak, we need to know about it right away.'

'This isn't connected with Delta Source,' Winter said, shaking her head. 'At least, not directly. She hasn't been here long enough for that.'

Leia frowned at her, trying to read her sense. There was a great deal of worry there, running squarely into an equally strong desire not to throw around hasty allegations. 'Is it Mara Jade?' she asked.

Winter hesitated. 'Yes. But again, I don't have any proof.'

'What *do* you have?'

'Not very much,' Winter said, tucking the blanket carefully around Jacen. 'Really only a short conversation with her when I was escorting her up from the medical section. She asked me what I did during the height of the Rebellion, and I told her about my job with Supply and Procurement. She then identified me as Targeter.'

Leia thought back. Winter had had so many code names during that time. 'Was that incorrect?'

'No, I had that name for a short time,' Winter said. 'Which is the point, really. I was only known as Targeter for a few weeks on Averam. Before Imperial Intelligence broke the cell there.'

'I see,' Leia said slowly. 'And Mara wasn't with the Averists?'

'I don't know,' Winter said, shaking her head. 'I never met more than a few of that group. That's why I've been searching the records. I thought there might be a complete listing somewhere.'

'I doubt it,' Leia said. 'Local cells like that almost never kept personnel files. It would be a group death warrant if it fell into Imperial hands.'

'I know.' Winter looked across the crib at her. 'Which rather leaves us at an impasse.'

'Perhaps,' Leia said, gazing past Winter and trying to pull together everything she knew about Mara. It wasn't all that much. As far as she knew, Mara had never claimed any past Alliance affiliation, which would tend to support Winter's suspicions. On the other hand, it had been less than two months since she'd enlisted Luke to help her free Karrde from a detention cell on Grand Admiral Thrawn's own flagship. That didn't make much sense if she was an Imperial agent herself. 'I think,' she told Winter slowly, 'that whatever side Mara was once on, she's not there any more. Any loyalty she has now is probably to Karrde and his people.'

Winter smiled faintly. 'Is that Jedi insight, Your Highness? Or just your trained diplomatic opinion?'

'Some of each,' Leia said. 'I don't think we have anything to fear from her.'

'I hope you're right.' Winter gestured. 'Shall I put Jaina to bed now?'

Leia looked down. Jaina's eyes were closed tightly, her tiny mouth making soft sucking motions at the empty air. 'Yes, thank you,' she said, giving her daughter's cheek one final caress. 'Is that reception for the Sarkan delegation still going on downstairs?' she asked as she rolled away from Jaina and stretched cramped muscles.

'It was when I passed by,' Winter said, picking Jaina up and setting her in the crib next to Jacen. 'Mon Mothma asked me to suggest you drop in for a few minutes if you had the chance.'

'Yes, I'll bet she did,' Leia said, getting off the bed and crossing to the wardrobe. One of the little side benefits of having twin infants on her hands was that she finally had an armor-plated excuse for getting out of these superficial government functions that always seemed to take up more time than they were worth. Now here was Mon Mothma, trying to chicane her back into that whole crazy runaround again. 'And I'm sorry to have to disappoint her,' she added. 'But I'm afraid I have something more urgent to do right now. Will you watch the twins for me?'

'Certainly,' Winter said. 'May I ask where you'll be?'

From the wardrobe Leia selected something more suitable for public wear than her dressing gown and started to change. 'I'm going to see what I can find out about Mara Jade's past,' she said.

She could sense Winter's frown all the way across the room. 'May I ask how?'

Leia smiled tightly. 'I'm going to ask her.'

He stood before her, his face half hidden by the cowl of his robe, his yellow eyes piercingly bright as they gazed across the infinite distance between them. His lips moved, but his words were drowned out by the throaty hooting of alarms all around them, filling Mara with an urgency that was rapidly edging into panic. Between her and the Emperor two figures appeared: the dark, imposing image of Darth Vader, and the smaller black-clad figure of Luke Skywalker. They stood before the Emperor, facing each other, and ignited their lightsabers. The blades crossed, brilliant red-white against brilliant green-white, and they prepared for battle.

And then, without warning, the blades disengaged . . . and

with twin roars of hatred audible even over the alarms, both turned and strode toward the Emperor.

Mara heard herself cry out as she struggled to rush to her master's aid. But the distance was too great, her body too sluggish. She screamed a challenge, trying to at least distract them. But neither Vader nor Skywalker seemed to hear her. They moved outward to flank the Emperor . . . and as they lifted their lightsabers high, she saw that the Emperor was gazing at her.

She looked back at him, wanting desperately to turn away from the coming disaster but unable to move. A thousand thoughts and emotions flooded in through that gaze, a glittering kaleidoscope of pain and fear and rage that spun far too fast for her to really absorb. The Emperor raised his hands, sending cascades of jagged blue-white lightning at his enemies. Both men staggered under the counterattack, and Mara watched with the sudden agonized hope that this time it might end differently. But no. Vader and Skywalker straightened, and with another roar of rage, they lifted their lightsabers high.

And then, over the raised lightsabers came a roll of distant thunder—

And with a jerk that nearly threw her out of her chair Mara snapped out of the dream.

She took a deep, shuddering breath against the flood of post-dream emotion; against the turmoil of pain, anger, and loneliness. But this time she wasn't going to have the luxury of working her way through the tangle in solitude. From outside her room she could vaguely sense another presence; and even as she rolled out of the desk chair into a reflexive combat crouch, the roll of thunder from her dream – a quiet knock – was repeated.

For a long moment she considered keeping quiet and seeing if whoever it was would decide the room was empty and go away. But the light from her room, she knew, would be visible beneath the old-style hinged door. And if the person out there was who she suspected, he wouldn't be fooled by silence, anyway. 'Come in,' she called.

The door unlocked and swung open . . . but it wasn't Luke Skywalker who stood there. 'Hello, Mara,' Leia Organa Solo nodded to her. 'Am I interrupting anything?'

'Not at all,' Mara said politely, suppressing a grimace. The last thing she wanted right now was company, particularly company that was in any way associated with Skywalker. But as long as she and Ghent were still stuck here it wouldn't be smart to deliberately alienate someone of Organa Solo's influence. 'I was just reading some of the news reports from the battle regions. Please come in.'

'Thank you,' Organa Solo said, stepping past her into the suite. 'I was looking over those same reports a little while ago. Grand Admiral Thrawn is certainly justifying the late Emperor's confidence in his ability.'

Mara threw her a sharp look, wondering what Skywalker had told her. But Organa Solo's eyes were turned toward the window and the lights of the Imperial City below. And what little Mara could discern of the other woman's sense didn't seem to be taunting. 'Yes, Thrawn was one of the best,' she said. 'Brilliant and innovative, with an almost compulsive thirst for victory.'

'Perhaps he needed to prove he was the equal of the other Grand Admirals,' Organa Solo suggested. 'Particularly given his mixed heritage and the Emperor's feelings toward non-humans.'

'I'm sure that was part of it,' Mara said.

Organa Solo took another step toward the window, her back still turned to Mara. 'Did you know the Grand Admiral well?' she asked.

'Not really,' Mara said cautiously. 'He communicated with Karrde a few times when I was there and visited our Myrkr base once. He had a big business going in Myrkr ysalamiri for a while – Karrde once figured they'd hauled five or six thousand of them out of there—'

'I meant, did you know him during the war,' Organa Solo said, turning finally to face her.

Mara returned her gaze steadily. If Skywalker had told her . . . but if he'd told her, why wasn't Mara in a detention cell

116

somewhere? No; Organa Solo had to be on a fishing expedition. 'Why should I have known Thrawn during the war?' she countered.

Organa Solo shrugged fractionally. 'There's been a suggestion made that you might once have served with the Empire.'

'And you wanted to make sure before you locked me up?'

'I wanted to see if you might have knowledge about the Grand Admiral we could use against him,' Organa Solo corrected.

Mara snorted. 'There isn't anything,' she said. 'Not with Thrawn. He has no patterns; no favorite strategies; no discernible weaknesses. He studies his enemies and tailors his attacks against psychological blind spots. He doesn't overcommit his forces, and he's not too proud to back off when it's clear he's losing. Which doesn't happen very often. As you're finding out.' She cocked an eyebrow. 'Any of that help you?' she added sarcastically.

'Actually, it does,' Organa Solo said. 'If we can identify the weaknesses he's planning to exploit, we might be able to anticipate the thrust of his attack.'

'That's not going to be easy,' Mara warned.

Organa Solo smiled faintly. 'No, but it gives us a place to start. Thank you for your help.'

'You're welcome,' Mara said, the words coming out automatically. 'Was there anything else?'

'No, I don't think so,' Organa said, stepping away from the window and heading for the door. 'I need to get back and get some sleep before the twins wake up again. And you'll probably want to be going to bed soon, too.'

'And I'm still free to move around the Palace?'

Organa Solo smiled again. 'Of course. Whatever you did in the past, it's clear you're not serving with the Empire now. Good night.' She turned to the door, reached for the handle—

'I'm going to kill your brother,' Mara told her. 'Did he tell you that?'

Organa Solo stiffened, just noticeably, and Mara could sense the ripple of shock run through that Jedi-trained calmness. Her hand, on the door handle, dropped to her side. 'No, he didn't,' she said, her back still to Mara. 'May I ask why?'

'He destroyed my life,' Mara told her, feeling the old ache deep in her throat and wondering why she was even telling Organa Solo this. 'You're wrong; I didn't just serve with the Empire. I was a personal agent of the Emperor himself. He brought me here to Coruscant and the Imperial Palace and trained me to be an extension of his will across the galaxy. I could hear his voice from anywhere in the Empire, and knew how to give his orders to anyone from a stormtrooper brigade all the way up to a Grand Moff. I had authority and power and a purpose in life. They knew me as the Emperor's Hand, and they respected me the same way they did him. Your brother took all that away from me.'

Organa Solo turned back to face her. 'I'm sorry,' she said. 'But there was no other choice. The lives and freedom of billions of beings—'

'I'm not going to debate the issue with you,' Mara cut her off. 'You couldn't possibly understand what I've been through.'

A shadow of distant pain crossed Organa Solo's face. 'You're wrong,' she said quietly. 'I understand very well.'

Mara glared at her; but it was a glare without any real force of hatred behind it. Leia Organa Solo of Alderaan, who'd been forced to watch as the first Death Star obliterated her entire world . . . 'At least you had a life to go to afterward,' she growled at last. 'You had the whole Rebellion – more friends and allies than you could even count. I had no-one.'

'It must have been hard.'

'I survived it,' Mara said briefly. 'So *now* are you going to have me hauled off to detention?'

Those Alderaanian-cultured eyebrows lifted slightly. 'You keep suggesting that I should have you locked up. Is that what you want?'

'I already told you what I want. I want to kill your brother.'

'Do you?' Organa Solo asked. 'Do you really?'

Mara smiled thinly. 'Bring him here and I'll prove it.'

Organa Solo studied her face, and Mara could feel the tenuous touch of her rudimentary Jedi senses as well. 'From what Luke's told me, it sounds like you've already had several chances to kill him,' Organa Solo pointed out. 'You didn't take them.'

'It wasn't from lack of intent,' Mara said. But it was a thought that had been gnawing at her as well. 'I just keep getting into situations where I need him alive. But that'll change.'

'Perhaps,' Organa Solo said, her eyes still moving across Mara's face. 'Or perhaps it's not really you who wants him dead.'

Mara frowned. 'What's *that* supposed to mean?'

Organa Solo's gaze drifted away from Mara to the window, and Mara could feel a tightening of the other woman's sense. 'I was at Endor a couple of months ago,' she said.

An icy sensation crawled up Mara's spine. She'd been at Endor, too, taken there to face Grand Admiral Thrawn . . . and she remembered what the space around the world of the Emperor's death had felt like. 'And?' she prompted. Even to herself, her voice sounded strained.

Organa Solo heard it, too. 'You know what I'm talking about, don't you?' she asked, her eyes still on the lights of the Imperial City. 'There's some shadow of the Emperor's presence still there. Some of that final surge of hatred and anger. Like a – I don't know what.'

'Like an emotional bloodstain,' Mara said quietly, the image springing spontaneously and vividly into her mind. 'Marking the spot where he died.'

She looked at Organa Solo, to find the other woman's eyes on her. 'Yes,' Organa Solo said. 'That's exactly what it was like.'

Mara took a deep breath, forcing the black chill from her mind. 'So what does that have to do with me?'

Organa Solo studied her. 'I think you know.'

YOU WILL KILL LUKE SKYWALKER. 'No,' Mara said, her mouth suddenly dry. 'You're wrong.'

'Am I?' Organa Solo asked softly. 'You said you could

hear the Emperor's voice from anywhere in the galaxy.'

'I could hear his *voice*,' Mara snapped. 'Nothing more.'

Organa Solo shrugged slightly. 'You know best, of course. It might still be worth thinking about.'

'I'll do that,' Mara said stiffly. 'If that's all, you can go.'

Organa Solo nodded, her sense showing no irritation at being dismissed like some minor underling. 'Thank you for your assistance,' she said. 'I'll talk with you later.'

With a final smile, she pulled the door open and left. 'Don't count on it,' Mara muttered after her, turning back to the desk and dropping into the chair. This had gone far enough. If Karrde was too preoccupied with business to get in touch with his contact man, then the contact man himself was going to get her and Ghent out of here. Pulling up her code file, she keyed for long-range comm access.

The response was prompt. UNABLE TO ACCESS, the words scrolled across her display. LONG-RANGE COMMUNICATIONS SYSTEM TEMPORARILY DOWN.

'Terrific,' she growled under her breath. 'How soon till it's back up?'

UNABLE TO DETERMINE. REPEATING, LONG-RANGE COMMUNICATIONS SYSTEM TEMPORARILY DOWN.

With a curse, she shut the terminal off. The whole universe seemed to be against her tonight. She picked up the data pad she'd been reading earlier, put it down again, and stood back up. It was late, she'd already fallen asleep once at her desk, and if she had any sense she would just give it up and go to bed.

Stepping across to the window, she leaned against the carved wooden frame and gazed out at the city lights stretching halfway to infinity. And tried to think.

No. It was impossible. Impossible, absurd, and unthinkable. Organa Solo could waste as much breath as she wanted spinning these clever speculations of hers. After five years of living with this thing, Mara ought to know her own thoughts and feelings. Ought to know what was real, and what wasn't.

And yet . . .

The image of the dream rose up before her. The Emperor,

gazing at her with bitter intensity as Vader and Skywalker closed in on him. The unspoken but tangible accusation in those yellow eyes: that it was her failure to take care of Skywalker at Jabba the Hutt's hideout that had caused this. That flood of powerless rage as the two lightsabers were lifted over him. That final cry, ringing for ever through her head—

YOU WILL KILL LUKE SKYWALKER.

'Stop it!' she snarled, slapping the side of her head hard against the window jamb. The image and words exploded into a flash of pain and a shower of sparks and vanished.

For a long time she just stood there, listening to the rapid thudding of her heartbeat in her ears, the conflicting thoughts chasing each other around her mind. Certainly the Emperor would have wanted Skywalker dead . . . but Organa Solo was still wrong. She had to be. It was Mara herself who wanted to kill Luke Skywalker, not some ghost from the past.

Far across the city, a multicolored light rippled gently against the surrounding buildings and clouds overhead, jolting her out of her musings. The clock at the ancient Central Gathering Hall, marking the hour as it had for the past three centuries. The light changed texture and rippled again, then winked out.

Half an hour past midnight. Lost in her thoughts, Mara hadn't realized it had gotten that late. And all of this wasn't accomplishing anything, anyway. She might as well go to bed and try to put the whole thing out of her mind long enough to get some sleep. With a sigh, she pushed away from the window—

And froze. Deep in the back of her mind, the quiet alarm bell had just gone off.

Somewhere nearby, there was danger.

She slid her tiny blaster out of its forearm holster, listening hard. Nothing. Glancing back once at the window, wondering briefly if anyone was watching her through the privacy laminate, she moved silently to the door. Putting her ear against it, she listened again.

For a moment there was nothing. Then, almost inaudible through the thick wood, she heard the sound of approaching footsteps. Footsteps with the kind of quiet but purposeful stride that she had always associated with combat professionals. She tensed; but the footsteps passed her door without pausing, fading away toward the far end of the hallway.

She waited a count of ten to let them get a good lead on her. Then, carefully, she opened her door and looked outside.

There were four of them, dressed in the uniforms of Palace security, walking in a bent diamond formation. They reached the hallway and slowed as the point man eased a quick look around it. His hand curbed slightly, and all four continued around the corner and disappeared. Heading toward the stairway that led down to the central sections of the palace below or up to the Tower and the permanent residential suites above.

Mara stared after them, her fatigue gone in a surge of adrenaline. The bent diamond formation, the obvious caution, the hand signal, and her own premonition of danger – they all pointed to the same conclusion.

Imperial Intelligence had penetrated the Palace.

She turned back toward her desk, stopped short with a quiet curse. One of the first tasks the team would have carried out would have been to get into the Palace's computer and comm systems. Any attempt to sound the alarm would probably be intercepted, and would certainly tip them off.

Which meant that if they were going to be stopped, she was going to have to do it herself. Gripping her blaster tightly, she slipped out of her room and headed after them.

She'd made it to the corner and was just easing forward for a careful look when she heard the quiet click of a blaster safety behind her. 'All right, Jade,' a voice murmured in her ear. 'Nice and easy. It's all over.'

CHAPTER 9

Admiral Drayson leaned back in his seat and shook his head. 'I'm sorry, Calrissian, General Bel Iblis,' he said for probably the tenth time since the session had begun. 'We just can't risk it.'

Lando took a deep breath, trying to scrape together a few last shards of patience. This was his sweat and work that Drayson was casually throwing away. 'Admiral—'

'It's not that much of a risk, Admiral,' Bel Iblis cut in smoothly and with far more courtesy than Lando had left at his disposal. 'I've shown you at least eight places we could draw an Assault Frigate from which would have it out of service less than ten days.'

Drayson snorted. 'At the rate he's going, Grand Admiral Thrawn could take three more sectors in ten days. You want to give him a shot at four?'

'Admiral, we're talking a single Assault Frigate here,' Lando said. 'Not a dozen Star Cruisers or an orbital battle station. What could Thrawn possibly have up his sleeve where one Assault Frigate could make or break the attack?'

'What could he do against a heavily defended shipyard with a single rigged freighter?' Drayson retorted. 'Face it, gentlemen: when you go up against someone like Thrawn, all the usual rules get tossed out the lock. He could spin a net out of this so transparent that we'd never even see it until it was too late. He's done it before.'

Lando grimaced; but it was hardly a frame of mind he could really blame Drayson for. A couple of months back, when he and Han had first been brought to Bel Iblis's hidden military base, he'd been three-quarters convinced himself that the whole thing was some gigantic and convoluted scheme that Thrawn had created for their benefit. It had taken him until after the *Katana* battle to finally be convinced otherwise, and it had taught him a valuable lesson. 'Admiral, we all agree that Thrawn is a brilliant tactician,' he said, choosing his words carefully. 'But we can't assume that everything that happens in the galaxy is part of some grand, all-encompassing scheme that he's dreamed up. He got my metal stockpiles and put Nomad City out of commission. Odds are that's all he wanted.'

Drayson shook his head. 'I'm afraid "odds are" isn't good enough, Calrissian. You find me proof that the Empire won't take advantage of a missing Assault Frigate and I'll consider loaning you one.'

'Oh, come on, Admiral—'

'And if I were you,' Drayson added, starting to gather his data cards together, 'I'd play down my connection with the whole Nkllon mining project. A lot of us still remember that it was your mole miners Thrawn used in his attack on the Sluis Van shipyards.'

'And it was his knowledge of them that kept that attack from succeeding,' Bel Iblis reminded the other quietly. 'A number of us remember that, too.'

'That assumes Thrawn actually intended to steal the ships,' Drayson shot back as he stood up from the table. 'Personally, I expect he was just as happy to have them put out of commission. Now if you'll excuse me, gentlemen, I have a war to run.'

He left, and Lando let out a quiet sigh of defeat. 'So much for that,' he said, pulling his own data cards together.

'Don't let it worry you,' Bel Iblis advised, getting up from his chair and stretching tiredly. 'It's not you and Nomad City so much as it is me. Drayson was always one of those who considered disagreement with Mon Mothma to be one step down from Imperial collaboration. Obviously, he still does.'

'I thought you and Mon Mothma had patched all that up,' Lando said, getting to his feet.

'Oh, we have,' Bel Iblis shrugged, circling the table and heading for the door. 'More or less. She's invited me back into the New Republic, I've accepted her leadership, and officially all is well. But old memories fade slowly.' His lip twisted slightly. 'And I have to admit that my departure from the Alliance after Alderaan could have been handled more diplomatically. You up on the President's Guests floor?'

'Yes. You?'

'The same. Come on – I'll walk you up.'

They left the conference room and headed down the arched hallway toward the turbolifts. 'You think he might change his mind?' Lando asked.

'Drayson?' Bel Iblis shook his head. 'Not a chance. Unless we can pry Mon Mothma out of the war room and get you a hearing, I think your only chance is to hope Ackbar gets back to Coruscant in the next couple of days. The importance of Nomad City aside, I imagine he still owes you a favor or two.'

Lando thought about that rather awkward scene back when he'd first told Ackbar that he was resigning his general's commission. 'Favors won't mean anything if he agrees that it might be a setup,' he said instead. 'Not after being burned once at Sluis Van.'

'True,' Bel Iblis conceded. He glanced down a cross corridor as they passed, and when he turned forward again Lando thought he could see a slight frown on his face. 'All of which is unfortunately complicated by the presence of this Delta Source thing the Empire's got planted here in the Palace. Just because Thrawn doesn't have any current plans for Nkllon doesn't mean he won't think some up once he finds out what we're going to do.'

'*If* he finds out,' Lando corrected. 'Delta Source isn't omniscient, you know. Han and Leia have managed to run some important missions past it.'

'Proving once again the basic strength of small groups. Still, the sooner you identify this leak and put it out of commission, the better.'

They passed another hallway, and again Bel Iblis glanced down it. And this time, there was no doubt about the frown. 'Trouble?' Lando asked quietly.

'I'm not sure,' Bel Iblis said. 'Shouldn't there be occasional guards in this part of the Palace?'

Lando looked around. They *were* rather alone out here.

'Could they all have been shifted down to the Sarkan reception for the evening?'

'They were here earlier,' Bel Iblis said. 'I saw at least two when I came down from my suite.'

Lando looked back along the hallway, an unpleasant sensation starting to crawl along his backbone. 'So what happened to them?'

'I don't know.' Bel Iblis took a deep breath. 'I don't suppose you're armed.'

Lando shook his head. 'Blaster's up in my room. I didn't think I'd need it here.'

'You probably don't,' Bel Iblis said, the fingertips of his right hand easing beneath his jacket as he looked around. 'There's probably some simple, perfectly innocuous explanation.'

'Sure,' Lando said, pulling out his comlink. 'Let's call in and find out what it is.' He thumbed the device on—

And as quickly shut it off as a soft squeal on static erupted from the speaker. 'I think the explanation just stopped being simple,' he said grimly. Suddenly his hand was itching to have a blaster in it. 'What now?'

'We find some way to alert Palace Security,' Bel Iblis said, looking around. 'All right. The turbolifts up ahead won't help us – they only serve the residential areas. But there's a stairway at the far end that leads down to Palace Central. We'll try that way.'

'Sounds good,' Lando nodded. 'Let's swing up to my suite first and pick up my blaster.'

'Good idea,' Bel Iblis agreed. 'We'll pass on the turbolift – stairs are over this way. Nice and quiet.'

The stairs were as deserted as the corridor behind them had been. But as Bel Iblis started out of the stairway door, he suddenly held up a warning hand. Moving to his side, Lando looked out on to the floor.

Ahead, moving cautiously down the hallway away from them, was a lone figure. A slender woman with red-gold hair, a small blaster gripped ready in her hand.

Mara Jade.

126

There was a soft whisper of metal on cloth as Bel Iblis drew his blaster. Motioning Lando to follow, he started silently down the hallway after her.

They had nearly caught up by the time she reached the far corner. There she paused, poised to look around it—

Bel Iblis leveled his blaster. 'All right, Jade,' he said quietly. 'Nice and easy. It's all over.'

For a second Lando was sure she was going to argue the point. She turned her head halfway, looking back over her shoulder as if targeting her opponents – 'Calrissian!' she said, and there was no mistaking the relief in her voice. Or the underlying tension, either. 'There are Imperials in the Palace, dressed as Security. I've just seen four of them.'

'Interesting,' Bel Iblis said, eyeing her closely. 'Where were you going?'

'I thought it might be a good idea to find out what they were up to,' she growled sarcastically. 'You want to help, or not?'

Bel Iblis eased a look around the corner. 'I don't see anyone. They've probably already headed down. Best guess is either the war room or the Sarkan reception.'

And suddenly, the whole thing clicked together in Lando's mind. 'No,' he said. 'They haven't gone down, they've gone *up*. They're after Leia's twins.'

Mara swore under her breath. 'You're right. Thrawn's promised them to that lunatic C'baoth. That has to be it.'

'You could be right,' Bel Iblis said. 'Where's your room, Calrissian?'

'Two doors back,' Lando told him, nodding over his shoulder.

'Get your blaster,' Bel Iblis ordered, peering again around the corner. 'You and Jade head down the hallway over there and find the main stairway. See if anyone's up there yet; maybe try to warn Leia and Solo. I'll go downstairs and scare up some reinforcements.'

'Be careful – they may have left a rear guard on the stairway down,' Mara warned.

'They'll certainly have one on the way up,' Bel Iblis

countered. 'Watch yourselves.' With one final look around the corner, he eased past and was gone.

'Wait here,' Lando told Mara, starting back toward his room. 'I'll be right back.'

'Just hurry it up,' she called after him.

'Right.'

He ran to his room; and as he keyed the door open, he threw a quick look back at Mara. She was still standing there, turned halfway around the corner, an intense yet strangely empty expression on the part of her face he could see.

That face. That somehow, somewhere familiar face. Fitting into a time and place and background he could almost but not quite make out in his mind's eye.

He shook off the thought. Whoever she had been, now was definitely not the time to try and figure it out. Han, Leia, and their children were in deadly danger . . . and it was up to him and Mara to get them out of it.

Turning back to his room, he hurried inside.

Leia Organa Solo. Leia Organa Solo. Wake up. You're in danger. Wake up. Leia Organa Solo, wake up—

With a gasp, Leia snapped out of the dream, the last remnants of that insistent voice echoing through her mind as she came awake. For a handful of dream-fogged heartbeats she couldn't remember where she was, and her eyes and Jedi senses flicked tensely around the darkened room as she struggled for recognition. Then the last of the sleep evaporated, and she was back in her suite in the Imperial Palace. Beside her, Han grunted gently in his sleep as he rolled over; across the room, the twins were huddled together in their crib: in the next room over, Winter was also asleep, no doubt dreaming in the laser-sharp images of her perfect memory. And outside the suite—

She frowned. There was someone at the outer door. No – more than one. Five or six of them at least, standing grouped around it.

She slipped out of bed, hands automatically scooping up her blaster and lightsaber from the floor as she did so. It was probably nothing – most likely simply a group of Security guards taking a moment for idle conversation among themselves before continuing on their rounds. Though if so, they were breaking several fairly strict rules about on-duty personnel. She would have to find a diplomatic but firm way of reminding them.

Padding silently on the thick carpet, she left the bedroom and headed across the living areas toward the door, working through the Jedi sensory enhancement routine as she walked. If she could hear and identify the guards' voices from inside the suite, she could warn them individually and privately in the morning.

She never made it to the door. Halfway across the living area, she stopped short as her enhanced hearing began to pick up a faint hum coming from ahead of her. She strained her ears, trying to ignore the sudden distraction of her own heartbeat as she listened. The sound was faint but very distinctive, and she knew she'd heard it somewhere before.

And then, abruptly, she had it: the hum of an electronic lock-breaker. Someone was trying to break into their suite.

And even as she stood there, frozen with shock, the lock clicked open.

There was no time to run and nowhere to run to . . . but the designers of the Tower hadn't been blind to this sort of danger. Lifting her blaster, hoping fervently the mechanism still worked, Leia fired two quick shots into the door.

The wood was one of the hardest and strongest known in the galaxy, and her shots probably didn't gouge their way more than a quarter of the way through. But it was enough. The embedded sensors had taken note of the attack; and even as the sound of the blasts thundered in Leia's enhanced hearing, the heavy metal security door slammed down along the wooden door's inside edge.

'Leia?' Han's voice demanded from behind her, sounding distant through the ringing in her ears.

'Someone's trying to break in,' she said, turning and hurrying back to where he stood in the bedroom doorway, blaster ready in his hand. 'I got the security door closed in time, but that won't hold them.'

'Not for long,' Han agreed, eyeing the door as Leia reached him. 'Get in the bedroom and call Security – I'll see what I can do about slowing them down.'

'All right. Be careful – they're serious about this.'

The words were barely out of her mouth when the whole room seemed to shake. The intruders, abandoning subtlety, had set to work blowing the outer door to splinters.

'Yeah, I'd call that serious,' Han seconded grimly. 'Get Winter and Threepio and grab the twins. We got some fast planning to do.'

The first sound that drifted down the delicate arch of the Tower staircase might have been a distant blaster shot – Mara couldn't tell for sure. The next one, a handful of seconds later, left no doubt.

'Uh-oh,' Calrissian muttered. 'That's trouble.'

Another shot echoed down the staircase. 'Sounds like a heavy blaster,' Mara said, listening hard. 'They must not have been able to get the door open quietly.'

'Or else they only want the twins,' Calrissian countered darkly, heaving himself away from the corner they'd paused at. 'Come on.'

'Hold it,' Mara said, grabbing his arm with her free hand as she studied the territory in front of them. The wide arch of the first flight of stairs ended at a presentation landing with an elaborate wrought-stone balustrade. Just visible from where they stood were the openings of two narrower stairways that continued upward, double-helix fashion, from opposite ends of the landing. 'That landing would be a good spot for a rear guard, and I don't feel like stopping a blaster bolt.'

Calrissian muttered something impatient sounding under his breath, but he stayed put. A moment later, he was probably glad he had. 'You're right – there's someone near the stairway to the left,' he murmured.

'Means there'll be one on the right, too,' Mara said, her eyes searching the contours and crevices of the balustrade's stone work as another blaster shot echoed down. Intelligence operatives liked lurking in shadows . . . 'And there's one on each side of the main stairway,' she added. 'About two meters out from the edges.'

'I see them,' Calrissian said. 'This isn't going to be easy.' He looked back over his shoulder, to where the stairway picked up again. 'Come on, Bel Iblis, get up here.'

'He'd better hurry,' Mara seconded, peering cautiously at the four Imperials and trying to remember the details of the Tower's layout. 'Organa Solo's door isn't going to last long.'

'Not nearly as long as that rear guard can hold us off,' Calrissian agreed, hissing softly between his teeth. 'Wait a minute. Stay here – I've got an idea.'

'Where are you going?' Mara demanded as he moved away from the corner.

'Main hangar,' Calrissian told her, heading for the stairway behind them. 'Chewie was down there earlier working on the *Falcon*. If he's still there, we can go up the outside of the Tower and get them out.'

'How?' Mara persisted. 'Those are transparisteel windows up there – you'll never blast through them without killing everyone inside.'

'I won't have to,' Calrissian said with a tightly sly smile. 'Leia's got a lightsaber. Keep these guys busy, OK?'

He sprinted to the stairway and vanished down it. 'Right,' Mara growled after him, turning her attention back to the Imperials up on the stairway. Had they spotted her and Calrissian skulking around down here? Probably. In which case, that guy at the leftmost stairway was probably standing too far out of cover just to bait her.

Well, she was willing to oblige. Switching her blaster to her left hand, she braced her wrist against the corner, took careful aim . . .

The shot from the other stairway spattered off the wall above her blaster, scattering hot splinters of stone across her hand. 'Blast!' she snarled, snatching her hand back and brushing the fragments off. So they wanted to play cute, did they? Fine – she could handle cute. Getting a fresh grip on her blaster, she eased back to the corner—

It was the sudden tingle of danger in the back of her mind that saved her life. She dropped to one knee; and as she did so, a pair of blaster shots from straight ahead flashed into the stonework where her head had been. Instantly, she threw herself backward to land on her side on the floor, eyes and blaster tracking toward where the shots had come from.

There were two of them, moving quietly toward her along the corridor on the opposite side of the stairway. She got off two quick shots as she rolled over onto her stomach, both of them missing. Shifting to a two-handed grip, trying to ignore the shots that were beginning to come uncomfortably close, she lined up her blaster on the rightmost of her assailants and fired twice.

He jerked and collapsed to the floor, his blaster still firing reflexively and uselessly into the ceiling. A shot sizzled past Mara's ear as she shifted aim toward the second assailant, another came even closer as his weapon tracked toward her—

And abruptly, the air over Mara's head was filled with a blazing storm of blaster fire. The Imperial across the way went down like a stuck bantha and lay still.

Mara twisted around. A half-dozen security guards were hurrying toward her from the lower staircase, weapons at the ready. Behind them was Bel Iblis. 'You all right?' he called to her.

'I'm fine,' she grunted, rolling further back from the corner. Just in time; the Imperials on the landing, their little surprise attack having fizzled, opened fire in full force. Mara got to her feet, ducking away from the rain of stone chips. 'Calrissian's gone down to the hangar,' she told Bel Iblis, raising her voice over the din.

'Yes, we passed him on the way up,' the other nodded as the security guards hurried forward. 'What happened here?'

'Couple of latecomers to the party,' Mara told him, jerking her head back toward the corridor. 'Probably on their way back from the comm section. Their friends on the landing tried to keep my attention while they sneaked up on me. Just about worked, too.'

'I'm glad it didn't,' Bel Iblis said, shifting his attention over her shoulder. 'Lieutenant?'

'Not going to be easy, sir,' the guard commander called over the noise. 'We've got an E-Web repeating blaster on its way up from the armory – soon as it gets here, we can cut them right off that landing. Until then, about all we can do is keep them busy and hope they do something stupid.'

Bel Iblis nodded slowly, his lips compressed into a tight line, a hint of strain around his eyes. It was a look Mara had seen only rarely, and then only on the faces of the best military commanders: the expression of a leader preparing to send men to their deaths. 'We can't wait,' he said. The strain was still there, but his voice was firm. 'The group upstairs will have Solo's door open well before that. We'll have to take them now.'

The guard commander took a deep breath. 'Understood, sir. Right, men, you heard the General. Let's find ourselves some cover and get to it.'

Mara took a step closer to Bel Iblis. 'They'll never do it in time,' she said quietly.

'I know that,' the other said tightly. 'But the more we can take out now, the fewer we'll have to deal with when the rest of them come downstairs.'

His gaze shifted again over her shoulder. 'When,' he added softly, 'they have hostages.'

There was one final stutter of heavy blaster fire, a vaguely metallic crash, and then silence. 'Oh, dear,' Threepio moaned from the corner where he was trying to make himself as inconspicuous as possible. 'I believe the front security door has failed.'

'Glad you're here to tell us these things,' Han said irritably, his eyes roving restlessly around Winter's bedroom. It was so much useless exercise, Leia knew – everything they could possibly use in their defense had already been moved into position. Winter's bed and memento chest were against the two doors leading out of here, and the wardrobe had been moved near the window and tipped on its side to serve as a makeshift firing barricade. And that was it. Until the intruders broke through one or both of the doors, there was nothing to do but wait.

Leia took a deep breath, trying to calm her racing heart. Ever since the first of these kidnapping attempts on Bimmisaari, she'd been able to think of it as the Imperials gunning for her and her alone – not an especially pleasant thought, but one that she'd become more or less accustomed to after years of warfare.

This time it was different. This time, instead of being after her and her unborn twins, they were after her babies. Babies they could physically take from her arms and hide away where she might never see them again.

She squeezed her lightsaber tightly. No. It was not going to happen. She wouldn't let it.

There was a vaguely wooden-sounding crash from outside. 'There goes the couch,' Han muttered. Another crash – 'And the chair. Didn't think they would slow 'em down any.'

'It was worth a try,' Leia said.

'Yeah.' Han snorted under his breath. 'You know, I've been telling you for months we needed more furniture in this place.'

Leia smiled tightly and squeezed his hand. Trust Han to try to take the edge off a tense situation. 'You have not,' she told him. 'You're never here anyway.' She looked back at Winter, sitting on the floor beneath the transparisteel windows with one twin cradled in each arm. 'How are they doing?'

'I think they're waking up,' Winter murmured back.

'Yes, they are,' Leia confirmed, giving each baby a quick mental caress with as much reassurance as she could manage.

'Try to keep them quiet,' Han muttered. 'Our pals out there don't need any help.'

Leia nodded, feeling a fresh tension squeezing her heart. Both bedrooms – theirs and Winter's – opened out into the living area of the suite, giving the attackers a fifty-fifty chance at picking the door their targets were hiding behind. With the kind of weaponry they obviously had, a wrong choice wouldn't lose them more than a few minutes; but a few minutes could easily mean the difference between life and death.

The thud of a heavy blaster shot came through the wall from the direction of their room, and for a moment Leia began to breathe again. But only for a moment. A second later the sound was repeated, this time from the door in front of them. Faced with two doors, the Imperials had decided to break down both.

She turned to Han, to find him looking at her. 'It'll still slow them down,' he reminded her, the words more soothing than the sense behind them. 'They have to split up their firepower. We've still got some time.'

'Now if we just had something to do with it,' Leia said, looking futilely around the room. Years of moving around the galaxy with the Rebellion's Supply and Procurement section had gotten Winter into the habit of traveling light, and there simply wasn't anything else in here that they could use.

Another volley of shots came from outside, followed by a faint splintering sound. The regular wooden doors would be down soon, leaving only the inner security doors. Leia looked around the room again, desperation starting to cloud her thoughts. The wardrobe, the bed, the memento chest; that was it. Nothing but the security doors, the transparisteel windows, and bare walls.

Bare walls . . .

She was suddenly and freshly aware of the lightsaber clutched in her hand. 'Han – why don't we just get out of here?' she said, the first cautious wisp of hope flicking through her. 'I can cut us through the wall to the next suite over with my lightsaber. And we wouldn't have to stop there – we could be halfway down the corridor before they get that door down.'

'Yeah, I already thought of that,' Han said tightly. 'Problem is, they probably thought of it, too.'

Leia swallowed. Yes – the Imperials would certainly be ready for them to try that. 'How about going down, then?'

she persisted. 'Or up? Do you think they'd be ready for us to go through the ceiling?'

'You've seen Thrawn in action,' Han countered. 'What do *you* think?'

Leia sighed, the brief glint of hope fading. He was right. If the Grand Admiral had planned this attack personally, they might as well open the security door and surrender right now. Everything they could possibly come up with would already have been anticipated in exquisite detail, with counters planned for each move.

She shook her head sharply. 'No,' she said aloud. 'He's not infallible. We've outthought him before, and we can do it again.' She turned around to look at Winter and the twins, still sleeping under the window.

The window . . .

'All right,' she said slowly. 'What if we go out the window?'

He stared at her. 'Out the window to where?'

'Wherever we can get to,' she said. The blasters outside were pounding at the security doors now. 'Up, down, sideways – I don't care.'

Han still had that astonished look on his face. 'Sweetheart, in case you hadn't noticed, those walls are flat stone. Even Chewie couldn't climb it without mountain gear.'

'That's why they won't expect us to go that way,' Leia said, glancing at the window again. 'Maybe I can carve out some hand- and foot-holds with the lightsabers—'

She stopped, giving the window a second look. It hadn't been a trick of the room's lighting: there were indeed a pair of headlights approaching. 'Han . . .'

He swiveled to look. 'Uh-oh,' he muttered. 'More company. Great.'

'Could it be a rescue team?' Leia suggested hesitantly.

'Doubt it,' Han shook his head, studying the approaching lights. 'It's only been a few minutes since the shooting started. Wait a minute . . .'

Leia looked back. Outside, the headlights had begun to flicker. She watched the pattern, trying unsuccessfully to match it with any code she knew—

'Captain Solo!' Threepio spoke up, sounding excited. 'As you know, I am fluent in over six million forms of communication—'

'It's Chewie,' Han cut him off, scrambling to his feet and waving both hands in front of the window.

'—and this signal appears to be related to one of the codes used by professional sabacc players when dealing with—'

'We've got to get rid of this window,' Han said, throwing a look back at the door. 'Leia?'

'Right.' Leia dropped her blaster and scrambled to her feet, lightsaber in hand.

'—cheating by third or fourth parties to the game—'

'Shut up, Goldenrod,' Han snapped at Threepio, helping Winter and the twins out from under the window. The lights outside were getting rapidly closer, and now Leia could make out the faint shape of the *Falcon* in the backwash of light from the city lights below. A memory flickered back: the Noghri kidnapping attempt on Bpfassh had used a fake *Falcon* as a lure. But the Imperials wouldn't have thought to use a sabacc player's code . . . would they?

It almost didn't matter. She would rather face enemies aboard a ship than sit here waiting for them to walk in on her like this. And well before they got on board, she ought to be able to sense whether it was Chewbacca out there or not. Stepping to the window, she ignited her lightsaber and raised it high—

And behind her, with a final explosive crash, the security door blew in.

Leia spun around, catching a brief glimpse through the smoke and sparks of two men pushing aside the memento chest and diving to the floor as Han grabbed her arm and yanked her to the floor. A covering volley of blaster fire spattered against the wall and window as she shut down her lightsaber and scooped up her blaster again. At her side Han was already returning fire, ignoring the danger as he crouched half protected by the wardrobe. Four more Imperials were at the doorway now, adding their contribution to the rapid splintering of the wardrobe. Leia clenched her teeth, firing back as well as long practice and the Force would let her, knowing full well how futile it was. The longer this firefight went on, the greater the chance that a stray shot would hit one of her babies—

And suddenly, unexpectedly, something touched her mind. A mental pressure; half suggestion, half demand. And what it told her . . .

She took a deep breath. 'Stop!' she shouted over the din. 'Stop shooting. We surrender.'

The firing hesitated, then came to a halt. Laying her blaster on top of the shattered wardrobe, she raised her hand as the two Imperials on the floor got cautiously to their feet and started forward. And tried to ignore Han's stunned disbelief.

The balustrade near the rightmost stairway erupted in a cloud of chips and stone dust as the concentrated fire of the security guards finally broke through it. The answering fire from the landing caught one of the guards as the balustrade collapsed, sending him flopping backward to lie still. Mara eased an inconspicuous eye around the corner, peering through the debris and the blinding flashes of blaster bolts, wondering if in all the mess they'd managed to take out the Imperial they were trying for.

They had. Through the clearing smoke she could make out the shape of a body, scorched and dust-covered. 'They got one,' she reported, turning back to Bel Iblis. 'Three to go.'

'Plus however many there are upstairs,' he reminded her, his face grim. 'Let's hope the legendary Solo luck extends to Leia and the babies and anyone else up there they take hostage.'

'That's the second time you've mentioned hostages,' Mara said.

Bel Iblis shrugged. 'A hostage screen is their only way out of here,' he said. 'And I'm sure they know it. Their only other option is to go up, and I've already told Calrissian to scramble some fighters to close off the airspace above the Palace. With the turbolift blocked, this stairway is it.'

Mara stared at him, an icy shiver running abruptly through

her. What with all the rush and commotion since this thing had started, she hadn't had time to pause and consider all the nuances of the situation. But now, Bel Iblis's words and her own distant memories had combined in a blinding flash of insight.

For a handful of heartbeats she stood there, thinking it through, wondering if it were real or a construct of her own imagination. But it held up. Logical, tactically brilliant, with Grand Admiral Thrawn's fingerprints all over it. It had to be the answer.

And it would have worked . . . except for a single flaw. Thrawn obviously didn't know she was here. Or didn't believe she'd really been the Emperor's Hand.

'I'll be back,' she told Bel Iblis, stepping around him and hurrying back down the hallway. She rounded a corner into a cross corridor, eyes studying the carved frieze running along the top of the wall. Somewhere along here would be the subtle marking she was looking for.

There it was. She stopped in front of the otherwise ordinary-looking paneling, glancing both ways down the corridor as she did so. Skywalker and Organa Solo might accept her past associations without any qualms, but she doubted anyone else here would be quite so blasé about it. But the corridor was deserted. Stretching up to the frieze, she slid two fingers into the proper indentations, letting the warmth of her hand soak into the sensors there.

And with a faint click the panel unlocked.

She slipped inside, closing the panel behind her, and looked around. Built more or less parallel to the turbolift shafts, the Emperor's private passageways were by necessity narrow and cramped. But they were well lit, dust-free, and soundproof. And, more importantly, they would take her past the Imperials on the presentation landing.

Two minutes and three staircases later, she was at the exit that opened out onto Organa Solo's floor. Taking a couple of deep breaths, preparing herself for combat, she stepped through the panel and out into the hallway.

With the battle raging three staircases below, she would

have expected to find a secondary rear guard stationed near their bolt-hole. She was right: two men in the by-now familiar Palace Security uniforms were crouched against the walls with their backs to her, keeping watch on the far end of the corridor. The noise of heavy blaster fire coming from the other direction was more than enough to cover her quiet footsteps, and it was likely neither of them had any idea she was even there as she shot them down. A quick check to make sure they were out of the fight, and she was heading down the corridor toward Organa Solo's suite.

She had reached it and was just starting to pick her way across the debris from the shattered outer door when the blaster fire from inside was suddenly punctuated by an explosive crash.

She clenched her teeth as the blasters of the defenders opened up, their noise mixing with that of the attackers. Rushing straight in without any attempt at stealth or cover would be a good way to get herself killed. But if she moved in more cautiously, someone in there was likely to be killed before she could get into firing position.

Unless . . .

Leia Organa Solo, she called silently, stretching out through the Force as she had earlier when Calrissian had gone for his blaster. No more certain now than she had been then that Organa Solo could even hear her. *It's Mara. I'm coming up behind them. Surrender. You hear me? Surrender. Surrender. Surrender.*

And as she reached the outer door she heard Organa Solo's shout, barely audible over the blaster fire. 'Stop! Stop shooting. We surrender.'

Carefully, Mara eased an eye around the door. There they were: four Imperials standing or kneeling at the blackened edges of the doorway, blasters trained warily inside, with two more inside starting to get up from prone positions across the ruined security door. None of them giving the slightest bit of attention in her direction.

Smiling tightly to herself, Mara leveled her blaster and opened fire.

She had two of them down before the others even woke to the fact that she was there. A third fell as he spun around, trying in vain to bring his blaster to bear on her. The fourth was nearly to firing position when a shot from inside the room sent him spinning to the floor.

Five seconds later, it was all over.

There was one survivor. Barely.

'We think it's the group's leader,' Bel Iblis told Han as the two of them strode down the corridor toward the medical wing. 'Tentatively identified as a Major Himron. Though we won't know for certain until he's conscious again. If then.'

Han nodded, throwing a quick glance at yet another pair of alert-looking guards as they passed. If nothing else, this little fiasco had sure gotten Security stirred up. About time, too. 'Any idea how they got in?'

'That's going to be one of my first questions,' Bel Iblis said. 'He's in intensive care – this way.'

Lando was waiting at the door with one of the medics when Han and Bel Iblis arrived. 'Is everyone OK?' Lando asked, eyes flicking up and down his friend. 'I sent Chewie up, but they told me I should stay here with the prisoner.'

'Everyone's fine,' Han assured him as Bel Iblis stepped past Lando and pulled the medic aside. 'Chewie was up there before I left, and he's helping Leia and Winter set up in another suite. By the way, thanks for coming up after us.'

'No charge,' Lando grunted. 'Especially since all we got to do was watch. What, you couldn't have held off your little fireworks display for two more minutes?'

'Don't look at me, pal,' Han countered. 'It was Mara's timing, not mine.'

A shadow seemed to cross Lando's face. 'Right. Mara.'

Han frowned at him. 'What's that supposed to mean?'

'I don't know,' Lando said, shaking his head. 'There's still something about her that bothers me. Remember back at Karrde's base on Myrkr, just before Thrawn dropped in and we had to go hide in the forest?'

'You said you thought you knew her from somewhere,' Han

141

said. It was a comment that had been stuck in the back of his mind all these months, too. 'You ever figure out where?'

'Not yet,' Lando growled. 'But I'm getting close. I know it.'

Han looked at Bel Iblis and the medic, thinking back to what Luke had said a couple of days later on their way off of Myrkr. That Mara had told Luke flat out that she wanted to kill him. 'Wherever you saw her, she seems to be on our side now.'

'Yeah,' Lando said darkly. 'Maybe.'

Bel Iblis beckoned them over. 'We're going to try to wake him up,' he said. 'Come on.'

They went inside. Surrounding the ICU bed were half a dozen medics and Emdee droids, plus three of Ackbar's top security officers. At Bel Iblis's nod one of the medics did something to the treatment wrap around the Imperial's upper arm; and as Han and Lando found places at the side of the bed, he coughed suddenly and his eyes fluttered open. 'Major Himron?' one of the security officers asked. 'Can you hear me, Major?'

'Yes,' the Imperial breathed, blinking a couple of times. His eyes drifted between the people standing around him . . . and it seemed to Han that he suddenly became more alert. 'Yes,' he repeated, stronger this time.

'Your attack has failed,' the officer told him. 'Your men are all dead, and we're not sure yet whether you're going to live.'

Himron sighed and closed his eyes. But that alertness was still in his face. 'Fortunes of war,' he said.

Bel Iblis leaned forward. 'How did you get into the Palace, Major?'

'Guess it can't . . . hurt now,' Himron murmured. His breathing was becoming labored. 'Back door. Put in . . . same time . . . private passage system. Locked from inside. She let us in.'

'Someone let you in?' Bel Iblis said. 'Who?'

Himron opened his eyes. 'Our contact here. Name . . . Jade.'

Bel Iblis threw Han a startled glance. 'Mara Jade?'

'Yes.' Himron closed his eyes again, let out a deep breath. 'Special agent of . . . Empire. Once called . . . Emperor's Hand.'

He fell silent, and seemed to sink a little deeper into the bed. 'That's all I can permit right now, General Bel Iblis,' the chief medic said. 'He needs rest, and we need to get him stabilized. In a day or two, perhaps, he'll be strong enough to answer more questions.'

'That's all right,' one of the security officers said, heading for the door. 'He's given us enough to start with.'

'Wait a minute,' Han called, starting after him. 'Where are you going?'

'Where do you think?' the officer retorted. 'I'm going to have Mara Jade put under arrest.'

'On what, the word of an Imperial officer?'

'He has no choice, Solo,' Bel Iblis said quietly, laying a hand on Han's shoulder. 'A precautionary detention is required after an accusation this serious. Don't worry – we'll get it straightened out.'

'We'd better,' Han warned. 'Imperial agent, my eye – she took out at least three of them up there—'

He broke off at the look on Lando's face. 'Lando?'

Slowly, the other focused on him. 'That's it,' he said quietly. 'That's where I saw her before. She was one of the new dancers at Jabba the Hutt's place on Tatooine when we were setting up your rescue.'

Han frowned. 'At Jabba's?'

'Yes. And I'm not sure . . . but in all that confusion before we left for the Great Pit of Carkoon, I seem to remember hearing her asking Jabba to let her come along on the Sail Barge. No, not asking – begging was more like it.'

Han looked down at the unconscious Major Himron. The Emperor's Hand? And Luke had said she wanted to kill him . . .

He shook off the thought. 'I don't care where she was,' he said. 'She still shot those Imperials off our backs up there. Come on – let's go help Leia get the twins settled. And then figure out what's going on around here.'

CHAPTER 10

The Whistler's Whirlpool tapcafe on Trogan was one of the best examples Karrde had ever seen of a good idea ruined by the failure of its designers to think their whole plan through. Situated on the coast of Trogan's most densely populated continent, the Whirlpool had been built around a natural formation called the Drinking Cup, a bowl-shaped rock pit open to the sea at its base. Six times a day, Trogan's massive tidal shifts sent the water level inside the bowl either up or down, turning it into a violent white-water maelstrom in the process. With the tapcafe's tables arranged in concentric circles around the bowl, it made for a nice balance between luxury and spectacular natural drama – a perfect drawing card for the billions of humans and aliens enamored of that combination.

Or so the designers and their backers had thought. Unfortunately, they'd rather overlooked three points: first, that such a place was almost by definition a tourist attraction, dependent on the vagaries of that market; second, that once the charm of the Whirlpool itself wore off, the centralized design pretty well precluded remodeling the place for any other type of entertainment; and, third, that even if such remodeling had occurred, the racket from the miniature breakers in the Drinking Cup would probably have drowned it out anyway.

The people of the Calius saj Leeloo on Berchest had turned their fizzled tourist attraction into a trade center. The people of Trogan had simply abandoned the Whistler's Whirlpool.

'I keep expecting someone to buy this place and refurbish it,' Karrde commented, looking around at the empty seats and tables as he and Aves walked down one of the aisles toward the Drinking Cup and the figure waiting there for them. The years of neglect showed, certainly, but the place wasn't nearly as bad as it could have been.

'I always liked it myself,' Aves agreed. 'Kind of noisy, but you get that almost everywhere you go these days.'

'Certainly made eavesdropping between tables difficult,' Karrde said. 'That alone made the place worthwhile. Hello, Gillespee.'

'Karrde.' Gillespee nodded in greeting, getting up from his table and offering his hand. 'I was starting to wonder if you were really going to show.'

'The meeting's not for another two hours,' Aves reminded him.

'Oh, come on,' Gillespee said with a sly grin. 'Since when does Talon Karrde ever arrive anywhere on time? Though you could have saved yourself the trouble – my people have already checked things out.'

'I appreciate the effort,' Karrde said. Which was not to say, of course, that he was going to pull his own people off that same job. With the Empire breathing down his neck and an Imperial garrison only twenty kilometers away, a little extra security wouldn't hurt. 'You have the guest list?'

'Right here,' Gillespee said, picking up a data pad and handing it over. 'Afraid it's not as long as I'd hoped.'

'That's all right,' Karrde assured him, running his eyes down the list. Small, certainly, but highly select, with some of the biggest names in smuggling coming personally. Brasck, Par'tah, Ellor, Dravis – that would be Billey's group; Billey himself didn't get around too much anymore – Mazzic, Clyngunn the ZeHethbra, Ferrier—

He looked up sharply. 'Ferrier?' he asked. '*Niles* Ferrier, the spaceship thief?'

'Yeah, that's him,' Gillespee nodded, frowning. 'He does smuggling, too.'

'He also works for the Empire,' Karrde countered.

'So do we,' Gillespee shrugged. 'Last I hear, so did you.'

'I'm not talking about smuggling merchandise to or from Imperial worlds,' Karrde said. 'I'm talking about working directly for Grand Admiral Thrawn. Doing such minor jobs

145

as snatching the man who located the *Katana* fleet for him.'

Gillespee's face tightened, just noticeably. Remembering, perhaps, his mad scramble off Ukio one step ahead of the Imperial invasion force in those same *Katana*-fleet ships. 'Ferrier did that?'

'And seemed to enjoy doing it,' Karrde told him, pulling out his comlink and thumbing it on. 'Lachton?'

'Right here,' Lachton's voice came promptly from the comlink.

'How do things look at the garrison?'

'Like a morgue on its day off,' Lachton said wryly. 'There hasn't been any movement in or out of the place for at least three hours.'

Karrde cocked an eyebrow. 'Indeed. That's very interesting. How about flights in or out? Or activity within the garrison grounds themselves?'

'Nothing of either,' Lachton said. 'No kidding, Karrde, the place looks completely dead. Must have gotten some new training holos in or something.'

Karrde smiled tightly. 'Yes, I'm sure that's it. All right, keep on them. Let me know immediately if there's activity of any sort.'

'You got it. Out.'

Karrde thumbed off the comlink and returned it to his belt. 'The Imperials aren't moving from their garrison,' he told the others. 'Apparently not at all.'

'Isn't that the way we want it?' Gillespee asked. 'They can't drop a hammer on the party if they're snugged up there in their barracks.'

'Agreed,' Karrde nodded. 'On the other hand, I've never yet heard of an Imperial garrison simply taking a day off.'

'Point,' Gillespee admitted. 'Unless this big campaign of Thrawn's has all these third-rate garrisons undermanned.'

'All the more reason for them to be running daily patrols as a visible show of force,' Karrde said. 'A man like Grand Admiral Thrawn counts on his opponents' perceptions to fill in the gaps in his actual strength.'

'Maybe we should cancel the meeting,' Aves suggested,

looking uneasily back at the entrance. 'Could be they're setting us up.'

Karrde looked past Gillespee to the churning water sloshing up the walls of the Drinking Cup. In just under two hours, the water would be at its lowest and quietest level, which was why he'd arranged the meeting for then. If he called it off now – admitted to all these big-time smugglers that the Empire had Talon Karrde jumping at shadows . . . 'No,' he said slowly. 'We'll stay. Our guests won't exactly be sitting here helpless, after all. And we should have adequate warning of any official moves against us.' He smiled thinly. 'Actually, it's almost worth the risk just to see what they have in mind.'

Gillespee shrugged. 'Maybe they're not planning anything at all. Maybe we chicaned Imperial Intelligence so good that they missed this completely.'

'That hardly sounds like the Imperial Intelligence we all know and love,' Karrde said, looking around. 'Still, we have two hours before the meeting. Let's see what we can arrange, shall we?'

They sat there in silence, each of the individuals and small groups sitting around its own table, while he made his pitch . . . and as he finished and looked around at them, Karrde knew they weren't convinced.

Brasck made it official. 'You speak well, Karrde,' the Brubb said, his thin tongue flicking out between his lips as he tasted the air. 'One might say passionately, if such a word could ever be said to apply to you. But you do not persuade.'

'Do I truly not persuade, Brasck?' Karrde countered. 'Or do I merely fail to overcome your reluctance to stand up to the Empire?'

Brasck's expression didn't change, but the pitted gray-green skin of his face – about all of him that was visible outside his body armor – turned a little grayer. 'The Empire pays well for smuggled goods,' he said.

[And for slaves as well?] Par'tah demanded in the singsong Ho'Din language. Her snakelike head appendages bounced gently as she snapped her mouth in a Ho'Din gesture

147

of contempt. [And for viyctiyms of kiydnap? You are no better than was the Hutt.]

One of Brasck's bodyguards shifted in his seat – a man, Karrde knew, who had escaped with Brasck from Jabba the Hutt's indentured servitude when Luke Skywalker and his allies had chopped off the head of that organization. 'No-one who knew the Hutt would say that,' he growled, jabbing a stiff finger on the table beside him for emphasis.

'We're not here to argue,' Karrde said before Par'tah or any of her entourage could respond.

'Why *are* we here?' Mazzic spoke up, lounging in his seat between a horn-headed Gotal and a decorative but vacant-faced woman with her hair done up in elaborate plaitlets around half a dozen large enameled needles. 'You'll forgive me, Karrde, but this sounds very much like a New Republic recruitment speech.'

'Yeah, and Han Solo's already pitched that one to us,' Dravis agreed, propping his feet up on his table. 'Billey's already said he wasn't interested in hauling the New Republic's cargo.'

'Too dangerous,' Clyngunn put in, shaking his shaggy black-and-white-striped mane. 'Far too dangerous.'

'Really?' Karrde said, feigning surprise. 'Why is it dangerous?'

'You must be joking,' the ZeHethbra rumbled, shaking his mane again. 'With Imperial harassment of New Republic shipping as it is, you take your life in clawgrip every time you lift off.'

'So what you're saying,' Karrde suggested, 'is that Imperial strength is becoming increasingly dangerous to our business activities?'

'Oh, no you don't, Karrde,' Brasck said, waving a large finger toward him. 'You're not going to persuade us into going along with this scheme by twisting our words.'

'I haven't suggested any schemes, Brasck,' Karrde said. 'All I've suggested is that we provide the New Republic with any useful information we might happen to come across in the course of our activities.'

148

'And you don't think the Empire would find this activity unacceptable?' Brasck asked.

[Siynce when do we care what the Empiyre thiynks?] Par'tah countered.

'Since Grand Admiral Thrawn took command,' Brasck said bluntly. 'I've heard stories of this warlord, Par'tah. It was he who forced my world under the Imperial shroud.'

'That ought to be a good reason for you to stand up to him,' Gillespee pointed out. 'If you're afraid of what Thrawn might do to you *now*, just think what'll happen to you if he gets the whole galaxy under the Imperial shroud again.'

'Nothing will happen to us if we don't oppose him,' Brasck insisted. 'They need our services too much for that.'

'That's a nice theory,' a voice spoke up from near the back of the group. 'But I can tell you right now it won't hold a mug's worth of vacuum.'

Karrde focused on the speaker. He was a big, thick-built human with dark hair and a beard, a thin unlit cigarra clenched in his teeth. 'And you are . . . ?' Karrde asked, though he was pretty sure he knew.'

'Niles Ferrier,' the other identified himself. 'And I can tell you flat out that minding your own business isn't going to do you a blame bit of good if Thrawn decides he wants you.'

'And yet he pays well,' Mazzic said, idly stroking the hand of his female companion. 'Or so I've heard.'

'You've heard that, huh?' Ferrier growled. 'Have you also heard that he grabbed me off New Cov and confiscated my ship? And then ordered me out on a nasty little errand for him aboard a bomb-rigged Intelligence bucket? Oh, and go ahead and guess what the penalty was going to be if we couldn't do it.'

Karrde looked around the room, listening to the gently sloshing water in the Drinking Cup behind him and holding his silence. This was hardly the way Solo had described Ferrier's involvement; and all other things being equal, he would probably trust Solo's rendition over the ship thief's. Still, it was always possible Solo had misinterpreted things.

149

And if Ferrier's story helped convince the others that the Empire had to be opposed . . .

'Were you paid for all your trouble?' Mazzic asked.

"Course I was paid,' Ferrier sniffed. 'That's not the point.'

'It is for me,' Mazzic said, turning back to look at Karrde. 'Sorry, Karrde, but I still haven't heard any good reason for me to stick my neck out this way.'

'What about the Empire's new traffic in clones?' Karrde reminded him. 'Doesn't that worry you?'

'I'm not especially happy about it, no,' Mazzic conceded. 'But I figure that's the New Republic's problem, not ours.'

[When does iyt become our problem?] Par'tah demanded. [When the Empiyre has replaced all smugglers wiyth these clones?]

'No-one's going to replace us with clones,' Dravis said. 'You know, Brasck is right, Karrde. The Empire needs us too much to bother us . . . provided we don't take sides.'

'Exactly,' Mazzic said. 'We're businessmen, pure and simple; and I for one intend to stay that way. If the New Republic can outbid the Empire for information, I'll be happy to sell it to them. If not—' He shrugged.

Karrde nodded, privately conceding defeat. Par'tah might be willing to discuss the matter further, and possibly one or two of the others. Ellor, perhaps – the Duro had so far stayed out of the conversation, which with his species was often a sign of agreement. But none of the rest were convinced, and pushing them further at this point would only annoy them. Later, perhaps, they might be willing to accept the realities of the Empire's threat. 'Very well,' he said. 'I think it's clear now where all of you stand on this. Thank you for your time. Perhaps we can plan to meet again after—'

And without warning, the back of the Whistler's Whirlpool blew in.

'Stay where you are!' an amplified voice shouted through the din. 'Face forward – no-one move. Everyone here is under Imperial detention.'

Karrde squinted over the heads of his suddenly frozen audience to the rear of the building. Through the smoke and dust he could see a double line of about thirty Imperial army troops crunching their way across the debris where the back wall had been, their flanks protected by two pairs of white-armored stormtroopers. Behind them, almost obscured by the haze, he could see two Chariot command speeders hovering in backup positions. 'So they came to the party after all,' he murmured.

'With a big hammer,' Gillespee agreed tightly from beside him. 'Looks like you were right about Ferrier.'

'Perhaps.' Karrde looked over at Ferrier, half expecting to see a triumphant smirk on the big man's face.

But Ferrier wasn't looking at him. His attention was slightly off to the side; not looking at the approaching troopers, but at a section of wall to the right of the new hole. Karrde followed the line of his gaze—

Just in time to see a solid black shadow detach itself from the wall and move silently up behind one set of flanking stormtroopers.

'On the other hand, perhaps not,' he told Gillespee, nodding slightly toward the shadow. 'Take a look – just past Ellor's shoulder.'

Gillespee inhaled sharply. 'What in hell's name is *that*?'

'Ferrier's pet Defel, I think,' Karrde said. 'Sometimes called wraiths – Solo told me about him. This is it. Everyone ready?'

'We're ready,' Gillespee said, and there were echoing murmurs from behind them. Karrde swept his gaze across his fellow smugglers and their aides, catching each pair of eyes in turn. They gazed back, their shock at the ambush rapidly turning to a cold anger . . . and they, too, were ready. The shadow of Ferrier's Defel reached the end of the approaching line of Imperials; and suddenly one of the stormtroopers was hurled bodily off his feet to slam crosswise into his companion. The nearest troopers reacted instantly, swinging their weapons to the side as they searched for the unseen attacker.

'Now,' Karrde murmured.

And from the corner of his eye he saw the long muzzles of two BlasTech A280 blaster rifles swing up over the rim of the Drinking Cup and open fire.

151

The first salvo cut through the center of the line, taking out a handful of the Imperials before the rest were able to dive for cover among the empty tables and chairs. Karrde took a long step forward, tipping over the nearest table and dropping to one knee behind it.

An almost unnecessary precaution. The Imperials' attention had been distracted away from their intended prisoners for a fatal half-second . . . and even as Karrde yanked out his weapon the entire room exploded into blaster fire.

Brasck and his bodyguards took out an entire squad of the troopers in the first five seconds, with a synchronized fire that showed the Brubb hadn't forgotten his mercenary background. Par'tah's entourage was concentrating on the other end of the line, their weapons smaller and less devastating than Brasck's heavy blaster pistols but more than enough to keep the Imperials pinned down. Dravis, Ellor, and Clyngunn were taking advantage of that cover fire to pick off the remaining troopers one by one. Mazzic, in contrast, was ignoring the nearer threat of the troopers to blast away at the Chariot command speeders outside.

A good idea, actually. 'Aves! Fein!' Karrde shouted over the din. 'Concentrate fire on the Chariots.'

There were shouts of acknowledgement from the edge of the Drinking Cup behind him, and the rifle blasts sizzling past his shoulder shifted their aim. Karrde eased a little over his table, caught a glimpse of Mazzic's female companion – her plaited hair down around her shoulders now and her face no longer blank – as she hurled the last of her enameled needles with lethal accuracy at one of the troopers. Another Imperial lunged up out of cover, bringing his rifle to bear on her, falling backward again as Karrde's shot caught him square in the torso. A pair of shots hit his cover table, sending clouds of splinters into the air and forcing him to drop to the floor. From outside came the sound of a massive explosion, echoed an instant later by a second blast.

And then, suddenly, it was all over.

Carefully, Karrde eased up over his table again. The others were doing likewise, weapons held at the ready as they surveyed the wreckage around them. Clyngunn was holding an arm gingerly out from his body as he dug in his beltpack for a bandage; Brasck's tunic was burned away in several places, the body armor beneath it blackened and blistered. 'Everyone all right?' Karrde called.

Mazzic straightened up. Even at this distance Karrde could see the white knuckles gripping his blaster. 'They got Lishma,' he said, his voice deadly quiet. 'He wasn't even shooting.'

Karrde dropped his gaze to the broken table at Mazzic's feet and the Gotal lying motionless and half hidden beneath it. 'I'm sorry,' he said, and meant it. He'd always rather liked the Gotal people.

'I'm sorry, too,' Mazzic said, jamming his blaster back into its holster and looking at Karrde with smoldering eyes. 'But the Empire's going to be a lot sorrier. OK, Karrde; I'm convinced. Where do I sign up?'

'Somewhere far away from here, I think,' Karrde said, peering out the shattered wall at the burning Chariots as he pulled out his comlink. No-one was moving out there, but that wouldn't last. 'They'll surely have backup on the way. Lachton, Torve – you there?'

'Right here,' Torve's voice came. 'What in space was all that?'

'The Imperials decided they wanted to play, after all,' Karrde told him grimly. 'Sneaked in with a couple of Chariots. Anyone stirring in either of your areas?'

'Not here,' Torve said. 'Wherever they came from, they didn't start at the spaceport.'

'Ditto here,' Lachton put in. 'Garrison's still quiet as a grave.'

'Let's hope it stays that way for a few more minutes,' Karrde said. 'Pass the word to the others; we're pulling back to the ship.'

'On our way. See you there.'

Karrde flicked off the comlink and turned around. Gillespee was just helping Aves and Fein pull themselves out over the lip of the Drinking Cup, the web harnesses that had held them suspended just beneath the rocky edge trailing behind them.

'Nicely done, gentlemen,' he complimented them. 'Thank you.'

'Our pleasure,' Aves grunted, popping his harness and accepting his blaster rifle back from Gillespee. Even with the water level at its lowest, he noticed, the turbulence had still managed to soak both men up to their knees. 'Time to make ourselves scarce?'

'Just as soon as we can,' Karrde agreed, turning back to the other smugglers. 'Well, gentlefolk, we'll see you in space.'

There was no ambush waiting for them by the *Wild Karrde*. No ambush, no fighter pursuit, no Imperial Star Destroyer lurking in orbit for them. From all appearances, the incident back at the Whistler's Whirlpool might just as well have been an elaborate mass hallucination.

Except for the destruction to the tapcafe, and the gutted Chariots, and the very real burns. And, of course, the dead Gotal.

'So what's the plan?' Dravis asked. 'You want us to help hunt down this clone pipeline you mentioned, right?'

'Yes,' Karrde told him. 'We know it goes through Poderis, so Orus sector is the place to start.'

'It once went through Poderis,' Clyngunn pointed out. 'Thrawn could have moved it by now.'

'Though presumably not without leaving some traces we can backtrack,' Karrde said. 'So. Have we an agreement?'

'My group's with you,' Ferrier put in promptly. 'Matter of fact, Karrde, if you want I'll see what I can do about getting your people some real fighting ships.'

'I may take you up on that,' Karrde promised. 'Par'tah?'

[We wiyll assiyst iyn the search,] Par'tah said, her voice about as angry as Karrde had ever heard it. The death of the Gotal was hitting her almost as hard as it had hit Mazzic. [The Empiyre must be taught a lesson.]

'Thank you,' Karrde said. 'Mazzic?'

'I agree with Par'tah,' he said coldly. 'But I think the lesson needs to be a bit more eye-catching. You go ahead and do your clone hunt – Ellor and I have something else in mind.'

Karrde looked at Aves, who shrugged. 'If he wants to go slap their hands, who are we to stop him?' the other murmured.

Karrde shrugged back and nodded. 'All right,' he said to Mazzic. 'Good luck. Try not to bite off more than you can chew.'

'We won't,' Mazzic said. 'We're heading out – see you later.'

At the far starboard edge of the viewport, two of the ships in their loose formation flickered with pseudomotion and vanished into hyperspace. 'That just leaves you, Brasck,' Karrde prompted. 'What do you say?'

There was a long, subtly voiced sigh from the comm speaker; one of many untranslatable Brubb verbal gestures. 'I cannot and will not stand against Grand Admiral Thrawn,' he said at last. 'To give information to the New Republic would be to invite his hatred and wrath upon me.' Another voiced sigh. 'But I will also not interfere with your activities or bring them to his attention.'

'Fair enough,' Karrde nodded. It was, in fact, far more than he had expected from Brasck. The Brubbs' fear of the Empire ran deep. 'Well, then. Let's organize our groups and plan to reconvene over Chazwa in, say, five days. Good luck, all.'

The others acknowledged and signed off, and one by one made their jumps to lightspeed. 'So much for staying neutral,' Aves sighed as he checked the nav computer. 'Mara's going to have a fit when she finds out. When is she coming back, by the way?'

'As soon as I can find a way to get her here,' Karrde said, feeling a twinge of guilt. It had been several days since he'd gotten the message that she and Ghent were ready to rejoin him, a message that had probably been several more days in reaching him in the first place. She was probably ready to bite hull metal by now. 'After that last raise in the Imperial price on us, there are probably twenty bounty hunters waiting off Coruscant for us to show up.'

Aves shifted uncomfortably. 'Is that what you think happened down there? Some bounty hunter got wind of the meeting and tipped off the Imperials?'

Karrde gazed out at the stars. 'I really don't know what all that was about,' he admitted. 'Bounty hunters generally avoid tipping off the authorities unless they already have a financial agreement. On the other hand, when the Imperials go to the effort of carrying out a raid, one expects them to do a more competent job of it.'

'Unless they were just tailing Gillespee and didn't know the rest of us were there,' Aves suggested hesitantly. 'Could be that three squads of troops and a couple of Chariots is all he rates.'

'I suppose that's possible,' Karrde conceded. 'Hard to believe their intelligence was that spotty, though. Well, I'll have our people on Trogan make some quiet inquiries. See if they can backtrack that unit and find out where the tip-off came from. In the meantime, we have a hunt to organize. Let's get to it.'

Niles Ferrier was smiling behind that unkempt beard of his, Pellaeon noticed as the stormtroopers escorted him across the bridge; a smug, highly self-satisfied type of smile that showed he had no idea whatsoever why he'd been brought to the *Chimaera*. 'He's here, Admiral,' Pellaeon murmured.

'I know,' Thrawn said calmly, his back to the approaching spaceship thief. Calmly, but with a deadly look in his glowing red eyes. Grimacing, Pellaeon braced himself. This wasn't going to be pretty.

The group reached Thrawn's command chair and halted. 'Niles Ferrier, Admiral,' the stormtrooper commander stated. 'As per orders.'

For a long moment the Grand Admiral didn't move, and as Pellaeon watched, the smirk on Ferrier's face slipped a bit. 'You were on Trogan two days ago,' Thrawn said at last, still not turning around. 'You met with two men currently wanted by the Empire: Talon Karrde and Samuel Tomas Gillespee. You also persuaded a small and unprepared task force under one Lieutenant Reynol Kosk to launch a rash attack on this meeting, an attack which failed. Is all this true?'

'Sure is,' Ferrier nodded. 'See, that's why I sent you that message. So you'd know—'

'Then I should like to hear your reasons,' Thrawn cut him off, swiveling his chair around at last to gaze up at the thief, 'why I should not order your immediate execution.'

Ferrier's mouth dropped open. 'What?' he said. 'But – I've gotten in with Karrde. He trusts me now – see? That was the whole idea. I can dig out the rest of his gang and deliver the whole bunch to you . . .' He trailed off, his throat bobbing as he swallowed.

'You were directly responsible for the deaths of four stormtrooprs and thirty-two Imperial army troops,' Thrawn continued. 'Also for the destruction of two Chariot command speeders and their crews. I am not the Lord Darth Vader, Ferrier – I do not spend my men recklessly. Nor do I take their deaths lightly.'

The color was starting to leave Ferrier's face. 'Sir – Admiral – I know that you've put a bounty on Karrde's whole group of almost—'

'But all that pales in comparison to the utter disaster you've created,' Thrawn cut him off again. 'Intelligence informed me of this meeting of smuggler chiefs almost four days ago. I knew the location, the timing, and the probable guest list . . . and I had already given the Trogan garrison precise instructions – *precise* instructions, Ferrier – to leave it strictly alone.'

Pellaeon hadn't thought Ferrier's face could get any paler. He was wrong. 'You—? But – sir – but . . . I don't get it.'

'I'm sure you don't,' Thrawn said, his voice deadly quiet. He gestured; and from his position beside Thrawn's chair the Noghri bodyguard Rukh took a step forward. 'But it's really quite simple. I know these smugglers, Ferrier. I've studied their operations, and I've made it a point to deal personally with each of them at least once over the past year. None of them wants to become entangled in this war, and without your staged attack I'm quite certain they would have left Trogan convinced that they could sit things out in traditional smuggler neutrality.'

He gestured again to Rukh, and suddenly the Noghri's

slender assassin's knife was in his hand. 'The result of your interference,' he continued quietly, 'has been to unite them against the Empire – precisely the turn of events I'd gone to great lengths to avoid.' His glowing eyes bored into Ferrier's face. 'And I do not appreciate having my efforts wasted.'

Ferrier's eyes flicked back and forth between Thrawn and the blade in Rukh's hand, his face now gone from pasty white to gray. 'I'm sorry, Admiral,' he said, the words coming out with obvious difficulty. 'I didn't mean – I mean, just give me another chance, huh? Just one more chance? I can deliver Karrde – I swear to you. Well, hey – I mean, never mind even Karrde. I'll deliver all of them to you.'

He ran out of words and just stood there looking sick. Thrawn let him hang for another few heartbeats. 'You are a small-minded fool, Ferrier,' he said at last. 'But even fools occasionally have their uses. You will have one more chance. One *last* chance. I trust I make myself clear.'

'Yes, Admiral, real clear,' Ferrier said, his head jerking up and down in something closer to a twitch than a nod.

'Good.' Thrawn gestured, and Rukh's knife vanished. 'You can start by telling me exactly what they have planned.'

'Sure.' Ferrier took a shuddering breath. 'Karrde, Par'tah, and Clyngunn are going to meet in – I guess three days now – at Chazwa. Oh – they know you're running your new clones through Orus sector.'

'Do they,' Thrawn said evenly. 'And they intend to stop it?'

'No – just find out where it's coming from. Then they're going to tell the New Republic. Brasck isn't going along, but he said he wouldn't stop them, either. Dravis is going to check with Billey and get back to them. And Mazzic and Ellor have something else planned – they didn't say what.'

He ran out of words, or air, and stopped. 'All right,' Thrawn said after a moment. 'This is what you're going to do. You and your people will meet Karrde and the others at Chazwa on schedule. You'll take Karrde a gift: an assault shuttle you stole from the Hishyim patrol station.'

'Rigged, right?' Ferrier nodded eagerly. 'Yeah, that was my idea, too – give 'em some rigged ships that—'

'Karrde will of course examine this gift thoroughly,' Thrawn interrupted him, his patience clearly becoming strained. 'The ship will therefore be in perfect condition. Its purpose is merely to establish your credibility. Assuming you still have any.'

Ferrier's lip twisted. 'Yes, sir. And then?'

'You will continue to report on Karrde's activities,' Thrawn told him. 'And from time to time I'll be sending you further instructions. Instructions which you will carry out instantly and without question. Is that clear?'

'Sure,' Ferrier said. 'Don't worry, Admiral, you can count on me.'

'I certainly hope so.' Deliberately, Thrawn looked at Rukh. 'Because I would hate to have to send Rukh to pay you a visit. I trust I make myself understood?'

Ferrier looked at Rukh, too, and swallowed hard. 'Yeah, I get it.'

'Good.' He swiveled his chair to face away from Ferrier again. 'Commander, escort our guest back to his ship and see that his people are checked out on the assault shuttle I've had prepared for them.'

'Yes, sir,' the stormtrooper commander said. He gave Ferrier a nudge, and the group turned and headed aft.

'Go with them, Rukh,' Thrawn said. 'Ferrier has a small mind, and I want it to leave here filled with the knowledge of what will happen if he trips over my plans again.'

'Yes, my lord,' the Noghri said, and slipped silently away after the departing ship thief.

Thrawn turned to Pellaeon. 'Your analysis, Captain?'

'Not a good situation, sir,' Pellaeon said, 'but not as bad as it might have been. We have a potential line on Karrde's group, if you can believe Ferrier. And in the meantime, he and his new allies won't be doing anything but following the decoy trail we've already prepared for the Rebellion.'

'And eventually they'll tire of that and again go their separate ways,' Thrawn agreed, his glowing eyes narrowed in thought. 'Particularly as the financial burden of lost Imperial business begins to take its toll. Still, that will take time.'

'What are the options?' Pellaeon asked. 'Take Ferrier up on his offer to give them booby-trapped ships?'

Thrawn smiled. 'I have something more useful and satisfying in mind, Captain. Eventually, I'm sure, some of the other smugglers will realize how unconvincing the Trogan attack really was. With a little judiciously planted evidence, perhaps we can persuade them that it was Karrde who was behind it.'

Pellaeon blinked. 'Karrde?' he repeated.

'Why not?' Thrawn asked. 'A deceitful and heavy-handed attempt, shall we say, to persuade the others that his fears about the Empire were justified. It would certainly lose Karrde any influence he might have over them, as well as possibly saving us the trouble of hunting him down ourselves.'

'It's something to think about, sir,' Pellaeon agreed diplomatically. The middle of a major offensive, in his opinion, was not the right time to be worrying about exacting vengeance on the dregs of the galaxy's underfringes. There would be plenty of time for that after the Rebellion had been pounded into dust. 'May I suggest, Admiral, that the stalled campaign of Ketaris requires your attention?'

Thrawn smiled again. 'Your devotion to duty is commendable, Captain.' He turned his head to gaze out the side viewport. 'No word yet from Coruscant?'

'Not yet, sir,' Pellaeon said, checking the comm log update just to be sure. 'But you remember what Himron said about first creating a data trail. He might have run into some delays.'

'Perhaps.' Thrawn turned back, and Pellaeon could see the slight tightness in his face. 'Perhaps not. Still, even if we fail to obtain the twins for our beloved Jedi Master, Major Himron's fingering of Mara Jade should succeed in neutralizing her as a threat to us. For the moment, that's what's important.'

He straightened in his chair. 'Set course for the Ketaris battle plane, Captain. We'll leave as soon as Ferrier is clear.'

CHAPTER 11

The bulky man was turning into the Grand Corridor when Han finally caught up with him, his expression that of a man in a hurry and in a rotten mood besides. But that was OK; Han wasn't in all that great a mood, either. 'Colonel Bremen,' he said, falling in step beside the man just as he passed the first of the slender purple-and-green ch'hala trees that lined both sides of the Grand Corridor. 'I want to talk to you a minute.'

Bremen threw him an irritated glance. 'If it's about Mara Jade, Solo, I don't want to hear it.'

'She's still under house arrest,' Han said anyway. 'I want to know why.'

'Gee, well, maybe it has something to do with that Imperial attack two nights ago,' Bremen said sarcastically. 'You suppose?'

'Could be,' Han agreed, batting at one of the ch'hala branches that was stretching a little too far from the trunk. The subtle turmoil of color taking place beneath the tree's transparent outer bark exploded into an angry red at the spot where the branch connected to it, the color shooting around the trunk in ripples as it slowly faded. 'I guess it all depends on how much we're listening to Imperial rumor these days.'

Bremen stopped short and spun to face him. 'Look, Solo, what do you want from me?' he snapped. A new flush of pale red rippled across the ch'hala tree Han had touched, and across the corridor a group of diplomats sitting around a conversation ring looked up questioningly. 'Look at the facts a minute, huh? Jade knew about the secret back door and the passages – she admits that outright. She was there on the scene before any alert was sounded – she admits that, too.'

'Well, so were Lando and General Bel Iblis,' Han said, feeling that thin plating of diplomacy that Leia had worked so hard to build starting to fail. 'You haven't got *them* locked up.'

'The situations are hardly similar, are they?' Bremen shot back. 'Calrissian and Bel Iblis have histories with the New Republic, and people here who vouch for them. Jade has neither.'

'Leia and I vouch for her,' Han told him, trying hard to ignore that whole thing about her wanting to kill Luke. 'Isn't that good enough? Or are you just mad at her for doing your job for you?'

It was the wrong thing to say. Bremen turned nearly as red as the ch'hala tree had, his face hardening to something you could use for hull metal. 'So she helped shoot some alleged Imperial agents,' he said frostily. 'That proves absolutely nothing. With a Grand Admiral pulling the strings out there, the entire raid could have been nothing more than an elaborate scheme to convince us she's on our side. Well, I'm sorry, but we're not buying today. She gets the full treatment: records search, background search, acquaintance correlation, and a couple of question/answer sessions with our interrogators.'

'Terrific,' Han snorted. 'If she's not on our side now, that'll put her there for sure.'

Bremen drew himself up to his full height. 'We're not doing this to be popular, Solo. We're doing this to protect New Republic lives – yours and your children's among them, if you recall. I presume Councilor Organa Solo will be at Mon Mothma's briefing; if she has any complaints or suggestions, she can present them there. Until then, I don't want to hear anything about Jade from anyone. Especially you. Is that clear, *Captain* Solo.'

Han sighed. 'Yeah. Sure.'

'Good.' Spinning around again, Bremen continued on his way down the corridor. Han watched him go, glowering at his back.

'You do have a way with people, don't you?' a familiar voice said wryly from beside him.

Han turned in mild surprise. 'Luke! When did you get back?'

'About ten minutes ago,' Luke told him, nodding down the

corridor. 'I called your room, and Winter told me you two had headed down here for a special meeting. I was hoping to catch you before you went in.'

'I'm not invited, actually,' Han said, throwing one last glare at Bremen's retreating back. 'And Leia stopped by Mara's room first.'

'Ah. Mara.'

Han looked back at his friend. 'She was here when we needed her,' he reminded the younger man.

Luke grimaced. 'And I wasn't.'

'That wasn't what I meant,' Han protested.

'I know,' Luke assured him. 'But I still should have been here.'

'Well . . .' Han shrugged, not really sure what to say. 'You can't always be here to protect her. That's what she's got me for.'

Luke threw him a wry smile. 'Right. I must have forgotten.'

Han looked over his shoulder. Other diplomats and Council aides were starting to show up, but no Leia yet. 'Come on – she must have gotten hung up somewhere. We can meet her halfway.'

'I'm surprised you're letting her walk around the Palace alone,' Luke commented as they headed back along the row of ch'hala trees.

'She's not exactly alone,' Han said dryly. 'Chewie hasn't let her out of his sight since the attack. The big fuzzball even sleeps outside our door at night.'

'Must give you a safe feeling.'

'Yeah. The kids'll probably grow up allergic to Wookiee hair.' He glanced over at Luke. 'Where were you, anyway? Your last message said you'd be back three days ago.'

'That was before I got stuck on—' Luke broke off, eyeing the people beginning to wander through the corridor. 'I'll tell you later,' he amended. 'Winter said that Mara was under house arrest?'

'Yeah, and it looks like she's going to stay there,' Han growled. 'At least till we can convince the bit-pushers down in Security that she's clear.'

'Yes,' Luke said hesitantly. 'Well, that might not be as easy as it sounds.'

Han frowned. 'Why not?'

Luke seemed to brace himself. 'Because she spent most of the war years as a personal assistant to the Emperor.'

Han stared at him. 'I hope you're kidding.'

'I'm not,' Luke said, shaking his head. 'He had her going all over the Empire doing jobs for him. They called her the Emperor's Hand.'

Which was what that Imperial major down in the medical wing had called her. 'That's great,' he told Luke, turning to face forward again. 'Just great. You could have told us.'

'I didn't think it was important,' Luke said. 'She's not with the Empire now, that's for sure.' He threw Han a significant glance. 'And I suppose most of us have things in our background we wouldn't want people talking about.'

'Somehow, I don't think Bremen and his Security hotshots are going to see it that way,' Han said grimly.

'Well, we'll just have to convince them—'

He broke off. 'What is it?' Han asked.

'I don't know,' Luke said slowly. 'I just felt a disturbance in the Force.'

Something cold settled into the pit of Han's stomach. 'What kind of disturbance?' he asked. 'You mean like danger?'

'No,' Luke said, his forehead wrinkled with concentration. 'More like surprise. Or shock.' He looked at Han. 'And I'm not sure . . . but I think it was coming from Leia.'

Han's hand dropped to the grip of his blaster, his eyes flicking around the corridor. Leia was up there with a former Imperial agent . . . and she was surprised enough for Luke to pick up on it. 'You think we should run?' he said quietly.

'No,' Luke said. His hand, Han noted, was fingering his lightsaber. 'But we can walk fast.'

From outside the door came the muffled voice of the G-2RD guard droid, and with a tired sigh Mara shut down her data pad and tossed it on the desk in front of her. Eventually, she assumed, Security would get tired of these polite little sweetness-coated interrogation sessions. But if they were, it wasn't showing yet. Reaching out with the Force, she tried to identify her visitor, hoping at least that it wasn't that Bremen character again.

It wasn't; and she had just enough time to get over her surprise before the door opened and Leia Organa Solo walked in.

'Hello, Mara,' Organa Solo nodded in greeting. Behind her, the guard droid closed the door, giving Mara a brief glimpse of an obviously unhappy Wookiee. 'I just stopped in to see how you were doing.'

'I'm just terrific,' Mara growled, still not sure whether getting Organa Solo instead of Bremen was a step up or a step down. 'What was all that about outside?'

'Leia shook her head, and Mara caught a flicker of the other woman's annoyance. 'Somebody in Security apparently decided you shouldn't have more than one guest at a time unless it was one of them. Chewie had to stay outside, and he wasn't very happy about it.'

'I take it he doesn't trust me?'

'Don't take it personally,' Leia assured her. 'Wookiees take these life-debts of theirs very seriously, you know. He's still pretty upset that he nearly lost all of us to that kidnap squad. Actually, at this point he probably trusts you more than he trusts anyone else in the Palace.'

'I'm glad *some*one does,' Mara said, hearing the bitterness in her voice. 'Maybe I should ask him to have a little talk with Colonel Bremen.'

Organa Solo sighed. 'I'm sorry about this, Mara. We've got a meeting downstairs in a few minutes and I'm going to try again to get you released. But I don't think Mon Mothma and Ackbar will OK it until Security finishes their check.'

And when they found out that she really *had* been the Emperor's Hand . . . 'I should have kept pushing Winter to get me a ship out of here.'

'If you had, the twins and I would be in Imperial hands now,' Organa Solo said quietly. 'On our way to be the prizes of his Jedi Master C'baoth.'

Mara felt her jaw tighten. Offhand, she couldn't think of many fates more horrible than that one. 'You've already thanked me,' she muttered. 'Let's just say you owe me one and leave it at that, OK?'

Organa Solo smiled slightly. 'I think we owe you a lot more than just one,' she said.

Mara looked her straight in the eye. 'Remember that when I kill your brother.'

Organa Solo didn't flinch. 'You still think you want to kill him?'

'I don't want to discuss it,' Mara told her, getting up from her chair and stalking over to the window. 'I'm doing fine, you're going to try to get me out, and we're all glad I saved you from C'baoth. Was there anything else?'

She could feel Organa Solo's eyes studying her. 'Not really,' the other said. 'I just wanted to ask why you did it.'

Mara stared out the window, feeling an uncomfortable swelling of emotion washing up against the heavy armor-plate she'd worked so hard to build up around herself. 'I don't know,' she said, vaguely surprised that she was even admitting it. 'I've had two days of solitary to think it over, and I still don't know. Maybe . . .' She shrugged. 'I guess it was just something about Thrawn trying to steal your children.'

For a minute Organa Solo was silent. 'Where did you come from, Mara?' she asked at last. 'Before the Emperor brought you to Coruscant.'

Mara thought back. 'I don't know. I remember the first time I met the Emperor, and the ride here in his private ship. But I don't have any memories of where I started from.'

'Do you remember how old you were?'

Mara shook her head. 'Not really. I was old enough to talk to him, and to understand that I would be leaving home and going with him. But I can't pin it down any closer than that.'

'How about your parents? Do you remember them?'

'Only a little,' Mara said. 'Not much more than shadows.' She hesitated. 'I have a feeling, though, that they didn't want me to go.'

'I doubt the Emperor gave them any choice in the matter,'

Organa Solo said, her voice suddenly gentle. 'What about you, Mara? Did *you* have any choice?'

Mara smiled tightly through a sudden inexplicable welling up of tears. 'So that's where you're going with this. You think I risked my life for your twins because I got taken from my home the same way?'

'Were you?'

'No,' Mara said flatly, turning back to face her. 'It wasn't like that. I just didn't want C'baoth getting his crazy grip on them. Just leave it at that.'

'All right,' Organa Solo said, in a voice that said she only half believed it. 'But if you ever want to talk more about it—'

'I know where to find you,' Mara finished for her. She still didn't believe she was telling Organa Solo all this . . . but down deep she had to admit that it felt strangely good to talk about it. Maybe she was getting soft.

'And you can call on me anytime,' Organa Solo smiled as she stood up. 'I'd better get downstairs to the briefing. See what Thrawn's fighting clones are up to today.'

Mara frowned. 'What fighting clones?'

It was Organa Solo's turn to frown. 'You don't know?'

'Know what?'

'The Empire's found some Spaarti cloning cylinders somewhere. They've been turning out huge numbers of clones to fight against us.'

Mara stared at her, an icy chill running through her. Clones . . . 'No-one told me,' she whispered.

'I'm sorry,' Organa Solo said. 'I thought everyone knew. It was the main topic of conversation in the Palace for nearly a month.'

'I was in the medical wing,' Mara said mechanically. Clones. With the *Katana*-fleet ships to fight from, and with the cold-blooded genius of Grand Admiral Thrawn to command them. It would be the Clone Wars all over again.

'That's right – I'd forgotten,' Organa Solo acknowledged. 'There was so much else going on.' She was looking oddly at Mara. 'Are you all right?'

'I'm fine,' Mara said, her voice sounding distant in her ears as the memories flashed across her mind like heat lightning. A forest – a mountain – a hidden and very private warehouse of the Emperor's personal treasures—

And a vast chamber full of cloning tanks.

'All right,' Organa Solo said, clearly not convinced but equally unwilling to press the point. 'Well . . . I'll see you later.' She reached again for the door handle—

'Wait.'

Organa Solo turned back. 'Yes?'

Mara took a deep breath. The very existence of the place had been a sacred trust, known to only a handful of people – the Emperor had made that clear time and time again. But for Thrawn to have a renewable army of clones to throw against the galaxy . . . 'I think I know where Thrawn's Spaarti cylinders are.'

Even with her rudimentary sensing abilities she could feel the wave of shock that rippled outward from Organa Solo. 'Where?' she asked, her voice tightly controlled.

'The Emperor had a private storehouse,' Mara said, the words coming out with difficulty. His wizened face seemed to hover before her, those yellow eyes gazing at her in silent and bitter accusation. 'It was beneath a mountain on a world he called Wayland – I don't know if it even had an official name. It was where he kept all of his private mementos and souvenirs and odd bits of technology he thought might be useful someday. One of the artificial caverns held a complete cloning facility he'd apparently appropriated from one of the clonemasters.'

'How complete was it?'

'Very,' Mara said with a shiver. 'It had a full nutrient delivery system in place, plus a flash-teaching setup for personality imprinting and tech training on the clones while they developed.'

'How many cylinders were there?'

Mara shook her head. 'I don't know for sure. It was arranged in concentric tiers, sort of like a sport arena, and it filled the whole cavern.'

'Were there a thousand cylinders?' Organa Solo persisted. 'Two thousand? Ten?'

'I'd say at least twenty thousand,' Mara told her. 'Maybe more.'

'Twenty thousand,' Organa Solo said, her face carved from ice. 'And he can turn out a clone from each one every twenty days.'

Mara stared at her. 'Twenty *days*?' she echoed. 'That's impossible.'

'I know. Thrawn's doing it anyway. Do you know Wayland's coordinates?'

Mara shook her head. 'I was only there once, and the Emperor flew the ship himself. But I know I could find it if I had access to charts and a nav computer.'

Organa Solo nodded slowly, her sense giving Mara the impression of wind racing through a ravine. 'I'll see what I can do. In the meantime—' Her eyes focused abruptly on Mara's face. 'You aren't to tell anyone what you've just told me. *Anyone*. Thrawn is still getting information out of the Palace . . . and this is well worth killing for.'

Mara nodded. 'I understand,' she said. Suddenly, the room was feeling chillier.

'All right. I'll try to get some extra security up here. If I can do it without drawing unwelcome attention.' She paused, cocking her head slightly to the side as if listening. 'I'd better go. Han and Luke are coming, and this isn't the right place for a council of war.'

'Sure,' Mara said, turning away from her to face the window. The lot was cast, and she had now irrevocably put herself on the side of the New Republic.

On the side of Luke Skywalker. The man she had to kill.

They held the council of war that night in Leia's office, the one place they knew for certain that the mysterious Delta Source had so far had no access to. Luke glanced around the room as he came in, thinking back again to the tangled series of events that had brought these people – these friends – into his life. Han and Leia, sitting together on the couch, sharing a brief moment of quietness together before the realities of a galaxy at war intruded once more. Chewbacca, sitting between them and the door, his bowcaster resting ready on his shaggy knees, determined not to fail again in the self-imposed duties of his life-debt. Lando, scowling at Leia's computer terminal and a list of what looked like some kind of current market prices displayed there. Threepio and Artoo, conversing off in a corner, probably catching each other up on recent news and whatever passed for gossip among droids. And Winter, sitting unobtrusively in another corner, tending to the sleeping twins.

His friends. His family.

'Well?' Han asked.

'I did a complete circle around the office area,' Luke told him. 'No beings or droids anywhere nearby. How about here?'

'I had Lieutenant Page come in personally and do a counterintelligence sweep,' Leia said. 'And no-one's come in since then. Everything should be secure.'

'Great,' Han said. 'Now can we find out what this is all about?'

'Yes,' Leia said, and Luke sensed his sister brace herself. 'Mara thinks she knows where the Empire's cloning facility is.'

Han sat up a little straighter, threw a quick look at Lando. 'Where?'

'On a planet the Emperor called Wayland,' Leia said. 'A code name, apparently – it's not on any list I can find.'

'What was it, one of the old clonemaster facilities?' Luke asked.

'Mara said it was the Emperor's storehouse,' Leia said. 'I got the impression that it was a sort of combination trophy room and equipment dump.'

'A private rat's nest,' Han said. 'Sounds like him. Where is it?'

'She doesn't have the coordinates,' Leia said. 'She was only there once. But she thinks she can find it again.'

'Why hasn't she said something about it before now?' Lando asked.

Leia shrugged. 'Apparently, she didn't know about the

clones until I said something. She was undergoing neural re-generation, remember, when everyone here was discussing it.'

'It's still hard to believe she could just miss the whole thing,' Lando objected.

'Hard, but not impossible,' Leia said. 'None of the general-distribution reports she had access to have ever mentioned the clones. And she hasn't exactly been what you'd call sociable around the Palace.'

'The timing here's still pretty convenient,' Lando pointed out. 'One might even say suspiciously convenient. Here she was, with practically free run of the Palace. Then she gets fingered by an Imperial commando leader and locked up – and suddenly she's dangling Wayland in front of us and wanting us to break her out.'

'Who said anything about breaking her out?' Leia asked, looking slightly aghast at the whole idea.

'Isn't that what she's offering?' Lando asked. 'To take us to Wayland if we get her out?'

'She's not asking anything,' Leia protested. 'And all *I'm* offering is to smuggle a nav computer in to her to get Wayland's location.'

'Afraid that won't do it, sweetheart,' Han shook his head. 'The coordinates would be a start, but a planet's a pretty big place to hide a storehouse in.'

'Especially one the Emperor didn't want found,' Luke agreed. 'Lando's right. We'll have to take her with us.'

Han and Lando turned to stare at him, and even Leia looked taken aback. 'You don't mean you're buying this whole thing,' Lando said.

'I don't think we have any choice,' Luke said. 'The longer we delay, the more clones the Empire's going to have to throw at us.'

'What about the backtrack you started?' Leia suggested. 'The one through Poderis and Orus sector?'

'That'll take time,' Luke said. 'This'll get us there a lot faster.'

'*If* she's telling the truth,' Lando countered darkly. 'If she isn't, you're off on a dead-end chase.'

'Or worse,' Han added. 'Thrawn's already tried once to get you and that C'baoth character together. This could be another trap.'

Luke looked at each of them in turn, wishing he knew how to explain it. Somewhere deep within him he knew that this was the right thing to do; that this was where his path was leading him. As it had been with that final confrontation with Vader and the Emperor, somehow his destiny and Mara's were joined together at this place in time. 'It's not a trap,' he said at last. 'At least, not on Mara's part.'

'I agree,' Leia said quietly. 'And I think you're right. We have to take her with us.'

Han shifted in his seat to stare at his wife. Shot a frown at Luke, looked back at Leia. 'Let me guess,' he growled. 'This is one of those crazy Jedi things, right?'

'Partly,' Leia conceded. 'But it's mostly just simple tactical logic. I don't think Thrawn would have tried so hard to convince us that Mara was a party to that kidnapping attempt unless he wanted us to disbelieve anything she might have told us about Wayland.'

'If you assume that, you also have to assume Thrawn figured the attempt would fail,' Lando pointed out.

'I assume Thrawn prepared for all contingencies,' Leia said. A muscle tightened in her cheek. 'And as you said, Han, there's also some Jedi insight involved here. I touched Mara's mind twice during that attack: once when she woke me up, then again when she came in behind the commandos.'

She looked at Luke, and in her sense he could see that she knew about Mara's vow to kill him. 'Mara doesn't like us very much,' she said aloud. 'But on some level I don't think that matters. She understands what a new round of Clone Wars would do to the galaxy, and she doesn't want that.'

'If she's willing to take me to Wayland, I'm going,' Luke added firmly. 'I'm not asking any of you to go along. All I want is your help getting Mon Mothma to release her.' He hesitated. 'And your blessing.'

For a long moment the room was silent. Han stared at the floor, his forehead creased with concentration, gripping Leia's hand tightly in both of his. Lando stroked at his mustache, saying nothing. Chewbacca fingered his bowcaster, rumbling softly under his breath; in the opposite corner Artoo was chirping away thoughtfully to himself. One of the twins – Jacen, Luke decided – moaned a little in his sleep, and Winter reached over to rub his back soothingly.

'We can't talk to Mon Mothma about it,' Han said at last. 'She'll go through channels, and by the time anyone's ready to do anything half the Palace will know about it. If Thrawn wants to shut Mara up for good, he'll have all the time he needs to do it.'

'What's the alternative?' Leia asked, her eyes suddenly cautious.

'What Lando already said,' Han told her bluntly. 'We break her out.'

Leia threw a startled look at Luke. 'Han! We can't do that.'

'Sure we can,' Han assured her. 'Chewie and me had to pop a guy out of an Imperial hotbox once, and it worked just fine.'

Chewbacca growled. 'It did too,' Han protested, looking over at him. 'It wasn't *our* fault they picked him up again a week later.'

'That's not what I meant,' Leia said, her voice pained. 'You're talking about a highly illegal action. Bordering on treason.'

Han patted her knee. 'The whole Rebellion was a highly illegal action bordering on treason, sweetheart,' he reminded her. 'When the rules don't work, you break 'em.'

Leia took a deep breath, let it out slowly. 'You're right,' she admitted at last. 'You're right. When do we do it?'

'*We* – that is, you – don't do it,' Han told her. 'It's going to be Luke and me. You and Chewie are staying here where it's safe.'

Chewbacca started to rumble something, broke off in midsentence. Leia looked at the Wookiee, at Luke – 'You don't need to come, Han,' Luke said, reading in his sister the fears he knew she couldn't voice. 'Mara and I can do it alone.'

'What, two of you are going to take out a whole cloning complex by yourselves?' Han snorted.

'We don't have much choice,' Luke said. 'As long as Delta Source is active there aren't too many other people we know we can trust. And the ones we can, like Rogue Squadron, are on active defense duty.' He waved a hand to encompass the room. 'We're pretty much it.'

'So we're it,' Han said. 'We'll still have a lot better chance with three than with two.'

Luke looked at Leia. Her eyes were haunted with fear for her husband's safety; but in her sense he could find only a reluctant acceptance of Han's decision. She understood the critical importance of this mission, and she was far too experienced a warrior not to recognize that Han's offer made sense.

Or perhaps, like Han, she didn't want Luke going off alone with the woman who wanted to kill him.

'All right, Han,' he said. 'Sure – we'll make it a party of three.'

'Might as well make it a party of four,' Lando sighed. 'The way things are going with my Nomad City petition, it doesn't look like I'm going to have much else to do. It'd be nice to pay them back a little for that.'

'Sounds good to me, pal,' Han nodded. 'Welcome aboard.' He turned to Chewbacca. 'OK, Chewie. Now what's *your* problem?'

Luke looked at Chewbacca in surprise. He hadn't noticed any problem there; but now that he was paying attention, he could indeed sense the turmoil in the Wookiee's emotions. 'What is it, Chewie?'

For a moment the other just rumbled under his breath. Then, with obvious reluctance, he told them. 'Well, we'd like to have you along, too,' Han told him. 'But someone's got to stay here and take care of Leia. Unless you think Palace Security's up to the job.'

Chewbacca growled a succinct opinion of Palace Security. 'Right,' Han agreed. 'That's why you're staying.'

Luke looked at Leia. She was looking at him, too, and he

could tell that she also recognized the dilemma. Chewbacca's original life-debt was to Han, and it pained him terribly to let Han go into this kind of danger without him. But Leia and the twins were also under the Wookiee's protection, and it would be equally unthinkable for him to leave them unguarded in the Palace.

And then, even as he tried to think of a solution, Luke saw his sister's eyes light up. 'I have an idea,' she said carefully.

They all listened to it, and to Han's obviously stunned surprise, Chewbacca agreed at once. 'You're kidding,' Han said. 'This is a joke, right? Yeah – it's a joke. 'Cause if you think I'm going to leave Leia and the twins—'

'It's the only way, Han,' Leia said quietly. 'Chewie's going to be miserable any other way.'

'Chewie's been miserable before,' Han shot back. 'He'll get over it. Come on, Luke – tell her.'

Luke shook his head. 'Sorry, Han. I happen to think it's a good idea.' He hesitated, but couldn't resist. 'I guess it's one of those crazy Jedi things.'

'Very funny,' Han growled. He looked around the room again. 'Lando? Winter? Come on, one of you say something.'

'Don't look at me, Han,' Lando said, holding up his hands. 'I'm out of this part of the discussion.'

'As for me, I trust Princess Leia's judgment,' Winter added. 'If she believes we'll be safe, I'm willing to accept that.'

'You've got a few days to get used to the idea,' Leia reminded him before Han could say anything more. 'Maybe we can change your mind.'

The look on Han's face wasn't encouraging. But he nodded anyway. 'Yeah. Sure.'

There was a moment of silence. 'So that's it?' Lando asked at last.

'That's it,' Leia confirmed. 'We've got a mission to plan. Let's get to it.'

CHAPTER 12

From the corner of the communications desk the intercom pinged. 'Karrde?' Dankin's voice came tiredly. 'We're coming up on the Bilbringi system. Breakout in about five minutes.'

'We'll be right there,' Karrde told him. 'Make sure the turbolasers are manned – no telling what we're going to run into.'

'Right,' Dankin said. 'Out.'

Karrde tapped off the intercom and keyed off the desk's decrypters. 'He sounds tired,' Aves commented from the other side of the desk as he put down his data pad.

'Almost as tired as you look,' Karrde said, giving the display he'd been studying one last scan before shutting it down as well. The report from his people on Anchoron, like the others before it: all negative. 'It must be too long since we've had to pull double shifts,' he added to Aves. 'No-one's used to it any more. I'll have to include that in future training exercises.'

'I'm sure the crew will love it,' Aves said dryly. 'We'd hate to have people think we were soft.'

'Contrary to our image,' Karrde agreed, standing up. 'Let's go; we'll finish sorting through these later.'

'For all the good it'll do,' Aves grunted. 'Are you absolutely sure those were clones Skywalker spotted on Berchest?'

'Skywalker was sure,' Karrde said as they left the office and headed for the bridge. 'I trust you're not suggesting the noble Jedi would have lied to me.'

'Not lied, no,' Aves shook his head. 'I'm just wondering if the whole thing could have been a setup. Something Thrawn deliberately dangled in front of you to put us off the real pipeline.'

'That thought has occurred to me,' Karrde agreed. 'Even

given Governor Staffa's indebtedness to us, we seemed to get in and out of the system just that little bit too easily.'

'You didn't mention these reservations when you were passing out search assignments back at Chazwa.'

'I'm sure similar thoughts have already occurred to each of the others,' Karrde assured him. 'Just as the thought has undoubtedly occurred to them that if there's an Imperial agent among us we should do our best to keep him believing we're buying Grand Admiral Thrawn's deception. If it *is* a deception.'

'*And* if there's an Imperial agent in the group,' Aves said.

Karrde smiled. ' "If we had some bruallki, we could have bruallki and Menkooro—'

'—if we had some Menkooro," ' Aves finished the old saying. 'You still think Ferrier's working for Thrawn, don't you?'

Karrde shrugged. 'It's only his word against Solo's that he wasn't a willing agent of the Empire in the *Katana*-fleet business.'

'That why you had Torve take that assault shuttle off to the Roche system?'

'Right,' Karrde nodded, wishing briefly that Mara was here. Aves was a good enough man, but he needed things laid out in front of him that Mara would have instantly picked up on her own. 'I know a couple of Verpine out there who owe me a favor. If the assault shuttle is rigged in any way, they'll find it.'

The door to the bridge slid open and they stepped inside. 'Status?' Karrde asked as he glanced through the viewport at the mottled sky of hyperspace rolling past.

'All systems showing ready,' Dankin said, yielding the helm seat to Aves. 'Balig, Lachton, and Corvis are at the turbolasers.'

'Thank you,' Karrde said, sitting down beside Aves at the copilot station. 'Stick around, Dankin; you're going to be captain today.'

'I'm honored,' Dankin said wryly, stepping over to the comm station and sitting down.

'What do you suppose this is all about?' Aves asked as he got the ship ready for breakout.

'No idea,' Karrde admitted. 'According to Par'tah, all Mazzic would say was that I might want to come by Bilbringi after our rendezvous with the others at Chazwa.'

'Probably the eye-catching lesson for the Empire he and Ellor were talking about at Trogan,' Aves said heavily. 'I don't think I'm going to like this.'

'Just remember that whatever happens we're innocent bystanders,' Karrde reminded him. 'An incoming freighter with an authorized delivery schedule and a cargo of Koensayr power converters. Perfectly legitimate.'

'As long as they don't look too close at any of it,' Aves said. 'OK, here we go.' He eased the hyperdrive levers forward, and the starlines appeared and collapsed again into a background of stars.

A background of stars, half-completed ships, service and construction vessels, and floating dockyard platforms. And, almost directly ahead of the *Wild Karrde*, a massive Golan II battle station bristling with armament.

They had arrived at the Imperial Shipyards of Bilbringi.

Dankin whistled softly. 'Look at all that new construction,' he said, his voice awed. 'They aren't kidding around, are they?'

'No, they're not,' Karrde agreed. 'Nor are they kidding around at Ord Trasi or Yaga Minor.' And if Thrawn was putting half as much effort into his cloning operation as he was into warship construction—

'Incoming freighter, this is Bilbringi Control,' an official-sounding voice from the comm cut him off. 'Identify yourself and your home port and state your business.'

'Dankin?' Karrde murmured.

Dankin nodded. 'Freighter *Hab Camber*, out of Valrar,' he said briskly into the comm. 'Captain Abel Quiller in command. Carrying a shipment of power converters for Dock Forty-seven.'

'Acknowledged,' the controller said. 'Stand by for confirmation.'

Aves tapped Karrde on the arm and pointed to the battle station ahead. 'They're launching an assault shuttle,' he said.

And launching it in the *Wild Karrde*'s direction. 'Hold course,' Karrde told him quietly. 'They may just be seeing how nervous we are.'

'Or else they're expecting trouble,' Aves countered.

'Or are cleaning up after it,' Dankin put in. 'If Mazzic's already been here—'

'Freighter *Hab Camber*, you're ordered to hold position there,' the controller broke in. 'An inspection team is on its way to examine your shipment order.'

Dankin keyed the comm. 'Why, what's wrong with it?' he asked with just the right mixture of puzzlement and annoyance. 'Look, I've got a business to run here – I haven't got time for any bureaucratic nonsense.'

'If you'd prefer, we can arrange to end all your scheduling problems right here and now,' the controller offered in a nasty voice. 'If that doesn't appeal to you, I'd suggest you prepare to receive boarders.'

'Acknowledged, Control,' Dankin growled. 'I just hope they're fast.'

'Control out.'

Dankin looked at Karrde. 'Now what?'

'We prepare to receive boarders,' Karrde said, letting his gaze sweep across the expanse of the shipyards. If Mazzic was keeping to the tentative schedule he'd given Par'tah, he ought to be showing up sometime soon.

He paused. 'Aves, get me a reading on those,' he said, pointing to a cluster of dark irregular spots drifting near the center of the shipyard area. 'They don't look like ships to me.'

'They're not,' Aves confirmed a few seconds later. 'Look to be midsize asteroids – maybe forty meters across each. I make the count . . . twenty-two of them.'

'Odd,' Karrde said, frowning at the sensor-focus display Aves had pulled up. There were over thirty small support craft in the area, he saw, with what seemed to be a similar number of maintenance-suited workers moving around the asteroids. 'I wonder what the Imperials are doing with that many asteroids.'

'Could be mining them,' Aves suggested hesitantly. 'I've never heard of anyone hauling the whole asteroid to a shipyard, though.'

'Neither have I,' Karrde nodded. 'It's just a thought . . . but I wonder if they could have something to do with Thrawn's magic superweapon. The one he hit Ukio and Woostri with.'

'That might explain the heavy security,' Aves said. 'Speaking of which, that assault shuttle's still coming. Are we going to let them board?'

'Unless you'd rather turn and run, I don't see many alternatives,' Karrde said. 'Dankin, how much scrutiny can our delivery schedule handle?'

'It can stand a lot,' Dankin said slowly. 'Depends a little on if they suspect something or if they're just being careful. Karrde, take a look about forty degrees to portside. That half-finished Imperial Star Destroyer – see it?'

Karrde swiveled in his seat. The Star Destroyer was, in fact, considerably more than half finished, with only the command superstructure and sections of the forward bastion ridgeline left to add. 'I see it,' he said. 'What about it?'

'There seems to be some activity around—'

And in midsentence, the starboard flank of the Star Destroyer blew up.

Aves whistled in startled awe. 'Scratch one warship,' he said as a section of the forward hull followed the flank to fiery oblivion. 'Mazzic, you think?'

'I don't think there's any doubt,' Karrde said, keying his main display for a closer view. For a moment, silhouetted against the boiling flames, he caught a glimpse of a half-dozen freighter-sized craft angling swiftly toward the shipyard perimeter. 'I also think they may have cut things a bit too fine,' he added, looking up again at the Star Destroyer. A group of disaster-control craft were already swarming in toward the burning ship, three squadrons of TIE fighters right behind them.

And then, abruptly, the focal point of the incoming fighter cloud shifted from the Star Destroyer to the vector the escaping freighters had taken. 'They've been spotted,' Karrde said grimly, giving the situation a quick assessment. Mazzic's group was outnumbered and outgunned, an imbalance that would likely get worse before they could get far enough out from the shipyard clutter to make their escape to hyperspace. The *Wild Karrde*'s three turbolasers would go a long way toward evening those odds; unfortunately, the center of action was too far away for them to make any significant difference to the outcome.

'We going to help him out?' Aves murmured.

'By all rights, we shouldn't lift a finger,' Karrde told him, keying the nav computer to start their own lightspeed calculation and tapping the intercom. 'Helping to salvage careless tactical planning only encourages more of the same. But I suppose we can't just sit here. Corvis?'

'Here,' Corvis's voice came.

'On my command you're to open fire on that approaching assault shuttle,' Karrde ordered. 'Balig and Lachton, you'll target the battle station. See how much chaos we can cause. At the same time, Aves, you'll bring us around on to a vector of—'

'Wait a minute, Karrde,' Dankin cut him off. 'There – fifty degrees portside.'

Karrde looked. There, straddling the same vector Mazzic's sabotage crew was escaping along, a pair of Corellian Gunships had shot in from hyperspace. A formation of TIE fighters that had been sweeping in from approximately that direction swerved to intercept, and were promptly blown into flaming dust. 'Well, well,' Karrde said. 'Perhaps Mazzic's tactics aren't as bad as I'd thought.'

'That's got to be Ellor's people,' Aves said.

Karrde nodded. 'Agreed. Corellian Gunships are a bit out of Mazzic's style – certainly out of his budget. It's a strategy that would certainly appeal to the legendary Duros cultural recklessness.'

'I'd have thought Corellian Gunships would be a strain on Ellor's budget, too,' Dankin commented. 'You think he stole them from the New Republic?'

' "Stole" is such a harsh word,' Karrde chided mildly. 'I

expect he considers them merely an informal loan. New Republic ships often use the line of Duros maintenance depots scattered through the Trade Spine, and Ellor has a silent interest in several of them.'

'I bet there'll be some complaints about the service this time around,' Aves said dryly. 'By the way, are we still planning to hit that assault shuttle?'

Karrde had almost forgotten about that. 'No, actually. Corvis, Balig, Lachton – power down those turbolasers. Everyone else: stand down from alert and prepare to receive Imperial inspectors.'

He got acknowledgements, and turned back to find Aves staring at him. 'We're not going to run?' the other asked carefully. 'Not even after that?' He nodded toward the firefight blazing off to portside.

'What's happening out there has absolutely nothing to do with us,' Karrde said, giving the other his best innocent look. 'We're an independent freighter with a cargo of power converters. Remember?'

'Yeah, but—'

'More to the point, it might be useful to see what happens in the aftermath of this raid,' Karrde went on, gazing back at the ships. With their immediate exit vector being covered by Ellor's gunships, and with the yards' capital ships too far away to reach them in time, the raiders looked well on their way to a relatively clean escape. 'Listen to their communications traffic, watch their cleanup and postraid security adjustments, get an assessment of how much damage was actually done. That sort of thing.'

Aves didn't look convinced, but he knew better than to argue the point. 'If you think we can pull it off,' he said doubtfully. 'I mean, with the bounty on us and all.'

'This is the last place an Imperial commander would expect us to show up,' Karrde assured him. 'Hence, no-one here will be watching for us.'

'Certainly not on a ship under the command of Captain Abel Quiller,' Dankin said, unstrapping and standing up. 'Impatient and bombastic, right?'

'Right,' Karrde said. 'But don't overdo the bombastic part. We don't want any hostility toward you, just contempt.'

'Got it,' Dankin nodded.

He left the bridge, and Karrde turned back to gaze at the smoldering wreckage of the now stillborn Star Destroyer. An eye-catching lesson, indeed, and one that Karrde would have argued strongly against if Mazzic and Ellor had asked his advice. But they hadn't, and they'd gone ahead and done it.

And now the lot was even more strongly cast than it had been after Trogan. Because Grand Admiral Thrawn would not let this go by without a swift and violent response. And if he could trace the attack back to Mazzic . . . and from there back to him . . .

'We're not going to be able to stop here,' he murmured, half to himself. 'We're going to have to organize. All of us.'

'What?' Aves asked.

Karrde focused on him. On that open and puzzled face, clever in its own way but neither brilliant nor intuitive. 'Never mind,' he told the other, smiling to take any possible sting out of the words.

He turned back to the approaching assault shuttle. And vowed that when this was over, he would find a way to get Mara back.

The last page scrolled across the display, and Thrawn looked up at the man standing at stiff attention before him. 'Have you anything to add to this report, General Drost?' he asked, his voice quiet.

Far too quiet, in Pellaeon's opinion. Certainly quieter than Pellaeon's voice would have been had *he* been in command here. Looking out the *Chimaera*'s viewport at the blackened wreckage that had once been a nearly completed and highly valuable Imperial Star Destroyer, it was all he could do to stand silently beside the Grand Admiral and not take Drost's head off. It was no more than the man deserved.

And Drost knew it. 'No, sir,' he said, his voice sounding strained.

Thrawn held his eyes a moment longer, then turned his gaze

out the viewport. 'Can you offer me any reason why you should not be relieved of command?'

The faintest of sighs escaped Drost's lips. 'No, sir,' he said again.

For a long moment the only sound was the muted background murmur of the *Chimaera*'s bridge. Pellaeon glowered at Drost's carved-stone face, wondering what his punishment would be. At the very least, a fiasco like this ought to earn him a summary court-martial and dismissal on charges of gross negligence. At the very most . . . well, there was always Lord Vader's traditional response to incompetence.

And Rukh was already standing close at hand behind Thrawn's command chair.

'Return to your headquarters, General,' Thrawn said. 'The *Chimaera* will be leaving here in approximately thirty hours. You have until then to design and implement a new security system for the shipyards. At that point I'll make my decision about your future.'

Drost glanced at Pellaeon, looked back at Thrawn. 'Understood, sir,' he said. 'I won't fail you again, Admiral.'

'I trust not,' Thrawn said, the bearest hint of veiled threat in his voice. 'Dismissed.'

Drost nodded and turned away, a freshly awakened determination in his step.

'You disapprove, Captain.'

Pellaeon forced himself to meet those glowing red eyes. 'I would have thought a more punitive response would be called for,' he said.

'Drost is a good enough man in his way,' Thrawn said evenly. 'His chief weakness is a tendency to become complacent. For the immediate future, at least, he should be cured of that.'

Pellaeon looked back at the wreckage outside the *Chimaera*'s viewport. 'A rather expensive lesson,' he said sourly.

'Yes,' Thrawn agreed. 'And it demonstrates precisely why I didn't want Karrde's smuggler associates stirred up.'

Pellaeon frowned at him. 'This was the smugglers? I assumed it was a Rebel sabotage squad.'

'Drost is under that same impression,' Thrawn said. 'But the method and execution here were quite different from the usual Rebel pattern. Mazzic, I think, is the most likely suspect. Though there are enough Duros elements woven into the style for Ellor's group to also have been involved.'

'I see,' Pellaeon said slowly. This put an entirely new spin on things. 'I presume that we'll be teaching them the folly of attacking the Empire.'

'I would like nothing better,' Thrawn agreed. 'And at the height of the Empire's power I wouldn't have hesitated to do so. Unfortunately, at this point such a reaction would be counter-productive. Not only would it harden the smugglers' resolve, but would risk bringing others of the galaxy's fringe elements into open hostility against us.'

'We surely don't need their assistance and services that badly,' Pellaeon said. 'Not now.'

'Our need for such vermin has certainly been reduced,' Thrawn said. 'That doesn't mean we're yet in a position to abandon them entirely. But that's not really the point. The problem is the dangerous fact that those in the fringe are highly experienced at operating within official circles without any official permission to do so. Keeping them out of places like Bilbringi would require far more manpower than we have to spare at present.'

Pellaeon ground his teeth. 'I understand that, sir. But we can't simply ignore an attack of this magnitude.'

'We won't,' Thrawn promised quietly, his eyes glittering. 'And when it comes, our response will be to the Empire's best advantage.' He swiveled his chair to face the center of the shipyards. 'In the meantime—'

'GRAND ADMIRAL THRAWN!'

The shout roared through the bridge like a violent thunderclap, filling it from aft to forward and echoing back again. Pellaeon wrenched himself around, reflexively scrabbling for the blaster he wasn't wearing.

Joruus C'baoth was striding toward them across the bridge,

his eyes flashing above his flowing beard. An angry radiance seemed to burn the air around him; behind him, the two stormtroopers guarding the entrance to the bridge were sprawled on the floor, unconscious or dead.

Pellaeon swallowed hard, his hand groping for and finding the reassuring presence of the ysalamir nutrient frame stretched across the top of the Grand Admiral's command chair. The frame rotated away from his touch as Thrawn swiveled to face the approaching Jedi Master. 'You wish to speak to me, Master C'baoth?'

'They have failed, Grand Admiral Thrawn,' C'baoth snarled at him. 'Do you hear me? Your commandos have failed.'

'I hear you,' Thrawn nodded calmly. 'What have you done to my guards?'

'*My* men!' C'baoth snapped, his voice again reverberating around the bridge. Even without the element of surprise, the trick was an effective one. 'Mine! *I* command the Empire, Grand Admiral Thrawn. Not you.'

Thrawn turned to the side and caught the eye of the portside crew pit officer. 'Call sick bay,' he ordered the man. 'Have them send a team.'

For a few painful heartbeats Pellaeon thought C'baoth was going to object or – worse – take the crew pit officer down, too. But all of his attention seemed to be focused on Thrawn. 'Your commandos have failed, Grand Admiral Thrawn,' he repeated, his voice now quiet and lethal.

'I know,' Thrawn said. 'All of them except the major in command appear to have been killed.'

C'baoth drew himself up. 'Then it is time for me to take this task upon myself. You will take me to Coruscant. Now.'

Thrawn nodded. 'Very well, Master C'baoth. We will load my special cargo, and then we shall go.'

It was clearly not the answer C'baoth was expecting. 'What?' he demanded, frowning.

'I said that as soon as the special cargo has been loaded aboard the *Chimaera* and the other ships we'll leave here for Coruscant,' Thrawn said.

C'baoth shot a look at Pellaeon, his eyes seeming to probe

for the information his Jedi senses were blinded to. 'What is this trick?' he growled, looking back at Thrawn.

'There is no trick,' Thrawn assured him. 'I've decided that a lightning thrust into the heart of the Rebellion will be the best way to shake their morale and prepare them for the next stage of the campaign. This will be that thrust.'

C'baoth looked out the viewport, his eyes searching the vast reaches of the Bilbringi shipyards. His gaze swept past the blackened hulk of the Star Destroyer . . . drifted to the asteroids clustered in the central sector . . .

'Those?' he demanded, jabbing a finger toward them. 'Are those your special cargo?'

'You're the Jedi Master,' Thrawn said. 'You tell me.'

C'baoth glared at him, and Pellaeon held his breath. The Grand Admiral was baiting him, Pellaeon knew – a rather dangerous game, in his opinion. The only people who knew precisely what Thrawn had in mind for those asteroids were currently protected by ysalamiri. 'Very well, Grand Admiral Thrawn,' C'baoth said. 'I will.'

He took a deep breath and closed his eyes, and the lines in his face sharpened with a depth of mental strain Pellaeon hadn't seen in the Jedi Master for a long time. He watched the other, wondering what he was up to . . . and suddenly, he understood. Out there, around the asteroids, were hundreds of officers and techs who had worked on the project, each of them with his own private speculations as to what the whole thing was about. C'baoth was reaching out to all those minds, trying to draw out those speculations and compile them into a complete picture—

'No!' he snapped suddenly, turning his flashing eyes on Thrawn again. 'You can't destroy Coruscant. Not until I have my Jedi.'

Thrawn shook his head. 'I have no intention of destroying Coruscant—'

'You lie!' C'baoth cut him off, jabbing an accusing finger at him. 'You always lie to me. But no more. No more. *I* command the Empire, and all its forces.'

He raised his hands above his head, an eerie blue-white

coronal sheen playing about them. Pellaeon cringed despite himself, remembering the lightning bolts C'baoth had thrown at them in the crypt on Wayland. But no lightning came. C'baoth simply stood there, his hands clutching at empty air, his eyes gazing toward infinity. Pellaeon frowned at him . . . and he was just considering asking C'baoth what he was talking about when he happened to glance down into the portside crew pit.

The crewers were sitting stiffly in their chairs, their backs parade-ground straight, their hands folded in their laps, their eyes staring blankly through their consoles. Behind them, the officers were equally stiff, equally motionless, equally oblivious. The starboard crew pit was the same as was the aft bridge. And on the consoles Pellaeon could see, which should have been active with incoming reports from other sectors of the ship, the displays had all gone static.

It was a moment Pellaeon had expected and dreaded since that first visit to Wayland. C'baoth had taken command of the *Chimaera*.

'Impressive,' Thrawn said into the brittle silence. 'Very impressive indeed. And what do you propose to do now?'

'Need I repeat myself?' C'baoth said, his voice trembling slightly with obvious strain. 'I will take this ship to Coruscant. To take my Jedi, not to destroy them.'

'It's a minimum of five days to Coruscant from here,' Thrawn said coldly. 'Five days during which you'll have to maintain your control of the *Chimaera*'s thirty-seven thousand crewers. Longer, of course, if you intend for them to actually fight at the end of that voyage. And if you intend for us to arrive with any support craft, that figure of thirty-seven thousand will increase rather steeply.'

C'baoth snorted contemptuously. 'You doubt the power of the Force, Grand Admiral Thrawn?'

'Not at all,' Thrawn said. 'I merely present the problems you and the Force will have to solve if you continue with this course of action. For instance, do you know where the Coruscant sector fleet is based, or the number and types of ships making it up? Have you thought about how you will neutralize Coruscant's orbital battle stations and ground-based systems? Do you know who is in command of the planet's defenses at present, and how he or she is likely to deploy the available forces? Have you considered Coruscant's energy field? Do you know how best to use the strategic and tactical capabilities of an Imperial Star Destroyer?'

'You seek to confuse me,' C'baoth accused. 'Your men – *my* men – know the answers to all those questions.'

'To some of them, yes,' Thrawn said. 'But you cannot learn the answers. Not all of them. Certainly not quickly enough.'

'I control the Force,' C'baoth repeated angrily. But to Pellaeon's ear there was a hint of pleading in the tone. Like a child throwing a tantrum that he didn't really expect to get him anywhere . . .

'No,' Thrawn said, his voice abruptly soothing. Perhaps he, too, had picked up on C'baoth's tone. 'The galaxy is not yet ready for you to lead, Master C'baoth. Later, when order has been restored, I will present it to you to govern as you please. But that time is not yet.'

For a long moment C'baoth remained motionless, his mouth working half invisibly behind his flowing beard. Then, almost reluctantly, he lowered his arms; and as he did so, the bridge was filled with muffled gasps and groans and the scraping of boots on steel decking as the crewers were released from the Jedi Master's control. 'You will never present the Empire to me,' C'baoth told Thrawn. 'Not of your own will.'

'That may depend on your ability to maintain that which I am in the process of re-creating,' Thrawn said.

'And which will not come to be at all without you?'

Thrawn cocked an eyebrow. 'You're the Jedi Master. As you gaze into the future, can you see a future Empire arising without me?'

'I see many possible futures,' C'baoth said. 'In not all of them do you survive.'

'An uncertainty faced by all warriors,' Thrawn nodded. 'But that was not what I asked.'

C'baoth smiled thinly. 'Never assume you are indispensable to my Empire, Grand Admiral Thrawn. Only I am that.'

He sent his gaze leisurely around the bridge, then drew himself to his full height. 'For now, however, I am pleased that you should lead my forces into battle.' He looked back sharply at Thrawn. 'You may lead; but you will not destroy Coruscant. Not until I have my Jedi.'

'As I have said already, I have no intention of destroying Coruscant,' Thrawn told him. 'For now, the fear and undermining of morale that accompany a siege will serve my purposes better.'

'*Our* purposes,' C'baoth corrected. 'Do not forget that, Grand Admiral Thrawn.'

'I forget nothing, Master C'baoth,' Thrawn countered quickly.

'Good,' C'baoth said, just as quietly. 'Then you may carry on with your duties. I will be meditating, should you require me. Meditating upon the future of my Empire.'

He turned and strode off the bridge; and Pellaeon let out a breath he hadn't realized he'd been holding. 'Admiral . . .'

'Signal the *Relentless*, Captain,' Thrawn ordered him, swiveling back around again. 'Tell Captain Dorja I need a five-hundred-man caretaker crew for the next six hours.'

Pellaeon looked down into the portside crew pit. Here and there one could see a crewer sitting properly at his station or an officer standing more or less vertically. But for the most part the crewers were collapsed limply in their seats, their officers leaning against walls and consoles or lying trembling on the deck. 'Yes, sir,' he said, stepping back to his chair and keying for comm. 'Will you be postponing the Coruscant operation?'

'No more than absolutely necessary,' Thrawn said. 'History is on the move, Captain. Those who cannot keep up will be left behind, to watch from a distance.'

He glanced back at the door through which C'baoth had departed. 'And those who stand in our way,' he added softly, 'will not watch at all.'

CHAPTER 13

They came in to Coruscant in the dead of night: ten of them, disguised as Jawas, slipping in through the secret entrance that Palace Security had carefully sealed and that Luke had now just as carefully unsealed. Getting to the Tower unseen was no problem – no-one had yet had the time to do anything about the Emperor's limited maze of hidden passageways.

And so they filed silently into the suite behind Luke . . . and for the first time Han found himself face-to-face with the bodyguards his wife had chosen to protect her and her children from the Empire.

A group of Noghri.

'We greet you, Lady Vader,' the first of the gray-skinned aliens said in a gravelly voice, dropping to the floor and spreading his arms out to his sides. The others followed suit, which should have been awkward or at least crowded in the narrow suite entryway. It wasn't, which probably said something about their agility. 'I am Cakhmaim, warrior of the clan Eikh'mir,' the Noghri continued, talking toward the floor. 'I lead the honor guard of the *Mal'ary'ush*. To your service and protection we commit ourselves and our lives.'

'You may rise,' Leia said, her voice solemnly regal. Han stole a glance at her, to find that her face and posture were just as stately as her voice. The sort of authority stuff that usually kicked in his automatic disobedience circuits. But on Leia it looked good. 'As the *Mal'ary'ush*, I accept your service.'

The Noghri got to their feet, making no more noise than they had getting down. 'My lieutenant, Mobvekhar clan Hakh'khar,' Cakhmaim said, indicating the Noghri to his right. 'He will lead the second watch.'

'My husband, Han Solo,' Leia responded, gesturing to Han. Cakhmaim turned to face him, and with a conscious effort

Han kept his hand away from his blaster. 'We greet you,' the alien said gravely. 'The Noghri honor the consort of the Lady Vader.'

The consort? Han threw a startled look at Leia. Her expression was still serious, but he could see the edge of an amused smile tugging at the corners of her mouth. 'Thanks,' Han growled. 'Nice meeting you, too.'

'And you, Khabarakh,' Leia said, holding her hand out to another of the Noghri. 'It's good to see you again. I trust the maitrakh of your family is well?'

'She is very well, my lady,' the Noghri said, stepping forward from the group to take her hand. 'She sends her greetings, as well as a renewed promise of her service.'

Behind the Noghri, the door opened and Chewbacca slipped inside. 'Any trouble?' Han asked him, glad of a distraction from all these pleasantries.

Chewbacca growled a negative, his eyes searching the group of aliens. He spotted Khabarakh and moved to the Noghri's side, rumbling a greeting. Khabarakh greeted him in turn. 'Which others will be under our protection, Lady Vader?' Cakhmaim asked.

'My aide, Winter, and my twins,' Leia said. 'Come, I'll show you.'

She headed toward the bedroom with Cakhmaim and Mobvekhar at her sides. The rest of the aliens began to spread out around the suite, giving special attention to the walls and doors. Chewbacca and Khabarakh headed off toward Winter's room together, conversing quietly between themselves.

'You still don't like this, do you?' Luke said from Han's side.

'Not really, no,' Han conceded, watching Chewbacca and Khabarakh. 'But I don't seem to have a lot of choices.'

He sensed Luke shrug. 'You and Chewie could stay here,' he offered. 'Lando, Mara, and I could go to Wayland by ourselves.'

'Or you could take the Noghri with you,' Han suggested dryly. 'At least out there you wouldn't have to worry about anyone seeing them.'

'No-one will see us here,' a gravelly voice mewed at his elbow.

Han jerked, hand dropping to his blaster as he spun around. There was a Noghri standing there, all right. He would have sworn none of the half-sized aliens were anywhere near him. 'You always sneak up on people like that?' he demanded.

The alien bowed his head. 'Forgive me, consort of the Lady Vader. I meant no offense.'

'They're great hunters,' Luke murmured.

'Yeah, I'd heard that,' Han said, turning back to Luke. Impressive, sure, but it was never the aliens' *ability* to protect Leia and the twins that he'd worried about. 'Look – Luke—'

'They're all right, Han,' Luke said quietly. 'Really they are. Leia's already trusted them once with her life.'

'Yeah,' Han said again. Tried to erase the image of Leia and the twins in Imperial hands . . . 'Everything go all right at the landing pad?'

'No problems,' Luke assured him. 'Wedge and a couple of his Rogue Squadron teammates were there to fly escort, and Chewie got the ship under cover. No-one saw us come into the Palace, either.'

'I hope you sealed the door behind you,' Han said. 'If another Imperial team gets in, Leia's going to have her hands full.'

'It's closed but not really sealed,' Luke shook his head. 'We'll have Cakhmaim seal it behind us.'

Han frowned at him, an unpleasant suspicion forming in his gut. 'You suggesting we go *now*?'

'Can you think of a better time?' Luke countered. 'I mean, the Noghri are here and the *Falcon*'s loaded and ready. And no-one's likely to miss Mara until morning.'

Han looked over Luke's shoulder, to where Leia was just emerging from the bedroom with her Noghri escort still in tow. It made sense – he had to admit that. But somehow he'd counted on him and Leia having a little more time together.

Except that the Empire would still be making clones during that time . . .

He grimaced. 'All right,' he grumbled. 'Sure. Why not?'

193

'I know,' Luke said sympathetically. 'And I'm sorry.'

'Forget it. How do you want to do this?'

'Lando and I will go get Mara out,' Luke said, all business again. Probably could tell that Han wasn't in the mood for sympathy. 'You and Chewie get the *Falcon* and pick us up. And don't forget to bring the droids.'

'Right,' Han said, feeling his lip twist. It wasn't bad enough that he had to leave Leia and his kids to go break into another Imperial stronghold – he had to have Threepio along yakking his overcultured metal head off, too. It just got better and better. 'You got the restraining bolt Chewie rigged up?'

'Right here,' Luke nodded, patting his jacket. 'I know where to attach it, too.'

'Just don't miss,' Han warned. 'You get a G-2RD droid going, and you'll have to take its head off to stop it.'

'I understand,' Luke nodded. 'We'll meet you out where we hid the Noghri ship – Chewie knows the place.' He turned and headed toward the door.

'Good luck,' Han muttered under his breath. He started to turn – 'What're *you* looking at?' he demanded.

The Noghri standing there bowed his head. 'I meant no offense, consort of the Lady Vader,' he assured Han. Turning away, he resumed his study of the wall.

Grimacing, Han looked around for Leia. OK, he'd leave tonight; but he wasn't going anywhere until he'd said goodbye to his wife. And in private.

The Emperor raised his hands, sending cascades of jagged blue-white lightning at his enemies. Both men staggered under the counterattack, and Mara watched with the sudden agonized hope that this time it might end differently. But no. Vader and Skywalker straightened, and with an electronic-sounding shriek of rage, they lifted their lightsabers high—

Mara snapped awake, her hand groping automatically under her bed for the blaster that wasn't there. That shriek had sounded like the start of an alarm from the G-2RD droid outside her room. An alarm that had been suddenly cut off . . .

Across the room, the lock clicked open. Mara's searching

hand touched the data pad she'd been reading from before going to sleep . . . and as the door swung open she hurled the instrument with all her strength at the dark figure silhouetted in the doorway.

The impromptu missile never reached him. The figure simply held up a hand, and the data pad skidded to a halt in midair. 'It's all right, Mara,' he murmured as he took another step into the room. 'It's just me – Luke Skywalker.'

Mara frowned through the darkness, stretching out with her mind toward the intruder. It was Skywalker, all right. 'What do you want?' she demanded.

'We're here to get you out,' Skywalker told her, stepping over to the desk and turning on a low light. 'Come on – you've got to get dressed.'

'I do, huh?' Mara retorted, squinting for a moment before her eyes adjusted to the light. 'Mind telling me where we're going?'

A slight frown creased Skywalker's forehead. 'We're going to Wayland,' he said. 'You told Leia you could find it.'

Mara stared at him. 'Sure, I told her that. When did I ever say I'd take anyone there?'

'You have to, Mara,' Skywalker said, his voice laced with that irritating idealistic earnestness of his. The same earnestness that had stopped her from killing that insane Joruus C'baoth back on Jomark. 'We're standing on the edge of a new round of Clone Wars here. We have to stop it.'

'So go stop it,' she retorted. 'This isn't my war, Skywalker.'

But the words were mere reflex, and she knew it. The minute she'd told Organa Solo about the Emperor's storehouse she had committed herself to this side of the war, and that meant doing whatever she was called on to do. Even if it meant taking them personally to Wayland.

With all those well-trained Jedi insights Skywalker must have seen that, too. Fortunately, he had the sense not to throw any of it back into her face. 'All right,' she growled, swinging her legs out of bed. 'Wait outside – I'll be right there.'

She had time while dressing to sweep the area with her far less trained Force abilities, and was therefore not surprised to find Calrissian waiting with Skywalker when she emerged from her suite. The condition of the G-2RD *was* a surprise, though. From the way that electronic shriek had been truncated, she'd expected to find the guard droid scattered around the hallway in several pieces; instead, it was standing perfectly intact beside her door, quivering slightly with mechanical rage or frustration. 'We put a restraining bolt on it,' Skywalker answered her unspoken question.

She looked and spotted the flat device attached to the droid's side. 'I didn't think you could restrain a guard droid.'

'It's not easy, but Han and Chewie knew a way to do it,' Skywalker said as the three of them hurried down the hallway toward the turbolifts. 'They thought this would make the prison break a little less conspicuous.'

Prison break. Mara threw a glance at Skywalker's profile, the word suddenly putting this whole thing into a new perspective. Here he was: Luke Skywalker, Jedi Knight, hero of the Rebellion, pillar of law and justice . . . and he'd just defied the entire New Republic establishment, from Mon Mothma on down, to get her out. Mara Jade, a smuggler to whom he owed not a single thing, and who in fact had promised to kill him.

All because he saw what needed to be done. And he trusted her to help him do it.

'A nice trick,' she murmured, glancing down a cross corridor as they passed, her eyes and mind alert for guards. 'I'll have to get Solo to teach it to me.'

Calrissian brought the airspeeder down at what appeared to be an old private landing pad. The *Millennium Falcon* was already there, an obviously nervous and impatient Chewbacca waiting for them at the open hatchway.

'About time,' Solo said as Mara followed Skywalker into the cockpit. They were barely aboard, she saw, and already he had the freighter in the air. He must be as nervous about this as the Wookiee. 'OK, Mara. Where do we go?'

'Set course for Obroa-skai,' she told him. 'That was the last stop before Wayland on that trip. I should be able to have the rest of it plotted out by the time we get there.'

'Let's hope so,' Solo said, reaching around to key the nav computer. 'Better strap in – we'll be making the jump to lightspeed as soon as we're clear.'

Mara slid into the passenger seat behind him, Skywalker taking the other one. 'What kind of assault force are we taking?' she asked as she strapped in.

'You're looking at it,' Solo grunted. 'You, me, Luke, Lando, and Chewie.'

'I see,' Mara said, swallowing hard. Five of them, against whatever defenses Thrawn would have set up to protect his most vital military base. Terrific. 'You sure we're not being unsporting about it?' she asked sarcastically.

'We didn't have a lot more than this at Yavin,' Solo pointed out. 'Or at Endor.'

She glared at the back of his head, willing the anger and hatred to flow. But all she felt was a quiet and strangely distant ache. 'Your confidence is so very reassuring,' she bit out.

Solo shrugged. 'You can get a lot of distance out of not doing what the other side expects you to,' he said. 'Remind me sometime to tell you how we got away from Hoth.'

Behind them, the door slid open and Chewbacca lumbered into the cockpit. 'Everything all set back there?' Solo asked him.

The Wookiee rumbled something that was probably an affirmation. 'Good. Run a quick check on the alluvial dampers – they were sparking red a while back.'

Another rumble, and the Wookiee got to work. 'Before I forget, Luke,' Solo added, 'you're in charge of those droids back there. I don't want to see Threepio fiddling with anything unless Chewie or Lando is with him. Got that?'

'Got it,' Skywalker said. He caught Mara's eye and threw her an amused grin. 'Threepio sometimes has extra time on his hands,' he explained. 'He's taken an interest in mechanical work.'

'And he's pretty bad at it,' Solo put in sourly. 'OK, Chewie, get ready. Here we go . . .'

He pulled back on the hyperdrive levers. Through the viewport the stars flared into starlines . . . and they were on their way. Five of them, on their way to invade an Imperial stronghold.

Mara looked over at Skywalker. And the only one of them who really trusted her was the one man she had to kill.

'Your first command since you resigned your commission, Han,' Skywalker commented into the silence.

'Yeah,' Solo said tightly. 'Let's just hope it's not my last.'

'The *Bellicose* task force has arrived, Captain,' the comm officer called up to the *Chimaera*'s command walkway. 'Captain Aban reports all ships at battle readiness, and requests final deployment orders.'

'Relay them to him, Lieutenant,' Pellaeon ordered, peering out the viewport at the new group of running lights that had appeared off to starboard and trying to suppress the growing sense of apprehension that was curling through his gut like wisps of poisoned smoke. It was all well and good for Thrawn to assemble the Empire's seasoned elite for what amounted to an extended hit-and-fade attack on Coruscant; what was not so well and good was the possibility that the raid might not stop there. C'baoth was aboard, and C'baoth's sole agenda these days seemed to be the capture of Leia Organa Solo and her twins. He'd already demonstrated his ability to take absolute control of the *Chimaera* and its crewers, an arrogant little stunt that had already delayed this operation by several hours. If he decided to do it again in the thick of battle off Coruscant . . .

Pellaeon grimaced, the ghostly memories of the Empire's defeat at Endor floating up before his eyes. The second Death Star had died there, along with Vader's Super Star Destroyer *Executor* and far too many of the best and brightest of the Empire's officer corps. If C'baoth's interference precipitated a repetition of that debacle – if the Empire lost both Grand Admiral Thrawn and his core Star Destroyer force – it might never again recover.

He was still gazing out the viewport at the gathering assault force, trying to suppress his concerns, when a rustle of uneasiness rippled across the bridge around him . . . and even without looking he knew what it meant.

C'baoth was here.

Pellaeon's command chair and its protecting ysalamir were a dozen long steps away – far too distant to reach without looking obvious about it. None of the other ysalamiri scattered around the bridge were within reach, either. It wouldn't do to go running around like a frightened field scurry in front of his crew, even if C'baoth was willing to let him.

And if the Jedi Master chose instead to paralyze him like he had the rest of the *Chimaera*'s crew at Bilbringi . . .

A shiver ran up Pellaeon's back. He'd seen the medical reports for those who'd had to recover in sick bay, and he had no desire to go through that himself. Aside from the discomfort and emotional confusion involved, such a public humiliation would severely diminish his command authority aboard his ship.

He could only hope that he'd be able to give C'baoth what he wanted without looking weak and subservient. Turning to face the approaching Jedi Master, he wondered if playing on this same fear of humiliation had been the way the Emperor had started his own rise to power. 'Master C'baoth,' he nodded gravely. 'What may I do for you?'

'I want a ship prepared for me at once,' C'baoth said, his eyes blazing with a strange inward fire. 'One with enough range to take me to Wayland.'

Pellaeon blinked. 'To Wayland?'

'Yes,' C'baoth said, looking out the viewport. 'I told you long ago that I would eventually take command there. That time has now come.'

Pellaeon braced himself. 'I was under the impression that you'd agreed to assist with the Coruscant attack—'

'I have changed my mind,' C'baoth cut him off sharply.

Sharply, but with a strange sense of preoccupation. 'Has something happened on Wayland?' Pellaeon asked.

C'baoth looked at him, and Pellaeon had the odd sense that the Jedi Master was really only noticing him for the first time.

'What happens or does not happen on Wayland is no concern of yours, Imperial Captain Pellaeon,' he said. 'Your only concern is to prepare me a ship.' He looked out the viewport again. 'Or do I need to choose my own?'

A movement at the rear of the bridge caught Pellaeon's eye: Grand Admiral Thrawn, arriving from his private command room to oversee the final preparations for the Coruscant assault. As Pellaeon watched, Thrawn's glowing red eyes flicked across the scene, taking in C'baoth's presence and pausing momentarily on Pellaeon's face and posture. He turned his head and nodded, and a stormtrooper with an ysalamir nutrient frame on his back stepped to Thrawn's side. Together, they started forward.

C'baoth didn't bother to turn around. 'You will prepare me a ship, Grand Admiral Thrawn,' he called. 'I wish to go to Wayland. Immediately.'

'Indeed,' Thrawn said, stepping to Pellaeon's side. The stormtrooper moved between and behind the two of them, finally bringing Pellaeon into the safety of the ysalamir's Force-empty bubble. 'May I ask why?'

'My reasons are my own,' C'baoth said darkly. 'Do you question them?'

For a long moment Pellaeon was afraid Thrawn was going to take him up on that challenge. 'Not at all,' the Grand Admiral said at last. 'If you wish to go to Wayland, you may of course do so. Lieutenant Tschel?'

'Sir?' the young duty officer said from the portside crew pit, stiffening to attention.

'Signal the *Death's Head*,' Thrawn ordered. 'Inform Captain Harbid that the Star Galleon *Draklor* is to be detached from his group and reassigned to me. Crew only; I'll supply troops and passengers.'

'Yes, sir,' Tschel acknowledged, and stepped over to the comm station.

'I did not ask for troops, Grand Admiral Thrawn,' C'baoth said, his face alternating between petulance and suspicion. 'Nor for other passengers.'

'I've been planning for some time to send General Covell

to take command of the Mount Tantiss garrison,' Thrawn said. 'As well as to supplement the troops already there. This would seem as good a time as any to do so.'

C'baoth looked at Pellaeon, then back at Thrawn. 'All right,' he said at last, apparently settling on petulance. 'But it will be *my* ship – not Covell's. *I* will give the orders.'

'Of course, Master C'baoth,' Thrawn said soothingly. 'I will so inform the general.'

'All right.' C'baoth's mouth worked uncertainly behind his long white beard, and for a moment Pellaeon thought he was going to lose control again. His head twitched to the side; then he was back in command of himself again. 'All right,' he repeated curtly. 'I will be in my chambers. Call me when my ship is ready.'

'As you wish,' Thrawn nodded.

C'baoth threw each of them another piercing look, then turned and strode away. 'Inform General Covell of this change of plans, Captain,' Thrawn ordered Pellaeon, watching C'baoth make his way across the bridge. 'The computer has a list of troops and crewers assigned as cloning templets; Covell's aides will arrange for them to be put aboard the *Draklor*. Along with a company of the general's best troops.'

Pellaeon frowned at Thrawn's profile. Covell's troops – and Covell himself, for that matter – had been slated to relieve the shock forces currently working their way across Qat Chrystac. 'You think Mount Tantiss is in danger?' he asked.

'Not any substantial danger, no,' Thrawn said. 'Still, it's possible our farseeing Jedi Master may indeed have picked up on something – unrest among the natives, perhaps. Best not to take chances.'

Pellaeon looked out the viewport at the star that was Coruscant's sun. 'Could it be something having to do with the Rebels?'

'Unlikely,' Thrawn said. 'There's no indication yet that they've even learned of Wayland's existence, let alone are planning any action against it. If and when that happens, we should have plenty of advance notice of their intentions.'

'Via Delta Source.'

'And via normal Intelligence channels.' Thrawn smiled slightly. 'It still disturbs you, doesn't it, to receive information from a source you don't understand?'

'A little, sir, yes,' Pellaeon admitted.

'Consider it a cultivation of your trust,' Thrawn said. 'Someday I'll turn Delta Source over to you. But not yet.'

'Yes, sir,' Pellaeon said. He looked aft, toward where C'baoth had disappeared from the bridge. Something about this was tickling uncomfortably in the back of his memory. Something about C'baoth and Wayland . . .

'You seem disturbed, Captain,' Thrawn said.

Pellaeon shook his head. 'I don't like the idea of him being inside Mount Tantiss, Admiral. I don't know why. I just don't like it.'

Thrawn followed his gaze. 'I wouldn't worry about it,' he said quietly. 'Actually, this is more likely to be a solution than a problem.'

Pellaeon frowned. 'I don't understand.'

Thrawn smiled again. 'All in good time, Captain. But now to the business at hand. Is my flagship ready?'

Pellaeon shook his thoughts away. Now, with the center of the Rebellion lying open before them, was not the time for nameless fears. 'The *Chimaera* is fully at your command, Admiral,' he gave the formal response.

'Good.' Thrawn sent his gaze around the bridge, then turned again to Pellaeon. 'Make certain the rest of the assault force is likewise, and inform them we'll be waiting until the *Draklor* has cleared the area.'

He looked out the viewport. 'And then,' he added softly, 'we'll remind the Rebellion what war is all about.'

CHAPTER 14

They stood there silently: Mara and Luke, waiting as the dark hooded shadow moved toward them, a lightsaber glittering in its hand. Back behind the figure an old man stood, craziness in his eyes and blue lightning in his hands. The shadow stopped and raised its weapon. Luke stepped away from Mara, lifting his own lightsaber, his mind filled with horror and dread—

The alarms wailed through the suite from the corridor outside, jolting Leia awake and shattering the nightmare into fragments of vivid color.

Her first thought was that the alarm was for Luke and Mara; her second was that another Imperial commando team had gotten into the Palace. But as she came awake enough to recognize the pitch of the alarm, she realized it was even worse.

Coruscant was under attack.

Across the room, the twins began to cry. 'Winter!' Leia shouted, grabbing her robe and throwing what she could in the way of mental comfort in the twins' direction.

Winter was already in the doorway, halfway into her own robe. 'That's a battle alert,' she called to Leia over the alarm.

'I know,' Leia said, tying the robe around her. 'I have to get to the war room right away.'

'I understand,' Winter said, peering intently at her face. 'Are you all right?'

'I had a dream, that's all,' Leia told her, snagging a pair of half-boots and pulling them on. Trust Winter to pick up on something like that, even in the middle of chaos. 'Luke and Mara were having a battle with someone. And I don't think they were expecting to win.'

'Are you sure it was just a dream?'

Leia bit at her lip as she fastened the half-boots. 'I don't know,' she had to admit. If it hadn't been a dream, but instead had been a Jedi vision . . . 'No – it had to be a dream,' she decided. 'Luke would be able to tell from space if C'baoth or another Dark Jedi was there. He wouldn't risk trying to carry out the mission under those conditions.'

'I hope not,' Winter said. But she didn't sound all that confident about it.

'Don't worry about it,' Leia assured her. 'It was probably

just a bad dream sparked by the alarms going off.' And fueled by a guilty conscience, she added silently, for letting Han and Luke talk her into letting them go to Wayland in the first place. 'Take care of the twins, will you?'

'We'll watch them,' Winter said.

We? Leia glanced around, frowning, and for the first time spotted Mobvekhar and the other two Noghri who'd taken up positions in the shadows around the crib. They hadn't been there when she went to bed, she knew, which meant they must have slipped in from the suite's main living area sometime in the minute or so since the alarm had gone off. Without her noticing.

'You may go without fear, Lady Vader,' Mobvekhar said solemnly. 'Your heirs will come to no harm.'

'I know,' Leia said, and meant it. She picked up her comlink from her nightstand, considered calling for information, but slipped it into the side pocket of her robe instead. The last thing the war room staff needed right now was to have to spend time explaining the situation to a civilian. She'd know soon enough what was happening. 'I'll be back when I can,' she told Winter. Grabbing her lightsaber, she left the suite.

The hallway outside was filled with beings of all sorts, some of them hurrying along on business, the rest milling around in confusion or demanding information from the security guards standing duty. Leia maneuvered her way past the guards and through the clumps of anxious discussion, joining a handful of sleep-tousled military aides hurrying toward the turbolifts. A full car was just preparing to leave as she arrived; two of the occupants, obviously recognizing Councilor Organa Solo, promptly gave up their places. The door slid shut behind her, barely missing a chattering pair of brown-robed Jawas who brazenly pushed their way aboard at the last instant, and they headed down.

The entire lower floor of the Palace was given over to military operations, starting with the support service offices on the periphery, moving inward to the offices of Ackbar and Drayson and other duty commanders, and on to the more vital and sensitive areas in the center. Leia cleared herself through at the duty station, passed between a towering pair of Wookiee guards, and stepped through the blast doors into the war room.

Bare minutes after the alarm had sounded, the place was already a scene of marginally controlled chaos as freshly awakened senior officers and aides hurried to battle positions. A single glance at the master tactical display showed that all the furor was fully justified: eight Imperial Interdictor Cruisers had appeared in a loose grouping around the one-one-six vector in Sector Four, their hyperdrive-dampening gravetic cones blocking all entry or exit from the region immediately around Coruscant. Even as she watched, a new group of ships flicked into the center of the cluster: two more Interdictors, plus an escort of eight *Katana*-fleet Dreadnaughts.

'What's going on?' an unfamiliar voice said at Leia's shoulder.

She turned. A young man – a kid, really – was standing there, scratching at a mop of tangled hair and frowning up at the tactical. For a moment she didn't recognize him; then her memory clicked. Ghent, the slicer Karrde had lent them to help crack the bank break-in code that the Imperials had framed Admiral Ackbar with. She'd forgotten he was still here. 'It's an Imperial attack,' she said.

'Oh,' he said. 'Can they do that?'

'We're at war,' she reminded him patiently. 'In war you can do just about anything the other side can't stop you from doing. How did you get in here, anyway?'

'Oh, I cut myself an entry code a while back,' he said, waving a vague hand, his eyes still on the tactical. 'Haven't had much to do lately. Can't you stop them?'

'We're certainly going to try,' Leia said grimly, looking around the room. Across by the command console she spotted General Rieekan. 'Stay out of the way and don't touch anything.'

She'd gotten two steps toward Rieekan when her brain suddenly caught up with her. Ghent, who'd cut himself a top-level access code because he didn't have anything better to do . . .

She spun around, took two steps back, and grabbed Ghent's

arm. 'On second thought, come with me,' she said, steering him through the chaos to a door marked CRYPT opening off the side of the war room. She keyed in her security code, and the door slid open.

It was a good-sized room, crowded to the gills with computers, decrypt techs, and interface droids. 'Who's in charge here?' Leia called as a couple of heads swung in her direction.

'I am,' a middle-aged man wearing a colonel's insignia said, taking a step back from one of the consoles into about the only bit of empty space in the room.

'I'm Councilor Organa Solo,' Leia identified herself. 'This is Ghent, an expert slicer. Can you use him?'

'I don't know,' the colonel said, throwing the kid a speculative look. 'Ever tackled an Imperial battle encrypt code, Ghent?'

'Nope,' Ghent said. 'Never seen one. I've sliced a couple of their regular military encrypts, though.'

'Which ones?'

Ghent's eyes went a little foggy. 'Well, there was one called a Lepido program. Oh, and there was something called the ILKO encrypt back when I was twelve. That was a tough one – took me almost two months to slice.'

Someone whistled softly. 'Is that good?' Leia asked.

The colonel snorted. 'I'd say so, yes. ILKO was one of the master encrypt codes the Empire used for data transfer between Coruscant and the original Death Star construction facility at Horuz. It took *us* nearly a month to crack it.' He beckoned. 'Come on over, son – we've got a console for you right here. If you liked ILKO, you're going to love battle encrypts.'

Ghent's face lit up, and he was picking his way between the other consoles as Leia slipped back into the war room.

To find that the battle was under way.

Six Imperial Star Destroyers had come in from hyperspace through the center gap of the Interdictor group, splitting into two groups of three and heading for the two massive midorbit Golan III battle stations. Their TIE fighters were swarming ahead of them, heading toward the defenders now beginning to emerge from the low-orbit space-dock facility and from Coruscant's surface. On the master visual display, occasional flashes of turbolaser fire flickered as both sides began to fire ranging shots.

General Rieekan was standing a few steps back from the main command console when Leia reached him. 'Princess,' he nodded gravely in greeting.

'General,' she nodded back breathlessly, throwing a quick look across the console displays. Coruscant's energy shield was up, the ground-based defenses were coming rapidly to full combat status, and a second wave of X-wings and B-wings were beginning to scramble from the space dock.

And standing in front of the raised command chair, barking out orders to everyone in sight, was Admiral Drayson.

'*Drayson?*' she demanded.

'Ackbar's on an inspection tour of the Ketaris region,' Rieekan said grimly. 'That leaves Drayson in charge.'

Leia looked up at the master tactical, a sinking feeling settling firmly in her stomach. Drayson was competent enough . . . but against Grand Admiral Thrawn, competent wasn't good enough. 'Has the sector fleet been alerted?'

'I think we got the word out to them before the shield went up,' Rieekan said. 'Unfortunately, one of the first things the Imperials hit was the out-orbit relay station, so there's no way of knowing whether or not they heard. Not without opening the shield.'

The sinking feeling sunk a little lower. 'Then this isn't just a feint to draw the sector fleet here,' Leia said. 'Otherwise, they'd have left the relay station alone so we could keep calling for help.'

'I agree,' Rieekan said. 'Whatever Thrawn has in mind, we seem to be it.'

Leia nodded, wordlessly, gazing up at the visual display. The Star Destroyers had entered the battle stations' outer kill zones now, and the black of space was beginning to sparkle with more serious turbolaser fire. Outside the main fire field, Dreadnaughts and other support ships were forming a perimeter to protect the Star Destroyers from the defenders rising toward them.

On the master tactical, a flicker of pale white light shot upward: an ion cannon blast from the surface, streaking toward the Star Destroyers. 'Waste of power,' Rieekan muttered contemptuously. 'They're way out of range.'

And even if they weren't, Leia knew, the electronics-disrupting charge would have had as much chance of hitting the battle station as any of the Star Destroyers it had been aimed at. Ion cannon weren't exactly known for tight-beam accuracy. 'We've got to get someone else in command here,' she said, looking around the war room. If she could find Mon Mothma and persuade her to put Rieekan in charge—

Abruptly, her eyes stopped their sweep. There, standing against the back wall, gazing up at the master tactical, was Sena Leikvold Midanyl. Chief adviser to General Garm Bel Iblis . . . who was considerably more than merely competent. 'I'll be back,' she told Rieekan, and headed off into the crowd.

'Councilor Organa Solo,' Sena said as Leia reached her, a tautness straining her face and sense. 'I was told to stay back here out of the way. Can you tell me what's happening?'

'What's happening is that we need Garm,' Leia said, glancing around. 'Where is he?'

'Observation gallery,' Sena said, nodding upward toward the semicircular balcony running around the back half of the war room.

Leia looked up. Beings of all sorts were beginning to pour into the gallery – government civilians, most of them, who were authorized this deep into the command floor but weren't cleared for access to the war room proper. Sitting alone to one side, gazing intently at the master displays, was Bel Iblis. 'Get him down here,' Leia told Sena. 'We need him.'

Sena seemed to sigh. 'He won't come down,' she said. 'Not unless and until Mon Mothma asks him to. His own words.'

Leia felt her stomach tighten. Bel Iblis had more than his share of stiff-necked pride, but this was no time for personal squabbles. 'He can't do that. We need his help.'

208

Sena shook her head minutely. 'I've tried. He won't listen to me.'

Leia took a deep breath. 'Maybe he'll listen to me.'

'I hope so.' Sena gestured toward the display, where one of Bel Iblis's Dreadnaughts had appeared from the space dock to join the rising wave of starfighters, Corellian Gunships, and Escort Frigates blazing toward the invaders. 'That's the *Harrier*,' she identified it. 'My sons Peter and Dayvid are aboard it.'

Leia touched her shoulder. 'Don't worry – I'll get him down here.'

The center section of the gallery was becoming almost crowded by the time she reached it. But the area around Bel Iblis was still reasonably empty. 'Hello, Leia,' he said as she came up to him. 'I thought you'd be down below.'

'I should be – and so should you,' Leia said. 'We need you down—'

'You have your comlink with you?' he cut her off sharply.

She frowned at him. 'Yes.'

'Get it out. Now. Call Drayson and warn him about those two Interdictors.'

Leia looked at the master tactical. The two Interdictor Cruisers that had come in late to the party were doing some fine-tune maneuvering, their hazy gravity-wave cones sweeping across one of the battle stations. 'Thrawn pulled this stunt on us at Qat Chrystac,' Bel Iblis went on. 'He uses an Interdictor Cruiser to define a hyperspace edge, then brings a ship in along an intersecting vector to drop out at a precisely chosen point. Drayson needs to pull some ships up on those flanks to be ready for whatever Thrawn's bringing in.'

Leia was already digging in her robe pocket. 'But we don't have anything here that can take on another Star Destroyer.'

'It's not a matter of taking it on,' Bel Iblis told her. 'Whatever's on its way will come in blind, with deflectors down and no targeting references. If our ships are in place, we'll get one solid free shot at them. That could make a lot of difference.'

'I understand,' Leia said, thumbing on her comlink and keying for the central switching operator. 'This is Councilor Leia Organa Solo. I have an urgent message for Admiral Drayson.'

'Admiral Drayson is occupied and cannot be disturbed,' the electronic voice said.

'This is a direct Council override,' Leia ordered. 'Put me through to Drayson.'

'Voice analysis confirmed,' the operator said. 'Council override is superseded by military emergency procedure. You may leave Admiral Drayson a message.'

Leia ground her teeth, throwing a quick glance at the tactical. 'Then put me through to Drayson's chief aide.'

'Lieutenant DuPre is occupied and cannot—'

'Cancel,' Leia cut it off. 'Get me General Rieekan.'

'General Rieekan is occupied—'

'Too late,' Bel Iblis said quietly.

Leia looked up. Two Victory-class Star Destroyers had suddenly appeared out of hyperspace, dropping in at point-blank range to their target battle stations exactly as Bel Iblis had predicted. They delivered massive broadsides, then angled away before the station or its defending Gunships could respond with more than token return fire. On the tactical, the hazy blue shell indicating the station's deflector shield flickered wildly before settling down again.

'Drayson's no match for him,' Bel Iblis sighed. 'He just isn't.'

Leia took a deep breath. 'You have to come down, Garm.'

He shook his head. 'I can't. Not until Mon Mothma asks me to.'

'You're behaving like a child,' Leia snapped, abandoning any attempt to be diplomatic about this. 'You can't let people die out there just because of personal pique.'

He looked at her; and as she glared back she was struck by the pain in his eyes. 'You don't understand, Leia,' he said. 'This has nothing to do with me. It has to do with Mon Mothma. After all these years, I finally understand why she does things the way she does. I've always assumed she was gathering more and more power to herself simply because she was in love with power. But I was wrong.'

'So why *does* she do it?' Leia demanded, not really interested in talking about Mon Mothma.

'Because with everything she does there are lives hanging in the balance,' he said quietly. 'And she's terrified of trusting anyone else with those lives.'

Leia stared at him . . . but even as she opened her mouth to deny it, all the pieces of her life these past few years fell suddenly into place. All the diplomatic missions Mon Mothma had insisted she go on, no matter what the personal cost in lost Jedi training and strained family life. All the trust she'd invested in Ackbar and a few others; all the responsibility that had been shifted on to fewer and fewer shoulders.

On to the shoulders of those few she could trust to do the job right.

'That's why I can't simply go down and take command,' Bel Iblis said into the silence. 'Until she's able to accept me – really accept me – as someone she can trust, she won't ever be able to give me any genuine authority in the New Republic. She'll always need to be hovering around in the background somewhere, watching over my shoulder to make sure I don't make any mistakes. She hasn't got the time for that, I haven't got the patience, and the friction would be devastating for everyone caught in the middle.'

He nodded toward the war room. 'When she's ready to trust me, I'll be ready to serve. Until then, it's better for everyone involved if I stay out of it.'

'Except for those dying out there,' Leia reminded him tightly. 'Let me call her, Garm. Maybe I can persuade her to offer you command.'

Bel Iblis shook his head. 'If you have to persuade her, Leia, it doesn't count. She has to decide this for herself.'

'Perhaps she has,' Mon Mothma's voice came from behind them.

Leia turned in surprise. With all her attention concentrated on Bel Iblis, she hadn't even noticed the older woman's approach. 'Mon Mothma,' she said, feeling the guilty

211

awkwardness of having been caught talking about someone behind her back. 'I—'

'It's all right, Leia,' Mon Mothma said. 'General Bel Iblis . . .'

Bel Iblis had risen to his feet to face her. 'Yes?'

Mon Mothma seemed to brace herself. 'We've had more than our share of differences over the years, General. But that was a long time ago. We were a good team once. There's no reason why we can't be one again.'

She hesitated again; and with a sudden flash of insight, Leia saw how incredibly difficult this was for her. How humiliating it was to face a man who'd once turned his back on her and to admit aloud that she needed his help. If Bel Iblis was unwilling to bend until she'd said the words he wanted to hear . . .

And then, to Leia's surprise, Bel Iblis straightened to a military attention. 'Mon Mothma,' he said formally, 'given the current emergency, I hereby request your permission to take command of Coruscant's defense.'

The lines around Mon Mothma's eyes smoothed noticeably, a quiet relief coloring over her sense. 'I would be very grateful if you would do so, Garm.'

He smiled. 'Then let's get to it.'

Together, they headed for the stairway down to the command floor; and with a newly humbled sense of her own limitations, Leia realized that probably half of what she'd just witnessed had passed her by completely. The long and perilous history Mon Mothma and Bel Iblis had shared had created an empathy between them, a bond and understanding far deeper than Leia's Jedi insights could even begin to track through. Perhaps, she decided, it was that empathy that formed the true underlying strength of the New Republic. The strength that would create the future of the galaxy.

If it could withstand the next few hours. Clenching her teeth, she hurried after them.

A pair of Corellian Gunships shot past the *Chimaera*, sending a volley of turbolaser fire spattering across the bridge deflector shield. A squadron of TIE fighters was right on their tail, sweeping into a Rellis flanking maneuver as they tried for a clear shot. Beyond them, Pellaeon spotted an Escort Frigate cutting into backup position across the Gunships' exit vector. 'Squadron A-4, move to sector twenty-two,' Pellaeon ordered. So far, as near as he could tell, the battle seemed to be going well.

'There they go,' Thrawn commented from beside him.

Pellaeon scanned the area. 'Where?' he asked.

'They're preparing to pull back,' Thrawn told him, pointing to one of the two Rebel Dreadnaughts that had joined the battle. 'Observe how that Dreadnaught is moving into cover position for a retreat. There – the second one is following suit.'

Pellaeon frowned at the maneuvering Dreadnaughts. He still didn't see it; but he'd never yet seen Thrawn wrong on such a call. 'They're abandoning the battle stations?'

Thrawn snorted gently. 'They never should have brought those ships out to defend them in the first place. Golan defense platforms can take considerably more punishment than their former ground commander apparently realized.'

'Their former ground commander?'

'Yes,' Thrawn said. 'At a guess, I'd say our old Corellian adversary has just been put in command of Coruscant's defense. I wonder what took them so long.'

Pellaeon shrugged, studying the battle area. The Grand Admiral was right: the defenders were starting to pull back. 'Perhaps they had to wake him up.'

'Perhaps.' Thrawn sent a leisurely look around the battle area. 'You see how the Corellian offers us a choice: stay here and duel with the battle stations, or follow the defenders down into range of the ground-based weaponry. Fortunately' – his eyes glittered – 'we have a third option.'

Pellaeon nodded. He'd been wondering when Thrawn would unveil his brilliant new siege weapon. 'Yes, sir,' he said. 'Shall I order the tractor launching?'

'We'll wait for the Corellian to pull his ships back a bit further,' Thrawn said. 'We wouldn't want him to miss this.'

'Understood,' Pellaeon said. Stepping back to his command chair, he sat down and confirmed that the asteroids and the hangar-bay tractor beams were ready.

And waited for the Grand Admiral's order.

'All right,' Bel Iblis said. '*Harrier*, begin pulling back – cover those Escort Frigates on your portside flank. Red leader, watch out for those TIE interceptors.'

Leia watched the tactical display, holding her breath. Yes; it was going to work. Unwilling to risk the ground-based weaponry, the Imperials were letting the defenders retreat back toward Coruscant. That left only the two battle stations still in danger, and they were proving themselves more capable of absorbing damage than Leia had realized they could. And even that would be ending soon – the Grand Admiral would know better than to be here when the sector fleet arrived. It was almost over, and they'd gotten through it.

'General Bel Iblis?' an officer at one of the monitor stations spoke up. 'We're getting a funny reading from the *Chimaera*'s hangar bay.'

'What is it?' Bel Iblis asked, stepping over to the console.

'It reads like the launching tractor beams being activated,' the officer said, indicating one of the multicoloured spots on the Star Destroyer silhouette centered in his display. 'But it's pulling far too much power.'

'Could they be launching a whole TIE squadron together?' Leia suggested.

'I don't think so,' the officer said, 'That's the other thing: near as we can tell, nothing at all left the bay.'

Beside Leia, Bel Iblis stiffened. 'Calculate the exit vector,' he ordered. 'All ships: sensor focus along that path for drive emissions. I think the *Chimaera*'s just launched a cloaked ship.'

Someone nearby swore feelingly. Leia looked up at the master visual display, her throat suddenly tight as the memory of that brief conversation she and Han had had with Admiral Ackbar flashed back to mind. Ackbar had been solidly convinced – and had convinced her – that the double-blind properties of the cloaking shield made it too user-dangerous to be an effective weapon. If Thrawn had found a way around that problem . . .

'They're firing again,' the sensor officer reported. 'And again.'

'Same from the *Death's Head*,' another officer put in. '—firing again.'

'Signal the battle stations to track and fire along those vectors,' Bel Iblis ordered. 'As close to the Star Destroyers as possible. We've got to find out what Thrawn's up to.'

The word was barely out of his mouth when there was a flash of light from the visual display. One of the Escort Frigates along the first projected vector was suddenly ablaze, its aft section trailing fiery drive gases as the whole ship spun wildly about its transverse axis. 'Collision!' someone barked. 'Escort Frigate *Evanrue* – impact with unknown object.'

'Impact?' Bel Iblis echoed. 'Not a turbolaser shot?'

'Telemetry indicates physical impact,' the other shook his head.

Leia looked back at the visual, where the *Evanrue* was now wreathed in burning gas as it fought to get its spin under control. 'Cloaking shields are supposed to be double-blind,' Leia said. 'How are they maneuvering?'

'Maybe they're not,' Bel Iblis said, his voice dark with suspicion. 'Tactical: give me a new track from point of impact with the *Evanrue*. Assume inert object; calculate impact velocity by distance to the *Chimaera*, and don't forget to factor in the local gravitational field. Feed probable location to the *Harrier*; order it to open fire as soon as it has the coordinates.'

'Yes, sir,' one of the lieutenants spoke up. 'Feeding to the *Harrier* now.'

'On second thought, belay that last,' Bel Iblis said, holding up a hand. 'Order the *Harrier* to use its ion cannon only – repeat, ion cannon only. No turbolasers.'

Leia frowned at him. 'You're trying to take the ship intact?'

'I'm trying to take it intact, yes,' Bel Iblis said slowly. 'But I don't think it's a ship.'

He fell silent. On the visual, the *Harrier*'s ion cannon began to fire.

215

The Dreadnaught opened fire, as indeed Thrawn had predicted it would. But only, Pellaeon noted with some surprise, with its ion cannon. 'Admiral?'

'Yes, I see,' Thrawn said. 'Interesting. I was right, Captain – our old Corellian adversary is indeed in command below. But he's allowed us to lead him by the nose only so far.'

Pellaeon nodded as understanding suddenly came. 'He's trying to knock out the asteroid's cloaking shield.'

'Hoping to take it intact.' Thrawn touched his control board. 'Forward turbolaser batteries: track and target asteroid number one. Fire on my command only.'

Pellaeon looked down at his magnified visual display. The Dreadnaught had found its target, its ion beams vanishing in midspace as they flooded down into the cloaking shield. It shouldn't be able to take much more of that . . .

Abruptly, the stars in that empty region vanished. For a couple of heartbeats there was complete blackness as the cloaking shield collapsed in on itself; then, just as abruptly, the newly uncloaked asteroid was visible.

The ion beams cut off. 'Turbolasers, stand by,' Thrawn said. 'We want them to have a good look first . . . Turbolasers: fire.'

Pellaeon shifted his attention to the viewport. The green fire lanced out, disappearing into the distance as they converged on their target. A second later, there was a faint flash from that direction, a flash that was repeated more strongly from his visual display. Another salvo – another – and another—

'Cease fire,' Thrawn said with clear satisfaction. 'They're welcome to whatever's left. Hangar bay: firing status.'

'We're up to seventy-two, sir,' the engineering officer reported, his voice sounding a little strained. 'But the power feedback shunt's starting to glow white. We can't keep up these dry firings much longer without burning out either the shunt or the tractor projector itself.'

'Close down dry firing,' Thrawn ordered, 'and signal the other ships to do likewise. How many total firings have there been, Captain?'

Pellaeon checked the figures. 'Two hundred eighty-seven,' he told the Grand Admiral.

'I presume all twenty-two actual asteroids are out?'

'Yes, sir,' Pellaeon confirmed. 'Most of them in the first two minutes. Though there's no way of knowing if they've taken up their prescribed orbits.'

'The specific orbits are irrelevant,' Thrawn assured him. 'All that matters is that the asteroids are somewhere in the space around Coruscant.'

Pellaeon smiled. Yes, they were . . . except that there were only a fraction of the number the Rebels thought were there. 'And now we leave, sir?'

'Now we leave,' Thrawn confirmed. 'For the moment, at least, Coruscant is effectively out of the war.'

Drayson nodded to the battle ops colonel and stepped back to the small group waiting for him a short distance behind the consoles. 'The final numbers are in,' he said, his voice sounding a little hollow. 'They can't be absolutely certain they didn't miss any through the battle debris. But even so . . . their count is two hundred eighty-seven.'

'Two hundred eighty-seven?' General Rieekan repeated, his jaw dropping slightly.

'That's the number,' Drayson nodded, turning his glare on Bel Iblis. As if, Leia thought, all this was somehow Bel Iblis's fault. 'What now?'

Bel Iblis was rubbing his cheek thoughtfully. 'For starters, I don't think the situation is quite as bad as it looks,' he said. 'From everything I've heard about how expensive cloaking shields are, I can't see Thrawn squandering the kind of resources three hundred of them would take. Especially when a much smaller number would do the job just as well.'

'You think the other tractor beam firings were faked?' Leia asked.

'They couldn't have been,' Rieekan objected. 'I was watching the sensor board. Those projectors were definitely drawing power.'

Bel Iblis looked at Drayson. 'You know more about Star Destroyers than the rest of us, Admiral. Is it possible?'

Drayson frowned off into the distance, professional pride momentarily eclipsing his personal animosity toward Bel Iblis. 'It could be done,' he agreed at last. 'You could run a feedback shunt from the tractor beam projector, either to a flash capacitor or a power dissipator somewhere else on the ship. That would let you run a sizable surge of power through the projector without it really doing anything.'

'Is there any way to tell the difference between that and an actual asteroid launch?' Mon Mothma asked.

'From this distance?' Drayson shook his head. 'No.'

'It almost doesn't matter how many are up there,' Rieekan said. 'Eventually, their orbits will decay, and letting even one hit ground would be a disaster. Until we've cleared them out, we can't risk lowering the planetary shield.'

'The problem being how we locate them,' Drayson agreed heavily. 'And how we know when we've gotten them all.'

A movement caught Leia's eye, and she looked over as a tight-faced Colonel Bremen joined them. 'Again, it could be worse,' Bel Iblis pointed out. 'The sector fleet can have the cut-orbit relay station replaced in a few hours, so at least we'll still be able to direct the New Republic's defense from here.'

'It'll also make it easier to transmit an all-worlds alert,' Bremen spoke up. 'Mara Jade's escaped.'

Mon Mothma inhaled sharply. 'How?' she asked.

'With help,' Bremen said grimly. 'The guard droid was deactivated. Some kind of jury-rigged restraining bolt. It erased that section of memory, too.'

'How long ago?' Rieekan asked.

'No more than a few hours.' Bremen glanced around the war room. 'We've had extra security on the command floor since the break was discovered, thinking they might have been planning some sabotage to coincide with the Imperials' attack.'

'That could still be the plan,' Bel Iblis said. 'Have you sealed off the Palace?'

'Like a smuggler's profit box,' Bremen said. 'I doubt they're still here, though.'

'We'll need to make certain of that,' Mon Mothma said. 'I want you to organize a complete search of the Palace, Colonel.'

Bremen nodded. 'Right away.'

Leia braced herself. They weren't going to be happy about this. 'Don't bother, Colonel,' she said, touching Bremen's arm to stop him as he turned to leave. 'Mara's not here.'

They all looked at her. 'How do you know?' Bel Iblis asked.

'Because she left Coruscant earlier tonight. Along with Han and Luke.'

There was a long silence. 'I wondered why Solo didn't come to the war room with you,' Bel Iblis said. 'You want to tell us what's going on?'

Leia hesitated; but surely none of these people could possibly have anything to do with the Delta Source security leak. 'Mara thinks she knows where the Empire's cloning facility might be. We thought it would be worth sending her and a small team to check it out.'

'*We* thought?' Drayson snapped. 'Who is this *we*?'

Leia looked him straight in the eye. 'My family and closest friends,' she said. 'The only people I can be absolutely certain aren't leaking information to the Empire.'

'That is a gross insult—'

'Enough, Admiral,' Mon Mothma cut him off calmly. Calmly, but there was a hardness around her eyes. 'Whatever reprimands may be due here can wait until later. Whether it was prudent or otherwise, the fact remains that they're on their way, and we need to decide how best to help them. Leia?'

'The most important thing to do is to pretend Mara's still here,' Leia said, the tightness in her chest easing slightly. 'She told me she'd only been to Wayland once, and she couldn't guess how long it would take her to reconstruct the route. The longer lead they have, the less time the Empire will have to rush reinforcements there.'

'What happens then?' Mon Mothma asked. 'Assuming they find it.'

'They'll try to destroy it.'

There was a moment of silence. 'By themselves,' Drayson said.

'Unless you have a spare fleet to lend them, yes,' Leia said.

Mon Mothma shook her head. 'You shouldn't have done it, Leia,' she said. 'Not without consulting the Council.'

'If I'd brought it to the Council, Mara might be dead now,' Leia said bluntly. 'If news leaked to the Empire that she could find Wayland, the next commando team they sent wouldn't stop at just trying to discredit her.'

'The Council is above suspicion,' Mon Mothma said, her voice turning chilly.

'Are all the Council members' aides?' Leia countered. 'Or the tactical people and supply officers and library researchers? If I'd suggested an attack on Wayland to the Council, all of those people would eventually have known about it.'

'And more,' Bel Iblis nodded. 'She has a point, Mon Mothma.'

'I'm not interested in laying blame, Garm,' Mon Mothma said quietly. 'Nor in defending anyone's little niche of power. I'm concerned about the possibility that all this was indeed a setup, Leia . . . and that it will cost your husband and brother their lives.'

Leia swallowed hard. 'We thought about that, too,' she said. 'But we decided it was worth the risk. And there was no-one else to do it.'

For a long minute no-one said anything. Then Mon Mothma stirred. 'You'll need to talk to everyone who knows Mara Jade is gone, Colonel,' she said to Bremen. 'If and when we obtain Wayland's location, we'll see what we can do about sending reinforcements to help them.'

'Provided we can be sure it isn't a trap,' Drayson added, glowering.

'Of course,' Mon Mothma agreed, avoiding Leia's eyes. 'For now, that's all we can do. Let's concentrate on Coruscant's immediate problems: defense, and finding those cloaked asteroids. General Bel Iblis—'

A tentative hand touched Leia's shoulder, and she turned

to find the slicer Ghent standing there. 'It's all over?' he muttered to her.

'The battle is, yes,' she said, glancing at Mon Mothma and the others. They were already knee-deep into a discussion about the asteroids, but eventually one of them was bound to notice Ghent and realize he wasn't supposed to be here. 'Come on,' she told him, steering him back towards the war room exit. 'I'll tell you all about it outside. What did you think of Imperial battle encrypt codes?'

'Oh, they're OK,' he said. 'The guys in there didn't let me do all that much, really. I didn't know their machines as well as they did. They had kind of a silly drill going, too.'

Leia smiled. The best and smoothest decrypting routine the New Republic's experts had come up with, and Ghent considered it a silly drill. 'People get into routines on the way they do things,' she said diplomatically. 'Maybe I can arrange for you to talk to the person in overall charge and offer some suggestions.'

Ghent waved a vague hand. 'Naw. Military types wouldn't like the way I do things. Even Karrde gets bent out by it sometimes. By the way, you know that pulse transmitter you've got going somewhere nearby?'

'The one Delta Source has been using?' Leia nodded. 'Counterintelligence has been trying to locate it since it started transmitting. But it's some sort of cross-frequency split-phase something-or-other, and they haven't had any luck.'

'Oh.' Ghent seemed to digest that. 'Well, that's a tech problem. I don't know anything about those.'

'That's all right,' Leia assured him. 'I'm sure you'll find other ways to help.'

'Yeah,' he said, digging a data card from his pocket. 'Anyway . . . here.'

She frowned as she took the card. 'What's this?'

'It's the encrypt code from the pulse transmitter.'

Leia stopped short. 'It's *what*?'

He stopped too, turning innocent eyes on her. 'The encrypt code that cross-frequency whatsis is using. I finally got it sliced.'

221

She stared at him. 'Just like that? You just went ahead and sliced it?'

He shrugged again. 'Well, sort of. I've been working on it for a month, you know.'

Leia gazed at the data card in her hand, a strange and not entirely pleasant thrill of excitement tingling through her. 'Does anyone know you have this?' she asked quietly.

He shook his head. 'I thought about giving it to that colonel in there before I left, but he was busy talking to someone.'

Delta Source's encrypt code . . . and Delta Source didn't know they had it. 'Don't tell anyone else,' she said. 'And I mean *anyone*.'

Ghent frowned, but shrugged. 'OK. Whatever you say.'

'Thank you,' Leia murmured, sliding the data card into her robe pocket. It was the key to Delta Source – deep within her, she knew that. All she needed was to find the right way to use it.

And to find it fast.

CHAPTER 15

The fortress of Hijarna had been crumbling slowly away for perhaps a thousand years before the Fifth Alderaanian Expedition had spotted it, keeping its silent, deserted vigil over its silent, deserted world. A vast expanse of incredibly hard black stone, it stood on a high bluff overlooking a plain that still bore the deep scars of massive destruction. To some, the enigmatic fortress was a tragic monument: a last-ditch attempt at defense by a desperate world under siege. To others, it was the brooding and malicious cause of both that siege and the devastation that had followed.

To Karrde, for the moment at least, it was home.

'You sure know how to pick 'em, Karrde,' Gillespee commented, propping his feet up on the edge of the auxiliary comm desk and looking around. 'How did you find this place, anyway?'

'It's all right there in the old records,' Karrde told him, watching his display as the decrypt program ran its course. A star map appeared, accompanied by a very short text . . .

Gillespee nodded toward Karrde's display. 'Clyngunn's report?'

'Yes,' Karrde said, pulling out the data card. 'Such as it is.'

'Nothing, right?'

'Pretty much. No indications of clone traffic anywhere on Poderis, Chazwa, or Joiol.'

Gillespee dropped his feet off the table and stood up. 'Well, that's that, then,' he said, stepping over to the fruit rack someone had laid out on a side table and picking himself out a driblis fruit. 'Looks like whatever the Empire had going in Orus sector has dried up. If there was anything going there in the first place.'

'Given the lack of a trail, I suspect the latter,' Karrde agreed, choosing one of the cards that had come from his contact on Bespin and sliding it into the display. 'Still, it was something we needed to know, one way or the other. Among other things, it frees us up to concentrate on other possibilities.'

'Yeah,' Gillespee said reluctantly as he went back to his seat. 'Well . . . you know, Karrde, this whole thing has been kind of strange. Smugglers, I mean, doing this kind of snoop work. Hasn't paid very much, either.'

'I've already told you we'll be getting some reimbursement from the New Republic.'

'Except that we don't have anything to sell them,' Gillespee pointed out. 'Never known anyone yet who paid for no delivery.'

Karrde frowned over at him. Gillespee had produced a wicked-looking knife from somewhere and was carefully carving a slice from the driblis fruit. 'This isn't about getting paid,' he reminded the other. 'It's about surviving against the Empire.'

'Maybe for you it is,' Gillespee said, studying the slice of fruit a moment before taking a bite. 'You've got enough sidelines going that you can afford to lay off business for a while. But, see, the rest of us have payrolls to meet and ships to keep fueled. The money stops coming in, our employees start getting nasty.'

'So you and the others want money?'

He could see Gillespee brace himself. 'I want money. The others want out.'

It was not, in retrospect, exactly an unexpected development. The white-hot anger toward the Empire that had been sparked by that attack at the Whistler's Whirlpool was cooling, and the habits of day-to-day business were beginning to reassert themselves. 'The Empire's still dangerous,' he said.

'Not to us,' Gillespee said bluntly. 'There hasn't been a single blip of Imperial attention directed toward us since the Whirlpool. They didn't mind us poking around Orus sector; they didn't even come down on Mazzic for that thing at the Bilbringi shipyards.'

'So they're ignoring us, despite provocation to do otherwise. Does that make you feel safe?'

Carefully, Gillespee sliced himself off another piece of fruit. 'I don't know,' he conceded. 'Half the time I think Brasck's right: that if we leave the Empire alone, it'll leave us alone. But I can't help thinking about that army of clones Thrawn chased me off Ukio with. I start thinking that maybe he's just too busy with the New Republic to bother with us right now.'

Karrde shook his head. 'Thrawn's never too busy to chase someone down if he wants them,' he said. 'If he's ignoring us, it's because he knows that's the best way to quiet any opposition. Next step will probably be to offer us transport contracts and pretend that we're all good friends again.'

Gillespee looked at him sharply. 'You been talking to Par'tah?'

'No. Why?'

'She told me two days ago that she's been offered a contract to bring a bunch of sublight engines to the Imperial shipyards at Ord Trasi.'

Karrde grimaced. 'Has she accepted?'

'Said she was still working out the details. But you know

Par'tah – she's always running right on the edge. Probably can't afford to say no.'

Karrde turned back to his display, the sour taste of defeat in his mouth. 'I suppose I can't really blame her,' he said. 'What about the others?'

Gillespee shrugged uncomfortably. 'Like I said, the money keeps going out. We have to have money coming in, too.'

And just like that, the reluctant coalition he'd tried to put together was falling apart. And the Empire hadn't had to fire a single shot to do it. 'Then I suppose I'll just have to go it alone,' he said, standing up. 'Thank you for your assistance. I'm sure you'll want to be getting back to business.'

'Now, don't get all huffy, Karrde,' Gillespee chided him, taking one last bite of fruit and getting to his feet. 'You're right, this clone stuff is serious business. If you want to hire my ships and people for your hunt, we'll be happy to help you out. We just can't afford to do it for free any more, that's all. Just let us know.' He turned toward the door—

'Just a minute,' Karrde called after him. A rather audacious thought had just occurred to him. 'Suppose I find a way to guarantee funding for everyone. You think the others would stay aboard, too?'

Gillespee eyed him suspiciously. 'Don't con me, Karrde. You don't have that kind of money lying around.'

'No. But the New Republic does. And under the current situation, I don't think they'd be averse to having a few more fighting ships on the payroll.'

'Uh-uh,' Gillespee shook his head firmly. 'Sorry, but privateer is a little out of my line.'

'Even if your duty consists entirely of collecting information?' Karrde asked. 'I'm not talking about anything more than what you were just doing in Orus sector.'

'Sounds like a dream assignment,' Gillespee said sardonically. 'Except for the tiny little problem of finding someone in the New Republic stupid enough to pay privateer rates for snoop duty.'

Karrde smiled. 'Actually, I wasn't planning to waste their

valuable time telling them about it. Have you ever met my associate Ghent?'

For a moment Gillespee just stared at him, looking puzzled. Then, abruptly, he got it. 'You wouldn't.'

'Why not?' Karrde countered. 'On the contrary, we'd be doing them a service. Why clutter their lives with these troublesome accounting details while they're trying to survive a war?'

'And since they'd have to pay anyway once we found the clone center for them . . . '

'Exactly,' Karrde nodded. 'We can consider this merely a prepayment for work about to be rendered.'

'Just as well they won't know about it until it's over,' Gillespee said dryly. 'Question is, can Ghent pull it off?'

'Easily,' Karrde assured him. 'Particularly since he's inside the Imperial Palace on Coruscant at the moment. I was planning to head that way soon to pick up Mara anyway; I'll simply have him slice into some sector fleet's records and write us in.'

Gillespee exhaled noisily. 'It's got possibilities – I'll give it that much. Don't know if it'll be enough to get the others back on board, though.'

'Then we'll just have to ask them,' Karrde said, stepping back to his desk. 'Invitations for, say, four days from now?'

Gillespee shrugged. 'Give it a try. What have you got to lose?'

Karrde sobered. 'With Grand Admiral Thrawn,' he reminded the other, 'that's not a question to ever ask lightly.'

The evening breezes moved through the crumbling walls and stone columns of the ruined fortress, occasionally whistling softly as it found its way through a small hole or crevice. Sitting with his back to one of the pillars, Karrde sipped at his cup and watched the last sliver of the sun disappear below the horizon. On the plain below, the long shadows stretching across the scarred ground were beginning to fade as the coming darkness of night began its inexorable move across the landscape.

All in all, rather symbolic of the way this galactic war had finally caught up with Karrde himself.

He took another sip from his cup, marveling once again at this whole absurd situation. Here he was: an intelligent, calculating, appropriately selfish smuggler who'd made a successful career out of keeping his distance from galactic politics. A smuggler, moreover, who'd sworn explicitly to keep his people out of this particular war. And yet, somehow, here he was, squarely in the middle of it.

And not only in the middle of it, but trying his best to drag other smugglers in after him.

· He shook his head in vague annoyance. This exact same thing, he knew, had happened to Han Solo sometime around the Big Yavin battle. He could remember being highly amused by Solo's gradual entanglement in the Rebel Alliance's nets of duty and responsibility. Looking at it from the inside of the net, the whole thing wasn't nearly so entertaining.

From across the battered courtyard came the faint sound of crunching gravel. Karrde turned to look at the line of stone pillars in that direction, his hand dropping to his blaster. No-one else was supposed to be here at the moment. 'Sturm?' he called softly. 'Drang?'

The familiar cackling/purr came in response, and Karrde let out a quiet sigh of relief. 'Over here,' he called to the animal. 'Come on – over here.'

The order was unnecessary. The vornskr was already loping around the pillars toward him, its muzzle low to the ground, the stub of its truncated whip tail wagging madly behind him. Probably Drang, Karrde decided: he was the more sociable of the two, and Sturm had a tendency to dawdle over his meals.

The vornskr skidded to a halt beside him, giving another of his strange cackle/purrs – a rather mournful one this time – as he pressed his muzzle up into Karrde's outstretched palm. It was Drang, all right. 'Yes, it's very quiet,' Karrde told him, running his hand back up across the animal's face and around to scratch at the sensitive skin behind his ears. 'But the others will be back soon. They've just gone out to check on the other ships.'

Drang gave another mournful cackle/purr and dropped into a half-crouch beside Karrde's chair, staring alertly out over the empty plain below. But whatever he was looking for, he didn't find it, and after a moment he growled deep in his throat and lowered his muzzle to rest on the stone. His ears twitched once, as if straining to hear a sound that wasn't there, and then they, too, folded back down.

'It's quiet down there, too,' Karrde agreed soberly, stroking the vornskr's fur. 'What do you suppose happened here?'

Drang didn't answer. Karrde gazed down at the vornskr's lean, muscled back, wondering yet again about these strange predators he'd so casually – perhaps even arrogantly – decided to make pets of. Wondering if he'd have thought twice about doing so if he'd realized that he was dealing with possibly the only animals in the galaxy who hunted via the Force.

It was a preposterous conclusion, on the face of it. Force sensitivity itself wasn't unheard of, certainly – the Gotal had a fairly useless form of it, and there were persistent rumors about the Duinuogwuin as well, to name just two. But all those who had such sensitivity were sentient creatures, with the high levels of intelligence and self-awareness that that implied. For nonsentient animals to use the Force this way was something new.

But it was a conclusion that the events of the past few months had forced him to. There had been his pets' unexpected reaction to Luke Skywalker at Karrde's Myrkr base. There'd been the similar and, again, previously unseen reaction to Mara aboard the *Wild Karrde*, just before the hunch she'd had that had saved them from that Imperial Interdictor Cruiser. There'd been the far more vicious reaction of the wild vornskrs toward both Mara and Skywalker during their three-day trek through the Myrkr forests.

Skywalker was a Jedi. Mara had shown some decidedly Jedi-like talents. And perhaps even more telling, the existence of the bizarre Force-empty bubbles created by Myrkr's ysalamiri could finally be explained if they were simply a form of defense or camouflage against predators.

Abruptly Drang's head snapped up, his ears stiffening as

he twisted halfway around. Karrde strained his ears . . . and a few seconds later he heard the faint sounds of the returning shuttle. 'It's all right,' he assured the vornskr. 'It's just Chin and the others, back from the ship.'

Drang held the pose a moment longer. Then, as if deciding to take Karrde's word for it, he turned and laid his head back down again. Looking out over a plain that, if Karrde's suspicion was right, was more silent even for him than it was for Karrde. 'Don't worry,' he soothed the animal, scratching again behind his ears. 'We'll be out of here soon. And I promise that the next place we go will have plenty of other life around for you to listen to.'

The vornskr's ears twitched, but that might have been just the scratching. Taking one last look at the fading colors of sunset, Karrde stood up, resettling his gun belt across his hips. There was no particular reason to go in yet, of course. The invitations had been written, encrypted, and transmitted, and for now there was nothing to do except wait for the replies. But suddenly it felt lonely out here. Much lonelier than it had a few minutes ago. 'Come on, Drang,' he said, reaching down for one last pat. 'Time to go in.'

The shuttle settled to the floor of the *Chimaera*'s hangar bay, release valves hissing over the heads of the stormtroopers moving purposefully into escort position around the lowering ramp. Pellaeon stayed where he was beside Thrawn, grimacing at the smell of the skid gases and wishing he knew what in the Empire the Grand Admiral was up to this time.

Whatever it was, he had a bad feeling that he wasn't going to like it. Thrawn could talk all he liked about how predictable these smugglers were; and maybe to him they were. But Pellaeon had had his own share of dealings with this sort of fringe scum, and he'd never yet seen a deal that hadn't gone sour one way or the other.

And none of *those* deals had started from the sheer audacity of an attack on an Imperial shipyard.

The ramp finished its descent and locked in place. The stormtrooper commander peered up into the shuttle and nodded . . . and, flanked by two black-clad fleet troopers, the prisoner descended to the deck.

'Ah – Captain Mazzic,' Thrawn said smoothly as the stormtroopers fell into escort positions around him. 'Welcome to the *Chimaera*. I apologize for this rather theatrical summons and any problems it may have created in your business scheduling. But there are certain matters that cannot be discussed other than face-to-face.'

'You're very funny,' Mazzic snarled. A marked contrast, Pellaeon thought, to the suave, sophisticated ladies' man that had been profiled in Intelligence's files. But then, the knowledge that one was facing an Imperial interrogation was enough to strip the civilized polish from any man. 'How did you find me?'

'Come now, Captain,' Thrawn admonished him calmly. 'Did you seriously think you could hide from me if I wanted you found?'

'Karrde managed it,' Mazzic shot back. Trying hard to put up a good front; but the manacled hands were working nervously at each other. 'You still haven't got him, have you?'

'Karrde's time will come,' Thrawn told him, his voice still calm but noticeably cooler. 'But we're not talking about Karrde. We're talking about you.'

'Yes, and I'm sure you're looking forward to it,' Mazzic growled, waving his manacled hands. 'Let's get it over with.'

Thrawn's eyebrows lifted slightly. 'You misunderstand, Captain. You're not here for punishment. You're here because I wanted to clear the air between us.'

Mazzic paused in midbluster. 'What are you talking about?' he asked suspiciously.

'I'm talking about the recent incident at the Bilbringi shipyards,' Thrawn said. 'No, don't deny it – I know it was you and Ellor who destroyed that unfinished Star Destroyer. And normally the Empire would exact an extremely high price for such an act. However, under these particular circumstances, I'm prepared to let it go.'

Mazzic stared at him. 'I don't understand.'

'It's very simple, Captain.' Thrawn gestured, and one of

Mazzic's escort began removing his restraints. 'Your attack on Bilbringi was in revenge for a similar attack against a smugglers' meeting you attended on Trogan. All well and good; except that neither I nor any senior Imperial officer authorized that attack. In fact, the garrison commander had explicit orders to leave your meeting alone.'

Mazzic snorted. 'You expect me to believe that?'

Thrawn's eyes glittered. 'Would you rather believe I was so incompetent that I allowed an inadequate field force to be sent on a mission?' he bit out.

Mazzic eyed him, still hostile but starting to look a little thoughtful, as well. 'I always thought we got away too easily,' he muttered.

'Then we understand each other,' Thrawn said, his voice calm again. 'And the matter is settled. The shuttle has orders to take you back to your base.' He smiled faintly. 'Or, rather, to the backup base your ship and crew will have fled to by now on Lelmra. Again, my apologies for the inconvenience.'

Mazzic's eyes darted around the hangar bay, his expression halfway between suspicion that this was a trick and an almost painfully eager hope that it wasn't. 'And I'm just supposed to believe you?' he demanded.

'You're welcome to believe anything you wish,' Thrawn said. 'But remember that I had you in my hand . . . and that I let you go. Good day, Captain.'

He started to turn away. 'So who were they?' Mazzic called after him. 'If they weren't Imperial troops, I mean?'

Thrawn turned back to face him. 'They were indeed Imperial troops,' he said. 'Our inquiries are still incomplete, but at the moment it appears that Lieutenant Kosk and his men were attempting to make a little extra money on the side.'

Mazzic stared. 'Someone *hired* them to hit us? Imperial troops?'

'Even Imperial troops are not always immune to the lure of bribery,' Thrawn said, his voice dark with an excellent imitation of bitter contempt. 'In this case, they paid for their treason with their lives. Be assured that the person or persons responsible will pay a similar price.'

'You know who it was?' Mazzic demanded.

'I believe I know,' Thrawn said. 'As yet, I have no proof.'

'Give me a hint.'

Thrawn smiled sardonically. 'Form your own hints, Captain. Good day.'

He turned and strode back toward the archway leading to the service and prep areas. Pellaeon waited long enough to watch Mazzic and his escort turn and start back up into the shuttle, then hurried to join him. 'Do you think you gave him enough, Admiral?' he asked quietly.

'It won't matter, Captain,' Thrawn assured him. 'We've given him all that's necessary; and if Mazzic himself isn't clever enough to finger Karrde, one of the other smuggler chiefs will be. In any case, it's always better to offer too little rather than too much. Some people automatically distrust free information.'

Behind them, the shuttle lifted from the deck and swung back around into space . . . and from the archway ahead a grinning figure emerged. 'Nicely done, Admiral,' Niles Ferrier said, shifting his cigarra to the other side of his mouth. 'You got him all squirmy and then tossed him back. He'll be thinking about that for a long time.'

'Thank you, Ferrier,' Thrawn said dryly. 'Your approval means so very much to me.'

For a second the ship thief's grin seemed to slip. Then, apparently, he decided to take the comment at face value. 'OK,' he said. 'So what's our next move?'

Thrawn's eyes flashed at the *our*, but he let it go. 'Karrde sent out a series of transmissions last night, one of which we intercepted,' he said. 'We're still decrypting it, but it can only be a call for another meeting. Once we have the location and time, they'll be provided to you.'

'And I'll go and help Mazzic finger Karrde,' Ferrier nodded.

'You'll do nothing of the sort,' Thrawn said sharply. 'You will sit in a corner and keep your mouth shut.'

Ferrier seemed to shrink back. 'OK. Sure.'

Thrawn held his gaze another moment. 'What you *will* do,' he continued at last, 'is to make certain that a certain data card is placed into Karrde's possession. Preferably in the office aboard his ship – that will be where Mazzic will probably look first.'

He motioned, and an officer stepped forward and handed Ferrier a data card. 'Ah,' Ferrier said slyly as he took it. 'Yeah, I get it. The record of Karrde's deal with this Lieutenant Kosk, huh?'

'Correct,' Thrawn said. 'That, plus the supporting evidence we've already inserted into Kosk's own personal records should leave no doubt that Karrde has been manipulating the other smugglers. I expect that to be more than adequate.'

'Yeah, they're a pretty nasty bunch, all right.' Ferrier turned the data card over in his hand, chewing on his cigarra. 'OK. So all I gotta do is get aboard the *Wild Karrde*—'

He broke off at the look on Thrawn's face. 'No,' the Grand Admiral said quietly. 'On the contrary, you'll stay as far away from his ship and private ground facilities as possible. In fact, you will never allow yourself to be alone while you're at his base.'

Ferrier blinked in surprise. 'Yeah, but . . .' Helplessly, he held up the data card.

Beside him, Pellaeon felt Thrawn's sigh of strained patience. 'Your Defel will be the one to plant the data card aboard the *Wild Karrde*.'

Ferrier's face cleared. 'Oh, yeah. Yeah. He can probably slip in and out without anyone even noticing.'

'He had better,' Thrawn warned; and suddenly his voice was icy cold. 'Because I haven't forgotten your role in the deaths of Lieutenant Kosk and his men. You owe the Empire, Ferrier. And that debt will be paid.'

Behind his beard, Ferrier's face had gone a little pale. 'I got it, Admiral.'

'Good,' Thrawn said. 'You'll remain on your ship until Decrypt obtains the location of Karrde's meeting for you. After that, you'll be on your own.'

'Sure,' Ferrier said, stuffing the data card into his tunic. 'So. After they take care of Karrde, what do I do?'

'You'll be free to go about your business,' Thrawn said. 'When I want you again, I'll let you know.'

Ferrier's lip twitched. 'Sure,' he repeated.

And on his face, Pellaeon saw that he was slowly starting to realize just how deep his debt to the Empire really was.

CHAPTER 16

The planet was green and blue and mottled white, pretty much like all the other planets Han had dropped in on over the years. With the minor exception that this one didn't have a name.

Or spaceports. Or orbit facilities. Or cities, power plants, or other ships. Or much of anything else.

'That's it, huh?' he asked Mara.

She didn't answer. Han looked over and found her staring at the planet hanging out there in front of them. 'Well, is it or isn't it?' he prompted.

'It is,' she said, her voice strangely hollow. 'We're here.'

'Good,' Han said, still frowning at her. 'Great. You going to tell us where this mountain is? Or are we just going to fly around and see where we draw fire from?'

Mara seemed to shake herself. 'It's about halfway between the equator and the north pole,' she said. 'Near the eastern edge of the main continent. A single mountain, rising out of forest and grassland.'

'OK,' Han said, feeding in the information and hoping the sensors wouldn't loop out and fail on him. Mara had made enough snide comments about the *Falcon* as it was.

Behind him, the cockpit door slid open, and Lando and Chewbacca came in. 'How about it?' Lando asked. 'We there?'

'We're there,' Mara said before Han could answer.

Chewbacca rumbled a question. 'No, seems to be a real low-tech place,' Han shook his head. 'No power sources or transmissions anywhere.'

'Military bases?' Lando asked.

'If they're there, I can't find 'em,' Han said.

'Interesting,' Lando murmured, peering over Mara's shoulder. 'I wouldn't have pegged the Grand Admiral as being the trusting sort.'

'The place was designed to be a private storehouse,' Mara reminded him tartly. 'Not a display ad for Imperial hardware. There weren't any garrisons or command centers scattered around for Thrawn to have moved into.'

'So whatever he's got will be stashed inside the mountain?' Han asked.

'Plus probably a few ground patrols just outside,' Mara said. 'But they won't have any fighter squadrons or heavy weaponry to throw at us.'

'That'll be a nice change,' Lando said wryly.

'Unless Thrawn decided to put up a couple of garrisons on his own,' Han pointed out. 'You and Chewie'd better charge up the quads, just in case.'

'Right.'

The two of them left. Han shifted into a general approach vector, then keyed for a sensor search. 'Trouble?' Mara asked.

'Probably not,' Han assured her, watching the displays. But there was nothing showing anywhere around them. 'A couple of times on the way in I thought I spotted something hanging around back there.'

'Calrissian thought he saw something when we changed course at Obroa-skai, too,' Mara said, peering down at the display. 'Could be something with a really good sensor stealth mode.'

'Or just a glitch,' Han said. 'The Fabritech's been giving us trouble lately.'

Mara craned her neck to look out to starboard. 'Could someone have followed us here from Coruscant?'

'Who knew we were coming?' Han countered. No, there was nothing there. Must have been his imagination. 'How much of this private storehouse did you see?'

Slowly, Mara turned back to face forward, not looking all

that convinced. 'Not much more than the route between the entrance and the throne room at the top,' she said. 'But I know where the Spaarti cylinder is.'

'How about the power generators?'

'I never actually saw them,' she said. 'But I remember hearing that the cooling system pulls in water from a river flowing down the northeastern slope of the mountain. They're probably somewhere on that side.'

Han chewed at his lip. 'And the main entrance is on the southwest side.'

'The *only* entrance,' she corrected. 'There's just the one way in or out.'

'I've heard that before.'

'This time it's true,' she retorted.

Han shrugged. 'OK,' he said. There was no point in arguing about it. Not until they'd looked the place over, anyway.

The cockpit door slid open, and he glanced over his shoulder to see Luke come in. 'We're here, kid,' he said.

'I know,' Luke said, moving forward to stand behind Mara. 'Mara told me.'

Han threw a look at Mara. Near as he could tell, she'd spent the whole trip avoiding Luke, which wasn't all that easy on a ship the size of the *Falcon*. Luke had returned the favor by staying out of her way, which wasn't much easier. 'She did, huh?'

'It's all right,' Luke assured him, gazing out at the planet ahead. 'So that's Wayland.'

'That's Wayland,' Mara said shortly, unstrapping and brushing past Luke. 'I'll be in back,' she said over her shoulder, and left.

'You two work so well together,' Han commented as the cockpit door slid shut behind her.

'Actually, we do,' Luke said, sliding into the copilot's seat Mara had just vacated. 'You should have seen us aboard the *Chimaera* when we went in to rescue Karrde. She's a good person to have at your side.'

Han threw him a sideways look. 'Except when she wants to slide a knife in it.'

236

'I'm willing to take my chances.' Luke smiled. 'Must be one of those crazy Jedi things.'

'This isn't funny, Luke,' Han growled. 'She hasn't given up on killing you, you know. She told Leia that back on Coruscant.'

'Which tells me that she really doesn't want to do it,' Luke countered. 'People don't usually go around announcing murder plans in advance. Especially not to the victim's family.'

'You willing to bet your life on that?'

Luke shrugged fractionally. 'I already have.'

The *Falcon* was skimming along the outer atmosphere now, and the computer had finally identified a probable location for Mount Tantiss. 'Well, if you ask me, this isn't a good time to be running short odds,' he told Luke, giving the sensor map a quick study. A straight-in southern approach, he decided – that would give them forest cover for both the landing and the overland trip.

'You have any suggestions?' Luke asked.

'Yeah, I've got one,' Han said, changing course toward the distant mountain. 'We leave her with the *Falcon* at the landing site.'

'Alive?'

At other times in his life, Han reflected, it wouldn't necessarily have been a ridiculous question. 'Of course alive,' he said stiffly. 'There are a lot of ways to keep her from getting into trouble.'

'You really think she'd agree to stay behind?'

'No-one said we had to ask her.'

Luke shook his head. 'We can't do that, Han. She needs to see this through.'

'Which part of it?' Han growled. 'Hitting the clone factory, or trying to kill you?'

'I don't know,' Luke said quietly. 'Maybe both.'

Han had never liked forests very much before joining the Rebel Alliance. Which wasn't to say he'd *dis*liked them, either. Forests were simply not something the average smuggler thought about very much. Most of the time you picked up and delivered in grimy little spaceports like Mos Eisley or Abregado-rae; and on the rare occasion where you met in a forest, you let the customer watch the forest while you watched the customer. As a result, Han had wound up with a vague sort of assumption that one forest was pretty much like another.

His stint with the Alliance had changed all that. What with Endor, Corstris, Fedje, and a dozen more, he'd learned the hard way that each forest was different, with its own array of plants, animal life, and general all-around headaches for the casual visitor. Just one of many subjects the Alliance had taught him more about than he'd really wanted to know.

Wayland's forest fit the pattern perfectly; and the first headache proved to be how to get the *Falcon* down through the dense upper leaf canopy without leaving a hole any wandering Imperial TIE pilot would have to be asleep to miss. They'd first had to find a gap – in this case made by a fallen tree – and then he'd had to basically run the ship in on its side, a lot trickier maneuver in a planetary gravity well than it was out in an asteroid field. The secondary canopy, which he didn't find out about until he was most of the way through the first, was the second headache, and he tore the tops off a line of those shorter trees before he got the *Falcon* stabilized and down, crunching a lot of underbrush in the process.

'Nice landing,' Lando commented dryly, rubbing his shoulder beneath the restraint strap as Han shut down the repulsorlifts.

'At least the sensor dish is still there,' Han said pointedly.

Lando winced. 'You're never going to let that go, are you?'

Han shrugged, keying in the life-form algorithms. Time to find out what was out there. 'You said you wouldn't get a scratch on her,' he reminded the other.

'Fine,' Lando grumped. 'Next time, *I'll* destroy the energy field generator and *you* can fly her down the Death Star's throat.'

Which wasn't all that funny. If the Empire got enough of its old resources back again, Thrawn just might try to build another of the blasted things.

'We're ready back here,' Luke said, poking his head into the cockpit. 'How's it look?'

'Not too bad,' Han said, reading off the display. 'Got a bunch of animals out there, but they're keeping their distance.'

'How big are these animals?' Lando asked, leaning over Han's shoulder to have a look at the display.

'And how many to a bunch?' Luke added.

'About fifteen,' Han told him. 'Nothing we can't handle if we need to. Let's go take a look.'

Mara and Chewbacca were waiting at the hatchway with Artoo and Threepio, the latter keeping his mouth shut for a change. 'Chewie and me'll go first,' Han told them, drawing his blaster. 'The rest of you stay sharp up here.'

He punched the controls, and the hatchway slid open as the entry ramp lowered, settling into the dead leaves with a muffled crunch. Trying to watch all directions at once, Han started down.

He spotted the first of the animals before he'd reached the bottom of the ramp: gray, with a freckling of white across its back, maybe two meters from nose to tail tuft. It was crouched at the base of a tree limb, its beady little eyes following him as he walked. And if its teeth and claws were anything to go by, it was definitely a predator.

Beside him, Chewbacca rumbled softly. 'Yeah, I see it,' Han muttered back. 'There are another fourteen out there somewhere, too.'

The Wookiee growled again, gesturing. 'You're right,' Han agreed slowly, eyeing the predator. 'It does kind of look familiar. Like those panthac things from Mantessa, maybe?'

Chewbacca considered, then growled a negative. 'Well, we'll figure it out later,' Han decided. 'Luke?'

'Right here,' Luke's voice came down from the hatchway.

'You and Mara start bringing the equipment down,' Han ordered, watching the predator closely. The sound of conversation didn't seem to be bothering it any. 'Start with the speeder bikes. Lando, you're high cover. Stay sharp.'

'Right,' Lando said.

From above came a handful of pops and clicks as the

transport restraints around the first two speeder bikes were knocked off, then the faint hum as the repulsorlifts were activated.

And with a sudden violent crackling of leaves and branches, the predator leaped.

'Chewie!' was all Han had time to shout before the animal was on top of him. He fired, the blaster bolt catching it square in the torso, and managed to duck as the carcass shot past his head. Chewbacca was roaring Wookiee battle cries, swinging his bowcaster around and firing again and again as more of the predators charged at them from out of the trees. From the hatchway someone shouted something and another shot flashed out.

And out of the corner of his eye, moving much too fast to avoid, Han saw a set of claws coming his direction.

He threw up his forearm across his face, ducking his head back as far out of the way as he could. An instant later he was knocked back off his feet as the predator slammed full-tilt into him. A moment of pressure and lancing pain as the claws dug through his camouflage jacket—

And then, suddenly, the weight was gone. He lowered his arm, just in time to see the predator bound on to the ramp and prepare for a spring into the *Falcon*. He twisted around and fired, just as a shot from inside the ship also caught it.

Chewbacca snarled a warning. Still on his back, Han swung around, to see three more of the animals bounding across the ground toward him. He dropped one with a pair of quick shots, and was trying to swing his blaster around to target the second when a pair of black-booted feet hit the ground just in front of him. The animals leaped upward into a blurred line of brilliant green and crashed to the ground.

Rolling over, Han scrambled back to his feet and looked around. Luke was standing in a half-crouch in front of him, lightsaber humming in ready position. On the other side of the ramp, Chewbacca was still on his feet with three of the speckled animals lying dead around him.

Han looked down at the dead predator beside him. Now that he had a good, close look at the thing . . .

'Watch out – there are three more over there,' Luke warned.

Han looked. Two of the animals were visible, crouched low down in the trees. 'They won't bother us. Any of them get into the ship?'

'Not very far into it,' Luke told him. 'What did you do that set them off?'

'We didn't do anything,' Han said, holstering his blaster. 'It was you and Mara turning on the speeder bikes.'

Chewbacca rumbled with sudden recognition. 'You got it, pal,' Han nodded. 'That's where we tangled with them, all right.'

'What are they?' Luke asked.

'They're called garrals,' Mara said from the ramp. Crouching down, her own blaster still drawn, she was peering at the carcasses scattered around Chewbacca. 'The Empire used to use them as watchdogs, usually near heavily wooded frontier garrisons where probe droid pickets weren't practical. There's something in the ultrasonic signature of a repulsorlift that's supposed to sound like one of their prey animals. Draws them like a magnet.'

'So that's why they were sitting here waiting for us,' Luke said, closing down his lightsaber but keeping it handy.

'They can hear a ship-sized repulsorlift coming in from kilometers away,' Mara said. Jumping down off the side of the ramp, she dropped to one knee beside one of the dead garrals and dug her free hand into the fur at its neck. 'Which means that if they've been radiotagged, the controllers in Mount Tantiss know we're here.'

'Great,' Han muttered, crouching down beside the dead garral at his feet. 'What do we look for, a collar?'

'Probably,' Mara said. 'Check around the legs, too.'

It took a few anxious minutes, but in the end they confirmed that none of the dead predators had been tagged.

'Must be descendants of the group they brought in to protect the mountain,' Lando said.

'Or else this is where they came from originally,' Mara said. 'I never saw their home planet listed.'

'It's trouble either way,' Han said, shoving the last carcass off the *Falcon*'s ramp to crunch into the leaf cover below. 'If we can't use the speeder bikes, it means we're walking.'

From up above came a low electronic whistle. 'Pardon me, sir,' Threepio asked. 'Does that also apply to Artoo and me?'

'Unless you've learned how to fly,' Han said.

'Well – sir – it occurs to me that Artoo in particular isn't really equipped for this sort of forest travel,' Threepio pointed out primly. 'If the cargo plat can't be used, perhaps other arrangements can be made.'

'The arrangement is that you walk like the rest of us,' Han said shortly. Getting into a long discussion with Threepio wasn't how he'd been planning to spend his day. 'You did it on Endor; you can do it here.'

'We didn't have nearly as far to go on Endor,' Luke reminded him quietly. 'We must be about two weeks' walk from the mountain here.'

'It's not that bad,' Han said, doing a quick estimate. It wasn't that bad, but it was bad enough. 'Eight or nine days, tops. Maybe a couple more if we run into trouble.'

'Oh, we'll run into trouble, all right,' Mara said sourly, sitting down on the ramp and dropping her blaster into her lap. 'Trust me on that one.'

'You don't expect the natives to be hospitable?' Lando asked.

'I expect them to welcome us with open crossbows,' Mara retorted. 'There are two different native species here, the Psadans and the Myneyrshi. Neither of them had any great love of humans even before the Empire moved in on Mount Tantiss.'

'Well, at least they won't be on the Empire's side,' Lando said.

'That's not likely to be a lot of comfort,' Mara growled. 'And whatever trouble they don't give us, the usual range of predators will. We'll be lucky to make it in twelve or thirteen days, not eight or nine.'

Han looked out at the forest, and as he did, something caught his eye. Something more than a little disturbing . . . 'So we'll figure on twelve,' he said. Suddenly it was critical

242

that they make tracks away from here. 'Let's get to it. Lando, Mara, you get the equipment packs sorted out for carrying. Chewie, go pull all the ration boxes out of the survival packs – that ought to do us for extra food. Luke, you and the droids head that way' – he pointed – 'and see what you can find in the way of a path. Maybe a dry creek bed – we ought to be close enough to the mountain to have some of those around.'

'Certainly, sir,' Threepio said brightly, starting down the ramp. 'Come, Artoo.'

There was a muttering of acknowledgement and the others headed into the ship. Han started toward the ramp; stopped as Luke put a hand on his arm. 'What's wrong?' he asked quietly.

Han jerked his head back toward the forest. 'Those garrals that were watching us? They're gone.'

Luke looked back. 'Did they all leave together?'

'I don't know. I didn't see them go.'

Luke fingered his lightsaber. 'You think it's an Imperial patrol?'

'Or else a flock of those prey animals Mara mentioned. You getting anything?'

Luke took a deep breath, held it a moment, then slowly let it out. 'I don't sense anyone else nearby,' he said. 'But they could just be out of range. You think we should abort the mission?'

Han shook his head. 'If we do, we'll lose our best shot at the place. Once they know we've found their clone factory, there won't be any point in pretending they're just some overlooked backwoods system any more. By the time we got back with a strike force, they'd have a couple of Star Destroyer fleets waiting for us.'

Luke grimaced. 'I suppose so. And you're right – if they tracked the *Falcon* in, the sooner we get away from it the better. Are you going to send the coordinates back to Coruscant before we go?'

'I don't know.' Han looked up at the *Falcon* looming above him, trying not to think about the Imperials getting their grubby little hands on it again. 'If that's a patrol out there, we'll never get the transmitter tuned tight enough to slide a message past them. Not the way it's been acting up lately.'

Luke glanced up, too. 'Sounds risky,' he said. 'If we get into trouble, they won't have any idea where to send a follow-up strike force.'

'Yeah, well, if we transmit through an Imperial patrol, I can guarantee that trouble,' Han growled. 'I'm open to suggestions.'

'How about if I stay behind for a few hours?' Luke suggested. 'If no patrols have shown up by then, it should be safe to transmit.'

'Forget it,' Han shook his head. 'You'd have to travel alone, and there's a better-than-even chance you wouldn't even be able to find us.'

'I'm willing to risk it.'

'I'm not,' Han said bluntly. 'And besides, every time you go off alone you wind up getting me in trouble.'

Luke smiled ruefully. 'It does seem that way sometimes.'

'Bet on it,' Han told him. 'Come on, we're wasting time. Get out there and find us a path.'

'All right,' Luke said with a sigh. But he didn't sound all that upset. Maybe he'd known all along that it wasn't a very smart idea. 'Come on, Threepio, Artoo. Let's go.'

The first hour was the hardest. The vague, pathlike trail Artoo had found dead-ended into a mass of thornbushes after less than a hundred meters, forcing them to push a path of their own through the dense undergrowth. In the process they disturbed more than plant life, and wound up spending several tense minutes shooting at a nest of six-legged, half-meter-long creatures that swarmed out biting and clawing at them. Fortunately, the claws and teeth were designed for much smaller game, and aside from a nicely matched set of tooth dents in Threepio's left leg, no-one suffered any damage before they could be driven away. Threepio moaned more about that than either the incident or the damage really deserved, the noise possibly attracting the brown-scaled animal that attacked a few minutes later. Han's quick blaster shot failed to stop the animal, and Luke had to use his lightsaber to cut it off Threepio's arm. The droid was even more inclined to moan after that; and Han was threatening to shut him down and leave him for the scavengers when they unexpectedly hit one of the dry creek beds they'd been hoping to find. With the easier terrain, and with no further animal attacks to slow them down, they made much better speed, and by the time the leaf canopy overhead began to darken with nightfall they'd made nearly ten kilometers.

'Brings back such wonderful memories, doesn't it?' Mara commented sarcastically as she got out of her backpack and dropped it beside one of the small bushes lining the creek bed.

'Just like back on Myrkr,' Luke agreed, using his lightsaber to cut away another of the thornbushes they'd become all too familiar with in the past few hours. 'You know, I never did find out what happened after we left.'

'About what you'd expect,' Mara told him. 'We cleared out about two steps ahead of Thrawn's AT-ATs. And then nearly got caught anyway when Karrde insisted on hanging around to watch.'

'Is that why you're helping us?' he asked her. 'Because Thrawn's put a death mark on Karrde?'

'Let's get one thing clear right now, Skywalker,' she growled. 'I work for Karrde, and Karrde has already said that we're staying neutral in this war of yours. The only reason I'm here is because I know a little about the Clone Wars era and don't want to see a bunch of cold-faced duplicates trying to overrun the galaxy again. The only reason *you're* here is that I can't shut the place down by myself.'

'I understand,' Luke said, cutting a second thornbush and closing down his lightsaber. Reaching out with the Force, he lifted the two bushes off the ground and lowered them into the creek bed. 'Well, it won't stop anything that's really determined to get at us,' he decided, studying the makeshift barrier. 'But it should at least slow them down.'

'For whatever that's worth,' Mara said, pulling out a ration bar and stripping off the wrapping. 'Let's just hope this isn't one of those lucky places where all the really big predators come out at night.'

'Hopefully, Artoo's sensors can spot them before they get too close,' Luke told her. Igniting his lightsaber again, he cut two more thornbushes for good measure.

And he was preparing to shut it down when he caught the subtle change in Mara's sense. He turned, to find her staring at his lightsaber, ration bar forgotten in her hand, a strangely haunted expression on her face. 'Mara?' he asked. 'You all right?'

Her gaze shifted almost guiltily away from him. 'Sure,' she muttered. 'I'm fine.' Throwing him a quick glare, she bit viciously into her ration bar.

'OK.' Closing down the lightsaber, Luke used the Force to move the newly cut thornbushes into place on top of the others. Still not much of a barrier, he decided. Maybe if he stretched a few of those vines between the trees . . .

'Skywalker.'

He turned. 'Yes?'

Mara was looking up at him. 'I have to ask,' she said quietly. 'You're the only one who knows. How did the Emperor die?'

For a moment Luke studied her face. Even in the fading light he could see the ache in her eyes; the bitter memories of the luxuriant life and glittering future that had been snatched away from her at Endor. But alongside the ache was an equally strong determination. However badly this might hurt, she truly did want to hear it. 'The Emperor was trying to turn me to the dark side,' he told her, long-buried memories of his own surging painfully back again. It had nearly been him, not the Emperor, who'd died that day. 'He almost succeeded. I'd taken one swing at him, and wound up fighting with Vader instead. I guess he thought that if I killed Vader in anger, I'd be opened to him through the dark side.'

'And so instead you ganged up on him,' she accused, her eyes flashing with sudden anger. 'You turned on him – both of you—'

'Wait a minute,' Luke protested. 'I didn't attack him. Not after that first swing.'

'What are you talking about?' she demanded. 'I saw you do it. Both of you moved in against him with your lightsabers. I saw you do it.'

Luke stared at her . . . and suddenly he understood. Mara Jade, the Emperor's Hand, who could hear his voice from anywhere in the galaxy. She'd been in contact with her master at the moment of his death, and had seen it all.

Except that, somehow, she'd gotten it wrong.

'I didn't move against him, Mara,' he told her. 'He was about to kill me when Vader picked him up and threw him down an open shaft. I couldn't have done anything even if I'd wanted to – I was still half paralyzed from the lightning bolts he'd hit me with.'

'What do you mean, if you'd wanted to?' Mara said scornfully. 'That was the whole reason you went aboard the Death Star in the first place, wasn't it?'

Luke shook his head. 'No. I went there to try and turn Vader away from the dark side.'

Mara turned away, and Luke could sense the turmoil within her. 'Why should I believe you?' she demanded at last.

'Why should I lie?' he countered. 'It doesn't change the fact that if I hadn't been there Vader wouldn't have turned on him. In that sense, I'm probably still responsible for his death.'

'That's right, you are,' Mara agreed harshly. But there was a moment of hesitation before she said it. 'And I won't forget it.'

Luke nodded silently, and waited for her to say more. But she didn't, and after a minute he turned back to the thorn-bushes. 'I'd go easy on those things if I were you,' Mara said from behind him, her voice cool and under control again. 'You don't want to trap us in an area this size if something big comes over the bushes.'

'Good point,' Luke said, understanding both the words and the meaning beneath them. There was a job to do, and until that job was finished, she still needed Luke alive.

At which point, she would have to face the destiny that had been prepared for her. Or would have to choose a new one.

Closing down his lightsaber, he stepped past Mara to where the others were busy setting up camp. Time to check on the droids.

CHAPTER 17

The door to the Assemblage chamber slid open and a small flood of beings and droids began pouring out into the Grand Corridor, chattering among themselves in the usual spectrum of different languages. Glancing at Winter as the two of them walked toward the crowd, Leia nodded.

It was show time.

'Anything else come in that I should know about?' she asked as they passed along the edge of the flow.

'There was an unusual follow-up to the Pantolomin report,' Winter said, her eyes flicking casually around the crowd. 'A bounty hunter there claims to have penetrated the Imperial shipyards at Ord Trasi and is offering to sell us information about their new building program.'

'I've dealt with my share of bounty hunters,' Leia said, trying not to look around the crowd as they passed through it. Winter was watching, and with her perfect memory she would remember everyone who was close enough to overhear their conversation. 'What makes Colonel Derlin think we can trust him?'

'He's not sure we can,' Winter said. 'The smuggler offered what he said was a free sample: the information that there are three Imperial Star Destroyers within a month of completion out there. Colonel Derlin said Wing Commander Harleys is drawing up a plan to confirm that.'

They were out of the Grand Corridor now, following along with the handful of beings who hadn't yet split off toward offices or other conference rooms. 'Sounds dangerous,' Leia said, dutifully running their prepared script out to the end. 'I hope he's not just going to do a fly-by.'

'The report didn't give any details,' Winter said. 'But there was an addendum asking about the possibility of borrowing a freighter from someone who does business with the Empire.'

The last of the officials turned off into a cross corridor, leaving them alone in the hallway with an assortment of techs, assistants, admin personnel, and other low-ranking members of the New Republic government. Leia threw a quick glance at each, decided there was no point in going through another script for their benefit. Looking at Winter, she nodded again, and together the two women headed toward the turbolifts.

They'd needed some place where Ghent could set up shop without word or even rumors of the project leaking out, and a search of the Palace's original blueprints had found them the ideal spot. It was an old backup power cell room, closed down and sealed years earlier, wedged in between the Sector Ordnance/Supply and Starfighter Command offices down on the command floor. Leia had cut a new entrance from a service corridor with her lightsaber; Bel Iblis had helped them run power cables and datalines; and Ghent had set up his decrypting program.

They had everything they needed. Except results.

Ghent was sitting in the room's single chair when they arrived, staring dreamily off into space with his feet propped up on the edge of his decrypter desk. They were both inside, and Winter had closed the door, before he even noticed their presence. 'Oh – hi,' he said, dropping his feet to the floor with a muffled thud.

'Not so loud, please,' Leia reminded him, wincing. The officers working on the other sides of the thin walls would probably ascribe any stray noises to the adjacent offices. But then again, they might not. 'Has General Bel Iblis brought the latest transmissions in yet?' she asked.

'Yeah – about an hour ago,' Ghent nodded, whispering almost inaudibly now. 'I just finished slicing 'em.'

He tapped a key, and a series of decrypted messages came up on the display. Leia stepped up behind his chair, reading down them. Details of upcoming military deployments, what seemed to be verbatim transcriptions of high-level diplomatic conversations, tidbits of idle Palace gossip – as always, Delta Source had covered the whole range from the significant to the trivial.

'There's one of ours,' Winter said, touching a spot on the display.

Leia read the item. An unconfirmed intelligence report from the Bpfassh system, suggesting that the *Chimaera* and its support ships had been spotted near Anchoron. That was one of theirs, all right. 'How many heard that one?' she asked Winter.

'Only forty-seven,' Winter told her, already busy with Ghent's data pad. 'It was just before three yesterday afternoon – during the second Assemblage session – and the Grand Corridor was fairly empty.'

Leia nodded and turned back to the display. By the time Winter had finished her list she'd identified two more of their decoy messages. By the time Winter had finished those, she'd found another five.

'Looks like that's it,' she said as Winter handed Ghent her first three lists and got to work on the others. 'Let's go ahead and run these through your sifter.'

'OK,' Ghent said, throwing one last look of awe at Winter before turning back to his console. Three days into this scheme, he still hadn't gotten over the way she could remember every single detail of fifty separate one-minute conversations. 'OK, let's see. Correlations . . . OK. We're down to a hundred twenty-seven possibilities. Mostly techs and admin types, looks like. Some off-world diplomats, too.'

Leia shook her head. 'None of those are likely to have access to all of this information,' she said, waving at the decrypt display. 'It has to be someone considerably higher up the command structure—'

'Wait a minute,' Ghent interrupted, raising a finger. 'You want a big fish; you got one. Councilor Sian Tevv of Sullust.'

Leia frowned at the display. 'That's impossible. He was one of the earliest leaders in the Rebel Alliance. In fact, I think he was the one who brought Nien Nunb and his private raiding squad over to us after the Empire forced them out of Sullust system.'

Ghent shrugged. 'I don't know anything about that. All I know is that he heard all fifteen of those little teasers that wound up on Delta Source's transmitter.'

'It can't be Councilor Tevv,' Winter spoke up absently, still working at the data pad. 'He wasn't present during any of these last six conversations.'

'Maybe one of his aides heard it,' Ghent offered. 'He didn't have to be there personally.'

Winter shook her head. 'No. One of his aides was present, but only for one of these conversations. More importantly, Councilor Tevv *was* present for two conversations the day before yesterday that Delta Source didn't transmit. Nine-fifteen in the morning and two-forty-eight in the afternoon.'

Ghent keyed up the relevant lists. 'You're right,' he confirmed. 'Didn't think about checking things that direction. Guess I'd better work up a better sifter program.'

Behind Leia their makeshift door swung open, and she turned to see Bel Iblis come in. 'Thought I'd find you here,' he nodded to Leia. 'We're about ready to give the Stardust plan its first try, if you want to come and watch.'

The latest scheme to locate the swarm of cloaked asteroids Thrawn had left in orbit around Coruscant. 'Yes, I do,' Leia said. 'Winter, I'll be in the war room when you're finished here.'

'Yes, Your Highness.'

Leia and Bel Iblis left the room and headed single-file down the service corridor. 'Find anything yet?' the general asked over his shoulder.

'Winter's still running yesterday's list,' Leia told him. 'So far we've got around a hundred thirty possibilities.'

Bel Iblis nodded. 'Considering how many of us there are working in the Palace, I'd say that qualifies as progress.'

'Maybe.' She hesitated. 'It's occurred to me that this scheme will only work if Delta Source is a single person. If it's a whole group, we may not be able to weed them out this way.'

'Perhaps,' Bel Iblis agreed. 'But I have a hard time believing we could have that many traitors here. Matter of fact, I still have trouble believing we have even one. I've always thought that Delta Source might be some kind of exotic recording system. Something Security simply hasn't been able to locate yet.'

'I've watched them do counterintelligence sweeps,' Leia said. 'I can't think how they could possibly have missed anything.'

'Unfortunately, neither can I.'

They arrived in the war room, to find General Rieekan and Admiral Drayson standing behind the main command console. 'Princess,' Rieekan greeted her gravely. 'You're just in time.'

Leia looked up at the master visual. An old transport had left the group of ships standing guard in far orbit and was making its careful way down toward the planet. 'How far in is it going to come?' Leia asked.

'We're going to start just above the planetary shield, Councilor,' Drayson told her. 'The postbattle analysis indicates that most of the cloaked asteroids probably wound up in low orbit.'

Leia nodded. And since those would be the ones most likely to sneak through if they opened the shield, it made all the more sense to start there.

Slowly, moving with the tentative awkwardness of a ship under remote control, the transport came closer in. 'All right,' Drayson said. 'Transport One control, cut drive and prepare to dump on my command. Ready . . . dump.'

For a moment nothing happened. Then, abruptly, a cloud of brilliant dust began to billow from the aft end of the transport, swirling around lazily in the ship's wake. 'Keep it coming,' Drayson said. '*Harrier*, stand by negative ion beams.'

'All dust is clear of the transport, Admiral,' one of the officers reported.

'Transport One control, pull her away,' Drayson ordered.

'But slowly,' Bel Iblis murmured. 'We don't want to carve exhaust grooves through the dust.'

Drayson threw an annoyed look back at him. 'Take it nice and slow,' he said grudgingly. 'Do we have any readings yet?'

'Coming in very strong, sir,' the officer at the sensor console reported. 'Between point nine-three and nine-eight reflection on all bands.'

'Good,' Drayson nodded. 'Keep a sharp eye on it. *Harrier?*'

'*Harrier* reports ready, sir,' another officer confirmed.

'Fire negative ion beam,' Drayson ordered. 'Lowest intensity. Let's see how this works.'

Leia peered up at the visual. The shimmering dust particles were beginning to clump together as ions from the departing transport's drive created random electrostatic charges throughout the cloud. Out of the corner of her eye, she saw the hazy line of an ion beam appear on the master tactical display and sweep across the cloud. Charging all the dust particles with the same polarity so that they would repel each other . . . and suddenly the coalescing dust cloud was expanding again, spreading out across the visual display like the opening of some exotic flower.

'Cease fire,' Drayson said. 'Let's see if that does it.'

For a long minute the flower continued to open, and Leia found herself staring intently at the hazy glitter. Unreasonably, of course. Given how much space there was out there, it was highly unlikely that this first dump would happen to be in the path of any of the orbiting asteroids. And even if it was, there still would be nothing for her to see on the visual. Except at the moment before its collapse, the cloaking shield seemed to twist light and sensor beams perfectly around itself, which meant there would be no dark spot cutting visibly through the dust.

'Cloud's starting to break up, Admiral,' the sensor officer reported. 'Dissipation ratio is up to twelve.'

'Solar wind's catching it,' Rieekan muttered.

'As expected,' Drayson reminded him. 'Transport Two control: go ahead and launch.'

A second transport emerged from among the orbiting ships and headed down toward the surface. 'This is definitely the slow way to do this,' Bel Iblis commented quietly.

'Agreed,' Rieekan said. 'I wish they hadn't lost that CGT array of yours out at Svivren. We could sure have used it here.'

Leia nodded. Crystal gravfield traps, originally designed to zoom in on the mass of sensor-stealthed ships from thousands of kilometers away, would be ideal for this job. 'I thought Intelligence had a lead on another one.'

'They've got leads on three,' Rieekan said. 'Problem is, they're all in Imperial space.'

'I'm still not convinced a CGT would do us all that much good here,' Bel Iblis said. 'This close in, I suspect that Coruscant's gravity would swamp any readings we got from the asteroids.'

'It would be tricky – no doubt about that,' Rieekan agreed. 'But I think it's our best chance.'

They fell silent as, on the visual, the second transport reached its target zone and repeated the procedure of the first. Again, nothing.

'That solar wind is going to be a real nuisance,' Bel Iblis commented as the third transport headed out. 'We may want to consider going with larger dust particles on the next batch.'

'Or shifting operations to the night side,' Rieekan suggested. 'That would at least cut back the effect—'

'Turbulence!' the sensor officer barked. 'Vector one-one-seven – bearing four-nine-two.'

There was a mad scramble for the sensor console. At the very edge of the still-expanding second dust cloud a hazy orange line had appeared, marking the turbulence created by the invisible asteroid's passage. 'Get a track on it,' Drayson ordered. '*Harrier*, fire at will.'

On the visual, red lines lanced out as the Dreadnaught's turbolasers began to sweep across the projected path. Leia watched the visual, hands gripping the sensor officer's chair back . . . and suddenly, there it was: a misshapen lump of rock, drifting slowly across the stars.

'Cease fire,' Drayson ordered. 'Well done, gentlemen. All right, *Allegiant*, it's your turn. Get your tech crew out there—'

He broke off. On the visual, a mesh of thin lines had appeared crisscrossing the dark bulk of the asteroid. For a brief moment they flared brilliantly, then faded away.

'Belay that order, *Allegiant*,' Drayson growled. 'Looks like

254

the Grand Admiral doesn't want anyone else getting a look at his little toys.'

'At least we found one of them,' Leia said. 'That's something.'

'Right,' Rieekan said dryly. 'Leaves just under three hundred to go.'

Leia nodded again and started to turn away. This was going to take a while, and she might as well get back to Winter and Ghent—

'Collision!' the sensor officer snapped.

She twisted back. On the visual the third transport was spinning wildly off course, its stern crushed and on fire, its cargo of dust spraying out in all directions.

'Can you get a track?' Drayson demanded.

The officer's hands were skating across his board. 'Negative – insufficient data. All I can do is a probability cone.'

'I'll take it,' Drayson said. 'All ships: open fire. Full-pattern bombardment; target cone as indicated.'

The cone had appeared on the tactical, and from the distant fleet turbolaser fire began to appear. 'Open the cone to fifty percent probability,' Drayson ordered. 'Battle stations, you take the outer cone. I want that target found.'

The encouragement was unnecessary. The space above Coruscant had become a fire storm, with turbolaser blasts and proton torpedoes cutting through the marked probability cone. The target zone stretched and expanded as the computers calculated the invisible asteroid's possible paths, the ships and battle stations shifting aim in response.

But there was nothing there . . . and after a few minutes Drayson finally conceded defeat.

'All units, cease fire,' he said, his voice tired. 'There's no more point. We've lost it.'

There didn't seem to be anything else to be said. In silence they stood and watched as the crippled transport, far out of range of the fleet's tractor beams, spun slowly toward the planetary shield and its impending death. Its crushed stern skimmed the shield, and the fire of burning drive gases was joined by the sharp blue-white edge of shattered atomic bonds.

A muffled flash as the stern broke away – a brighter flash as the bow hit the shield – scatterings of dark debris against the flame as the hull began to break up—

And with a final spattering of diffuse fire it was gone.

Leia watched the last flickers fade away, running through her Jedi calming exercises and forcing the anger from her mind. Allowing herself the luxury of hating Thrawn for doing this to them would only fog her own intellect. Worse, such hatred would be a perilous step toward the dark side.

There was a breath of movement at her shoulder, and she turned to see Winter at her side. The other woman was gazing up at the visual, a look of ancient pain deep in her eyes. 'It's all right,' Leia assured her. 'There wasn't anyone aboard.'

'I know,' Winter murmured. 'I was thinking about another transport I saw go down like that over Xyquine. A passenger transport . . .'

She took a deep breath, and Leia could see the conscious effort as she put her always-vivid past away from her. 'I'd like to speak with you, Your Highness, whenever you're finished here.'

Leia reached out past Winter's carefully neutral expression and touched her sense. Whatever the news was, it wasn't good. 'I'll come now,' she said.

They left the war room and circled back past the turbolifts to the service corridor and their secret decrypt room. And the news was indeed not good.

'This can't be,' Leia said, shaking her head as she reread Ghent's analysis. 'We *know* there's a leak in the Palace.'

'I've checked it backwards, forwards, and from the inside out,' Ghent said. 'It comes up the same every time. Feed in everyone who heard and didn't hear the stuff Delta Source sent out; feed in everyone who heard or didn't hear the stuff Delta Source *didn't* send out; and you come out with the same answer every time. A straight, flat zero.'

Leia keyed the data pad for a replay and watched as the list of names dwindled with each sifting until it was gone. 'Then Delta Source has to be more than one person,' she said.

'I already ran that,' Ghent said, waving his hands helplessly.

'It doesn't work, either. You wind up having to have at least fifteen people. Your security here can't be that bad.'

'Then he's picking and choosing what he transmits. Sending some of what he hears but not all of it.'

Ghent scratched at his cheek. 'I suppose that could be it,' he said reluctantly. 'I don't know, though. You look at some of the really stupid stuff he's sent – I mean, there was one in that last transmission that was nothing but a couple of Arcona talking about what one of them was going to name her hatchlings. Either this guy doesn't remember too good or else he's got a really weird priority list.'

The door opened, and Leia turned as Bel Iblis stepped in. 'I saw you leave,' the general said. 'Have you found something?'

Wordlessly, Leia handed him the data pad. Bel Iblis glanced over it, then read it through more carefully. 'Interesting,' he said at last. 'Either the analysis is wrong, or Winter's memory is starting to fail her . . . or Delta Source is on to us.'

'How do you figure that?' Leia asked.

'Because he's clearly no longer transmitting everything he hears,' Bel Iblis said. 'Something must have aroused his suspicions.'

Leia thought back to all those staged conversations. 'No,' she said slowly. 'I don't believe it. I never picked up even a hint of malice or suspicion.'

Bel Iblis shrugged. 'The alternative is to believe we have a whole spy nest here. Wait a minute, though – this isn't quite as bad as it sounds. If we assume he didn't catch on right away, we should still be able to use the data from the first two days to cut the suspect list down to a manageable number.'

Leia felt her stomach tighten. 'Garm, we're talking about over a hundred trusted members of the New Republic here. We can't go around accusing that many people of treason. Councilor Fey'lya's accusations against Admiral Ackbar were bad enough – this would be orders of magnitude worse.'

'I know that, Leia,' Bel Iblis said firmly. 'But we can't let the Empire continue to listen in on our secrets. Offer me an alternative and I'll take it.'

Leia bit at her lip, her mind racing. 'What about that comment you made on the way to the war room?' she asked. 'You said you thought Delta Source might be nothing but an exotic recording system.'

'If it is, it's somewhere in the Grand Corridor,' Winter said before Bel Iblis could answer. 'That's where all the conversations that were transmitted took place.'

'Are you sure?' Bel Iblis frowned.

'Absolutely,' Winter said. 'Every one.'

'That's it, then,' Leia said, feeling the first stirrings of excitement. 'Somehow, someone's planted a recording system in the Grand Corridor.'

'Don't get excited,' Bel Iblis cautioned. 'I know it sounds good, but it's not that easy. Microphone systems have certain well-defined characteristics, all of which are quite well known and can be readily picked up by a competent counter-intelligence sweep.'

'Unless it goes dormant when counterintelligence comes by,' Ghent suggested. 'I've seen systems that do that.'

Bel Iblis shook his head. 'But then you're talking something with at least minimal decision-making capabilities. Anything that close to droid-level intelligence would—'

'Hey!' Ghent interrupted excitedly. 'That's it. Delta Source isn't a person – it's a droid.'

Leia looked at Bel Iblis. 'Is that possible?'

'I don't know,' the general said slowly. 'Implanting secondary espionage programming in a droid is certainly feasible. The problem is how to get that programming in past the Palace's usual security procedures, and then avoiding the counterintelligence sweeps.'

'It would have to be a droid that has a good reason to hang around the Grand Corridor,' Leia said, trying to think it through. 'But who can also leave without attracting notice whenever a sweep gets under way.'

'And given the sort of high-level traffic that passes through the Grand Corridor, those sweeps are pretty frequent,' Bel Iblis agreed. 'Ghent, can you get into Security's records and pull a list of sweep times over the past three or four days?'

'Sure,' the kid shrugged. 'Probably take me a couple of hours, though. Unless you don't care if they spot me.'

Bel Iblis looked at Leia. 'What do you think?'

'We certainly don't want him to get caught,' Leia said. 'On the other hand, we don't want to give Delta Source free rein of the Palace any longer than we have to.'

'Your Highness?' Winter asked. 'Pardon me, but it seems to me that if the sweeps are that frequent, all we need to do is watch the Grand Corridor until one gets under way and then see which droids leave.'

'It's worth a try,' Bel Iblis said. 'Ghent, you get started on Security. Leia, Winter – let's go.'

'They're coming,' Winter's voice came softly from the comlink nestled in Leia's palm.

'You sure they're Palace Security?' Bel Iblis's voice said.

'Yes,' Winter said. 'I've seen Colonel Bremen giving them orders. And they have droids and equipment with them.'

'Sounds like this is it,' Leia murmured, surreptitiously raising her hand near her mouth and hoping the three Kubaz sitting across the lounge/conversation ring from her wouldn't notice the odd behavior. 'Watch carefully.'

There were acknowledging murmurs from both of them. Lowering her hand back to her lap, Leia looked around. This was it, all right: possibly the clearest shot at Delta Source they were likely to get. With an Assemblage meeting just letting out and a Council meeting about to start, the Grand Corridor was crowded with high-ranking officials. With officials, their aides and assistants, and their droids.

On one level, Leia had always known how common droids were in the Imperial Palace. On another level, as she was rapidly coming to realize, she'd had no idea how many of them there actually were. There were quite a few 3PO protocol droids visible from where she sat, most of them accompanying groups of offworld diplomats but some also in the entourages of various Palace officials. Hovering over the crowd on repulsorlifts, a set of insectoid SPD maintenance droids were systematically cleaning the carvings and cut-glass windows

259

that alternated along the walls. A line of MSE droids scuttled past along the far wall, delivering messages too complex for comm transmissions or too sensitive for direct data transfer and trying hard not to get stepped on. At the next of the greenish-purple ch'hala trees down the line, occasionally visible through the crowd, an MN-2E maintenance droid was carefully pruning away dead leaves.

Which one of them, she wondered, had the Empire turned into a spy?

'They're starting,' Winter reported quietly. 'Lining up across the Corridor—'

There was a sudden rustle of sound from the comlink, as if Winter had put her hand across the microphone. Another series of muffled sounds; and Leia was wondering if she should go and investigate when a man's voice came on. 'Councilor Organa Solo?'

'Yes,' she said cautiously. 'Who is this?'

'Lieutenant Machel Kendy, Councilor,' he said. 'Palace Security. Are you aware that a third person is tapping into your comlink signal?'

'It's not a tap, Lieutenant,' Leia assured him. 'We were holding a three-way discussion with General Bel Iblis.'

'I see,' Kendy said, sounding a little disappointed. Probably thought he'd stumbled on to Delta Source. 'I'll have to ask you to suspend your conversation for a few minutes, Councilor. We're about to do a sweep of the Grand Corridor, and we can't have stray comlink transmissions in the area.'

'I understand,' Leia said. 'We'll wait until you're finished.'

She shut off the comlink and replaced it in her belt, her heart beginning to thud in her ears. Twisting casually around in her seat, she made sure she could see the entire end of the Grand Corridor. If there was an espionage droid present, he'd be shuffling this direction as soon as he noticed the sweep team coming from the other end.

Overhead, the hovering cleaning droids had been joined by a new set of SPDs, moving down the corridor as they methodically checked the upper walls and convoluted contours of the vaulted ceiling for any microphones or recording systems that might have somehow been planted there since the last sweep. Directly beneath them, Leia could see Lieutenant Kendy and his squad, walking through the milling diplomats in a militarily straight line stretched across the corridor and watching the displays of their shoulder-slung detectors. The line reached her lounge area, passed it, and continued without incident to the end of the corridor. There the squad waited, letting the SPD droids and a group of wall-hugging MSEs finish their part of the sweep and catch up. Re-formed again, the entire group disappeared down the hallway toward the Inner Council offices.

And that was that. The entire Grand Corridor had been swept, and had obviously come up negative . . . and not a single droid had scurried out ahead of the sweep.

Something off to the side caught her eye. But it was just the MN-2E maintenance droid she'd notice earlier, rolling up to the ch'hala tree that sprouted out of the floor beside her conversation ring. Clucking softly to itself, the droid began poking delicate feelers through the branches, hunting for dead or dying leaves.

Dead or dying. Rather like their theory.

With a sigh, she pulled out her comlink. 'Winter? Garm?'

'Here, Your Highness,' Winter's voice came promptly.

'So am I,' Bel Iblis added. 'What happened?'

Leia shook her head. 'Absolutely nothing,' she told them. 'As far as I could tell, none of the droids even twitched.'

There was a short pause. 'I see,' Bel Iblis said at last. 'Well . . . it may just be that our droid doesn't happen to be here today. What we need to do is send Winter back to Ghent and have her add droids into the list.'

'What do you think, Winter?' Leia asked.

'I can try,' the other woman said hesitantly. 'The problem will be identifying specific droids. Externally, one 3PO protocol droid looks basically like any other.'

'We'll take whatever you can get,' Bel Iblis said. 'It's here, though, somewhere close by. I can feel it.'

Leia held her breath, stretching out with her Jedi senses.

She didn't have Bel Iblis's fine-honed warrior's intuition, nor did she have Luke's far deeper Jedi skill. But she could sense it, too. Something about the Grand Corridor . . . 'I think you're right,' she told Bel Iblis. 'Winter, you'd better head down and get busy on this.'

'Certainly, Your Highness.'

'I'll come with you, Winter,' Bel Iblis volunteered. 'I want to see what's happening with the Stardust plan.'

Leia shut off the comlink and leaned back in her seat, fatigue and discouragement seeping into her mind despite her best efforts to hold it back. It had seemed like such a good idea, using Ghent's decrypt to try to identify Delta Source. But so far every lead had simply melted away from in front of them.

And time was running out. Even if they were able to keep Ghent's work a secret – which was by no means certain – each of these failed gambits simply brought them closer to the inevitable day when Delta Source would finally notice all the activity and shut down. And when that happened, their last chance to identify the Imperial spy in their midst would be gone.

And that would be a disaster. Not because of the leak itself – Imperial Intelligence had been stealing information since the Rebel Alliance was first formed, and they'd managed to live through it. What was infinitely more dangerous to the New Republic was the deepening aura of suspicion and distrust that Delta Source's mere existence had already spread through the Palace. Councilor Fey'lya's discredited accusations against Admiral Ackbar had already shown what such distrust could do to the delicate multi-species coalition that made up the New Republic. If that leadership was found to contain a genuine Imperial agent . . .

Across the conversation ring the three Kubaz got to their feet and headed away, circling around behind the ch'hala tree and the MN-2E droid working alongside it and disappearing into the traffic flow down the corridor. Leia found herself staring at the droid, watching as it eased a manipulator arm carefully through the branches toward a small cluster of dead leaves, clucking softly to itself all the while. She'd had a brief run-in with an Imperial espionage droid on the Noghri home planet of Honoghr, a run-in which could have spelled disaster for her and genocide for the remnants of the Noghri race. If Bel Iblis was right – if Delta Source was, in fact, merely a droid and not a traitor . . .

But it didn't really help. The Empire simply could not have infiltrated an espionage droid into the Palace without the collaboration of one or more of the beings here. Security invariably did a complete screening of every droid that came into the Palace, whether on a permanent or temporary basis, and they knew exactly what to look for. Hidden secondary espionage programming would show up like a burst of pale red against the subtle background pattern on that ch'hala tree—

Leia frowned, staring at the tree, as her chain of thought jolted to a halt. Another small burst of red appeared on the slender trunk as she watched, sending a pale red ring rippling outward and around the trunk until it faded into the quiet purple background turmoil. Another flicker followed, and another, and another, chasing each other around the trunk like ripples from a dripping water line. All of them more or less the same size; all of them originating from the same place on the trunk.

And each of them exactly in time with one of the clucking noises from the MN-2E droid.

And suddenly then it hit her, like a violent wave of icy water. Fumbling at her belt with suddenly trembling fingers, she keyed for the central operator. 'This is Councilor Organa Solo,' she identified herself. 'Get me Colonel Bremen in Security.

'Tell him I've found Delta Source.'

They had to dig nearly eight meters down before they found it: a long, fat, age-tarnished tube half buried in the side of the ch'hala tree's taproot with a thousand slender sampling leads feeding into one end and a direct-transmission fiber snaking out the other. Even then, it took another hour and

263

the preliminary report before Bremen himself was finally convinced.

'The techs say it's like nothing they've ever seen before,' the security chief told Leia, Bel Iblis, and Mon Mothma as they stood on the scattered dirt around the uprooted ch'hala tree. 'But apparently it's reasonably straightforward. Any pressure on the ch'hala tree's trunk – including the pressure created by sound waves – sets off small chemical changes in the inner layers of bark.'

'Which is what creates the shifting colors and patterns?' Mon Mothma asked.

'Right,' Bremen nodded, wincing slightly. 'Obvious in hindsight, really – the pattern changes are far too fast to be anything but biochemical in origin. Anyway, those implanted tubes running up into the trunk continuously sample the chemicals and shunt the information back down to the module on the taproot. The module takes the chemical data, turns it back into pressure data, and from there back into speech. Some other module – maybe farther down the taproot – sorts out the conversations and gets the whole thing ready for encrypting and transmission. That's all there is to it.'

'An organic microphone,' Bel Iblis nodded. 'With no electronics anywhere in sight for a counterintelligence sweep to pick up.'

'A whole series of organic microphones,' Bremen corrected, glancing significantly at the twin rows of trees lining the Grand Corridor. 'We'll get rid of them right away.'

'Such a brilliant plan,' Mon Mothma mused. 'And so very like the Emperor. I'd always wondered how he obtained some of the information he used against us in the Senate.' She shook her head. 'Even after his death, it seems, his hand can move against us.'

'Well, this part's about to be stilled, anyway,' Bel Iblis said. 'Let's get a team up here, Colonel, and dig up some trees.'

CHAPTER 18

In the distance, far across the scarred plain, there was a glimmer of reflected light. 'Mazzic's coming,' Karrde commented.

Gillespee turned his attention from the refreshments table and squinted out past the crumbling fortress wall. 'Someone's coming, anyway,' he agreed, putting down his cup and the cold bruallki he'd been munching on and wiping his hands on his tunic. Pulling out his macrobinoculars, he peered through them. 'Yeah, it's him,' he confirmed. 'Funny – he's got two other ships with him.'

Karrde frowned at the approaching spot. 'Two other ships?'

'Take a look,' Gillespee said, handing over the macrobinoculars.

Karrde held them up to his eyes. There were three incoming, all right: a sleek space yacht and two slender, highly vicious-looking ships of an unfamiliar design. 'You suppose he's brought some guests?' Gillespee asked.

'He didn't say anything about guests when he checked in with Aves a few minutes ago,' Karrde said. Even as he watched, the two flanking ships left the formation, dropping to the plain below and vanishing into one of the deep ravines crisscrossing it.

'Maybe you'd better check.'

'Maybe I'd better,' Karrde agreed, handing back the macrobinoculars and pulling out his comlink. 'Aves? You have some ID on our incoming?'

'Sure do,' Aves's voice came back. 'Gimmicked IDs on all of them, but we read them as the *Distant Rainbow*, the *Skyclaw* and the *Raptor*.'

Karrde grimaced. The designs might not be familiar, but the names certainly were. Mazzic's personal transport and two of his favorite customized fighters. 'Thank you,' he said, and shut down the comlink.

'Well?' Gillespee asked.

Karrde returned the comlink to his belt. 'It's just Mazzic,' he said.

'What's that about Mazzic?' Niles Ferrier's voice put in.

Karrde turned. The ship thief was standing behind them at the refreshments table, a generous helping of charred pirki nuts cupped in one hand. 'I said Mazzic was coming,' he repeated.

'Good,' Ferrier nodded, popping one of the nuts into his mouth and cracking it loudly between his teeth. 'About time. Finally get this meeting going.'

He sauntered off, crunching as he went, nodding at Dravis and Clyngunn as he passed. 'I thought you didn't want him here,' Gillespee muttered.

Karrde shook his head. 'I didn't. Apparently, the feeling wasn't universal.'

Gillespee frowned. 'You mean someone else invited him? Who?'

'I don't know,' Karrde admitted, watching as Ferrier wandered over to the corner where Ellor and his group had gathered. 'I haven't found a way to ask around without looking either petty, suspicious, or overbearing. Anyway, it's probably quite innocent. Someone assuming that all those at the original Trogan meeting should continue to be involved.'

'The lack of an invitation notwithstanding?'

Karrde shrugged. 'Perhaps that was assumed to be an oversight. At any rate, calling attention to it at this point would only create friction. Some of the others already seem resentful that I've apparently taken over management of the operation.'

Gillespee tossed the last bit of bruallki into his mouth. 'Yeah, maybe it's innocent,' he said darkly. 'But maybe it's not.'

'We're keeping a good watch on the likely approaches,' Karrde reminded him. 'If Ferrier's made a deal with the Empire, we'll see them coming in plenty of time.'

'I hope so,' Gillespee grunted, surveying the refreshments

table for his next target. 'I hate running on a full stomach.'

Karrde smiled; and he was starting to turn away when his comlink beeped. He pulled it out and flicked it on, eyes automatically turning to the sky. 'Karrde,' he said into it.

'This is Torve,' the other identified himself . . . and from the tone Karrde knew something was wrong. 'Could you step downstairs a minute?'

'Certainly,' Karrde said, his other hand dropping to his side and the blaster holstered there. 'Should I bring anyone?'

'No need – we're not having a party or anything here.'

Translation: reinforcements were already on their way. 'Understood,' Karrde said. 'I'll be right there.'

He shut off the comlink and returned it to his belt. 'Trouble?' Gillespee asked, eyeing Karrde over his glass.

'We've got an intruder,' Karrde said, glancing around the courtyard. None of the other smugglers or their entourages seemed to be looking his direction. 'Do me a favor and keep an eye on things here.'

'Sure. Anyone in particular I should watch?'

Karrde looked at Ferrier, who had now left Ellor and was heading toward Par'tah and her fellow Ho'Din. 'Make sure Ferrier doesn't leave.'

The main part of the base had been set up three levels below the top remaining floors of the ruined fortress, in what had probably been the kitchens and ancillary prep areas for a huge high-ceilinged room that had probably been a banquet area. The *Wild Karrde* was berthed in the banquet chamber itself – a moderately tight fit for a ship its size, but offering the twin advantages of reasonable concealment plus the possibility for a quick exit should that become necessary. Karrde arrived at the high double doors to find Fynn Torve and five of the crewers from the *Starry Ice* waiting with drawn blasters. 'Report,' he said.

'We think someone's in there,' Torve told him grimly. 'Chin was taking the vornskrs for a walk around the ship and saw something moving in the shadows along the south wall.'

The wall closest to the *Wild Karrde*'s lowered entrance ramp. 'Anyone currently aboard the ship?'

'Lachton was working on the secondary command console,' Torve said. 'Aves told him to sit tight on the bridge with his blaster pointed at the door until we got someone else there. Chin grabbed some of the *Etherway* people who were hanging around and started searching through the south-end rooms; Dankin is doing the same with the north-end ones.'

Karrde nodded. 'That leaves the ship for us, then. You two' – he pointed to two of the *Starry Ice* crewers – 'will stay here and guard the doors. Nice and easy; let's go.'

They pulled open one of the double doors and slipped inside. Directly ahead, the *Wild Karrde*'s stern rose up darkly in front of them; 150 meters beyond it, glimpses of the blue Hijarna sky could be seen through the broken fortress wall. 'I wish we had better lighting in here,' Torve muttered as he looked around.

'It looks easier to hide in than it really is,' Karrde assured him, pulling out his comlink. 'Dankin, Chin, this is Karrde. Report.'

'Nothing so far in the north-end rooms,' Dankin's voice came promptly. 'I sent Corvis for some portable sensor equipment, but he's not back yet.'

'Nothing here either, Capt',' Chin added.

'All right,' Karrde said. 'We're coming in around the starboard side of the ship and heading for the entryway. Be ready to give us cover fire if we need it.'

'We're ready, Capt'.'

Karrde slid the comlink back in his belt. Taking a deep breath, he headed out.

They searched the ship, the banquet chamber, and all the offices and storerooms on the periphery. And in the end, they found no-one.

'I must have imagined it,' Chin said morosely as the searchers gathered together at the foot of the *Wild Karrde*'s entrance ramp. 'Sorry, Capt'. Truly sorry.'

'Don't worry about it,' Karrde said, looking around the banquet chamber. Cleared or not, there was still an uneasy feeling tugging at him. Like someone was watching and laughing . . . 'We all misread things sometimes. If this was, in fact, a misreading. Torve, you're certain you and Lachton covered the entire ship?'

'Every cubic meter of it,' Torve said firmly. 'If anyone sneaked into the *Wild Karrde*, he was out long before we got here.'

'What about those vornskr pets of yours, sir?' one of the *Starry Ice* crewers asked. 'Are they any good at tracking?'

'Only if you're hunting ysalamiri or Jedi,' Karrde told him. 'Well. Whoever was here seems to be gone now. Still, we may have driven him off before he finished whatever it was he came to do. Torve, I want you to set up a guard detail for the area. Have Aves alert the duty personnel aboard the *Starry Ice* and *Etherway*, as well.'

'Right,' Torve said, pulling out his comlink. 'What about our guests upstairs? Should we warn them, too?'

'What are we, their mothers?' one of the other crewers snorted. 'They're big boys – they can look out for themselves.'

'I'm sure they can,' Karrde reproved him mildly. 'But they're here at my invitation. As long as they're under our roof, they're under our protection.'

'Does that include whoever sent the intruder Chin spotted?' Lachton asked.

Karrde looked up at his ship. 'That will depend on what the intruder was sent to do,' he said. And speaking of his guests, it was time he got back to them. Mazzic would have joined them by now, and Ferrier wasn't the only one impatient for the meeting to begin. 'Lachton, as soon as Corvis gets here with those scanners I want the two of you to run a complete check of the ship, starting with the exterior hull. Our visitor may have left us a gift, and I don't want to fly out of here with a homing beacon or timed concussion bomb aboard somewhere. I'll be up in the conference area if you need me.'

He left them to their work, feeling once again Mara Jade's absence from the group. One of these days, he was going to have to make the time to go back to Coruscant and get her and Ghent back.

Assuming he was allowed to do so. His information sources

had picked up a vague and disturbing rumor that an unnamed woman had been caught giving assistance to an Imperial commando force on Coruscant. Given Mara's obvious disdain for Grand Admiral Thrawn, it was unlikely she would actually give his Empire any help. But on the other hand, there were many in the New Republic starting to edge toward a kind of war hysteria . . . and given her shadowy history, Mara was an obvious candidate for that kind of accusation. All the more reason for him to get her off Coruscant.

He reached the upper courtyard to find that Mazzic had indeed arrived. He was standing with the Ho'Din group, talking earnestly with Par'tah, with the deceptively decorative female bodyguard he'd had at Trogan an aloof half-step back from the conversation, trying to look inconspicuous.

As were the pair of men just behind her. And the four standing around them a few meters away. And the six scattered elsewhere around the edges of the courtyard.

Karrde paused in the arched entrance, a quiet warning alarm going off in the back of his head. For Mazzic to bring a pair of fighting ships to protect him en route was one thing. To bring a full squad of enforcers into a friendly meeting was something else entirely. Either the Imperial attack on Trogan had made him uncharacteristically nervous . . . or else he wasn't planning for the meeting to remain quite so friendly.

'Hey – Karrde,' Ferrier called, beckoning him over. 'Come on – let's get this meeting out of the bay.'

'Certainly,' Karrde said, putting on his best host's smile as he walked into the room. Too late now to bring some of his own people up here for balance. He would just have to hope that Mazzic was merely being cautious. 'Good afternoon, Mazzic. Thank you for coming.'

'No problem,' Mazzic said, his eyes cool. He didn't smile back.

'We have more comfortable seats prepared in a room back this way,' Karrde said, gesturing to his left. 'If you'd all care to follow me—'

'I have a better idea,' Mazzic interrupted. 'What do you say we hold this meeting inside the *Wild Karrde*?'

Karrde looked at him. Mazzic returned the gaze evenly, his face not giving anything away. Apparently, he was not merely being cautious. 'May I ask why?' Karrde asked.

'Are you suggesting you have something to hide?' Mazzic countered.

Karrde allowed himself a cool smile. 'Of course I have things to hide,' he said. 'So does Par'tah; so does Ellor; so do you. We're business competitors, after all.'

'So you won't allow us aboard the *Wild Karrde*?'

Karrde looked at each of the smuggler chiefs in turn. Gillespee, Dravis, and Clyngunn were frowning, clearly with no idea at all as to what this was all about. Par'tah's Ho'Din face was difficult to read, but there was something about her stance that seemed oddly troubled. Ellor was avoiding his eyes entirely. And Ferrier—

Ferrier was smirking. Not obviously – almost invisibly, in fact, behind that beard of his. But enough. More than enough.

And now, far too late, he finally understood. What Chin had seen – and what all of them had subsequently failed to catch – had been Ferrier's shadowy Defel.

Mazzic's men were here. Karrde's were three levels down, guarding his ship and base against a danger that was long gone. And all his guests were waiting for his answer. 'The *Wild Karrde* is berthed down below,' he told them. 'If you'd care to follow me?'

Dankin and Torve were conversing together at the foot of the *Wild Karrde*'s entrance ramp as the group arrived. 'Hello, Captain,' Dankin said, looking surprised. 'Can we help you?'

'No help needed,' Karrde said. 'We've decided to hold the meeting aboard ship, that's all.'

'Aboard ship?' Dankin echoed, his eyes flicking over the group and obviously not liking what he saw. Small wonder: among the smuggler chiefs, aides, and bodyguards, Mazzic's enforcers stood out like a landing beacon cluster. 'I'm sorry – I wasn't informed,' he added, hooking the thumb of his right hand casually into the top of his gun belt.

'It was a rather spur-of-the-moment decision,' Karrde told him. Out of the corner of his eye, he could see the rest of his people in the banquet chamber beginning to drift from their assigned tasks as they spotted Dankin's hand signal. Drifting into encirclement positions . . .

'Oh, sure,' Dankin said, starting to look a little embarrassed. 'Though the place really isn't set up for anything this fancy. I mean, you know what the wardroom looks like—'

'We're not interested in the decor,' Mazzic interrupted. 'Please step aside – we have business to attend to.'

'Right – I understand that,' Dankin said, looking even more embarrassed but holding his ground. 'Problem is, we've got a scanning crew aboard right now. It'll foul up the readings if we get more people coming and going.'

'So foul them up,' Ferrier put in. 'Who do you think you are, anyway?'

Dankin didn't get a chance to come up with an answer to that one. A whiff of perfume-scented air brushed across the side of Karrde's face, and the hard knob of a blaster muzzle dug gently into his side. 'Nice try, Karrde,' Mazzic said, 'but it won't work. Call them off. Now.'

Carefully, Karrde looked over his shoulder. Mazzic's decorative bodyguard looked back, her eyes cool and very professional. 'If I don't?'

'Then we have a firefight,' Mazzic said bluntly. 'Right here.'

There was a quiet ripple of movement through the group. 'Would someone like to tell me what's going on here?' Gillespee murmured uncertainly.

'I'll tell you inside the ship,' Mazzic said, his eyes steady on Karrde. 'Assuming we all live to get in there. That part's up to our host.'

'I won't surrender my people to you,' Karrde said quietly. 'Not without a fight.'

'I have no interest in your people,' Mazzic told him. 'Or your ship, or your organization. This is a personal matter, between you and me. And our fellow smugglers.'

'Then let's have it out,' Dankin suggested. 'We'll clear a space, you can choose weapons—'

'I'm not talking some stupid private feud,' Mazzic cut him off. 'This is about treachery.'

'About *what*?' Gillespee asked. 'Mazzic—'

'Shut up, Gillespee,' Mazzic said, throwing a quick glare at him. 'Well, Karrde?'

Slowly, Karrde looked around the group. There were no allies here; no friends who would stand firmly by him against whatever these phantom charges were that Mazzic and Ferrier had concocted. Whatever respect any of them might have for him, whatever favors they might owe him – all of that was already forgotten. They would watch while his enemies took him down . . . and then they would each take a piece of the organization he'd worked so hard to build.

But until that happened, the men and other beings here were still his associates. And still his responsibility.

'There's not enough room in the wardroom for anyone but the eight of us,' he told Mazzic quietly. 'All aides, bodyguards, and your enforcers will have to stay out here. Will you order them to leave my people alone?'

For a long minute Mazzic studied his face. Then he nodded, a single curt jerk of his head. 'As long as they're not provoked, they won't bother anyone. Shada, get his blaster. Karrde . . . after you.'

Karrde looked at Dankin and Torve and nodded. Reluctantly, they moved away from the ramp and he started up. Followed closely by the people he'd once hoped to make into a unified front against the Empire.

He should have known better.

They settled into the wardroom, Mazzic nudging Karrde into a chair in one corner as the others found places around the table facing him. 'All right,' Karrde said. 'We're here. Now what?'

'I want your data cards,' Mazzic said. 'All of them. We'll start with the ones in your office.'

Karrde nodded over his shoulder. 'Through the door and down the corridor to the right.'

'Access codes?'

'None. I trust my people.'

Mazzic's lip twisted slightly. 'Ellor, go get them. And bring a couple of data pads back with you.'

Wordlessly, the Duro stood up and left. 'While we're waiting,' Karrde said into the awkward silence, 'perhaps I could present the proposal I invited you to Hijarna to hear.'

Mazzic snorted. 'You've got guts, Karrde – I'll give you that. Guts and style. Let's just sit quiet for now, OK?'

Karrde looked at the blaster pointed at him. 'Whatever you wish.'

Ellor returned a minute later, carrying a tray full of data cards with two data pads balanced on top. 'OK,' Mazzic said as the Duro sat down beside him. 'Give one of the data pads to Par'tah and start going through them. You both know what to look for.'

[[I must acknowledge at the beginning,]] Ellor said, [[that I do not like this.]]

[Iy agree,] Par'tah said, her head appendages writhing like disturbed snakes. [To fiyght openly agaiynst a competiytor iys part of busiyness. But thiys iys diyfferent.]

'This isn't about business,' Mazzic said.

'Of course not,' Karrde agreed. 'He's already said he has no interest in the organization. Remember?'

'Don't try playing on my words, Karrde,' Mazzic warned. 'I hate that as much as I hate being led around by the nose.'

'I'm not leading anyone by the nose, Mazzic,' Karrde said quietly. 'I've dealt squarely with all of you since this whole thing began.'

'Maybe. That's what we're here to find out.'

Karrde looked around the table, remembering back to the chaos that had flooded through the twilight world of smuggling after the collapse of Jabba the Hutt's organization. Every group in the galaxy had scrambled madly to pick up the pieces, snatching ships and people and contracts for themselves, sometimes fighting viciously for them. The larger organizations, particularly, had profited quite handsomely from the Hutt's demise.

He wondered if Aves would be able to beat them off. Aves, and Mara.

'Anything yet?' Mazzic asked.

[We wiyll tell you iyf there iys,] Par'tah said, her off-pitch tone betraying her displeasure with the whole situation.

Karrde looked at Mazzic. 'Would you mind at least telling me what it is I've allegedly done?'

'Yeah, I want to hear it, too,' Gillespee seconded.

Mazzic leaned back in his seat, resting his gun hand on his thigh. 'It's very simple,' he said. 'That attack on Trogan – the one where my friend Lishma was killed – appears to have been staged.'

'What do you mean, staged?' Dravis asked.

'Just what I said. Someone hired an Imperial lieutenant and his squad to attack us.'

Clyngunn rumbled deep in his throat. 'Imperial troops do not work for hire,' he growled.

'This group did,' Mazzic told him.

'Who said so?' Gillespee demanded.

Mazzic smiled tightly. 'The most knowledgeable source there is. Grand Admiral Thrawn.'

There was a moment of stunned silence. Dravis found his voice first. 'No kidding,' he said. 'And he just happened to mention this to you?'

'They picked me up poking around Joiol system and took me to the *Chimaera*,' Mazzic said, ignoring the sarcasm. 'After the incident at the Bilbringi shipyards I thought I was in for a rough time. But Thrawn told me he'd just pulled me in to clear the air, that no-one in the Empire had ordered the Trogan attack and that I shouldn't hold them responsible for it. And then he let me go.'

'Having conveniently implied that I was the one you should hold responsible?' Karrde suggested.

'He didn't finger you specifically,' Mazzic said. 'But who else had anything to gain by getting us mad at the Empire?'

'We're talking a Grand Admiral here, Mazzic,' Karrde reminded him. 'A Grand Admiral who delights in leisurely and convoluted strategies. And who has a personal interest in destroying me.'

Mazzic smiled tightly. 'I'm not just taking Thrawn's word

for this, Karrde. I had a friend do a little digging through Imperial military records before I came here. He got me the complete details of the Trogan arrangement.'

'Imperial records can be altered,' Karrde pointed out.

'Like I said, I'm not taking their word for it,' Mazzic retorted. 'But if we find the other end of the deal here' – he lifted his blaster slightly – 'I'd say that would be hard evidence.'

'I see,' Karrde murmured, looking at Ferrier. So that was what his Defel had been doing down here. Planting Mazzic's hard evidence. 'I suppose it's too late to mention that we had an intruder down here a few minutes before you arrived.'

Ferrier snorted. 'Oh, right. Nice try, Karrde, but a little late.'

'A little late for what?' Dravis asked, frowning.

'He's trying to throw suspicion on someone else, that's all,' Ferrier said contemptuously. 'Trying to make you think one of us planted that data card on him.'

'What data card?' Gillespee scoffed. 'We haven't found any data card.'

[[Yes, we have,]] Ellor said softly.

Karrde looked at him. Ellor's flat face was stiff, his emotions unreadable as he silently handed his data pad to Mazzic. The other took it; and his face, too, hardened. 'So there it is,' he said softly, laying the data pad on the table. 'Well. I suppose there's nothing else to say.'

'Wait a second,' Gillespee objected. 'There is too. Karrde's right about that intruder – I was with him upstairs when the alert came through.'

Mazzic shrugged. 'Fine; I'll play. What about it, Karrde? What did you see?'

Karrde shook his head, trying to keep his eyes off the muzzle of Mazzic's blaster. 'Nothing, unfortunately. Chin thought he saw some movement near the ship, but we weren't able to locate anyone.'

'I didn't notice all that many places out there where anyone could hide,' Mazzic pointed out.

'A human couldn't, no,' Karrde agreed. 'On the other hand, it didn't occur to us at the time just how many shadows there were along the walls and near the doors.'

276

'Meaning you think it was my wraith, huh?' Ferrier put in. 'That's typical, Karrde – fire off a few hints and try to fog the issue. Well, forget it – it won't work.'

Karrde frowned at him. At the aggressive face but wary eyes . . . and suddenly he realized he'd been wrong about the setup here. Ferrier and Mazzic were not, in fact, working together on this. It was Ferrier alone, probably under Thrawn's direction, who was trying to bring him down.

Which meant Mazzic honestly thought Karrde had betrayed them all. Which meant, in turn, that there might still be a chance to persuade him otherwise. 'Let me try this, then,' he said, shifting his attention back to Mazzic. 'Would I really be so careless as to leave a record of my treachery here where anyone could find it?'

'You didn't know we'd be looking for it,' Ferrier said before Mazzic could answer.

Karrde cocked an eyebrow at him. 'Oh, so now it's "we," Ferrier? You're assisting Mazzic on this?'

'He's right, Karrde – stop trying to fog the issue,' Mazzic said. 'You think Thrawn would go to all this effort just to take you down? He could have done that straight-out at Trogan.'

'He couldn't touch me at Trogan,' Karrde shook his head. 'Not with all of you there watching. He would have risked stirring up the entire fringe against him. No, this way is much better. He destroys me, discredits my warnings about him, and retains both your goodwill and your services.'

Clyngunn shook his shaggy head. 'No. Thrawn is not like Vader. He would not waste troops in a deliberately failed attack.'

'I agree,' Karrde said. 'I don't think he ordered the Trogan attack, either. I think someone else planned that raid, and that Thrawn's simply making the best use of it he can.'

'I suppose you're going to try and put that one on me, too,' Ferrier growled.

'I haven't accused anyone, Ferrier,' Karrde reminded him mildly. 'One might think you had a guilty conscience.'

'There he goes – fogging things again,' Ferrier said, looking around the table before turning his glare back to Karrde. 'You already practically flat out accused my wraith of planting that data card in here.'

'That was your suggestion, not mine,' Karrde said, watching the other closely. Thinking on his feet obviously wasn't Ferrier's strong point, and the strains were starting to show. If he could push just a little harder . . . 'But since we're on the subject, where *is* your Defel?'

'He's on my ship,' Ferrier said promptly. 'Over in the western courtyard with everyone else's. He's been there since I landed.'

'Why?'

Ferrier frowned. 'What do you mean, why? He's there because he's part of my crew.'

'No, I mean why isn't he outside the *Wild Karrde* with the rest of the bodyguards?'

'Who said he was a bodyguard?'

Karrde shrugged. 'I simply assumed he was. He was playing that role on Trogan, after all.'

'That's right, he was,' Gillespee said slowly. 'Standing over against the wall. Where he was all ready to hit the Imperials when they came in.'

'Almost as if he knew they were coming,' Karrde agreed.

Ferrier's face darkened. 'Karrde—'

'Enough,' Mazzic cut him off. 'This isn't evidence, Karrde, and you know it. Anyway, what would Ferrier have to gain by setting up an attack like that?'

'Perhaps so he could be inconspicuous in helping us fight it off,' Karrde suggested. 'Hoping it would soothe our suspicions about his relationship with the Empire.'

'Twist all the words you want,' Ferrier said, jabbing a finger at the data pad sitting on the table beside Mazzic. 'But that data card doesn't say *I* hired Kosk and his squad. It says *you* did. Personally, I think we've heard enough of this—'

'Just a minute,' Mazzic interrupted, turning to face him. 'How do you know what the data card says?'

'You told us,' Ferrier said. 'You said it was the other half of the—'

'I never mentioned the lieutenant's name.'

The room was suddenly very quiet ... and behind his beard, Ferrier's face had gone pale. 'You must have.'

'No,' Mazzic said coldly. 'I didn't.'

'No-one said it,' Clyngunn rumbled.

Ferrier glared at him. 'This is insane,' he spat, some of his courage starting to come back. 'All the evidence points straight to Karrde – and you're going to let him off just because I happened to hear this Kosk's name somewhere? Maybe one of the stormtroopers on Trogan shouted it during the fight – how should I know?'

'Well, then, here's an easier question,' Karrde said. 'Tell us how you learned the time and location of this meeting. Given your lack of an invitation.'

Mazzic shot a look at him. 'You didn't invite him?'

Karrde shook his head. 'I've never really trusted him, not since I heard about his role in Thrawn's acquisition of the *Katana* fleet. He wouldn't have been at Trogan at all if Gillespee hadn't made that invitation more or less open to anyone.'

'Well, Ferrier?' Dravis prompted. 'Or are you going to claim one of us told you?'

There were tight lines at the corners of Ferrier's eyes. 'I picked up the transmission to Mazzic,' he muttered. 'Decrypted it; figured I ought to be here.'

'Pretty fast decrypting work,' Gillespee commented. 'Those were good encrypt codes we were using. You kept a copy of the original encrypted transmission, of course?'

Ferrier stood up. 'I don't have to sit here and listen to this,' he growled. 'Karrde's the one on trial here, not me.'

'Sit down, Ferrier,' Mazzic said softly. His blaster was no longer pointed at Karrde.

'But *he's* the one,' Ferrier insisted. His right hand shot out, forefinger pointed accusingly at Karrde. 'He's the one who—'

'Watch out!' Gillespee snapped.

But it was too late. With his right hand waving out in front of him as a diversion, Ferrier's left hand had dipped into his waist sash and was now back out in front of him.

Holding a thermal detonator.

'All right, hands on the table,' he snarled. 'Drop it, Mazzic.'

Slowly, Mazzic laid his blaster on the table. 'You can't possibly get out of here, Ferrier,' he bit out. 'It'll be a toss-up between Shada and my enforcers.'

'They'll never even get a shot at me,' Ferrier said, reaching over to pick up Mazzic's blaster. 'Wraith! Get in here!'

Behind him, the wardroom door slid open and a black shadow moved silently into the room. A black shadow with red eyes and a hint of long white fangs.

Clyngunn swore, a roiling ZeHethbra curse. 'So Karrde was right about all of it. You have betrayed us to the Empire.'

Ferrier ignored him. 'Watch them,' he ordered, shoving Mazzic's blaster at the shadow and drawing his own. 'Come on, Karrde – we're going to the bridge.'

Karrde didn't move. 'If I refuse?'

'I kill you all and take the ship up myself,' Ferrier told him shortly. 'Maybe I should do that anyway – Thrawn'd probably pay a good bounty on all of you.'

'I concede the point,' Karrde said, getting to his feet. 'This way.'

They reached the bridge without incident. 'You're flying,' Ferrier instructed, gesturing toward the helm with his blaster as he took a quick look at the displays. 'Good – I figured you'd have it ready to go.'

'Where are we going?' Karrde asked, sitting down in the helm seat. Through the viewport, he could see some of his people, oblivious to his presence up here as they maintained their uneasy standoff with Mazzic's enforcers.

'Out, up, and over,' Ferrier told him, motioning toward the broken fortress wall ahead with his blaster. 'We'll start with that.'

'I see,' Karrde said, keying for a preflight status report with his right hand and letting his left drop casually to his knee. Just above it, built into the underside of the main console, was a knee panel with the controls for the ship's external lights. 'What happens then?'

'What do you think?' Ferrier retorted, crossing over to the comm station and giving it a quick look. 'We get out of here.

You got any other ships on comm standby?'

'The *Starry Ice* and *Etherway*,' Karrde said, turning the exterior running lights on and then off three times. Outside the viewport, frowning faces began turning to look up at him. 'I trust you're not going to try to go very far.'

Ferrier grinned at him. 'What, you afraid I'll steal your precious freighter?'

'You're not going to steal it,' Karrde said, locking eyes with him. 'I'll destroy it first.'

Ferrier snorted. 'Big talk from someone on the wrong end of a blaster,' he said contemptuously, hefting the weapon for emphasis.

'I'm not bluffing,' Karrde warned him, turning on the running lights again and risking a casual look out the viewport. Between the warning flicker of lights and the sight of Ferrier holding a blaster on him, the crowd out there had presumably caught on to what was happening. He hoped so, anyway. If they hadn't, the *Wild Karrde*'s unannounced departure would probably trigger a firefight.

'Sure you're not,' Ferrier grunted, dropping into the copilot station beside him. 'Relax – you're not going to have to be a hero. I'd like nothing better than to take the *Wild Karrde* off your hands, but I know better than to try to run a ship like this with half a crew. No, all you're going to do is take me back to my ship. We'll get out of here and lay low until all this blows over.' He threw one last look at the displays and nodded. 'OK. Let's go.'

Mentally crossing his fingers, Karrde eased in the repulsorlifts and nudged the ship forward, half expecting a barrage of blaster shots from the crowd of aides and bodyguards outside. But no-one opened fire as he maneuvered carefully through the jagged stone edging the opening and out into the open air. 'Yeah, they're all gone from in there, all right,' Ferrier said casually into the silence. 'Probably scrambling to get back to their ships so they can chase after us.'

'You don't seem worried about it.'

'I'm not,' Ferrier said. 'All you have to do is get me to my ship a little ahead of them. You can do that, right?'

Karrde looked over at the blaster pointed at him. 'I'll do my best.'

They made it easily. Even as the *Wild Karrde* settled to the cracked stone beside a modified Corellian Gunship the others were just beginning to appear from the archways leading into the main part of the fortress, a good couple of minutes away. 'Knew you could do it,' Ferrier complimented him sarcastically, standing up and keying the intercom. 'Wraith? Hit the door. We're out of here.'

There was no response. 'Wraith? You hear me?'

'He will not be hearing anything for a while,' Clyngunn's voice rumbled back. 'If you want him, you will have to carry him.'

Viciously, Ferrier slapped off the intercom. 'Fool. I should have known better than to trust a stupid wraith with anything. Better yet, I should have killed all of you right at the start.'

'Perhaps,' Karrde said. He nodded across the courtyard toward the approaching bodyguards and enforcers. 'I don't think you have time to correct that oversight now.'

'I'll just have to do it later,' Ferrier shot back. 'I could still take care of you, though.'

'Only if you're willing to die along with me,' Karrde countered, shifting slightly in his seat to show that his left hand was holding down one of the knee panel switches. 'As I said, I'd rather destroy the ship than let you have it.'

For a long moment he thought Ferrier was going to try it anyway. Then, with obvious reluctance, the ship thief shifted his aim and sent two shots sizzling into the fire-control section of the control board. 'Another time, Karrde,' he said. He stepped back to the bridge door, threw a quick look outside as it opened, and then slipped through.

Karrde took a deep breath, exhaled it slowly. Releasing the landing light switch he'd been holding down, he stood up. Fifteen seconds later, he spotted Ferrier through the viewport as he sprinted alone toward his Gunship.

Reaching carefully past the sizzling hole in his control board, he keyed the intercom. 'This is Karrde,' he said. 'You can unbarricade the door now; Ferrier's left. Do you need any medical help or assistance with your prisoner?'

'No, to both,' Gillespee assured him. 'Defel might be good at sneaking around, but they're not much good as jailers. So Ferrier just abandoned him here, huh?'

'No more or less than I would have expected from him,' Karrde said. Outside the viewport, Ferrier's Gunship was rising on its repulsorlifts, rotating toward the west as it did so. 'He's lifting now. Warn everyone not to leave the ship – he's bound to have something planned to discourage pursuit.'

And he did. The words were barely out of Karrde's mouth when the hovering ship ejected a large canister into the air overhead. There was a flash of light, and suddenly the sky exploded into a violently expanding tangle of metal mesh. The net stretched itself out across the courtyard and settled to the ground, throwing off sparks where it draped itself across the parked ships.

'A Conner net,' Dravis's voice came from behind him. 'Typical ship-thief trick.'

Karrde turned. Dravis, Par'tah, and Mazzic were standing just inside the door, looking through the viewport at the departing Gunship. 'We have plenty of people outside it,' he reminded them. 'It shouldn't take long to get it burned off.'

[He must not be allowed to escape,] Par'tah insisted, making a Ho'Din gesture of contempt toward the Gunship.

'He won't,' Karrde assured her. The Gunship was streaking low across the plain, staying out of range of anything the netter ships might still be able to fire at him. 'The *Etherway* and *Starry Ice* are standing ready, north and south of here.' He turned back and lifted an eyebrow toward Mazzic. 'But under the circumstances, I think Mazzic should have the honor.'

Mazzic gave him a tight smile. 'Thank you,' he said softly, pulling out his comlink. 'Griv, Amber. Gunship on the way. Take it.'

Karrde looked back. The Gunship was nearly to the horizon now, starting its vertical climb toward space . . . and as he watched, Mazzic's two fighters rose behind it from their hiding places and gave pursuit.

'I guess I owe you an apology,' Mazzic said from behind him.

Karrde shook his head. 'Forget it,' he said. 'Or, better, don't forget it. Keep it as a reminder of the way Grand Admiral Thrawn does business. And what people like us ultimately mean to him.'

'Don't worry,' Mazzic said softly. 'I won't forget.'

'Good,' Karrde said briskly. 'Well, then. Let's get our people out there busy on this net – I'm sure we'd all prefer to be off Hijarna before the Empire realizes their scheme has failed.'

In the distance, just above the horizon, there was a brief flare of light. 'And while we're waiting,' Karrde added, 'I still have a proposal to present to you.'

CHAPTER 19

'All right,' Han told Lando, his fingers searching along the edge of Artoo's left leg for a better handhold. 'Get ready.'

The droid twittered something. 'He reminds you to be careful,' Threepio translated, standing nervously just far enough out of their way not to get yelled at. 'Do remember that the last time—'

'We didn't drop him on purpose,' Han growled. 'If he'd rather wait for Luke, he's welcome.'

Artoo twittered again. 'He says that will not be necessary,' Threepio said primly. 'He trusts you implicitly.'

'Glad to hear it,' Han said. There were, unfortunately, no better handholds. He'd have to talk to Industrial Automaton about that someday. 'Here we go, Lando: lift.'

Together they strained; and with a jolt that wrenched Han's back the droid came up and out of the tangle of tree roots that he'd somehow gotten entwined around his wheels. 'There you go,' Lando grunted as they dropped the droid more or less gently back into the dirt and leaves of the dry creek bed. 'How's it feel?'

The explanation this time was longer. 'He says there appears to have been only minimal damage,' Threepio said. 'Mainly cosmetic in nature.'

'Translation: he's rusting,' Han muttered, rubbing the small of his back as he turned around. Five meters further down the creek bed, Luke was using his lightsaber to carefully slice through a set of thick vines blocking their path. Beside him, Chewbacca and Mara were crouched with weapons drawn, ready to shoot the snakelike creatures that sometimes came boiling out when you cut into them. Like everything else on Wayland, they'd learned about that one the hard way.

Lando walked up beside him, brushing a few last bits of acidic tree root off his hands. 'Fun place, isn't it?' he commented.

'I should have brought the *Falcon* down closer,' Han grumbled. 'Or moved it closer in when we found out we couldn't use the speeder bikes.'

'If you had, we might be dodging Imperial patrols right now instead of fighting acid root and vine snakes,' Lando said. 'Personally, I'd call that a fair trade.'

'I suppose so,' Han agreed reluctantly. In the near distance something gave out with a complicated whistle, and something else whistled back. He looked that direction, but between the brush and vines and two different levels of trees he couldn't see anything.

'Doesn't sound much like a predator,' Lando said.

'Maybe.' Han looked back over his shoulder, to where Threepio was talking soothingly to Artoo as he inspected the squat droid's latest acid burns. 'Hey – short stuff. Get your scanners busy.'

Obediently, Artoo extended its little antenna and began moving it back and forth. For a minute it clucked to itself, then jabbered something. 'He says there are no large animals anywhere within twenty meters,' Threepio said. 'Beyond that—'

'He can't read through the undergrowth,' Han finished for

him. It was getting to be a very familiar conversation. 'Thanks.'

Artoo retracted his sensor, and he and Threepio resumed their discussion. 'Where do you suppose they've all gone?' Lando asked.

'The predators?' Han shook his head. 'Beats me. Maybe the same place the natives went.'

Lando looked around, exhaling gently between his teeth. 'I don't like it, Han. They've got to know by now that we're here. What are they waiting for?'

'Maybe Mara was wrong about them,' Han suggested doubtfully. 'Maybe the Empire got tired of sharing the planet with anyone else and wiped them out.'

'That's a cheerful thought,' Lando said. 'Still wouldn't explain why the predators have ignored us for the past two and a half days.'

'No,' Han agreed. But Lando was right: there *was* something out there watching them. He could feel it deep in his gut. Something, or somebody. 'Maybe the ones that got away after that first fight passed the word down the wire to leave us alone.'

Lando snorted. 'Those things were dumber than space slugs, and you know it.'

Han shrugged. 'Just a thought.'

Ahead, the greenish glow vanished as Luke closed down his lightsaber. 'Looks clear,' he called softly back. 'You get Artoo out?'

'Yeah, he's all right,' Han said, stepping up behind them. 'Any snakes?'

'Not this time.' Luke pointed with his lightsaber at one of the trees bordering the creek bed. 'Looks like we just missed having to tangle with another group of clawbirds, though.'

Han looked. There, in one of the lower branches, was another of the plate-sized mud-and-grass nests. Threepio had brushed against one of them the day before, and Chewbacca was still nursing the slashes he'd gotten in his left arm before they'd managed to shoot or lightsaber the predator birds that had come out of it. 'Don't touch it,' he warned.

'It's OK – it's empty,' Luke assured him, nudging it with the tip of the lightsaber. 'They must have moved on.'

'Yeah,' Han said slowly, taking a step closer to the nest. 'Right.'

'Something wrong?'

Han looked back at him. 'No,' he said, trying hard to sound casual. 'No problem. Why?'

Behind Luke, Chewbacca rumbled deep in his throat. 'Let's get moving,' Han added before Luke could say anything. 'I want to get a little further before it gets dark. Luke, you and Mara take the droids and head out. Chewie and me'll take the rear.'

Luke wasn't going for it – he could tell that from the kid's face. But he just nodded. 'All right. Come on, Threepio.'

They started down the creek bed, Threepio complaining as usual the whole way. Lando threw Han a look of his own, but followed after them without comment.

Beside him, Chewbacca growled a question. 'We're going to find out what happened to the clawbirds, that's what,' Han told him, looking back at the nest. It didn't look damaged, like it should have if a predator had got it. 'You're the one who can smell fresh meat ten paces upwind. Start sniffing.'

It turned out not to take much in the way of Wookiee hunting skill. One of the birds was lying beside a bush just on the other side of the tree, its wings stretched out and stiff. Very dead.

'What do you think?' Han asked as Chewbacca gingerly picked it up. 'Some predator?'

Chewbacca rumbled a negative. His climbing claws slid from their sheaths, probing at a dark-brown stain on the feathers under the left wing. He found a cut, dug a single claw delicately into it.

And growled. 'You sure it was a knife?' Han frowned, peering at the wound. 'Not some kind of claw?'

The Wookiee rumbled again, pointing out the obvious: if the bird had been killed by a predator, there shouldn't have been anything left but feathers and bones.

'Right,' Han commented sourly as Chewbacca dropped the

287

clawbird back beside the bush. 'So much for hoping the natives weren't around. Must be pretty close, too.'

Chewbacca growled the obvious questions. 'Beats me,' Han told him. 'Maybe they're still checking us out. Or waiting for reinforcements.'

The Wookiee rumbled, gesturing at the bird, and Han took another look. He was right: the way the wound was placed meant that the wings had been open when it had been killed. Which meant it had been killed in flight. By a single stab. 'You're right – they're not going to need any reinforcements,' he agreed. 'Come on, let's catch up with the others.'

Solo had wanted them to keep going until it got dark, but after another disagreement between Skywalker's astromech droid and a tangle of acid vines, he gave up and called a halt.

'So what's the word?' Mara asked as Skywalker dropped his pack beside hers and stretched his shoulder muscles. 'We going to have to carry it?'

'I don't think so,' Skywalker said, looking over his shoulder to where Calrissian and the Wookiee had the R2 on its side and were tinkering with its wheels. 'Chewie thinks he'll be able to fix it.'

'You ought to trade it in on something that wasn't designed to travel on a flat metal deck.'

'Sometimes I've wished,' Skywalker conceded, sitting down beside her. 'All things considered, though, he does pretty well. You should have seen how far across the Tatooine desert he got the first night I had him.'

Mara looked past the droids to where Solo was setting up his bedroll and keeping one eye on the forest around them. 'You going to tell me what Solo was talking to you about back there? Or is it something I'm not supposed to know?'

'He and Chewie found one of the clawbirds from that empty nest,' Skywalker said. 'The one near the second vine cluster we had to cut through today. It had been killed by a knife thrust.'

Mara swallowed, thinking back to some of the stories she'd heard when she was here with the Emperor. 'Probably the

Myneyrshi,' she said. 'They were supposed to have made an art of that kind of close-blade combat.'

'Did they have any feelings one way or the other about the Empire?'

'Like I told you before, they don't like humans,' Mara told him. 'Starting with the ones who came here as colonists long before the Emperor found the planet.'

She looked at Skywalker, but he wasn't looking back. He was staring at nothing, a slight frown creasing his forehead.

Mara took a deep breath, stretching out with the Force as hard as she could. The sounds and smells of the forest wove their way into her mind, flattening into the overall pattern of life around her. Trees, bushes, animals and birds . . .

And there, just at the edge of her consciousness, was another mind. Alien, unreadable . . . but a mind just the same.

'Four of them,' Skywalker said quietly. 'No. Five.'

Mara frowned, concentrating on the sensation. He was right: there was more than one mind out there. But she couldn't quite separate the various components out from the general sense.

'Try looking for deviations,' Skywalker murmured. 'The ways the minds are different from each other. That's the best way to resolve them.'

Mara tried it; and to her slightly annoyed surprise discovered that he was right. There was the second mind . . . the third . . .

And then, suddenly, they were gone.

She looked sharply at Skywalker. 'I don't know,' he said slowly, still concentrating. 'There was a surge of emotion, and then they just turned and left.'

'Maybe they didn't know we were here,' Mara suggested hesitantly, knowing even as she said it how unlikely that was. Between the Wookiee roaring at everything that came at them and the protocol droid whining about everything else, it was a wonder the whole planet didn't know they were there.

'No, they knew,' Skywalker said. 'In fact, I'm pretty sure they were coming directly toward us when they were—' He shook his head. 'I want to say they were scared away. But that doesn't make any sense.'

Mara looked at the double leaf-canopy overhead. 'Could we have picked up an Imperial patrol?'

'No.' Skywalker was positive. 'I'd know if there were any other humans nearby.'

'Bet that comes in handy,' Mara muttered.

'It's just a matter of training.'

She threw him a sideways look. There'd been something odd in his voice. 'What's that supposed to mean?'

He grimaced, a quick tightening of his mouth. 'Nothing. Just . . . I was thinking about Leia's twins. Thinking about how I'm going to have to train them some day.'

'You worried about when to start?'

He shook his head. 'I'm worried about being able to do it at all.'

She shrugged. 'What's to do? You teach them how to hear minds and move objects and use lightsabers. You did that with your sister, didn't you?'

'Yes,' he agreed. 'But that was when I thought that was all there was to it. It's really just the beginning. They're going to be strong in the Force, and with that strength comes responsibility. How do I teach them that? How do I teach them wisdom and compassion and how not to abuse their power?'

Mara studied his profile as he gazed out into the forest. This wasn't just word games; he was really serious about it. Definitely a side of the heroic, noble, infallible Jedi she hadn't seen before. 'How does anyone teach anyone else that stuff?' she said. 'Mostly by example, I suppose.'

He thought about it, nodded reluctantly. 'I suppose so. How much Jedi training did the Emperor give you?'

YOU WILL KILL LUKE SKYWALKER. 'Enough,' she said shortly, shaking the sound of the words from her mind and trying to stifle the flash of reflexive hatred that came with them. 'All the basics. Why? – you checking for wisdom and compassion?'

'No.' He hesitated. 'But as long as we've got a few more

days until we reach Mount Tantiss, it might be a good idea to go over it again. You know – a refresher course sort of thing.'

She looked at him, an icy chill running through her. He was just a little bit too casual about this . . . 'Have you seen something about what's ahead of us?' she asked suspiciously.

'Not really,' he said. But there was that brief hesitation again. 'A few images and pictures that didn't make any sense. I just think it would be a good idea for you to be as strong in the Force as possible before we go in.'

She looked away from him. *YOU WILL KILL LUKE SKYWALKER.* 'You'll be there,' she reminded him. 'What do I need to be strong in the Force for?'

'For whatever purpose your destiny calls you to,' he said, his voice quiet but firm. 'We have an hour or so left before sundown. Let's get started.'

Wedge Antilles slid into his place on the long semicircular bench beside the other starfighter squadron commanders, glancing around the Star Cruiser war room as he did so. A good crowd already, and more were still filing in. Whatever Ackbar had planned, it was going to be big.

' 'Lo, Wedge,' someone grunted in greeting as he sat down beside Wedge. 'Fancy meeting you here.'

Wedge looked at him in mild surprise. Pash Cracken, son of the legendary General Airen Cracken, and one of the best starfighter commanders in the business. 'I could say the same about you, Pash,' he said. 'I thought you were out in Atrivis sector, babysitting the Outer Rim comm center.'

'You're behind the times,' Pash said grimly. 'Generis fell three days ago.'

Wedge stared at him. 'I hadn't heard,' he apologized. 'How bad was it?'

'Bad enough,' Pash said. 'We lost the whole comm center, more or less intact, and most of the sector fleet supply depots. On the plus side, we didn't leave them any ships they could use. And we were able to make enough trouble on our way out to let General Kryll sneak Travia Chan and her people out from under the Imperials' collective snout.'

'That's something, I guess,' Wedge said. 'What was it got you, numbers or tactics?'

'Both,' Pash said with a grimace. 'I don't think Thrawn was there personally, but he sure planned out the assault. I've got to tell you, Wedge, that those clones of his are the creepiest things I've ever tangled with. It's like going up against stormtroopers: same rabid dedication, same cold-blooded machine-precision fighting. The only difference is that they're everywhere now instead of just handling shock-troop duty.'

'Tell me about it,' Wedge agreed soberly. 'We had to fight off two TIE fighter squadrons of the things in the first Qat Chrystac assault. They were pulling stunts I didn't think TIEs were capable of.'

Pash nodded. 'General Kryll figures Thrawn must be picking his best people for his cloning templets.'

'He'd be stupid to do anything else. What about Varth? Did he make it out?'

'I don't know,' Pash said. 'We lost contact with him during the retreat. I'm still hoping he was able to punch through the other side of the pincer and hook up with one of the units at Fedje or Ketaris.'

Wedge thought about the handful of times he'd gone nose-to-nose with Wing Commander Varth over something, usually involving spare parts or maintenance time. The man was a bitter, caustic-mouthed tyrant, with the single redeeming talent of being able to throw his starfighters against ridiculous odds and then get them back out again. 'He'll make it,' Wedge said. 'He's too contrary to roll over and die just for the Empire's convenience.'

'Maybe.' Pash nodded toward the center of the room. 'Looks like we're ready to start.'

Wedge turned back as the buzz of conversation around them faded away. Admiral Ackbar was standing by the central holo table, flanked by General Crix Madine and Colonel Bren Derlin. 'Officers of the New Republic,' Ackbar greeted them gravely, his large Mon Calamari eyes rotating to take in the entire war room. 'None of you needs to be reminded that in the past few weeks our war against the remnants of the Empire has changed from what was once called a mopping-up exercise to a battle for our very survival. For the moment, the advantage of resources and personnel is still ours; but even as we speak that advantage is in danger of slipping away. Less tangible but no less serious are the ways in which Grand Admiral Thrawn is seeking to undermine our resolve and morale. It is time for us to throw both aspects of this attack back into the Empire's face.' He looked at Madine. 'General Madine.'

'I assume that you've all been briefed on the innovative form of siege the Imperials have created around Coruscant,' Madine said, tapping his light-pointer gently against his left palm. 'They've been making some progress in clearing out the cloaked asteroids; but what they really need to get the job done is a crystal gravfield trap. We've been assigned to get them one.'

'Sounds like fun,' Pash muttered.

'Quiet,' Wedge muttered back.

'Intelligence has located three of them,' Madine continued. 'All in Imperial-held space, naturally. The simplest one to go after is at Tangrene, helping to guard the new Ubiqtorate base they're putting together there. Lots of cargo and construction ships moving around, but relatively few combat ships. We've managed to insert some of our people into the cargo crew, and they report the place is ripe for the taking.'

'Sounds a lot like Endor,' someone commented from the bench across from Wedge. 'How can we be sure it isn't a trap?'

'Actually, we're pretty sure it is,' Madine said with a tight smile. 'That's why we're going here instead.'

He touched a switch. The holo projector rose from the center of the table, and a schematic appeared in the air above it. 'The Imperial shipyards at Bilbringi,' he identified it. 'And I know what you're all saying to yourselves: it's big, it's well defended, and what in the galaxy is the high command thinking about? The answer is simple: it's big, it's well defended, and it's the last place the Imperials will expect us to hit.'

'Moreover, if we succeed, we will have severely damaged their shipbuilding capability,' Ackbar added. 'As well as putting to rest the growing belief in Grand Admiral Thrawn's infallibility.'

Which assumed, of course, that Thrawn *was* fallible. Wedge thought about pointing that out, decided against it. Everyone here was probably already thinking it, anyway.

'The operation will consist of two parts,' Madine went on. 'We certainly don't want to disappoint the Imperials planning the trap for us at Tangrene, so Colonel Derlin will be in charge of creating the illusion that that system is indeed our target. While he does that, Admiral Ackbar and I will be organizing the actual attack on Bilbringi. Any questions?'

There was a moment of silence. Then, Pash raised his hand. 'What happens if the Imperials pick up on the Bilbringi attack and miss the Tangrene preparations entirely?'

Madine smiled thinly. 'We'd be most disappointed in them. All right, gentlemen, we have an assault force to organize. Let's get started.'

The bedroom was dark and warm and quiet, murmuring with the faint nighttime noises of the Imperial City outside the windows and the more subtle sounds of the sleeping infants across the room. Listening to the sounds, inhaling the familiar aromas of home, Leia stared at the ceiling and wondered what had awakened her.

'Do you require anything, Lady Vader?' a soft Noghri voice came from the shadows beside the door.

'No, Mobvekhar, thank you,' Leia said. She hadn't made any noise – he must have picked up on the change in her breathing pattern. 'I'm sorry; I didn't mean to disturb you.'

'You did not,' the Noghri assured her. 'Are you troubled?'

'I don't know,' she said. It was starting to come back now. 'I had – not a dream, exactly. More like a subconscious flash of insight. A piece of a puzzle trying to fit into place.'

'Do you know which piece?'

Leia shook her head. 'I don't even know which puzzle.'

'Did it relate to the siege of stones in the sky above?'

Mobvekhar asked. 'Or with the mission of your consort and the son of Vader?'

'I'm not sure,' Leia said, frowning with concentration into the darkness and running through the short-term memory enhancement techniques Luke had taught her. Slowly, the half-remembered dream images started to sharpen . . . 'It was something Luke said. No. It was something *Mara* said. Something Luke *did*. They fit together somehow. I don't know how . . . but I know it's important.'

'Then you will find the answer,' Mobvekhar said firmly. 'You are the Lady Vader. The *Mal'ary'ush* of the Lord Vader. You will succeed at whatever goal you set for yourself.'

Leia smiled in the darkness. It wasn't just words. Mobvekhar and the other Noghri truly believed that. 'Thank you,' she said, taking a deep breath and feeling a renewing of her own spirit. Yes, she would succeed. If for no other reason than to justify the trust that the Noghri people had placed in her.

Across the room, she could sense the restlessness and growing hunger that meant the twins would be waking up soon. Reaching past the lightsaber half hidden beneath her pillow, she pulled her robe over to her. Whatever this important puzzle piece was she'd stumbled on, it would wait until morning.

CHAPTER 20

The last surviving Rebel ship flickered with pseudomotion and vanished into hyperspace . . . and after a thirty-hour battle, the heart of Kanchen sector was finally theirs. 'Secure the fleet from full battle status, Captain,' Thrawn ordered, his voice grimly satisfied as he stood at the side viewport. 'Deploy for planetary bombardment, and have Captain Harbid transmit our terms of surrender to the Xa Fel government.'

'Yes, sir,' Pellaeon said, keying in the order.

Thrawn half turned to face him. 'And send a further message to all ships,' he added. 'Well done.'

Pellaeon smiled. Yes; the Grand Admiral did indeed know how to lead his men. 'Yes, sir,' he said, and transmitted the message. On his board, a light went on: a preflagged message had just come through decrypt. He pulled it up, skimmed through it—

'A report from Tangrene?' Thrawn asked, still gazing out at the helpless world lying below them.

'Yes, sir,' Pellaeon nodded. 'The Rebels have sent two more freighters into the system. Long-range scans suggest that they offloaded something in the outer system on the way in, but Intelligence has so far been unable to locate or identify the drops.'

'Instruct them not to try,' Thrawn said. 'We don't want our prey frightened off.'

Pellaeon nodded, marveling once again at the Grand Admiral's ability to read his opponents. Up until twenty hours ago he would have sworn the Rebels wouldn't be audacious enough to commit this many forces to a battle just to get hold of a CGT array. Apparently, they were. 'We're also getting reports of Rebel ships drifting quietly into the Tangrene area,' he added, skimming down the report again. 'Warships, starfighters, support craft – the whole range.'

'Good,' Thrawn said. But there was something preoccupied and troubled about the way he clasped his hands behind his back.

A message appeared on Pellaeon's board: the Xa Fel government had accepted Harbid's terms. 'Word from the *Death's Head*, Admiral,' he said. 'Xa Fel has surrendered.'

'Not unexpectedly,' Thrawn said. 'Inform Captain Harbid that he will handle the landings and troop deployments. You, Captain, will reconfigure the fleet into defensive formation until planetary defenses have been secured.'

'Yes, sir.' Pellaeon frowned at the Grand Admiral's back. 'Is anything wrong, Admiral?'

'I don't know,' Thrawn said slowly. 'I'll be in my private command room, Captain. Join me there in one hour.'

He turned and favored Pellaeon with a tight smile. 'Perhaps by then I'll have an answer to that question.'

Gillespee finished reading and handed the data pad across the table to Mazzic. 'You never cease to amaze me, Karrde,' he said, his voice just loud enough to be heard over the tapcafe's background noise. 'Where in space do you dig this stuff up from, anyway?'

'Around,' Karrde said, waving his hand vaguely. 'Just around.'

'That doesn't tell me mynock spit,' Gillespee complained.

'I don't think it was meant to,' Mazzic said dryly, handing the data pad back to Karrde. 'I agree; it's very interesting. The question is whether we can believe it.'

'The information itself is reliable,' Karrde said. 'My interpretation of it, of course, is certainly open to question.'

Mazzic shook his head. 'I don't know. It seems like a pretty desperate move to me.'

'I wouldn't say desperate,' Karrde disagreed. 'Call it instead a return to the bold tactics the Rebel Alliance used to be known for. Personally, I think a move like this is long overdue – they've allowed themselves to be put on the defensive far longer than they should have.'

'That doesn't change the fact that if this doesn't work they're going to lose a lot of ships,' Mazzic pointed out. 'Up to two entire sector fleets, if you can believe these numbers.'

'True,' Karrde agreed. 'But if it does work, they get a major victory against Thrawn and an equally major lift in morale. Not to mention a CGT array.'

'Yeah, that's another thing,' Gillespie put in. 'What do they need a CGT for, anyway?'

'It supposedly has something to do with the reason Coruscant has been closed to civilian traffic for the past few days,' Karrde said. 'That's all I know.'

Mazzic leaned back in his seat and fixed Karrde with a speculative look. 'Forget what they need it for. What are you proposing we do about it?'

Karrde shrugged. 'It looks to me like the New Republic is

fairly desperate to get their hands on a CGT. If they're willing to fight for one, I assume they'd be even more willing to pay for one.'

'Seems reasonable,' Mazzic agreed. 'So what do you want us to do, sneak into Tangrene before they get there?'

'Not really,' Karrde shook his head. 'I thought that while everyone was busy fighting at Tangrene, we'd pick up the CGT at Bilbringi.'

Mazzic's smile vanished. 'You're joking.'

'Not a bad idea, really,' Gillespee put in, slowly swirling the remains of the drink in his cup. 'We slip in before the attack starts, then grab the CGT and run.'

'Through half the Imperial fleet?' Mazzic countered. 'Come on – I've seen the kind of firepower they keep there.'

'I doubt they'll have more than a skeleton defense there.' Karrde raised an eyebrow. 'Unless you seriously think Thrawn won't anticipate and prepare for the new Republic's move on Tangrene.'

'Point,' Mazzic conceded. 'They can't afford to let the New Republic have a victory there, can they?'

'Particularly not at Tangrene,' Karrde nodded. 'That's where General Bel Iblis successfully hit them once before.'

Mazzic grunted and pulled the data pad over in front of him again. Karrde let him reread the information and analysis, giving the tapcafe a leisurely scan as he waited. Near the main entrance, Aves and Gillespee's lieutenant Faughn were sitting together at one of the tables, doing a good job of looking inconspicuous. Across the way at the rear entrance, Mazzic's bodyguard Shada was playing the flirtatious hostess role for Dankin and Torve, the whole routine being convincingly leered at by Rappapor and Oshay, two more of Gillespee's people. Three more tables of backup forces were scattered elsewhere throughout the tapcafe, primed and ready. This time, none of them were taking any chances with Imperial interference.

'It won't be easy,' Mazzic warned at last. 'Thrawn was furious about that raid we pulled. They've probably redone their whole security setup by now.'

'All the better,' Karrde said. 'They won't have found the holes in it yet. Are you in or out?'

Mazzic looked down at the data pad. 'I might be in,' he growled. 'But only if you can get a confirmation on the time of this Tangrene thing. I don't want Thrawn anywhere within a hundred light-years of Bilbringi when we hit the place.'

'That shouldn't be a problem,' Karrde said. 'We know the systems where the New Republic is assembling their forces. I'll send some of my people to poke around and see what they can turn up.'

'What if they can't get anything?'

Karrde smiled. 'I need to have Ghent write us on to their payroll anyway,' he pointed out. 'As long as he's in the system, he might as well check on their battle plans, too.'

For a moment Mazzic just stared at him. Then, suddenly, the frown vanished and he actually chuckled. 'You know, Karrde, I've never seen anyone play both ends against the middle the way you do. OK. I'm in.'

'Glad to have you,' Karrde nodded. 'Gillespee?'

'I've already seen Thrawn's clones in action,' Gillespee reminded him grimly. 'You bet I'm in. Besides, if we win maybe I can get that land back the Empire stole from me on Ukio.'

'I'll put in a good word for you with the New Republic,' Karrde promised. 'All right, then. I'm taking the *Wild Karrde* to Coruscant, but I'll be leaving Aves behind to coordinate my part of the attack group. He'll give you the operations plan when you check in.'

'Sounds good,' Mazzic said as they all got to their feet. 'You know, Karrde, I just hope I'm around to see the day the New Republic catches up with you. Whether they give you a medal or just shoot you – either way, it'll be a terrific show.'

Karrde smiled at him. 'I rather hope to be there that day myself,' he said. 'Good flights, gentlemen; I'll see you at Bilbringi.'

The brilliant green turbolaser blast flashed downward from the fuzzy-looking Star Destroyer in the distance beyond. It splashed slightly against the unseen energy shield, then reappeared a short distance away, continuing onward—

'Stop,' Admiral Drayson said.

The record froze, the hazy splash of turbolaser fire looking angular and rather artificial as it sat there in stop-frame mode on the main display. 'I apologize for the quality here,' Drayson said, stepping over to tap it with his light-pointer. 'Macrobinocular records can be enhanced only so much before the algorithms start breaking down. But even so, I think you can all see what's happening. The Star Destroyer's blast is not, in fact, penetrating Ukio's planetary shield. What appears to be that same blast is actually a second shot, fired from a cloaked vessel *inside* the shield.'

Leia peered at the hazy picture. It didn't seem nearly that obvious to her. 'Are you sure?' she asked.

'Quite sure,' Drayson said, touching his light-pointer to the empty space between the splash and the continuing green fire. 'We have spectral and energy-line data on the beams themselves; but this gap by itself is really all the proof we need. That's the bulk of the second ship – most likely a *Carrack*-class light cruiser, from the size.'

He lowered the light-pointer and looked around the table. 'In other words, the Empire's new superweapon is nothing more than an extremely clever fraud.'

Leia thought about that meeting in Admiral Ackbar's rooms, back when he was under suspicion of treason. 'Ackbar once warned Han and me that a Grand Admiral would find ways to use a cloaking shield against us.'

'I don't think you'd find anyone arguing that point,' Drayson nodded. 'At any rate, this should put an end to this particular gambit. We'll put out an alert to all planetary forces that if the Empire tries it again, all they need to do is direct a saturation fire at the spot where the turbolaser blasts appear to penetrate the shield.'

'Fraud or not, it was still one highly impressive show,' Bel Iblis commented. 'The position and timing were exquisitely handled. What do you think, Leia – that insane Jedi Luke locked horns with on Jomark?'

'I don't think there's any doubt,' Leia said, a shiver running through her. 'We've already seen this kind of coordination between forces in Thrawn's earlier campaigns. And we know from Mara that C'baoth and Thrawn are working together.'

Mentioning Mara's name was a mistake. There was a general, uncomfortable shifting in seats around the table as the emotional sense in the room chilled noticeably. They'd all heard Leia's reasoning for her unilateral decision to release Mara, and none of them had liked it.

Bel Iblis broke the awkward silence first. 'Where did this macrobinocular record come from, Admiral?'

'From that smuggler, Talon Karrde,' Drayson said. He threw a significant look at Leia. 'Another outsider who came here offering valuable information that didn't pan out.'

Leia bristled. 'That's not fair,' she insisted. 'The fact we lost the *Katana* fleet wasn't Karrde's fault.' She looked at Councilor Fey'lya, sitting silently at the table, doing his private Bothan penance. If Fey'lya hadn't been making that insane bid for power . . .

She looked back at Drayson. 'It was nobody's fault,' she added quietly, releasing at last the final lingering dregs of resentment at Fey'lya and allowing them to drain away. The recognition of his failure was already paralyzing the Bothan. She couldn't allow long-dead anger to do the same to her.

Bel Iblis cleared his throat. 'I think what Leia's trying to say is that without Karrde's help we might have lost more than just the *Katana* fleet. Whatever you think of smugglers in general or Karrde in particular, we owe him.'

'Interesting that you should say that, General,' Drayson said dryly. 'Karrde seems to feel the same way. In exchange for this record and certain other minor items of intelligence, he's drawn rather liberally from a special New Republic credit line.' He looked at Leia again. 'A line apparently set up by Councilor Organa Solo's brother.'

Commander Sesfan, Ackbar's representative to the Council, rolled his huge Mon Calamari eyes toward Leia. 'Jedi Skywalker authorized payments to a smuggler?' he said, his gravelly voice sounding astonished.

'He did,' Drayson confirmed. 'Completely without authorization, of course. We'll close it off immediately.'

'You'll do no such thing,' Mon Mothma's quiet voice came from the head of the table. 'Whether Karrde is officially on our side or not, he's clearly willing to help us. That makes him worthy of our support.'

'But he is a smuggler,' Sesfan objected.

'So was Han,' Leia reminded him. 'So was Lando Calrissian, once. Both of them became generals.'

'*After* they joined us,' Sesfan countered. 'Karrde has made no such commitment.'

'It doesn't matter,' Mon Mothma said. Her voice was still quiet, but there was steel beneath it. 'We need all the allies we can get. Official or otherwise.'

'Unless he's setting us up,' Drayson pointed out darkly. 'Gaining our trust with things like this macrobinocular record so that he can feed us disinformation later. And in the meantime profiting rather handsomely from it.'

'We'll simply have to make certain we spot any such duplicity,' Mon Mothma told him. 'But I don't believe that will happen. Luke Skywalker is a Jedi . . . and he, clearly, has some trust in this man Karrde. Regardless, for now, our focus should be on those parts of our destiny which are in our hands. Admiral Drayson, have you the latest report on the Bilbringi operation?'

'Yes,' Drayson nodded, pulling out a data card. He inserted it into the display slot, and as he did so, Leia heard the faint beep of a comlink from beside her. Winter pulled the device from her belt and acknowledged softly into it. Leia couldn't make out the reply, but she felt the sudden flicker in Winter's sense. 'Trouble?' she murmured.

'If I may have everyone's attention?' Drayson said, just a little too loudly.

Leia returned back to him, feeling her face warm, as Winter pushed her chair back and slipped over to the door. Drayson threw a glare at her back, apparently decided it wasn't worth invoking the usual sealed-room rule. The door slid open at Winter's touch and an unseen person pressed a data card into

302

her hand. The door slid shut again – 'Well?' Drayson demanded. 'I trust this is something that couldn't wait?'

'I'm certain it could have,' Winter said coolly, giving Drayson her full anticluster gaze as she returned to her seat and sat down. 'For you, Your Highness,' she said, handing Leia the data card. 'The coordinates of the planet Wayland.'

A ripple of surprise went around the room as Leia took the card. 'That was fast,' Drayson said, his voice tinged with suspicion. 'I was under the impression this place was going to be a lot harder to find.'

Leia shrugged, trying to suppress her own twinge of uneasiness. That had been her impression, too. 'Apparently it wasn't.'

'Show it to us,' Mon Mothma said.

Leia slid the data card into the slot and keyed for a visual. A sector map appeared on the main display, with familiar names floating beside several of the stars. In the center, surrounded by a group of unlabeled stars, one of the systems flashed red. At the bottom of the map was a short list of planetary data and a few lines of text. 'So that's the Emperor's rat's nest,' Bel Iblis murmured, leaning forward as he studied it. 'I always wondered where he hid all those interesting little tidbits that seemed to mysteriously vanish from official storehouses and depots.'

'If that's really the place,' Drayson murmured.

'I presume you can confirm the information came from Captain Solo,' Mon Mothma said, looking at Winter.

Winter hesitated. 'It didn't come from him, exactly,' she said.

Leia frowned at her. 'What do you mean, not exactly? Was it from Luke?'

A muscle in Winter's cheek twitched. 'All I can say is that the source is reliable.'

There was a short moment of silence as everyone digested that. 'Reliable,' Mon Mothma said.

'Yes,' Winter nodded.

Mon Mothma threw a look at Leia. 'This Council is not accustomed to having information withheld from it,' she said. 'I want to know where these coordinates came from.'

'I'm sorry,' Winter said quietly. 'It's not my secret to tell.'

'Whose secret is it?'

'I can't tell you that, either.'

Mon Mothma's face darkened. 'It doesn't matter,' Bel Iblis put in before she could speak. 'Not for right now. Whether this planet is the actual cloning center or not, there's nothing we can do about it until the Bilbringi operation is over.'

Leia looked at him. 'We're not sending any backup?'

'Impossible,' Sesfan growled, shaking his huge Mon Calamari head. 'All available ships and personnel are already committed to the Bilbringi attack. Too many regions and systems have been left undefended as it is.'

'Especially when we don't even know if this is the right place,' Drayson added. 'It could just as easily be an Imperial trap.'

'It's not a trap,' Leia insisted. 'Mara's not working for the Empire any more.'

'We only have your word for that—'

'It still doesn't matter,' Bel Iblis cut him off, his senatorial voice cutting through the growing argument. 'Look at the bottom of the map, Leia – it says all indications are that their landing was undetected. Would you really want to risk that element of surprise by sending another ship in after them?'

Leia felt her stomach tighten. Unfortunately, he had a point.

'Then perhaps the Bilbringi attack should be postponed,' Fey'lya said.

Leia turned to look at him, dimly aware that the whole table was doing likewise. It was practically the first time the Bothan had spoken at a Council meeting since his bid for power had ignominiously collapsed out at the *Katana* fleet. 'I'm afraid that's out of the question, Councilor Fey'lya,' Mon Mothma said. 'Aside from all the preparations that would have to be discarded, it's absolutely imperative that we clear out these cloaked asteroids hanging over our heads.'

'Why?' Fey'lya demanded, a rippling wave running through the fur of his neck and down his shoulders. 'The shield protects us. We have adequate supplies for many months. We have full communication with the rest of the New Republic. Is it merely the fear of looking weak and helpless?'

'Appearances and perceptions are important to the New Republic,' Mon Mothma reminded him. 'And properly so. The Empire rules by force and threat; we rule instead by inspiration and leadership. We cannot be perceived to be cowering here in fear of our lives.'

'This is beyond image and perception,' Fey'lya insisted, the fur fluttering across the back of his head. 'The Bothan people knew the Emperor – knew his desires and his ambitions, perhaps better than all who were not his allies and servants. There are things in that storehouse which must never again see light. Weapons and devices which Thrawn will some day find and use against us unless we prevent him from doing so.'

'And we will do so,' Mon Mothma assured him. 'And soon. But not until we've damaged the Bilbringi shipyards and obtained a CGT array.'

'And what of Captain Solo and Councilor Organa Solo's brother?'

The lines around Mon Mothma's mouth tightened. For all the rigid military logic, Leia could see that she didn't like abandoning them there, either. 'All we can do for them right now is to continue with our plans,' she said quietly. 'To draw the Grand Admiral's attention toward our supposed attack on Tangrene.' She looked at Drayson. 'Which we were about to discuss. Admiral?'

Drayson stepped up to the display again. 'We'll start with the current status of preparations for the Tangrene feint,' he said, keying his light-pointer to call up the proper display.

Leia threw a sideways glance at Fey'lya, and at the obvious signs of agitation still visible in the Bothan's face and fur movements. What was in the mountain, she wondered, that he was so afraid Thrawn would get hold of?

Perhaps it was just as well she didn't know.

Pellaeon stepped into the dimly lit entry room just outside Thrawn's private command room, his eyes darting around. Rukh was here somewhere, waiting to play his little Noghri games. He took a step toward the door to the main chamber, took another—

There was a touch of air on the back of his neck. Pellaeon spun around, hands snapping up in half-remembered academy self-defense training.

There was no-one there. He looked around again, searching for where the Noghri might have taken cover—

'Captain Pellaeon,' the familiar catlike voice mewed from behind him.

He spun back again. Again, no-one was there; but even as his eyes searched the walls and nonexistent cover, Rukh stepped around from behind him. 'You are expected,' the Noghri said, gesturing with his slender assassin's knife toward the main door.

Pellaeon glared at him. Someday, he promised himself darkly, he would persuade Thrawn that a Grand Admiral of the Empire didn't need an arrogant alien bodyguard to protect him. And when that happened, he was going to take a very personal pleasure in having Rukh killed. 'Thank you,' he growled, and went in.

He'd expected the command room to be filled with Thrawn's usual eclectic collection of alien art, and he was right. But with one minor difference: even to Pellaeon's untrained eye it was clear that two very different styles of art were being represented. They were spread out along opposite sides of the room, with a large tactical holo of the Tangrene system filling the center.

'Come in, Captain,' Thrawn called from the double display ring as Pellaeon paused in the doorway. 'What news from Tangrene?'

'The Rebels are still moving forces into strike positions,' Pellaeon told him, making his way between the sculptures and the tactical holo toward Thrawn's command chair. 'Sneaking their devious way into our trap.'

'How very convenient of them.' Thrawn gestured to his right. 'Mon Calamari art,' he identified it. 'What do you think?'

Pellaeon gave it a quick look as he came up to the double

306

display ring. It looked about as repulsive and primitive as the Mon Calamari themselves. 'Very interesting,' he said aloud.

'Isn't it,' Thrawn agreed. 'Those two pieces in particular – they were created by Admiral Ackbar himself.'

Pellaeon eyed the indicated sculptures. 'I didn't know Ackbar had any interest in art.'

'A minor one only,' Thrawn said. 'These were composed some time ago, before he joined the Rebellion. Still, they provide useful insights into his character. As do those,' he added, gesturing to his left. 'Artwork once chosen personally by our Corellian adversary.'

Pellaeon looked at them with new interest. So Senator Bel Iblis had picked these out himself, had he? 'Where were these from, his old Imperial Senate office?'

'Those were,' Thrawn said, indicating the nearest group. 'Those were from his home; those from his private ship. Intelligence found these records, more or less accidentally, in the data from our last Obroa-skai information raid. So the Rebels continue to edge toward our trap, do they?'

'Yes, sir,' Pellaeon said, glad to be getting back to something he could understand. 'We've had two more reports of Rebel support ships moving into positions at the edge of the Draukyze system.'

'But not obviously.'

Pellaeon frowned. 'Excuse me, Admiral?'

'What I mean is that they're being highly secretive about their preparations,' Thrawn said thoughtfully. 'Quietly detaching intelligence and support ships from other assignments; moving and reforming sector fleets to free capital ships for service – that sort of thing. Never obviously. Always making Imperial Intelligence work hard to put the pieces together.'

He looked up at Pellaeon, his glowing red eyes glittering in the dim light. 'Almost as if Tangrene was indeed their true target.'

Pellaeon stared at him. 'Are you saying it isn't?'

'That's correct, Captain,' Thrawn said, gazing out at the artwork.

Pellaeon looked at the Tangrene holo. Intelligence had put a 94 per cent probability on this. 'But if they're not going to hit Tangrene . . . then where?'

'The last place we would normally expect them,' Thrawn said, reaching over to touch a switch on his command board. Tangrene system vanished, to be replaced by—

Pellaeon felt his jaw drop. '*Bilbringi?*' He wrenched his eyes back to his commander. 'Sir, that's . . .'

'Insane?' Thrawn cocked a blue-black eyebrow. 'Of course it is. The insanity of men and aliens who've learned the hard way that they can't match me face-to-face. And so they attempt to use my own tactical skill and insight against me. They pretend to walk into my trap, gambling that I'll notice the subtlety of their movements and interpret that as genuine intent. And while I then congratulate myself on my perception' – he gestured at the Bilbringi holo – 'they prepare their actual attack.'

Pellaeon looked at Bel Iblis's old artwork. 'We might want to wait for confirmation before we shift any forces from Tangrene, Admiral,' he suggested cautiously. 'We could intensify Intelligence activity in the Bilbringi region. Or perhaps Delta Source could confirm it.'

'Unfortunately, Delta Source has been silenced,' Thrawn said. 'But we have no need of confirmation. 'This *is* the Rebels' plan, and we will not risk tipping our hand with anything so obvious as a heightened Intelligence presence. They believe they've deceived me. Our overriding task now is to make certain they continue to believe that.'

He smiled grimly. 'After all, Captain, it makes no difference whether we crush them at Tangrene or at Bilbringi. No difference whatsoever.'

CHAPTER 21

The lopsided-helix shape of the seed pod hovered a meter and a half in front of Mara, practically daring her to strike it down. She eyed it darkly, Skywalker's lightsaber held ready in an unorthodox but versatile two-handed grip. She'd already missed the pod twice; she didn't intend to do so a third time. 'Don't rush it,' Skywalker cautioned her. 'Concentrate, and let the Force flow into you. Try to anticipate the pod's motion.'

Easy for him to say, she thought sourly; after all, he was the one controlling it. The pod twitched a millimeter closer, daring her again . . .

And suddenly, she decided she was tired of this game. Reaching out with the Force, she got a grip of her own on the pod. Briefly immobilized, it managed a single tremor before she jabbed the lightsaber straight out, stabbing it nearly dead center. 'There,' she said, closing down the weapon. 'I did it.'

She'd expected Skywalker to be angry. To her mild surprise, and not so mild annoyance, he wasn't in the least. 'Good,' he said encouragingly. 'Very good. It's difficult to split your attention between two separate mental and physical activities that way. And you did it well.'

'Thanks,' she muttered, tossing the lightsaber away from her toward the bushes. It curved smoothly around in midair as Skywalker pulled it back to land in his outstretched hand. 'So is that it?' she added.

Skywalker looked over his shoulder. Solo and Calrissian were hunched over the protocol droid, which had stopped complaining about Wayland's terrain, vegetation, and animal life and was instead complaining about what crunching through that stone crust had done to its foot. Skywalker's astromech droid was hovering nearby with its sensor antenna extended, running through its usual repertoire of encouraging noises. A couple of steps away, the Wookiee was rummaging through one of their packs, probably for some tool or other.

'I think we've got time for a few more exercises,' Skywalker decided, turning back to face her. 'That technique of yours is very interesting – Obi-wan never taught me anything about using the tip of the lightsaber blade.'

'The Emperor's philosophy was to use everything you had available,' Mara said.

'Somehow, that doesn't surprise me,' Skywalker said dryly. He held out the lightsaber. 'Let's try something else. Go ahead and take the lightsaber.'

Reaching out with the Force, Mara snatched it away from his loose grip, wondering idly what he would do if she tried sometime to ignite the weapon first. She wasn't sure she could handle anything as small as a switch, but it'd be worth trying just to see him scramble away from the blade.

And if, in the process, she happened to accidentally kill him . . .

YOU WILL KILL LUKE SKYWALKER.

She squeezed the lightsaber hard. *Not yet*, she told the voice firmly. *I still need him.* 'All right,' she growled. 'What now?'

He didn't get a chance to answer. Behind him, the astro-mech droid suddenly started squealing excitedly.

'What?' Solo demanded, his blaster already out of its holster.

'He says he's just noticed something worth investigating there to the side,' the protocol droid translated, gesturing to his left. 'A group of vines, I believe he's saying. Though I could be mistaken – with all the acid damage—'

'Come on, Chewie, let's check it out,' Solo cut him off, getting to his feet and starting up the shallow slope of the creek bed.

Skywalker caught Mara's eye. 'Come on,' he said, and started off after them.

There wasn't very far to go. Just inside the first row of trees, hidden from view by a bush, was another set of vines like the ones they'd had to occasionally cut through the last couple of days.

Except that this group had already been cut. Cut, and then

bunched up out of the way like a pile of thick, tangled rope.

'I think that ends any discussion as to whether someone out there is helping us along,' Calrissian said, studying one of the cut ends.

'I think you're right,' Solo said. 'No predator would have bunched them up like this.'

The Wookiee rumbled something under his breath and pulled on the bush in front of the vines. To Mara's surprise, it came away from the ground without any effort at all. 'And wouldn't have bothered with camouflage, either,' Calrissian said as the Wookiee turned it over. 'Knife cut, looks like. Just like the vines.'

'And like the clawbird from yesterday,' Solo agreed grimly. 'Luke? We been getting company?'

'I've sensed some of the natives,' Skywalker said. 'But they never seem to come very close before they leave again.' He looked back downslope at the protocol droid, waiting anxiously for them in the creek bed. 'You suppose it has anything to do with the droids?'

Solo snorted. 'You mean like on Endor, when those fuzzball Ewoks thought Threepio was a god?'

'Something like that,' Skywalker nodded. 'They could be getting close enough to hear either Threepio or Artoo.'

'Maybe.' Solo looked around. 'When do they come around?'

'Mostly around sundown,' Skywalker said. 'So far, anyway.'

'Well, next time they do, let me know,' Solo said, jamming his blaster back into its holster and starting back down the slope to the creek bed. 'It's about time we all had a little chat together. Come on, let's get moving.'

The darkness was growing thicker, and the camp nearly put together for the night, when the wisps of sensation came. 'Han?' Luke called softly. 'They're here.'

Han nodded, tapping Lando on the back as he drew his blaster. 'How many?'

Luke focused his mind, working at separating the distinct

parts out of the overall sensation. 'Looks like five or six of them, coming in from that direction.' He pointed to the side.

'Is that just in the first group?' Mara asked.

First group? Luke frowned, letting his focus open up again. She was right: there was a second group coming up behind the first. 'That's just the first group,' he confirmed. 'Second group . . . I get five or six there, too. I'm not sure, but they might be a different species from the first.'

Han looked at Lando. 'What do you think?'

'I don't like it,' Lando said, fingering his blaster uneasily. 'Mara, how well do these species usually get along?'

'Not all that well,' she said. 'There was some trade and other stuff going on when I was here; but there were also stories about long, three-way wars between them and the human colonists.'

Chewbacca growled a suggestion: that the aliens might be joining forces against them. 'That's a fun thought,' Han said. 'How about it, Luke?'

Luke strained, but it was no use. 'Sorry,' he said. 'There's plenty of emotion there, but I don't have any basis for figuring out what kind.'

'They've stopped,' Mara said, her face tight with concentration. 'Both groups.'

Han grimaced. 'I guess this is it. Lando, Mara – you stay here and guard the camp. Luke, Chewie, let's go check 'em out.'

They headed up the rocky slope and into the forest, moving as quietly as possible among the bushes and dead leaves underfoot. 'They know we're coming yet?' Han muttered over his shoulder.

Luke stretched out with the Force. 'I can't tell,' he said. 'But they don't seem to be coming any closer.'

Chewbacca rumbled something Luke didn't catch. 'Could be,' Han said. 'It'd be pretty stupid to hold a council of war this close to their target, though.'

And then, ahead and to their left, Luke caught a shadowy movement beside a thick tree trunk. 'Watch it!' he warned, his lightsaber igniting with a *snap-hiss*. In the green-white light from the blade a small figure in a tight-fitting hooded garment could be seen as it ducked back behind the trunk, barely getting out of the way as Han's quick shot blew a sizable pit in one side of the trunk. Chewbacca's bowcaster bolt was a split second behind Han's, gouging out a section of the trunk on the other side. Through the erupting cloud of smoke and splinters the figure could be seen briefly as it darted from the rapidly decreasing cover of its chosen tree toward another, thicker trunk. Even as Han swung his blaster to track it, a strange warbling split the air, sounding like a dozen alien birds—

And with a roar that was part recognition, part understanding, and part relief, Chewbacca swung the end of his bowcaster into Han's blaster, sending the shot wide of its intended target. 'Chewie—!' Han barked.

'No – he's right,' Luke cut him off. Suddenly, it had all come together for him, too. 'You – stop.'

The order was unnecessary. The shadowy figure had already come to a halt, standing unprotected in the open, its hooded face shaded from the faint light of Luke's lightsaber.

Luke took a step toward it. 'I'm Luke Skywalker,' he said formally. 'Brother of Leia Organa Solo, son of the Lord Darth Vader. Who are you?'

'I am Ekhrikhor clan Bakh'tor,' the gravelly Noghri voice replied. 'I greet you, son of Vader.'

The clearing Ekhrikhor led them to was close, only twenty meters or so further along the vector Luke had started them on in the first place. The aliens were there, all right: two different types, five of each, standing on the far side of a thick fallen tree trunk. On the near side stood two more Noghri in those camouflaged outfits of theirs with the hoods thrown back. Propped up on the log between the two sides was some sort of compact worklight, giving off just enough of a glow for Han to pick out the details of the nearest aliens.

It wasn't very encouraging. The group on the right were a head taller than the Noghri facing them and maybe a head shorter than Han. Covered with lumpy plates, they looked

313

more like walking rock piles than anything else. The group on the left were nearly as tall as Chewbacca, with four arms each and a shiny, bluish-crystal skin that reminded Han of the brownish thing they'd had to shoot off Threepio their first day here. 'Friendly-looking bunch,' he muttered to Luke as their group moved toward the last line of trees between them and the clearing.

'They are the Myneyrshi and Psadans,' Ekhrikhor said. 'They have been seeking to confront you.'

'And you've been driving them off?' Luke asked.

'They sought to confront,' the Noghri repeated. 'We could not permit that.'

They stopped just inside the clearing. A rustle ran through the aliens, one that didn't sound all that friendly. 'I get the feeling we aren't all that welcome,' Han said. 'Luke?'

Beside him, he felt Luke shake his head. 'I still can't read anything solid,' he said. 'What's this all about, Ekhrikhor?'

'They have indicated they wish a conversation with us,' the Noghri said. 'Perhaps to decide whether they will seek to give us battle.'

Han gave the aliens a quick once-over. They all seemed to be wearing knives, and there were a couple of bows in evidence, but he didn't see anything more advanced. 'They better hope they brought an army with them,' he said.

'We don't want to fight at all if we can avoid it,' Luke reproved him mildly. 'How are you going to communicate with them?'

'One of them learned a little of the Empire's basic when the storehouse was being built beneath the mountain,' Ekhrikhor said, pointing to the Myneyrsh standing closest to the work light. 'He will attempt to translate.'

'We might be able to do a little better.' Luke raised his eyebrows at Han. 'What do you think?'

'It's worth a try,' Han agreed, pulling out his comlink. It was about time Threepio earned his keep, anyway. 'Lando?'

'Right here,' Lando's voice came instantly. 'You find the aliens?'

'Yeah, we found them,' Han said. 'Plus a surprise or two.

Have Mara bring Threepio here – if she heads out the way we went she'll run right into us.'

'Got it,' Lando said. 'What about me?'

'I don't think this bunch will give us any trouble,' Han said, giving the aliens another once-over. 'You and Artoo might as well stay there and keep an eye on the camp. Oh, and if you see some short guys with camouflage suits and lots of teeth, don't shoot. They're on our side.'

'I'm glad,' Lando said dryly. 'I think. Anything else?'

Han looked at the groups of shadowy aliens, all of them staring straight back at him. 'Yeah – cross your fingers. We might be about to pick up some allies. Or else a whole lot of trouble down the road.'

'Right. Mara and Threepio are on their way. Good luck.'

'Thanks.' Shutting off the comlink, Han returned it to his belt. 'They're coming,' he told Luke.

'There is no need for them to guard your camp,' Ekhrikhor said. 'The Noghri will protect it.'

'That's OK,' Han said. 'It's getting crowded enough here as it is.' He eyed Ekhrikhor. 'So I was right. We *were* followed in.'

'Yes,' Ekhrikhor said, bowing his head. 'And for that deception I beg your forgiveness, consort of the Lady Vader. I and others did not feel it entirely honorable; but Cakhmaim clan Eikh'mir wished our presence to be kept hidden from you.'

'Why?'

Ekhrikhor bowed again. 'Cakhmaim clan Eikh'mir felt hostility from you in the Lady Vader's suite,' he said. 'He believed you would not willingly accept a guard of Noghri to accompany you.'

Han looked at Luke, caught the kid's halfway try at hiding a grin. 'Well, next time you see Cakhmaim, you tell him that I stopped passing up free help years ago,' he told Ekhrikhor. 'But as long as we're discussing hostility, you can knock off that "consort of the Lady Vader" stuff. Call me Han, or Solo. Or Captain. Or practically anything else.'

'Han clan Solo, maybe,' Luke murmured.

315

Ekhrikhor brightened. 'That is good,' he said. 'We beg your forgiveness, Han clan Solo.'

Han looked at Luke. 'I think you've been adopted,' Luke said, fighting that grin again.

'Yeah,' Han said. 'Thanks. A lot.'

'A little rapport never hurts,' Luke pointed out. 'Remember Endor.'

'I'm not likely to forget,' Han growled, feeling his lip twist. Sure, the little fuzzballs there had done their bit in that final battle against the second Death Star. That didn't change the fact that being made part of an Ewok tribe was one of the more ridiculous things he'd ever had to go through.

Still, the Ewoks had overwhelmed the Imperial troops by sheer weight of numbers. The Noghri, on the other hand – 'How many of you are there here?' he asked Ekhrikhor.

'There are eight,' the other replied. 'Two each have traveled before, after, and on either side of you during your journey.'

Han nodded, feeling a grudging trickle of unwilling respect for these things. Eight of them, silently killing or driving away predators and natives. Day and night both. *And* still finding time on top of it to clear their path of nuisances like clawbirds and vine snakes.

He looked down at Ekhrikhor. No, the adoption process didn't feel quite so ridiculous this time around.

From somewhere behind them came a familiar shuffling sound. Han turned, and a moment later the equally familiar golden figure of Threepio traipsed into view. Beside him and a half-step behind was Mara, blaster in hand. 'Master Luke,' Threepio called, his voice its usual mixture of relieved and anxious and just plain prissy.

'Over here, Threepio,' Luke called back. 'Think you can do some translation for us?'

'I'll do my best,' the droid said. 'As you know, I am fluent in over six million forms of communica—'

'I see you found the natives,' Mara cut him off, giving the group by the log a quick survey as she and Threepio stepped into the clearing. Her eyes fell on Ekhrikhor – 'And a little surprise, too,' she added, her blaster quietly shifting its aim toward the Noghri.

'It's all right – he's a friend,' Luke assured her, reaching toward her blaster.

'I don't think so,' Mara said, twitching the weapon to the side out of his reach. 'They're Noghri. They work for Thrawn.'

'We serve him no longer,' Ekhrikhor told her.

'That's true, Mara, they don't,' Luke said.

'Maybe,' Mara said. She still wasn't happy about it, but at least her blaster wasn't pointed exactly at Ekhrikhor any more.

Across the clearing, the Myneyrsh nearest the log pulled what seemed to be a bleached-white stuffed clawbird from a shoulder pouch. Speaking inaudibly under his breath, he laid it in front of him beside the worklight. 'What's that?' Han asked. 'Lunch?'

'It is called the *satna-chakka*,' Ekhrikhor said. 'It is a bond of peace while this meeting lasts. They are ready to begin. You – Threepio-droid – come with me.'

'Of course,' Threepio said, not sounding exactly thrilled by the whole arrangement. 'Master Luke . . . ?'

'I'll come with you,' Luke soothed. 'Han, Chewie – you stay here.'

'No argument from me,' Han said.

With a clearly reluctant Threepio in tow, Luke and the Noghri headed toward the log. The head Myneyrsh raised its upper two hands over his head, palm inwards. '*Bidaesi charaa*,' he said, his voice surprisingly melodious. '*Lyaaunu baaraemaa dukhnu phaeri*.'

'He announces the arrival of the strangers,' Threepio said precisely. 'Presumably, that refers to us. He fears, however, that we will bring danger and trouble again to his people.'

Beside Han, Chewbacca rumbled a sarcastic comment. 'No, they're not much for small talk,' Han agreed. 'Not much for diplomacy, either.'

'We bring hope to your people,' the chief Noghri countered. 'If you let us pass, we will free you from the domination of the Empire.'

Threepio translated, the melodious Myneyrshi words still

coming out prissy, in Han's opinion. One of the lumpy Psadans made a chopping gesture and said something that sounded like a faint and distant scream with consonants scattered around in it. 'He says that the Psadan people have long memories,' Threepio translated. 'Apparently, deliverers have come before but nothing has ever changed.'

'Welcome to the real world,' Han muttered.

Luke threw a look at him over his shoulder. 'Ask him to explain, Threepio,' he told the droid.

Threepio complied, quiet-screaming back at the Psadan and then throwing in a Myneyrshi translation, too, just to show he could do it. The Psadan's answer went on for several minutes, and Han's ears were starting to hurt by the time he was done.

'Well,' Threepio said, tilting his head and settling into the professor mode Han had always hated. 'There are many details – but I will pass those by for now,' he added hastily, probably at a look from one of the Noghri. 'The humans who came as colonists were the first invaders. They drove the native peoples from some of their lands, and were stopped only when their lightning bows and metal birds – those are their terms, of course – began to fail. Much later came the Empire, who as we know built into the forbidden mountain. They enslaved many of the native peoples to help on the project and drove others from their lands. After the builders left came someone who called himself the Guardian, and he, too, sought control over the native peoples. Finally, the one who called himself the Jedi Master came, and in a battle that lit up the sky he defeated the Guardian. For a time the native peoples thought they might be freed, but the Jedi Master brought humans and native peoples to himself and forced them to live together beneath the shadow of the forbidden mountain. Finally, the Empire has returned.' Threepio tilted his head back again. 'As you can see, Master Luke, we are merely the last in a long line of invaders.'

'Except that we're not invaders,' Luke said. 'We're here to free them from the rule of the Empire.'

'I understand that, Master Luke—'

'I know you do,' Luke interrupted the droid. 'Tell *them* that.'

'Oh. Yes. Of course.'

He started into his translation. 'You ask me, I don't think they've had it all that bad,' Han muttered to Chewbacca. 'The Empire took whole planets away from some people.'

'Primitives always have this reaction to visitors,' Mara said. 'They usually have long memories, too.'

'Yeah. Maybe. You suppose that Jedi Master they were talking about was your pal C'baoth?'

'Who else?' Mara said grimly. 'This must be where Thrawn found him.'

Han felt his stomach tighten. 'You think he's here now?'

'I don't sense anything,' Mara said slowly. 'Doesn't mean he can't come back.'

The head Myneyrsh was talking again. Han let his gaze drift around the clearing. Were there other Myneyrshi and Psadans out there keeping an eye on the big debate? Luke hadn't said anything about backups, but they'd have to be crazy not to have them somewhere nearby.

Unless Ekhrikhor's pals had already taken care of them. If this didn't work, it could turn out to be handy having the Noghri around.

The Myneyrsh finished its speech. 'I'm sorry, Master Luke,' Threepio apologized. 'They say they have no reason to assume we are any different than all those they have already spoken of.'

'I understand their fears,' Luke nodded. 'Ask them how we can prove our good intentions.'

Threepio started to translate; and as he did so, a hard Wookiee elbow jabbed into Han's shoulder. 'What?' Han asked.

Chewbacca nodded toward his left, his bowcaster already up and tracking. Han followed the movement with his eyes – 'Uh-oh.'

'What is it?' Mara demanded.

Han opened his mouth; then, suddenly, there wasn't time to tell her. The wiry predator Chewbacca had spotted slinking

319

through the tree branches had stopped slinking and was coiling itself to spring at the discussion group. 'Look out!' he snapped instead, bringing his blaster up.

Chewbacca was faster. With a Wookiee hunter's roar, he fired, the bowcaster bolt slicing the predator nearly in half. It fell off its perch, crunching into the dead leaves, and lay still.

And over by the log, the whole group of Myneyrshi snarled.

'Watch it, Chewie,' Han warned, shifting his aim toward the aliens.

'That might have been a mistake,' Mara said tensely. 'You're not supposed to fire weapons at a truce conference.'

'You're not supposed to let the conference get eaten, either,' Han retorted. Beside the Myneyrshi, the five Psadans had started to shake, and he hoped Ekhrikhor's pals had the rest of the area covered. 'Threepio – tell them.'

'Certainly, Captain Solo,' Threepio said, sounding about as nervous as Han felt. '*Mulansaar—*'

The head Myneyrsh cut him off with a chopping motion of its two left arms. 'You!' he warbled in passable Basic, jabbing all four hands at Han. 'He have lightning bow?'

Han frowned at him. Of course Chewbacca had a weapon – so did all the rest of them. He glanced up at the Wookiee . . . and suddenly he understood. 'Yes, he has,' he told the Myneyrsh, lowering his blaster. 'He's our friend. We don't keep slaves like the Empire did.'

Threepio started into his translation, but the Myneyrsh was already jabbering away to his friends. 'Nice work,' Mara murmured. 'I hadn't thought of that. But you're right – the last Wookiees they saw here would have been Imperial slaves.'

Han nodded. 'Let's hope it makes a difference.'

The discussion ran on for a few more minutes, mostly between the Myneyrshi and the Psadanas. Threepio tried for a while to keep up a running translation, but it quickly degenerated into not much more than a reporting of the highlights. The Myneyrshi, apparently, were starting to think this was their chance to get rid of the oppression of first the Empire and then the Jedi Master himself. The Psadans didn't like the Imperials any more than the Myneyrshi, but the thought of facing up to C'baoth was making them skittish.

'We aren't asking you to fight alongside us,' Luke told them when he was finally able to get their attention back. 'Our battle is our own, and we will handle it ourselves. All we ask is your permission to travel through your territory to the forbidden mountain and your assurance that you won't betray us to the Empire.

Threepio did his double translation, and Han braced himself for another argument. But there wasn't one. The head Myneyrsh raised his upper hands again, and with his lower hands picked up the bleached clawbird and offered it to Luke. 'I believe he is offering you safe conduct, Master Luke,' Threepio said helpfully. 'Though I could be wrong – their dialect has survived relatively intact, but gestures and movements are often—'

'Tell him thank you,' Luke said, nodding as he accepted the clawbird. 'Tell him we accept their hospitality. And that they won't be sorry they helped us.'

'General Covell?' the militarily precise voice came over the intercom from the shuttle cockpit. 'We should be on the surface in just a few more minutes.'

'Acknowledged,' Covell said. He keyed the intercom off and turned to the shuttle's only other passenger. 'We're almost there,' he said.

'Yes, I heard,' C'baoth said, his amusement echoing through his voice. And through Covell's mind. 'Tell me, General Covell, are we at the end of our voyage or at the beginning?'

'The beginning, of course,' Covell told him. 'The voyage we have set upon will have no end.'

'And what of Grand Admiral Thrawn?'

Covell felt a frown crease his forehead. He hadn't heard this question before, at least not said this particular way. But even as he hesitated, the answer came soothingly into his thoughts. As all answers did now. 'It's the beginning of Grand Admiral Thrawn's ending,' he said.

C'baoth laughed softly, the amusement rippling pleasantly through Covell's mind. Covell thought about asking what was funny, but it was easier and far more agreeable to just sit back and enjoy the laughter. And anyway, he knew perfectly well what it was that was funny.

'You do, don't you,' C'baoth agreed, shaking his head. 'Ah, General, General. It's so very ironic, isn't it? From the very beginning – from that very first meeting in my city – Grand Admiral Thrawn has had the answer within his grasp. And yet even now he is as far from understanding as he was then.'

'Is it about power, Master C'baoth?' Covell asked. This was a familiar topic, and even without the prompting in his mind he would have remembered his lines.

'It is indeed, General Covell,' C'baoth said gravely. 'I told him at the very beginning that true power didn't lie in the conquering of distant worlds. Or in battles and war and the crushing of faceless rebellions.'

He smiled, his eyes glittering brightly in Covell's mind. 'No, General Covell,' he said softly. 'This – *this* – is true power. Holding another's life in the palm of your hand. Having the power to choose his path, and his thoughts, and his feelings. To rule his life, and decree his death.' Slowly, theatrically, C'baoth held out his hand, palm upward. 'To command his soul.'

'Something not even the Emperor ever understood,' Covell reminded him.

Another ripple of pleasure rolled through Covell's mind. It was so satisfying to see the Master enjoying his game. 'Not even the Emperor,' C'baoth agreed, his eyes and thoughts drifting far away. 'He, like the Grand Admiral, saw power only as how far outside himself he could reach. And it destroyed him, as I could have told him it would. For if he'd truly commanded Vader . . .' He shook his head. 'In many ways he was a fool. But perhaps it was not his destiny to be otherwise. Perhaps it was the will to grasp hold of this power. The first . . . but not the last.'

Covell nodded, swallowing against a dry throat. It was not

pleasant when C'baoth left him like this, even for a little bit. Especially not when there was this strange loneliness along with it . . .

But of course, the Master knew that. 'Do you ache with my loneliness, General Covell?' he said, warming Covell's mind with another smile. 'Yes, of course you do. But be patient. The time is coming when we shall be many. And when that time is here, we will never be lonely again. Observe.'

He felt the distant sense as he did all others now: filtered and focused and structured through the Master's perfect mind. 'You see, I was right,' C'baoth said, reaching out to examine that sense. 'They are here. Skywalker and Jade both.' He smiled at Covell 'They will be the first, General Covell – the first of our many. For they will come to me, and when I have shown to them the true power, they will understand and will join us.' His eyes drifted away again. 'Jade will be first, I think,' he added thoughtfully. 'Skywalker has resisted once, and will resist again; but the key to his soul is even now waiting for me in the mountain below. But Jade is another matter. I have seen her in my meditations – have seen her coming to me and kneeling at my feet. She will be mine, and Skywalker will follow. One way or another.'

He smiled again. Covell smiled back, pleased at the Master's own pleasure and by the thought of others who would be there to warm his mind.

And then, without any warning, it all went dark. Not loneliness, not the way it had been. But a sort of emptiness . . .

By and by, he felt his head being roughly lifted by his chin. C'baoth was there, in a way, staring into his eyes. 'General Covell!' the Master's voice thundered. Thundered strangely, too. Covell could hear it, but it wasn't really there. Not like it should have been. 'Can you hear me?'

'I can hear you,' Covell said. His own voice sounded strange, too. He looked past C'baoth's face, to the interesting pattern of lines on the shuttle bulkhead.

He felt himself being shaken. 'Look at me!' C'baoth demanded.

Covell did so. That was odd, too, because he could see the Master but he wasn't really there. 'Are you still there?'

The Master's face changed. Something – was it called a smile? – came across it. 'Yes, General, I am here,' the distant voice said. 'I no longer touch your mind, but I am still your Master. You will continue to obey me.'

Obey. An odd concept, Covell thought. Not like simply doing what was natural. 'Obey?'

'You will do as I tell you,' C'baoth said. 'I will give you things to say, and you will repeat every word.'

'All right,' Covell said. 'If I do that, will you come back?'

'I will,' the Master promised. 'Despite Grand Admiral Thrawn's treachery. With your obedience – with you doing what I tell you – we will together destroy his betrayal of us. And then we will never be apart again.'

'The emptiness will be gone?'

'Yes. But only if you do what I say.'

The other men came a little later. The Master stayed at his side the whole time, and he said all the words the Master told him to say. They all went somewhere, and then the men left, and the Master left, too.

He stared off across the place they'd left him in, watching the patterns of lines and listening to the emptiness all around him. Eventually, he fell asleep.

A strange sort of birdcall warbled off in the distance, and instantly the background crackle of insects and scuttling animals ceased. But apparently there was no immediate danger, and a minute later the nighttime sounds and activity resumed. Shifting her position against her chosen tree trunk, Mara eased her aching back muscles and wished this whole thing was over.

'There is no need for you to stay awake,' a soft Noghri voice said at her shoulder. 'We will guard.'

'Thanks,' Mara said shortly. 'If it's all the same to you, I'll do my job.'

The Noghri was silent a moment. 'You still do not trust us, do you?'

Actually, she hadn't thought all that much about it one way or the other. 'Skywalker trusts you,' she said. 'Isn't that good enough?'

'It is not approval we seek,' the Noghri told her. 'Only the chance to repay our debt.'

She shrugged. They'd protected the camp, they'd tackled the always tricky job of first contact with the Myneyrshi and Psadans, and now here they were protecting the camp again. 'If it's a debt to the New Republic, I'd say you're doing a pretty good job of it,' she conceded. 'You finally figured out Thrawn and the Empire had been stringing you along?'

There was a quiet click, like needle teeth coming together. 'You knew about that?'

'I heard rumors,' Mara said, recognizing how potentially dangerous this ground was but not really caring. 'More like jokes, really. I never knew how much of it was true.'

'Most likely all of it,' the Noghri said calmly. 'Yes. I can see how our lives and deaths could be amusing to our enslavers. We will convince them otherwise.'

No white-hot rage, no fanatical hatred. Just a simple, icy determination. About as dangerous as you could get. 'How are you going to do that?' she asked.

'When the time is right the Noghri will turn upon their enslavers. Some on Imperial worlds, some on transporting ships. And five groups will come here.'

Mara frowned. 'You knew about Wayland?'

'Not until you led us here,' the other said. 'But we know now. We have sent the location to those waiting at Coruscant. By now they will have passed the word on to others.'

Mara snorted quietly. 'You have a lot of confidence in us, don't you?'

'Our missions complement each other,' the Noghri assured her, his gravelly mewing somehow sounding grimmer. 'You have set for yourselves the task of destroying the cloning facility. With the help of the son of Vader we do not doubt you will succeed. For ourselves, the Noghri have chosen the task of eliminating every last reminder of the Emperor's presence on Wayland.'

Probably the last relics of the Emperor's presence anywhere. Mara turned that idea over in her mind, wondering why it didn't seem to grieve or anger her. Probably she was just tired. 'Sounds like a big project,' she said instead. 'Who is this son of Vader you're expecting to show up and help us?'

There was a brief silence. 'The son of Vader is already with you,' the Noghri said, sounding puzzled. 'You serve him, as do we.'

Mara stared at him through the darkness . . . and suddenly her heart seemed to freeze in her chest. 'You mean . . . *Skywalker*?'

'You did not know?'

Mara turned away from him, staring down at the sleeping form no more than a meter away from her feet, a horrible numbness flooding through her. Suddenly, finally, after all these years, the last elusive piece had fallen into place. The Emperor didn't want her to kill Skywalker for his own sake. It was, instead, one final act of vengeance against his father.

YOU WILL KILL LUKE SKYWALKER.

And in the space of a few heartbeats everything Mara had believed about herself – her hatred, her mission, her entire life – had turned from certainty to confusion.

YOU WILL KILL LUKE SKYWALKER. YOU WILL KILL LUKE SKYWALKER. YOU WILL KILL LUKE SKYWALKER.

'No,' she muttered at the voice through clenched teth. 'Not like that. *My* decision. *My* reasons.'

But the voice continued unabated. Perhaps it was her resistance and defiance fueling it now, or perhaps the deeper power in the Force that Skywalker had given her over the past few days had made her more receptive to it.

YOU WILL KILL LUKE SKYWALKER. YOU WILL KILL LUKE SKYWALKER.

But you are another matter, Mara Jade.

Mara jerked, the sudden motion banging the back of her head against the tree trunk behind her. Another voice; but this one wasn't coming from inside her. It was coming from—

I have seen you in my meditations, the voice continued placidly. *Have seen you coming to me and kneeling at my feet. You will be mine, and Skywalker will follow. One way or another.*

Mara shook her head violently, trying to shake away the words and thoughts. The second voice seemed to laugh; then, suddenly, the words and laughter disappeared beneath a distant but steady pressure against her mind. Setting her teeth, she pushed back against it. Dimly, she heard the voice laugh again at her efforts—

And then, with a suddenness that made her catch her breath, the pressure was gone.

'Are you all right?' Skywalker's voice asked quietly.

Mara looked down. Skywalker had risen up on one elbow, his silhouetted face turned toward her. 'Did you hear it, too?' she asked.

'I didn't hear any words. But I felt the pressure.'

Mara looked up toward the leaf canopy overhead. 'It's C'baoth,' she said. 'He's here.'

'Yes,' Skywalker said; and she could hear the apprehension in his voice. Small wonder – he'd faced C'baoth once, back on Jomark, and nearly lost out to him.

'So what now?' Mara asked, rubbing at the sweat around her mouth with a shaking hand. 'We abort the mission?'

The silhouette shrugged. 'How? We're only a couple of days from the mountain. It'd take us a lot longer than that to get back to the *Falcon*.'

'Except that the Imperials know we're here now.'

'Maybe,' Skywalker said slowly. 'But maybe not. Did the contact cut off suddenly for you, too?'

She frowned; and suddenly it hit her. 'You think they moved some ysalamiri around him?'

'Or else strapped him into one of those frames you were using on Jomark,' Skywalker said. 'Either way, it would imply he was a prisoner.'

Mara thought about that. If so, he might not be interested in telling his captors about the invaders moving toward the mountain.

She looked sharply at him as another thought suddenly occurred to her. 'Did you know C'baoth was going to come?'

she demanded. 'Is that why you wanted me to practice my old Jedi training?'

'I didn't know he'd be here,' Skywalker said. 'But I knew we would eventually have to face him again. He said that himself on Jomark.'

Mara shivered. *Kneeling at my feet* . . . 'I don't want to face him, Skywalker.'

'Neither do I,' he said softly. 'But I think we have to.'

He sighed; and then, quietly, he peeled off the top of his bedroll and got to his feet. 'Why don't you go get some sleep,' he said, stepping over to her side. 'I'm awake now anyway; and you took the brunt of that attack.'

'All right,' Mara said, too tired to argue. 'If you need any help, call me.'

'I will.'

She picked her way across Calrissian and the Wookiee to her bedroll and crawled into it. Her last memory, as she dropped off to sleep, was of the voice in the back of her mind.

YOU WILL KILL LUKE SKYWALKER . . .

CHAPTER 22

The report came in from Mount Tantiss during ship's night and was waiting for him when Pellaeon arrived on the bridge in the morning. The *Draklor* had reached Wayland more or less on schedule six hours previously, had off-loaded its passengers, and had left the system bound for Valrar as per orders. General Covell had refused to take command until local morning—

Pellaeon frowned. *Refused to take command?* That didn't sound like Covell.

'Captain Pellaeon?' the comm officer called up to him. 'Sir, we're getting a holo transmission from Colonel Selid on Wayland. It's marked urgent.'

'Put it through to the aft bridge hologram pod,' Pellaeon

instructed, getting up from his command chair and heading aft. 'Signal the Grand Admiral to – never mind,' he interrupted himself as, through the archway, he spotted Thrawn and Rukh coming up the steps into the aft bridge.

Thrawn saw him, too. 'What's wrong, Captain?'

'Urgent message from Wayland, sir,' Pellaeon said, gesturing toward the hologram pod. The image of an Imperial officer was already waiting, and even in a quarter-size holo, Pellaeon could see the younger man's nervousness.

'Probably C'baoth,' Thrawn predicted darkly. They reached position in front of the hologram pod, and Thrawn nodded to the image. 'Colonel Selid, this is Grand Admiral Thrawn. Report.'

'Sir,' Selid said, his parade-ground posture stiffening even more. 'I regret to inform you, Admiral, of the sudden death of General Covell.'

Pellaeon felt his mouth fall open a couple of centimeters. 'How?' he asked.

'We don't know yet, sir,' Selid said. 'He apparently died in his sleep. The medics are still running tests, but so far all they can suggest is that large portions of the General's brain had simply shut down.'

'Brain tissue does not 'simply' shut down, Colonel,' Thrawn said. 'There has to be a reason for it.'

Selid seemed to wince. 'Yes, sir. I'm sorry, sir; I didn't mean it that way.'

'I know you didn't,' Thrawn assured him. 'What about the rest of the passengers?'

'The medics are checking them all now,' Selid said. 'No problems so far. Rather, they're checking all those still within the garrison. General Covell's troops – the company that arrived on the *Draklor* with him – had already been dispersed outside the mountain when he died.'

'What, the whole company?' Pellaeon asked. 'What for?'

'I don't know, sir,' Selid said. 'General Covell gave the orders. After the big meeting, I mean, before he died.'

'Perhaps we'd better have the story from the beginning, Colonel,' Thrawn cut him off. 'Tell me everything.'

329

'Yes, sir.' Selid visibly pulled himself together. 'General Covell and the others were landed via shuttle approximately six hours ago. I tried to turn over command of the garrison to him, but he refused. He then insisted on having a private word with his troops in one of the officers' mess halls.'

'Which troops?' Thrawn asked. 'The whole garrison?'

'No, sir, just the ones who'd accompanied him on the *Draklor*. He said he had some special orders to give them.'

Pellaeon looked at Thrawn. 'I'd have thought he'd have had plenty of time aboard ship for special orders.'

'Yes,' Thrawn agreed. 'One would think so.'

'Maybe it was C'baoth's idea, sir,' Selid suggested. 'He was at the general's side from the minute they got off the shuttle. Muttering, sort of, the whole time.'

'Was he, now,' Thrawn said thoughtfully. His voice was calm, but there was something beneath it that sent a shiver up Pellaeon's back. 'Where is Master C'baoth now?'

'Up in the Emperor's old royal chambers,' Selid said. 'General Covell insisted they be opened for him.'

'Would he be above the ysalamiri influence up there?' Pellaeon murmured.

Thrawn shook his head. 'I doubt it. According to my calculations, the entire mountain and some of the surrounding area should be within the Force-empty bubble. What happened then, Colonel?'

'The general spent about fifteen minutes talking to his troops,' Selid said. 'When he came out, he told me that he'd given them secret orders that had come directly from you, Admiral, and that I wasn't to interfere.'

'And then they left the mountain?'

'After stripping one of the supply rooms of field gear and explosives, yes,' Selid said. 'Actually, they spent a couple more hours inside the garrison before leaving. Familiarizing themselves with the layout, the general said. After they left, C'baoth escorted the general to his quarters and then was himself escorted to the royal chambers by two of my stormtroopers. I put the rest of the garrison back on to standard nighttime routine, and that was it. Until this morning, when the orderly found the general.'

'So C'baoth wasn't with Covell at the time of his death?' Thrawn asked.

'No, sir,' Selid said. 'Though the medics don't think the general lived very long after C'baoth left him.'

'And he was with the general up until that time.'

'Yes, sir.'

Pellaeon threw Thrawn a sideways look. The Grand Admiral was staring at nothing, his glowing red eyes narrowed to slits. 'Tell me, Colonel, what was your impression of General Covell?'

'Well . . .' Selid hesitated. 'I'd have to say I was a bit disappointed, sir.'

'How so?'

'He just wasn't what I was expecting, Admiral,' Selid said, sounding distinctly uncomfortable. Pellaeon didn't blame him: criticizing one senior officer in front of another was a serious breach of military etiquette. Especially between different branches of the service. 'He seemed . . . *distant* is the word I'd have to use, sir. He implied that my security was poor and that he would be making some important changes, but he wouldn't talk to me about them. In fact, he hardly spoke to me the whole time he was here. And it wasn't just me – he was short with the other officers who tried to talk to him, as well. That was his privilege, of course, and he may have just been tired. But it didn't seem to fit with what I'd heard of the general's reputation.'

'No, it doesn't,' Thrawn said. 'Is the hologram pad in the Emperor's old throne room operational, Colonel?'

'Yes, sir. Though C'baoth may not be in the throne room itself.'

'He will be,' Thrawn said coldly. 'Connect me with him.'

'Yes, sir.'

Selid's image vanished, replaced by the pause symbol. 'You think C'baoth did something to Covell?' Pellaeon asked quietly.

'I see no other likely explanation,' Thrawn said. 'My guess

331

is that our beloved Jedi Master was trying to take over Covell's mind, perhaps even replacing entire sections of it with his own. When they hit the ysalamir bubble and he lost that direct contact, there wasn't enough of Covell left to keep him alive for long.'

'I see.' Pellaeon turned his head away from the Grand Admiral, a darkening anger flowing through him. He'd warned Thrawn about what C'baoth might do. Had warned him over and over again. 'What are you going to go about it?'

The pause symbol vanished before Thrawn could answer; but it wasn't the standard quarter-size figure that replaced it. Instead, a huge image of C'baoth's face suddenly glared out at them, jolting Pellaeon an involuntary step backwards.

Thrawn didn't even twitch. 'Good morning, Master C'baoth,' the Grand Admiral said, his voice mirror smooth. 'I see you've discovered the Emperor's private hologram setting.'

'Grand Admiral Thrawn,' C'baoth said, his own voice cold and arrogant. 'Is this how you reward my work on behalf of your ambitions? By an act of betrayal?'

'If there is betrayal, it's on your side, Master C'baoth,' Thrawn said. 'What did you do to General Covell?'

C'baoth ignored the question. 'The Force is not so easily betrayed as you think,' he said. 'And never forget this, Grand Admiral Thrawn: With my destruction will come your own. I have foreseen it.'

He stopped, glaring back and forth at the two of them. For a handful of heartbeats Thrawn remained silent. 'Are you finished?' he asked at last.

C'baoth frowned, the play of uncertainty and nervousness easily visible in the magnified face. For all its intimidating majesty, the Emperor's personal hologram setting clearly had its own set of drawbacks. 'For now,' C'baoth said. 'Have you some feeble defense to offer?'

'I have nothing to defend, Master C'baoth,' Thrawn said. 'It was you who insisted on going to Wayland. Now tell me what you did to General Covell.'

'You will first restore the Force to me.'

'The ysalamiri will stay where they are,' Thrawn said. 'Tell me what you did to General Covell.'

For a moment the two men glared at each other. C'baoth's glare crumbled first, and for a moment it looked as if he was going to fold. But then the old man's jaw jutted out, and once again he was the arrogant Jedi Master. 'General Covell was mine to do with as I pleased,' he said. 'As is everything in my Empire.'

'Thank you,' Thrawn said. 'That's all I need to know. Colonel Selid?'

The huge face vanished and was replaced by Selid's quarter-size image. 'Yes, Admiral?'

'Instructions, Colonel,' Thrawn told him. 'First of all, Master C'baoth is hereby placed under arrest. You may allow him free run of the royal chambers and Emperor's throne room but he is not to leave there. All control circuits from those floors will be disconnected, of course. Secondly, you're to initiate inquiries as to precisely where General Covell's troops were seen within the mountain before they left.'

'Why don't we ask the troops themselves, sir?' Selid suggested. 'They presumably have comlinks with them.'

'Because I'm not certain we could trust their answers,' Thrawn told him. 'Which brings me to my third order. None of the troops which left the mountain under General Covell's orders are to be allowed back in.'

Selid's jaw dropped visibly. 'Sir?'

'You heard correctly,' Thrawn told him. 'Another transport will arrive for them in a few days, at which time they'll be rounded up and taken off the planet. But under no circumstances are they to be allowed back into the mountain.'

'Yes, sir,' Selid said, floundering. 'But – sir, what do I tell them?'

'You may tell them the truth,' Thrawn said quietly. 'That their orders came not from General Covell, and certainly not from me, but from a traitor to the Empire. Until Intelligence can sort through the details, the entire company will be considered as under suspicion, as unwitting accomplices to treason.'

The word seemed to hang before them in the air. 'Understood, sir,' Selid said at last.

'Good,' Thrawn said. 'You are of course reinstated as garrison commander. Any questions?'

Selid drew himself up. 'No, sir.'

'Good. Carry on, Colonel. *Chimaera* out.'

The figure vanished from the hologram pod. 'Do you think it's safe to leave C'baoth there, sir?' Pellaeon asked.

'There's nowhere in the Empire safer,' Thrawn pointed out. 'At least, not yet.'

Pellaeon frowned. 'I don't understand.'

'His use to the Empire is rapidly nearing an end, Captain,' Thrawn said, turning and walking beneath the archway into the main section of the bridge. 'However, he still has one last role to play in our long-term consolidation of power.'

He paused at the aft edge of the command walkway. 'C'baoth is insane, Captain – that we both agree on. But such insanity is in his mind. Not in his body.'

Pellaeon stared at him. 'Are you suggesting we *clone* him?'

'Why not?' Thrawn asked. 'Not at Mount Tantiss itself, certainly, given the conditions there. Most likely not at the speed which that facility allows, either – that's all well and good for techs and TIE fighter pilots, but not a project of this delicacy. No, I envision bringing such a clone to childhood and then allowing it to grow to maturity at a normal pace for its last ten or fifteen years. Under suitable upbringing conditions, of course.'

'I see,' Pellaeon said, struggling to keep his voice steady. A young C'baoth – or maybe two or ten or twenty of them – running loose around the galaxy. This was an idea that was going to take some getting used to. 'Where would you set up this other cloning facility?'

'Somewhere absolutely secure,' Thrawn said. 'Possibly on one of the worlds in the Unknown Regions where I once served the Emperor. You'll instruct Intelligence to begin searching for a suitable location after we've crushed the Rebels at Bilbringi.'

Pellaeon felt his lip twitch. Right: the dangerously ethereal

Bilbringi attack. What with this C'baoth thing, he'd almost forgotten the main business of the day. Or his reservations concerning it. 'Yes, sir. Admiral, I'm forced to remind you that all the evidence still indicates Tangrene as the probable point of attack.'

'I'm aware of the evidence, Captain,' Thrawn said. 'Nevertheless, they will be at Bilbringi.'

He sent his gaze leisurely around his bridge, his glowing red eyes missing nothing. And the crewers knew it. At every station, from the crew pits to the lateral consoles, there were the subtle sounds and movements of men aware that their commander was watching and striving to show him their best. 'And so will we,' the Grand Admiral added to Pellaeon. 'Set course for Bilbringi, Captain. And let us prepare to meet our guests.'

Wedge drained the last of his cup and set it back on the chipped and stained wood of the small table, glancing across the noisy Mumbri Storve cantina as he did so. The place was as crowded as it had been when he, Janson, and Hobbie had come in an hour earlier, but the texture of the crowd had changed quite a bit. Most of the younger people had left, couples and groups both, and had been replaced by an older and decidedly seedier-looking bunch. The fringe types were drifting in; which meant it was time for them to be drifting out.

His fellow Rogue Squadron pilots knew it, too. 'Time to go?' Hobbie suggested, his voice just audible over the noise.

'Right,' Wedge nodded, getting to his feet and fumbling in his pouch for a coin that would cover this last round. His *civilian* pouch; and he really hated the awkward things. But it would hardly do for them to go wandering around town in full New Republic uniforms, complete with the distinctive Rogue Squadron patches.

He found a proper-size coin and dropped it into the center of the table as the others stood up. 'Where to now?' Janson asked, hunching his shoulders slightly to stretch out his back muscles.

'Back to the base, I think,' Wedge told him.

'Good,' Janson grunted. 'Morning's going to come early enough as it is.'

Wedge nodded as he turned and headed toward the exit. Morning could come anytime it wanted to, of course: well before then they were going to be off this planet and driving hard toward their assigned rendezvous point outside the Bilbringi shipyards.

They wove their way between the crowded tables; and as they did so, a tall, thin man shoved his chair back almost into Wedge's knees and got unsteadily to his feet. 'Watch out,' he slurred, half turning to throw his arm across Wedge's shoulders and much of his weight against Wedge's side.

'Easy, friend,' Wedge grunted, struggling to regain his balance. Out of the corner of his eye he saw Janson step to the tall man's other side and put a supporting arm around him—

'Easy sounds good to me,' the man murmured, the slurring abruptly gone as his arm tightened around Wedge's shoulders. 'All four of us – nice and easy now, let's help the poor old drunk out of here.'

Wedge stiffened. Tracked, blindsided, and caught . . . and in the flip of an X-wing they had suddenly gone from a simple night on the town to serious trouble. With him and Janson tangled up like this, only Hobbie was left with a clear gun hand. And their assailant surely hadn't forgotten to have some backup around.

The tall man must have felt Wedge's tension. 'Hey – play it smooth,' he admonished quietly. 'Don't remember me, huh?'

Wedge frowned at the face practically leaning against his. It didn't look familiar; but on the other hand, at this range he probably wouldn't recognize his own mother. 'Should I?' he murmured back.

The other did a little more staggering. 'I'd have thought so,' he said in an injured voice. 'You go up against a Star Destroyer with someone, he ought to remember you. Especially out in the middle of nowhere.'

Wedge frowned a little harder at the face, dimly aware that the whole group had started walking. In the middle of nowhere . . . ?

And suddenly, it hit him. The *Katana* fleet, and Talon Karrde's people coming out of nowhere to lend their assistance and firepower against the Imperials. And afterwards the brief, preoccupied introductions aboard the Star Cruiser . . . 'Aves?'

'That wasn't so hard, was it?' the other said approvingly. 'Told you you could do it if you tried. Come on, now – nice and easy and don't let's draw any more attention to ourselves than we need to.'

There didn't seem to be any real option other than to comply; but even as Wedge continued toward the exit, he kept his eyes moving, looking for something they could use to get them out of this. Karrde and his people had supposedly agreed to funnel information back to the New Republic, but that was a far way from being allies together. And if the Empire had threatened them . . . or just bought them outright . . .

But no opportunity for escape presented itself before they got out the doors. 'This way,' Aves said, abandoning his drunk act and hurrying down the dimly lit and sparsely populated street.

Janson caught Wedge's eye and raised his eyebrows questioningly. Wedge shrugged slightly in return and set off after Aves. It could still be some sort of trap, but at this point the vague fears were being rapidly overtaken by simple curiosity. Something was going on, and he wanted to find out what.

He didn't have long to wonder about it. Two buildings down from the Mumbri Storve, Aves turned and disappeared into a darkened entryway. Wedge followed, half expecting to run into a half-dozen blaster muzzles. But Aves was alone. 'What now?' he asked as Janson and Hobbie joined them.

Aves nodded toward the street outside the entryway. 'Watch,' he said. 'If I'm right – here he comes.'

Wedge looked. A walrus-faced Aqualish strode quickly by, throwing a quick glance into the entryway as he passed. His stride broke, just noticeably; then he caught himself and picked up his pace. He passed the other side of the entryway—

There was a muffled thud, and suddenly the Aqualish was back in the entryway, his slack and obviously unconscious form being supported by two grim-faced men. 'Any trouble?' Aves asked.

'Naw,' one of the men said as they dropped the Aqualish none too gently to the ground near the back of the entryway. 'They're a lot meaner than they are smart.'

'This one was smart enough,' Aves said. 'Take a good look at him, Antilles. Maybe next time you'll recognize an Imperial spy when you pick one up.'

Wedge looked down at the alien. 'An Imperial spy, huh?'

'A free-lancer, anyway,' Aves shrugged. 'Just as dangerous.'

Wedge looked back at him, trying to keep his expression neutral. 'I suppose we ought to thank you,' he said.

One of the other men, busy searching the Aqualish's clothing, snorted under his breath. 'I'd think you should, yeah,' Aves said. 'If it hadn't been for us, you'd have been a juicy little item in the next Imperial Intelligence report.'

'I suppose we would have,' Wedge conceded, exchanging glances with Hobbie and Janson. But then, that had been the idea of the whole charade. To do their bit to convince Grand Admiral Thrawn that Tangrene was still the New Republic's intended target. 'What are you going to do with him?' he asked Aves.

'We'll take care of him,' Aves said. 'Don't worry, he won't be making any reports anytime soon.'

Wedge nodded. One evening, shot completely to flinders. Still, it was nice to know Karrde's people were still on their side. 'Thanks again,' he said, and meant it this time. 'I owe you one.'

Aves cocked his head. 'You want to pay off the debt right now?'

'How?' Wedge asked cautiously.

'We've got a little job in the works,' Aves said, waving a hand vaguely toward the night sky. 'We know you do, too. It would help a lot if we could time ours to go while you're keeping Thrawn occupied.'

Wedge frowned at him. 'What, you want me to tell you when our operation is starting?'

'Why not?' Aves said reasonably. 'Like I said, we already know it's in the works. Bel Iblis's repeat performance, and all that.'

Wedge looked at his pilots again, wondering if they appreciated the irony of this as much as he did. Here they stood, an evening's worth of subtle hints gone straight down the proton tubes; and now they were being asked for an outright confirmation of the whole operation. Colonel Derlin's decoy team couldn't have set things up better if they'd tried. 'I'm sorry,' he said slowly, putting some genuine regret into his voice. 'But you know I can't tell you that.'

'Why not?' Aves asked patiently. 'Like I said, we already know most of it already. I can prove that if you want.'

'Not here,' Wedge said quickly. The goal was to plant hints, not to be so obvious that it aroused suspicion. 'Someone might hear you.'

Janson tapped his arm. 'Sir, we need to get back,' he murmured. 'There's a lot of work yet to do before we leave.'

'I know, I know,' Wedge said. Good old Janson; just the angle he'd been searching for. 'Look, Aves, I tell you what I'll do. Are you going to stick around here for a while?'

'I could. Why?'

'Let me talk to my unit commander,' Wedge said. 'See if I can get a special clearance for you.'

Aves' expression showed pretty clearly what he thought of that idea. 'It's worth a try,' he said diplomatically instead. 'How soon can you get an answer?'

'I don't know,' Wedge said. 'He's as busy as all the rest of us, you know. I'll try to get back to you one way or the other; but if you haven't heard from me in about twenty-eight hours, don't expect to.'

Aves might have smiled slightly. Wedge couldn't tell in the dim light. 'All right,' he said, grumbling a bit. 'I suppose it's better than nothing. You can leave any messages with the night bartender at the Dona Laza tapcafe.'

'OK,' Wedge said. 'We've got to go. Thanks again.'

Together, he and the other two pilots left the entryway and crossed the street. They were two blocks away before Hobbie spoke. 'Twenty-eight hours, huh? Pretty clever.'

'I thought so,' Wedge agreed modestly. 'Leaving here then would get us to Tangrene just about on time for the big battle.'

'Let's just hope he's planning to sell that information to the Empire,' Janson murmured. 'It'd be a shame to have wasted the whole evening.'

'Oh, he'll sell it, all right,' Hobbie snorted. 'He's a smuggler. What else would he want it for?'

Wedge thought back to the *Katana* battle. Maybe that was indeed all Karrde and his gang were: fringe scum, always for sale to the highest bidder. But somehow, he didn't think so. 'We'll find out soon enough,' he told Hobbie. 'Come on. Like Janson said, we've got a lot of work to do.'

CHAPTER 23

The last page scrolled across the display and stopped. SEARCH SUMMARY ENDED. NEXT REQUEST?

'Cancel,' Leia said, leaning back in her desk chair and looking out the window. Another dead end. Just like the last one, and the one before that. It was beginning to look like the Research librarians had been right: if there was any information on the old Clone Wars cloning techniques still in the Old Senate Library, it was buried away so deeply that no-one would ever find it.

Across the room, she caught a flicker of returning consciousness. Standing up, she crossed to the crib and looked down on her children. Jacen was indeed awake, cooing to himself and making a serious effort to study his fingers. Beside him, Jaina was still asleep, her pudgy lips hanging open just enough to whistle softly with every breath. 'Hi, there,' Leia murmured to her son, picking him up out of the crib and cradling him in her arms. He looked up at her, his fingers momentarily forgotten, and smiled his wonderful toothless smile. 'Well, thank you,' she said, smiling back and caressing his cheek. 'Come on – let's go see what's happening out in the big world.'

She carried him to the window. Beneath them, the Imperial City was in full midmorning mayhem, with ground vehicles and air-speeders buzzing along in all directions like frantic insects. Beyond the city, the snow-tipped peaks of the Manarai Mountains to the south were dazzling in the morning sunshine. Beyond the mountains, the sky was a deep and cloudless blue; and beyond the sky—

She shivered. Beyond the sky was the planetary energy shield. And the Empire's invisible, deadly asteroids.

Jacen gurgled. Leia looked back down at him, found him studying her with what she could almost imagine to be concern. 'It's all right,' she assured him, holding him a little closer and bouncing him gently in her arms. 'It's all right. We'll find them all and get rid of them – don't you worry.'

Behind her, the door opened and Winter came into the room, a hover tray floating along in front of her. 'Your Highness,' she greeted Leia in a soft voice. 'I thought you might like some refreshment.'

'Yes, I would, thank you,' Leia said, sniffing at the gentle aroma of spiced paricha rising from the pot on the tray. 'Anything happening downstairs?'

'Nothing interesting,' Winter said, pushing the tray over to a side table and starting to unload it. 'The search teams haven't found any new asteroids since yesterday morning. I understand General Bel Iblis has been suggesting they may already have cleared them all out.'

'I doubt Admiral Drayson believes that.'

'No,' Winter agreed, holding out a steaming mug and waiting as Leia shifted Jacen to a one-armed grip. 'Neither does Mon Mothma.'

Leia nodded as she accepted the mug. To be honest, she didn't really believe it herself. No matter how expensive these cloaking shields might be to produce, she couldn't see the Empire going to this much trouble for anything fewer than

341

seventy cloaked asteroids. And there could easily be twice that many. The twenty-one they'd found hardly even scratched the surface.

'How is the research going?' Winter asked, pouring a mug for herself.

'It's not,' Leia had to admit. From one insoluble problem to another, it seemed. 'Though I don't know why that should surprise me. The Council Research specialists have already been all through the records, and they didn't find anything.'

'But you're a Jedi,' Winter reminded her. 'You have the Force.'

'Not enough of it, apparently,' Leia shook her head. 'At least, not enough to guide me to the right archive. If there is a right archive. I'm not sure any more that there is.'

For a minute they sipped in silence. Leia savored the soft flavor of the hot paricha, acutely aware that this could easily be her last taste of it for a while. All supplies of the root from which the drink was made had to be imported from offplanet.

'I was talking to Mobvekhar yesterday,' Winter said into her thoughts. 'He said you'd spoken to him about a clue of some sort. Something that Mara Jade had said.'

'Something that Mara said, coupled with something Luke did,' Leia nodded. 'Yes, I remember; and I still think there's an important key in there somewhere. I just can't figure out what it is.'

At her waist, her comlink beeped. 'I knew it couldn't last,' Leia sighed, putting her mug down and pulling the comlink out. Mon Mothma had promised her a complete morning off; obviously, that promise was about to be bent a little. 'Councilor Organa Solo,' she said into the device.

But it wasn't Mon Mothma. 'Councilor, this is Central Communications,' a brisk military voice said. 'There's a civilian freighter called the *Wild Karrde* holding position just outside the sentry line. The captain insists on speaking with you personally. Do you want to talk to him, or shall we just go ahead and chase him out of the system?'

So Karrde had finally come to pick up his people. Or else had been listening to rumors and had decided to poke around

Coruscant a little for himself. Either way, it was trouble. 'Better let me talk to him,' she told the controller.

'Yes, Councilor.'

There was a quiet click. 'Hello, Karrde,' Leia said. 'This is Leia Organa Solo.'

'Hello, Councilor,' Karrde's cool, well-modulated voice replied. 'It's nice to talk to you again. I trust you received my package?'

Leia had to think back. Right – the macrobinocular record of the Ukio attack. 'Yes, we did,' she acknowledged. 'Allow me to express the New Republic's gratitude.'

'Your gratitude has already been amply expressed,' Karrde said dryly. 'Were there any unpleasant repercussions over the payment arrangements?'

'On the contrary,' Leia said, bending the truth only a bit. 'We'd be happy to pay equivalent rates for more information of that quality.'

'I'm glad to hear that,' Karrde said. 'Are you by any chance also in the market for technology?'

Leia blinked. It wasn't a question she'd been expecting. 'What sort of technology?' she asked.

'The semirare sort,' he said. 'Why don't you give me clearance to come down and we'll discuss it.'

'I'm afraid that won't be possible,' Leia said. 'All nonessential traffic in and out of Coruscant has been restricted.'

'Only the nonessential traffic?'

Leia grimaced. So he *had* been listening to rumors. 'What exactly have you heard?'

'Assorted whispers only,' he said. 'Only one of which really concerns me. Tell me about Mara.'

'What about Mara?' Leia asked guardedly.

'Is she under arrest?'

Leia threw a look at Winter. 'Karrde, this isn't something we should be discussing—'

'Don't give me that,' Karrde cut her off, his voice suddenly hard. 'You owe me. More to the point, you owe her.'

'I'm aware of that,' Leia countered, letting her own voice cool a degree or two. 'If you'll let me finish, this isn't

343

something we should be discussing on an open channel.'

'Ah. I see.' If he was feeling any embarrassment over his mistake, it didn't show in his voice. 'Let's try this. Is Ghent available?'

'He's around somewhere.'

'Find him and get him on a terminal with comm system access. Tell him to program in one of my personal encrypt codes – his choice. That should give us enough privacy.'

Leia thought about it. It should at least filter out casual eavesdropping by other civilian ships in the system. Whether any Imperial probe droids lurking out there would be fooled was another question. 'It's a start, at least,' she agreed. 'I'll go find him.'

'I'll be waiting.'

The signal went silent. 'Trouble?' Winter asked.

'Probably,' Leia said. She looked down at Jacen, a strange tingling in the back of her mind. There it was again: the eerie feeling that a vital piece of information was hovering in the darkness just out of reach. Luke and Mara were involved with it, she'd already decided. Could Karrde be involved, too? 'He's come to plead Mara's case . . . and I don't think he's going to be happy to find her gone. Take care of the twins, please – I have to find Ghent and get down to the war room.'

The data checklist ran to the end and stopped. 'Looks OK,' Ghent told Leia, peering at the display and making one final adjustment to the encrypt scheme. 'You're not going to lose more than a syllable here or there, anyway. Go ahead.'

'Just be careful what you say,' Bel Iblis reminded her. 'There could still be probe droids out there listening in, and there's no guarantee the Imperials haven't broken Karrde's encrypt codes. Don't say anything they don't already know.'

'I understand,' Leia nodded. She sat down and tapped the switch the comm officer indicated. 'We're ready here, Karrde.'

'So am I,' Karrde's voice came back. It sounded a bit lower in pitch than normal, but otherwise seemed to be coming through fine. 'Why is Mara under arrest?'

'There was a break-in by an Imperial commando team a

few weeks ago,' Leia said, choosing her words carefully. 'The leader of the team implicated Mara as an accomplice.'

'That's absurd,' Karrde scoffed.

'I agree,' Leia said. 'But an accusation like that has to be investigated.'

'And what have your investigators discovered?'

'What some of us already knew,' Leia said. 'That she was once a member of the Emperor's personal staff.'

'Is that why you're still holding her?' Karrde demanded. 'For things she might or might not have done years ago?'

'We're not worried about her past,' Leia said, starting to sweat a little. She hated misleading Karrde this way, particularly after all the assistance he'd given them. But if there were probe droids listening, she needed to make it look like Mara was still under suspicion. 'Certain members of the Council and high command are concerned about her current loyalties.'

'Then those members are fools,' Karrde bit out. 'I'd like to talk with her.'

'I'm afraid that's impossible,' Leia said. 'She's not being allowed access to external communications.'

There was a faint sound from the speaker; an encrypt glitch or a sigh, Leia couldn't tell which. 'Tell me why I can't land,' Karrde said. 'I've heard the rumors. Tell me the truth.'

Leia looked up at Bel Iblis. There was a sour look on his face, but he gave a reluctant nod. 'The truth is we're under siege,' she told Karrde. 'The Grand Admiral has placed a large number of cloaked asteroids into orbit around Coruscant. We don't know what their orbits are, or even how many of them are there. Until we find and destroy all of them the planetary shield has to stay up.'

'Indeed,' Karrde murmured. 'Interesting. I'd heard about the Empire's hit-and-fade, but there hasn't been anything at all about any asteroids. Most of the rumors have suggested merely that you'd suffered severe damage and were trying to cover it up.'

'That sounds like the sort of story Thrawn would circulate,'

Bel Iblis growled. 'A little jab at our morale to keep him amused between attacks.'

'He's adept at all aspects of warfare,' Karrde agreed. But to Leia's ear, there was something odd in his tone. 'How many of these asteroids have you found so far? I presume you've been looking.'

'We've found and destroyed twenty-one,' she told him. 'That's twenty-two gone, counting the one the Imperials destroyed to keep us from capturing it. But our battle date indicates he could have launched as many as two hundred eighty-seven.'

Karrde was silent a moment. 'That's still not all that many for the volume of space involved. I'd be willing to risk coming through it.'

'We're not worried about you,' Bel Iblis put in. 'We're thinking of what would happen in Coruscant if a forty-meter asteroid got through the shield and hit the surface.'

'I could make it in through a five-second gap,' Karrde offered.

'We're not opening one,' Leia said firmly. 'I'm sorry.'

There was another faint sound from the speaker. 'In that case, I suppose I have no choice but to make a deal. You said earlier that you'd be willing to pay for information. Very well. I have something you need; and my price is a few minutes with Mara.'

Leia frowned up at Bel Iblis, got an equally puzzled look in return. Whatever Karrde was angling for, it wasn't obvious to him, either. What *was* obvious was that she couldn't very well promise to let him talk to Mara. 'I can't make any promises,' she told him. 'Tell me what the information is, and I'll try to be fair.'

There was a moment of silence as he thought it over. 'I suppose that's the best offer I'm ging to get,' he said at last. 'All right. You can lower your shield any time now. The asteroids are all gone.'

Leia stared at the speaker. 'What?'

'You heard me,' Karrde said. 'They're gone. Thrawn left you twenty-two; you've destroyed twenty-two. The siege is over.'

'How do you know?' Bel Iblis asked.

'I was at the Bilbringi shipyards shortly before the Empire's hit-and-fade attack,' Karrde told him. 'We observed a group of twenty-two asteroids being worked on under close security. At the time, of course, we didn't know what the Empire was doing with them.'

'Did you make any records while you were there?' Bel Iblis asked.

'I have the *Wild Karrde*'s sensor data,' he said. 'If you're ready, I'll drop it to you.'

'Go ahead.'

The data-feed light went on, and Leia looked up at the master visual display. It was the inside of the Bilbringi shipyards, all right – she recognized it from New Republic surveillance flights. And there in the center, surrounded by support craft and maintenance-suited workers—

'He's right,' Bel Iblis murmured. 'Twenty-two of them.'

'That doesn't prove there aren't any more, sir,' the officer at the sensor console pointed out. 'They could have put together another group at Ord Trasi or Yaga Minor.'

'No,' Bel Iblis shook his head. 'Aside from the logistics problems involved, I can't imagine Thrawn spreading his cloaking technology around more than he has to. The last thing he can afford would be for us to get our hands on a working model.'

'Or even a systems readout,' Karrde agreed. 'If you found a weakness, one of his chief advantages over you would be gone. All right: I've delivered on my end of the deal. How about yours?'

Leia looked at Bel Iblis helplessly. 'Why do you want to talk with her?' the general asked.

'If it matters, one of the hardest parts of being locked up is the feeling that you've been deserted,' Karrde said coolly. 'I imagine Mara's feeling that – I know I did when I was Thrawn's unwilling guest aboard the *Chimaera*. I want to let her know – in person – that she hasn't been forgotten.'

'Leia?' Bel Iblis murmured. 'What do we do?'

Leia stared at the general, hearing his words but not really registering them. There it was, right in front of her: the key she'd been searching for. Karrde's imprisonment aboard the *Chimaera* . . .

'Leia?' Bel Iblis repeated, frowning.

'I heard you,' she said, the words sounding distant and mechanical in her ears. 'Let him land.'

Bel Iblis threw a glance at the deck officer. 'Perhaps we should—'

'I said let him land,' Leia snapped with more fire than she'd intended. Suddenly, all the pieces had fallen into place . . . and the picture they formed was one of potential disaster. 'I'll take responsibility.'

For a moment, Bel Iblis studied her face. 'Karrde, this is Bel Iblis,' he said slowly. 'We'll give you your five-second opening. Stand by for landing instructions.'

'Thank you,' Karrde said. 'I'll talk to you soon.'

Bel Iblis gestured to the deck officer, who nodded and got busy. 'All right, Leia,' he said, turning back to her. 'What's going on?'

Leia took a deep breath. 'It's the cloning, Garm. I know how Thrawn's growing them so fast.'

The whole war room had gone dead quiet. 'Tell me,' Bel Iblis said.

'It's the Force,' she told him. It was so obvious – so utterly obvious – and yet she'd missed it completely. 'Don't you see? When you make an exact duplicate of a sentient being, there's a natural resonance or something set up through the Force between that duplicate and the original. *That's* what warps the mind of a clone that's been grown too fast – there's not enough time for the mind to adapt to the pressure on it. It can't adjust; so it breaks.'

'All right,' Bel Iblis said dubiously. 'How is Thrawn getting around the problem?'

'It's very simple,' Leia said, a shiver running through her. 'He's using ysalamiri to block the Force away from the cloning tanks.'

Bel Iblis's face went rigid. Across the silent war room, someone swore softly. 'It was Karrde's rescue from the

Chimaera that was the key,' Leia went on. 'Mara told me that the Empire had taken five or six thousand ysalamiri out of the forests on Myrkr. But they weren't loading them on to their warships, because when she and Luke went after Karrde Luke had no problem using the Force.'

'Because the ysalamiri were on Wayland,' Bel Iblis nodded. He looked sharply at Leia, the texture of his sense abruptly changing. 'Which means that when the team gets to the mountain—'

'Luke will be helpless,' Leia nodded, her throat tight. 'And he won't even suspect it until it's too late.'

She shivered again, the dream she'd had the night of the Imperial attack suddenly coming back to her. Luke and Mara, facing a crazed Jedi and another unknown threat. She'd soothed herself at the time with the knowledge that Luke would be able to sense C'baoth's presence on Wayland and take steps to avoid him. But with the ysalamiri there, he might walk right into the other's hands.

No. *Would* walk into C'baoth's hands. Somehow, at this instant, she knew that he would. What she'd seen that night hadn't been a dream, but a Jedi vision.

'I'll talk to Mon Mothma,' Bel Iblis was saying, his face grim. 'Even with Bilbringi, maybe we can shake some ships loose to go to their assistance.'

Turning, he headed quickly toward the exit and the turbolifts beyond it. For a moment Leia watched him, listening as the war room broke its self-imposed trance and came slowly back to life. He'd try, she knew; but she also knew that he would fail. Mon Mothma, Commander Sesfan, and Bel Iblis himself had already said it: there simply weren't enough resources available to hit both Wayland and the Bilbringi shipyards at the same time. And she knew all too well that not everyone on the Council would believe that the threat of cloaked asteroids had ended. At least, not enough to call off the Bilbringi attack.

Which meant there was exactly one person left who could go to the aid of her husband and brother.

Taking a deep breath, Leia headed off after Bel Iblis. There was a great deal she had to do before Karrde arrived.

There were three of them waiting when Karrde emerged from the ship, skulking beneath the canopy overhanging the pad accessway tunnel. Karrde spotted them from the top of the *Wild Karrde*'s entrance ramp, and despite the shadows had two of them identified before he was halfway down. Leia Organa Solo was there, with Ghent fidgeting behind her. The third figure, standing behind both of the others, was short and wore the coarse brown robe of a Jawa. What a desert scavenger was doing there Karrde couldn't guess . . . but as the group stepped out of the shadows toward him and he got his first good look at Organa Solo's face, it became clear that he was about to find out. 'Good morning, Councilor,' he greeted her, inclining his head slightly. 'Good to see you, Ghent. I trust you've been making yourself useful?'

'I suppose so,' Ghent said, shifting nervously from one foot to the other. Far too nervously, even for him. 'They say so, anyway.'

'Good.' Karrde shifted his attention to the third of the party. 'And your friend is . . . ?'

'I am Mobvekhar clan Hakh'khar,' a gravelly voice mewed.

Karrde resisted the urge to take a half-step backward. Whatever it was hiding under that robe, it most certainly wasn't a Jawa. 'He's my bodyguard,' Organa Solo said.

'Ah.' With an effort, Karrde pulled his eyes away from whatever it was that was being concealed by the dark hood. 'Well,' he said, waving a hand toward the accessway. 'Shall we go?'

Organa Solo shook her head. 'Mara's not here.'

Karrde threw a look at Ghent, who was looking even more uncomfortable. 'You told me she was.'

'I only agreed with you that she'd been arrested,' Organa Solo said. 'I couldn't say anything more then – there may have been Imperial probe droids listening in.'

With an effort, Karrde fought down his annoyance. They were all on the same side here, after all. 'Where is she?'

'On a planet called Wayland,' Organa Solo said. 'Along with Luke and Han and some others.'

Wayland? Karrde couldn't recall ever hearing of that world before. 'And what's on Wayland that they find so interesting?' he asked.

'Grand Admiral Thrawn's cloning facility.'

Karrde stared at her. 'You found it?'

'We didn't,' Organa Solo said. 'Mara did.'

Karrde nodded mechanically. So they'd found the cloning facility on their own. All that work he'd put in organizing the other smuggler groups: gone like dumped Kessel spice. The work, the risk, not to mention the money he'd planned to pay them with. 'You're certain the cloning facility is there?'

'We'll find out soon enough,' Organa Solo said, gesturing to the ship behind him. 'I need you to take me there. Right away.'

'Why?'

'Because the expedition's in danger,' Organa Solo said. 'They may not know it yet, but they are. And if they're still on the timetable we were sent, we have a chance of getting to them before it's too late.'

'She told me all about it on the way up here,' Ghent added hesitantly. 'I think we ought to . . .'

He trailed off as Karrde sent a look his way. 'I sympathize with your people, Councilor,' he said. 'But there are other matters that also need my attention.'

'Then you abandon Mara,' Organa Solo reminded him.

'I have no particular feelings for Mara,' Karrde countered. 'She's a member of my organization; nothing more.'

'Isn't that enough?'

For a moment Karrde gazed at her. She held his gaze evenly, calling his bluff . . . and in her eyes, he could see that she knew perfectly well that it *was* a bluff. He couldn't simply walk away and abandon Mara to her death, any more than he could abandon Aves or Dankin or Chin. Not if there was anything he could do to prevent it. 'It's not that easy,' he said quietly. 'I have responsibilities to the rest of my people, as well. At the moment they're preparing to launch a raid with

351

the hope of obtaining a crystal gravfield trap to sell you.'

A flicker of surprise flashed across Organa Solo's face. 'A crystal gravfield trap—?'

'It's not the one you're trying for,' Karrde assured her. 'But we've scheduled it for the same time, hoping your attack will distract the enemy. I need to be there.'

'I see,' Organa Solo murmured, apparently deciding to pass over the question of how Karrde could have known about the Tangrene raid. 'Will the *Wild Karrde* make all that much difference in that raid?'

Karrde looked at Ghent. It wouldn't make any difference at all, not with Mazzic and Ellor and the others reinforcing the impressive group Aves had already pulled together. The problem was that if they left now – and the way Organa Solo was talking, she meant for him to turn around and head straight back into space – there wouldn't be any chance of turning Ghent loose on the New Republic's computer system and rerouting the funds he needed to pay the other groups.

Unless he could get the money another way. 'It can't be done,' he told Organa Solo firmly. 'I can't simply walk out on my people. At least, not without—'

Abruptly, the Jawa-robed alien snapped his fingers. Karrde paused in midsentence, watching in fascination as the creature slipped noiselessly back into the accessway tunnel, a slender knife appearing somehow in his hand. He disappeared through the door, and for a moment there was silence. Karrde raised his eyebrows at Organa Solo, got a slight shrug in return—

There was a sudden squeal from inside the accessway door, followed by a sudden flurry of half-visible commotion. Karrde found his blaster in his hand; and he was bringing it to bear on the figures when all the activity abruptly stopped. A moment later, the alien reappeared, forcing a half-crouched figure before him.

An all-too-familiar figure. 'Well, well,' Karrde said, lowering his blaster but not holstering it. 'Councilor Fey'lya, I believe. Reduced to eavesdropping at doorways?'

'He is unarmed,' the robed alien said in his gravelly voice.

'Release him, then,' Organa Solo said.

The alien complied. Fey'lya straightened up, his fur rippling madly across his head and torso as he tried to salvage what he could of his composure. 'I protest this improper treatment,' he said, his voice somewhat less melodious than the Bothan norm. 'And I was not eavesdropping. General Bel Iblis informed me of Councilor Organa Solo's revelation concerning the cloning facility on Wayland. I came here, Captain Karrde, to urge you to assist Councilor Organa Solo in her wish to go to Wayland.'

Karrde smiled tightly. 'Where she would be conveniently out of your way? Thank you, but I believe we've already been through this together.'

The Bothan drew himself up. 'This is not about politics. Without her warning, the team on Wayland may not survive. And without their survival, the Emperor's storehouse may not be destroyed before the Grand Admiral can remove some of its contents to a safe place.'

His violet eyes locked with Karrde's. 'And that would be a disaster. To both the Bothan people and to the galaxy.'

For a moment Karrde studied him, wondering what was there that Fey'lya was so worried about. Some weapon or technology that Thrawn hadn't found yet? Or was it more personal than that? Unpleasant or embarrassing information, perhaps, either about Fey'lya or the Bothan people generally?

He didn't know, and he suspected Fey'lya wouldn't tell. But the particulars didn't really matter. 'Potential disasters to the Bothan people don't worry me,' he told Fey'lya. 'How much do they worry you?'

There was an uncertain ripple of the fur across Fey'lya's shoulders. 'It would be a disaster for the galaxy as well,' he said.

'So you said,' Karrde agreed. 'I repeat: How much does it worry you?'

And this time Fey'lya got it. His eyes narrowed, his fur rippling with obvious contempt. 'How much worry will it take?' he demanded.

'Nothing unreasonable,' Karrde assured him. 'Merely a credit of, say, seventy thousand?'

'Seventy *thousand*?' Fey'lya echoed, aghast. 'What exactly do you think—'

'That's my price, Councilor,' Karrde cut him off. 'Take it or leave it. And if Councilor Organa Solo is correct, we don't have time for any long discussions.'

Fey'lya hissed like an angry predator. 'You're no better than a foul mercenary,' he snarled, his voice about as vicious as Karrde had ever heard a Bothan get. 'You drain out the lifeblood of the Bothan people—'

'Spare me the lecture, Councilor,' Karrde said. 'Yes or no?'

Fey'lya hissed again. 'Yes.'

'Good,' Karrde nodded, looking at Organa Solo. 'Is the credit line your brother set up for me still there?'

'Yes,' she said. 'General Bel Iblis knows how to access it.'

'You can deposit the seventy thousand there,' Karrde told Fey'lya. 'And bear in mind that we'll be stopping to check on it before we reach Wayland. In case you had any thoughts about backing out.'

'*I* am honorable, smuggler,' Fey'lya snarled. 'Unlike others present.'

'I'm glad to hear that,' Karrde said. 'Honorable beings are so difficult to find. Councilor Organa Solo?'

She took a deep breath. 'I'm ready,' she said.

They were off Coruscant and nearly ready for the jump to lightspeed before Leia finally asked the question she'd worried about since coming aboard. 'Are we really going to stop to check on Fey'lya's funds?'

'With time as critical as you suggest?' Karrde countered. 'Don't be silly. But Fey'lya doesn't know that.'

Leia watched him for a moment as he handled the *Wild Karrde*'s helm. 'The money's not really important to you, is it?'

'Don't believe that, either,' he advised her coolly. 'I have certain obligations to meet. If Fey'lya hadn't been willing to cooperate, your New Republic would have had to do so.'

'I see,' Leia murmured.

He must have heard something in her voice. 'I mean that,'

he insisted, throwing a brief and entirely unconvincing scowl at her. 'I'm here because it suits my purposes. Not for the sake of your war.'

'I said I understood,' Leia agreed, smiling privately to herself. The words were different; but the look on Karrde's face was almost identical. *Look, I ain't in this for your revolution, and I'm not in it for you, Princess. I expect to be well paid. I'm in it for the money.* Han had said that to her after that stormy escape from the first Death Star. At the time, she'd believed it.

Her smile faded. He and Luke had saved her life then. She wondered if she'd be in time now to save theirs.

CHAPTER 24

The entrance to Mount Tantiss was a glint of metal nestled cozily beneath an overhang of rock and vegetation. Between them and it, just visible from their hilltop vantage point, was a clearing with a small city lying in it. 'What do you think?' Luke asked.

'I think we find another way in,' Han told him, bracing his elbows a little harder into the dead leaves and trying to hold the macrobinoculars steady. He'd been right; there was a stormtrooper guard station just off the metal doors. 'You never want the front door, anyway.'

Luke tapped his shoulder twice: the signal that he'd picked up someone coming. Han froze, listening. Sure enough, there was a faint sound of clumping feet in the underbrush. A minute later, four Imperial troops in full field gear came out of the trees a few meters further down the hill. They walked straight past Han and Luke without so much as looking up, disappearing back into the trees a few steps later. 'Starting to get pretty thick,' Han muttered.

'I think it's just the proximity to the mountain,' Luke said. 'I still don't get any indication that they know we're out here.'

Han grunted and shifted his view to the village poking out of the clearing down below them. Most of the buildings were squat, alien-looking things, with one really good-sized one facing into an open square. His angle wasn't all that good, but it looked like there were a bunch of Psadans hanging around near the front of the big one. A town meeting, maybe? 'I don't see any sign of a garrison down there,' he said, sweeping the macrobinoculars slowly across the village. 'Must be working directly out of the mountain.'

'That should make it easier to get around it.'

'Yeah,' Han said, frowning as he swung the macrobinoculars back to the town square. That crowd of Psadans he'd noticed a minute ago had shifted into a sort of semicircle now, facing a couple more of the walking rock piles standing with their backs to the big building. And it was definitely getting bigger.

'Trouble?' Luke murmured.

'I don't know,' Han said slowly, wedging his elbows a little tighter and kicking the magnification up a notch. 'There's a big meeting going on down there. Two Psadans . . . but they don't seem to be talking. Just holding something.'

'Let me try,' Luke offered. 'There are Jedi techniques for enhancing vision. Maybe they'll work on a macrobinocular image.'

'Go ahead,' Han said, handing over the macrobinoculars and squinting at the sky. There were a few wispy clouds visible up there, but nothing that looked like it was going to become a general overcast anytime soon. Figure two hours till sundown; another half hour of light after that—

'Hmm,' Luke said.

'What is it?'

'I'm not exactly sure,' Luke said, lowering the macrobinoculars. 'But it looks to me like what they're holding is a data pad.'

Han looked out toward the city. 'I didn't know they used data pads.'

'Neither did I,' Luke said, his voice suddenly going all strange.

356

Han frowned at him. The kid was just staring at the mountain a funny look on his face. 'What's wrong?'

'It's the mountain,' he said, staring hard at it. 'It's dark. All of it.'

Dark? Han frowned at the mountain. It looked fine to him. 'What are you talking about?'

'It's dark,' Luke repeated slowly. 'Like Myrkr was.'

Han looked at the mountain. Looked back at Luke. 'You mean, like in a bunch of ysalamiri cutting off the Force?'

Luke nodded. 'That's what it feels like. I won't know for sure until we're closer.'

Han looked back at the mountain, feeling his stomach curling up inside him. 'Great,' he muttered. 'Just great. Now what?'

Luke shrugged. 'We go on. What else is there?'

'Getting back to the *Falcon* and getting out of here, that's what,' Han retorted. 'Unless you're really hot to walk into an Imperial trap.'

'I don't think it's a trap,' Luke said, shaking his head thoughtfully. 'Or at least, not a trap for us. Remember how that contact I told you about with C'baoth was suddenly cut off?'

Han rubbed his cheek. He could see what Luke was getting at, all right: the ysalamiri were here for C'baoth, not him. 'I'm still not sure I buy that,' he said. 'I thought C'baoth and Thrawn were on the same side. Mara said that herself.'

'Maybe they had a falling out,' Luke suggested. 'Or maybe Thrawn was using him from the start and now doesn't need him any more. If the Imperials don't know we're here, the ysalamiri must have been meant for him.'

'Yeah, well, it doesn't matter much who they were meant for,' Han pointed out. 'They'll block you just as well as they will C'baoth. It'll be like Myrkr all over again.'

'Mara and I did OK on Myrkr,' Luke reminded him. 'We can handle it here. Anyway, we've come too far to back out now.'

Han grimaced. But the kid was right. Once the Empire gave up on this deserted-planet routine, chances were the next New

Republic team wouldn't even make it into the atmosphere. 'You going to tell Mara before we get there?'

'Of course.' Luke looked up at the sky. 'But I'll tell her on the way. We'd better get moving while we still have daylight.'

'Right,' Han said, giving the area one last look before he got to his feet. Force or no Force, it was up to them. 'Let's go.'

The others were waiting just around the other side of the hill. 'How's it look?' Lando asked as Han and Luke rejoined them.

'They still don't know we're here,' Han told him, looking around for Mara. She was sitting on the ground near Threepio and Artoo, concentrating on a set of five stones she'd gotten to hover in the air in front of her. Luke had been teaching her this kind of stuff for days, and Han had finally given up trying to talk the kid out of it. It looked like the lessons were going to be a waste of time now, anyway. 'You ready to take us to this back door of yours?'

'I'm ready to start looking for it,' she said, still keeping the stones in the air. 'As I told you before, I only saw the air system equipment from inside the mountain. I never saw the intakes themselves.'

'We'll find them,' Luke assured her, passing Han and walking over to the droids. 'How are you doing, Threepio?'

'Quite well, thank you, Master Luke,' the droid answered primly. 'This route is so much better than many of the earlier ones.' Beside him, Artoo trilled something. 'Artoo finds it so, as well,' Threepio added.

'Don't get attached to it,' Mara warned, finally letting the stones drop as she stood up. 'There probably won't be any Myneyrshi trails up the mountain for us to follow. The Empire discouraged native activity anywhere nearby.'

'But don't worry,' Luke soothed the droids. 'The Noghri will help us find a path.'

'Freighter *Garret's Gold*, you're cleared for final approach,' the brisk voice of Bilbringi Control came over the *Etherway*'s bridge speaker. 'Docking Platform Twenty-five.

Straight-vector as indicated to the buoy; it'll feed you the course to follow to the platform.'

'Acknowledged, Control,' Aves said, keying in the course that had come up on the nav display. 'What about the security fields?'

'Stay on the course you're given and you won't run into them,' the controller said. 'Deviate more than about fifteen meters any direction and you'll get a good bump on the nose. From the looks of it, I don't think your nose can afford any more bumps.'

Aves threw a glare at the speaker. One of these days he was going to get real tired of Imperial sarcasm. 'Thank you,' he said, and keyed off.

'Imperials are such fun to work with, aren't they?' Gillespee commented from the copilot station.

'I like to imagine what his expression is going to be like when we burn out of here with their CGT,' Aves said.

'Let's hope we're not around to find out for sure,' Gillespee said. 'Pretty complicated flight system they've got here.'

'It wasn't like this before that raid of Mazzic's,' Aves said, gazing ahead through the viewport. Half a dozen shield generators were visible along his approach vector, floating loose around the area and defining the flight path the buoy would supposedly give him. 'Probably supposed to keep anyone else from flying around the shipyards any old way they want to.'

'Yeah,' Gillespee said. 'I just hope they've got all the glitches out of the system.'

'Me, too,' Aves agreed. 'I don't want them to know how much of a bump this ship can really take.'

He glanced down at his board, confirming his vector and then checking the time. The New Republic fleet ought to be hitting Tangrene in a little over three hours. Just enough time for the *Etherway* to dock, unload the specially tweaked tractor beam burst capacitors they were courteously donating to the Empire's war effort, and get into backup position for Mazzic's attempt to grab the CGT from the main command center eight docking platforms away.

'There goes Ellor,' Gillespee commented, nodding off to starboard.

Aves looked. It was the *Kai Mir*, all right, with the *Klivering* running in flanking position beside it. Beyond it, he could see the *Starry Ice* drifting in toward a docking platform near the perimeter. Near as he could tell, everything seemed to be falling into place.

Though with someone like Thrawn in charge, appearances didn't mean much. For all he knew, the Grand Admiral might already know all about this raid, and was just waiting for everybody to sneak in under the net before wrapping it around them.

'You ever hear anything else from Karrde?' Gillespee asked, a little too casually.

'He's not deserting us, Gillespee,' Aves growled. 'If he says he has something more important to do, then he has something more important to do. Period.'

'I know,' Gillespee said, his voice noncommittal. 'Just thought some of the others might have asked.'

Aves grimaced. Here they went again. He'd have thought that opening up Ferrier's treachery at Hijarna would have settled this whole thing once and for all. He should have known better. 'I'm here,' he reminded Gillespee. 'So are the *Starry Ice*, the *Dawn Beat*, the *Lastri's Ort*, the *Amanda Fallow*, the—'

'Yeah, right, I get the point,' Gillespee interrupted. 'Don't get huffy at me – my ships are here, too.'

'Sorry,' Aves said. 'I'm just getting tired of everybody always being so suspicious of everybody else.'

Gillespee shrugged. 'We're smugglers. We've had a lot of practice at it. Personally, I'm surprised the group's held together this long. What do you think he's doing?'

'Who, Karrde?' Aves shook his head. 'No idea. But it'll be something important.'

'Sure.' Gillespee pointed ahead. 'That the marker buoy?'

'Looks like it,' Aves agreed. 'Get ready to copy the course data. Ready or not, here we go.'

*　　*　　*

The orders came up on Wedge's comm screen, and he gave them a quick check as he keyed for the squadron's private frequency. 'Rogue Squadron, this is Rogue Leader,' he said. 'Orders: we're going in with the first wave, flanking Admiral Ackbar's Command Cruiser. Hold position here until we're cleared for positioning. All ships acknowledge.'

The acknowledgements came in, crisp and firm, and Wedge smiled tightly to himself. There'd been some worry among Ackbar's staff, he knew, that the long flight here to the rendezvous point might take the edge off those units that had first had to carry out decoy duty near the supposed Tangrene jump-off point. Wedge didn't know about the others, but it was clear that Rogue Squadron was primed and ready for battle.

'You suppose Thrawn got our message, Rogue Leader?' Janson's voice came into Wedge's thoughts.

Their message . . . ? Oh, right – that little conversation outside the Mumbri Storve cantina with Talon Karrde's friend Aves. The one Hobbie had been firmly convinced would be going straight to Imperial Intelligence. 'I don't know, Rogue Five,' Wedge told him. 'Actually, I sort of hope it didn't.'

'Kind of a waste of time if it didn't.'

'Not necessarily,' Wedge pointed out. 'Remember, he said they had some other scheme on line that they wanted to coordinate with ours. Anything that hits or distracts the Empire can't help but do us some good.'

'They've probably just got some smuggling drop planned,' Rogue Six sniffed. 'Hoping to run it through while the Imperials are looking the other way.'

Wedge didn't reply. Luke Skywalker seemed to think Karrde was quietly on the New Republic's side, and that was good enough for him. But there wasn't any way he was going to convince the rest of his squadron of that. Someday, maybe, Karrde would be willing to take a more open stand against the Empire. Until then at least in Wedge's opinion, everyone who wasn't on the Grand Admiral's side was helping the New Republic, whether they admitted it or not.

Sometimes, even, whether they knew it or not.

His comm display changed: the vanguard cone of Star Cruisers had made it into their launch formation. Time for their escort ships to do the same. 'OK, Rogue Squadron,' he told the others. 'We've got the light. Let's get to our places.'

Easing power to his X-wing's drive, he headed off toward the running lights ahead. Two and a half hours, if the rest of the fleet assembly stayed on schedule, and they'd be dropping out of light-speed within spitting distance of the Bilbringi shipyards.

A shame, he thought, that they wouldn't be able to see the looks on the Imperials' faces.

The latest group of reports from the Tangrene region scrolled across the display. Pellaeon skimmed through them, scowling blackly to himself. No mistake – the Rebels were still there. Still slipping forces into the region; still doing nothing to draw attention to themselves. And in two hours, if Intelligence's projections were even halfway accurate, they would be launching an attack on an effectively undefended system.

'They're doing quite well, aren't they, Captain?' Thrawn commented from beside him. 'A very convincing performance all around.'

'Sir,' Pellaeon said, fighting to keep his voice properly deferential. 'I respectfully suggest that the Rebel activity is not any kind of performance. The preponderance of evidence points to Tangrene as their probable target. Several key starfighter units and capital ships have clearly been assembled at likely jump-off points—'

'Wrong, Captain,' Thrawn cut him off coolly. 'That's what they want us to believe, but it's nothing more than a carefully constructed illusion. The ships you refer to pulled out of those sectors between forty and seventy hours ago, leaving behind a few men with the proper uniforms and insignia to confuse our spies. The bulk of the force is even now on its way to Bilbringi.'

'Yes, sir,' Pellaeon said with a silent sigh of defeat. So that was it. Once again, Thrawn had chosen to ignore his arguments – as well as all the evidence – in favor of nebulous hunches and intuitions.

362

And if he was wrong, it wouldn't be simply the Tangrene Ubiqtorate base that would be lost. An error of that magnitude would shake the confidence and momentum of the entire Imperial war machine.

'All war is risk, Captain,' Thrawn said quietly. 'But this is not as large a risk as you seem to think. If I'm wrong, we lose one Ubiqtorate base – important, certainly, but hardly critical.' He cocked a blue-black eyebrow. 'But if I'm right, we stand a good chance of destroying two entire Rebel sector fleets. Consider the impact that will have on the current balance of power.'

'Yes, sir,' Pellaeon said dutifully.

He could feel Thrawn's eyes on him. 'You don't have to believe,' the Grand Admiral told him. 'But be prepared to be proved wrong.'

'I very must hope so, sir,' Pellaeon said.

'Good. Is my flagship ready, Captain?'

Pellaeon felt his back stiffen a bit in old parade-ground reflex. 'The *Chimaera* is fully at your command, Admiral.'

'Then prepare the fleet for hyperspace.' The glowing eyes glittered. 'And for battle.'

There were no real paths up Mount Tantiss; but as Luke had predicted, the Noghri had a knack for terrain. They made remarkably good time, even with the droids slowing them down, and as the sun was disappearing below the trees, they reached the air intakes.

It was not, however, exactly the way Luke had envisioned it.

'Looks more like a retractable turbolaser turret than an air system,' he commented to Han as they moved cautiously through the trees toward the heavy metal mesh and the even heavier metal structure the mesh was set into.

'Reminds me of the bunker we had to break into on Endor,' Han muttered back. 'Except with a screen door. Easy – they might have intruder detectors.'

Anywhere else, Luke would have reached out into the tunnel with the Force. Here, within the ysalamiri effect surrounding him, it was like being blind.

363

Like being on Myrkr again.

He looked at Mara, wondering if she was having similar thoughts and memories. Perhaps so. Even in the fading light, he could see the tension in her face, an anxiety and fear that hadn't been there before they entered the ysalamiri bubble. 'So what now?' she growled, flashing a brief glare at him before looking away again. 'We just sit around until morning?'

Han had his macrobinoculars trained on the intake. 'Looks like a computer outlet there on the wall under the overhang,' he said. 'The rest of you stay put – I'll take Artoo over and try plugging him in.'

Beside Han, Chewbacca rumbled a warning. 'Where?' Han muttered, drawing his blaster.

The Wookiee pointed with one hand as he unlimbered his bowcaster with the other.

The whole group froze, weapons ready . . . and it was then that Luke first heard the faint sounds of distant blaster fire. From several kilometers away, he thought, possibly somewhere down the mountain. But without his Jedi enhancement techniques, there was no way to know for sure.

From much closer came a birdlike warbling. 'A group of Myneyrshi approach,' Ekhrikhor said, listening intently to the signaling. 'The Noghri have stopped them. They wish to come forward and speak.'

'Tell them to stay there,' Han said, hesitating just a second before holstering his blaster. Pulling the bleached *satnachakka* clawbird out of a pocket of his jacket, he beckoned to Threepio. 'Come on, Goldenrod, let's go find out what they want.'

Ekhrikhor muttered an order, and one of the Noghri moved silently to Han's side. Chewbacca stepped to the other side, and with a helplessly protesting Threepio trailing along they all headed off into the trees.

Artoo gurgled uncomfortably, his dome head swiveling back and forth between Luke and the departing Threepio. 'He'll be all right,' Luke assured him. 'Han won't let anything happen to him.'

The squat droid grunted, probably expressing his opinion

of the depths of Han's concern for Threepio. 'We may have more problems than Threepio's health to worry about in a minute,' Lando said grimly. 'I thought I heard blaster fire from down the mountain.'

'I did, too,' Mara nodded. 'Probably coming from the storehouse entrance.'

Lando looked over his shoulder at the massive air intake. 'Let's see if we can get that vent open. At least it'll give us another direction to go if we need to jump.'

Luke looked at Mara, but she was avoiding his eyes again. 'All right,' he told Lando. 'I'll go first; you bring Artoo.'

Cautiously, he moved through the trees toward the intakes. But if there were any anti-intruder defenses, they didn't seem to be working anymore. He made it in under the metal overhang without incident, and with the wind of the inrushing air ruffling through his hair he studied the mesh. At this distance he could see that it was more like a heavy grating, with each strand of what had looked like mesh actually a plate extending several centimeters back into the tunnel. A formidable barrier, but nothing his lightsaber couldn't handle.

There was the sound of a footstep through leaves, and he turned as Lando and Artoo came up. 'The outlet's over there, Artoo,' he told the droid, pointing to the socket in the side wall. 'Plug in and see what you can find out.'

The droid warbled acknowledgement, and with Lando's help maneuvered his way across the rough ground.

'It's not just going to open up for you,' Mara said from behind him.

'Artoo's going to check it out,' Luke told her, peering at her face. 'You all right?'

He'd expected a sarcastic comment or at least a withering glare. He wasn't prepared for her to reach out and grip his hand. 'I want you to promise me something,' she said in a low voice. 'Whatever it costs, don't let me go over to C'baoth's side. You understand? Don't let me join him. Even if you have to kill me.'

Luke stared at her, an eerie chill running through him.

'C'baoth can't force you to his side, Mara,' he said. 'Not without your cooperation.'

'Are you sure of that? *Really* sure?'

Luke grimaced. There was so much he didn't know yet about the Force. 'No.'

'Neither am I,' Mara said. 'That's what worries me. C'baoth told me back on Jomark that I'd be joining him. He said it again here, too, the night he arrived.'

'He may have been mistaken,' Luke suggested hesitantly. 'Or lying.'

'I don't want to risk it.' She gripped Luke's hand tighter. 'I'm not going to serve him, Skywalker. I want you to promise that you'll kill me before you let him do that to me.'

Luke swallowed hard. Even without the Force, he could hear in her voice that she meant it. But for a Jedi to promise to cut someone down in cold blood . . . 'I'll promise you this,' he said instead. 'Whatever happens in there, you won't have to face him alone. I'll be there to help you.'

She turned her face away. 'What if you're already dead?'

So it was down to this: the same battle she'd been fighting with herself since the day they met. 'You don't have to do it,' he said quietly. 'The Emperor's dead. That voice you hear is just a memory he left behind inside you.'

'I know that,' she snapped, a touch of fire flickering through the cold dread. 'You think that makes it any easier to ignore?'

'No,' he conceded. 'But you can't use the voice as an excuse, either. Your destiny is in your hands, Mara. Not C'baoth's or the Emperor's. In the end you're the one who makes the decisions. You have that right . . . and that responsibility.'

From the forest came the sound of footsteps. 'Fine,' Mara growled, dropping Luke's hand and taking a step back away from him. 'You spout philosophy if you want to. Just remember what I said.' Spinning around, she turned to face the approaching group. 'So what's going on, Solo?'

'We've picked up some allies,' he said, throwing what looked like a frown in Luke's general direction. 'Sort of allies, anyway.'

'Hey – Threepio,' Lando called, waving to him. 'Come over here, will you, and tell me what Artoo's all excited about.'

'Certainly, sir,' Threepio said, shuffling over to the computer terminal.

Luke looked back at Han. 'What do you mean, sort of allies?'

'It's kind of confusing,' Han said. 'At least the way Threepio translates it. They don't want to help us, they just want to go in and fight the Imperials. They followed us because they figured we'd find a back door they could get in through.'

Luke studied the group of silent four-armed aliens towering over the Noghri guarding them. All wore four or more long knives and carried crossbows – not exactly the sort of weapons to use against armored Imperial troops. 'I don't know. What do you think?'

'Hey, Han,' Lando called softly before Han could answer. 'Come here. You'll want to hear this.'

'What?' Han asked as they went over to the computer terminal.

'Tell them, Threepio,' Lando said.

'Apparently, there is an attack taking place at the main entrance to the mountain,' Threepio said in that perennially surprised manner of his. 'Artoo has picked up several reports detailing perimeter-guard troop movements into the area—'

'Who's attacking?' Han cut him off.

'Apparently, some of the Psadans from the city,' Threepio said. 'According to the gate reports, they demanded the release of their Lord C'baoth before they attacked.'

Han looked at Luke. 'The data pad.'

'Makes sense,' Luke agreed. A message from C'baoth, inciting them to attack. 'I wonder how he managed to smuggle it out to them.'

'Confirms he's been locked up, anyway,' Mara put in. 'I hope they've got some good guards on his cell.'

'Pardon me, Master Luke,' Threepio said, cocking his head to one side, 'but as to the data pad Captain Solo mentioned,

I would suggest it arrived the same way the weapons did. According to reports—'

'What kind of weapons?' Han said.

'I was getting to that, sir,' Threepio said, sounding a bit huffy. 'According to gate reports, the attackers are armed with blasters, portable missile launchers, and thermal detonators. All quite modern versions, if reports are to be believed.'

'Never mind where they got them from,' Lando said. 'The point is that we've got a custom-cut diversion here. Let's use it while it's still there.'

Chewbacca rumbled suspiciously. 'You're right, pal,' Han agreed, peering into the grating. 'It's awfully convenient timing. But Lando's right – we might as well go for it.'

Lando nodded. 'OK, Artoo. Shut it all down.'

The squat droid chirped acknowledgment, his computer arm rotating in the socket. The inflow of air across Luke's face began to decrease, and a minute later had stopped completely.

Artoo warbled again. 'Artoo reports that all operating systems for this intake have been shut down,' Threepio announced. 'He warns, however, that once the duty cycle has ended, the dust barriers and driving fields may be reactivated from a central location.'

'Better get moving, then,' Luke said, igniting his lightsaber and stepping over to the intake. Four careful slices later, they had their entrance.

'Looks clear,' Han said, climbing gingerly through the opening and stepping over to the limited protection of the side wall. 'Got maintenance lights showing up down the tunnel a ways. Artoo, you get us any floor plans for this place?'

The droid jabbered as he rolled through the opening. 'I'm terribly sorry, sir,' Threepio said. 'He has full schematics for the air-duct system itself, but he says that further information on the facility was not available at this terminal.'

'There'll be other terminals down the line,' Lando said. 'Are we leaving a rear guard?'

'One of the Noghri will stay,' Ekhrikhor mewed at Han's elbow. 'He will keep the exit clear.'

'Fine,' Han said. 'Let's go.'

They were fifty meters down the tunnel and approaching the first of the dim maintenance lights Han had spotted before Luke suddenly noticed that the silent Myneyrshi had followed them in. 'Han?' he murmured, gesturing behind them.

'Yeah, I know,' Han said. 'What did you want me to do, tell them to go home?'

Luke looked back again. He was right, of course. But knives and crossbows against blasters . . . 'Ekhrikhor?'

'What is your command, son of Vader?'

'I want you to assign two of your people to go with those Myneyrshi,' he told the Noghri. 'They're to guide them and help them with their attacks.'

'But it is you we must protect, son of Vader,' Ekhrikhor objected.

'You will be protecting me,' Luke said. 'Every Imperial the Myneyrshi can pin down will be one less for us to worry about. But they can't pin any troops down if they're killed in the first sortie.'

The Noghri made an unhappy-sounding noise in the back of his throat. 'I hear and obey,' he said reluctantly. He gestured to two of the Noghri; and as Luke watched them drop back down the tunnel he caught a quick look at Mara's face as she passed one of the lights. The dread was still there, but along with it was a grim determination. Whatever was waiting ahead for them, she was ready to face it.

He could only hope that he was, too.

'There it is,' Karrde announced, pointing ahead to the mountain rising out of the forest and the gathering shadows of twilight.

'You sure?' Leia asked, stretching out with the Force as hard as she could. Back at Bespin, during that mad escape from Lando's Cloud City, she'd been able to sense Luke's call from almost this far away. Here, now, there was nothing at all.

'That's where their nav feed seems to be leading us,' Karrde told her. 'Unless they've seen through Ghent's little deception and are sending us to some sort of decoy spot.' He glanced over his shoulder at her. 'Anything?'

'No.' Leia looked out at the mountain, her stomach tightening painfully. After all their hopes and effort, they were too late. 'They must already be inside.'

'They're heading into trouble, then,' Ghent spoke up from the comm station where he was still fiddling with the fine-tuning on his counterfeit Imperial ID code. 'Flight control says they've got a riot going on at the entrance. They're diverting us to a secondary maintenance area about ten kilometers north.'

Leia shook her head. 'We're going to have to risk contacting them.'

'Too dangerous,' Dankin, the copilot, said. 'If they catch us using a non-Imperial comlink channel, we're likely to get shot down.'

'Perhaps there is another way,' Mobvekhar said, moving to Leia's side. 'Ekhrikhor clan Bakh'tor will have left a guard at their entrance point. There is a Noghri recognition signal that can be created with landing lights.'

'Go ahead,' Karrde said. 'We can always claim a malfunction if the garrison notices. Chin, Corvis – watch your scopes.'

Stepping over to Dankin's board, the Noghri keyed the landing lights on and off a half-dozen times. Leia stared out the viewport, trying to watch the whole mountain at once. If Han and the others had gone in above the dusk line—

'Got it,' Corvis's voice came from his turbolaser turret. 'Bearing zero-zero-three mark seventeen.'

Leia looked over Karrde's shoulder as the coordinates came up on his nav display. There it was, faint but visible: a flickering light. 'They are there,' Mobvekhar confirmed.

'Good,' Karrde said. 'Ghent, acknowledge that we're proceeding to that secondary maintenance area as ordered. Better find a seat and strap down, Councilor; we're about to have an unexpected repulsorlift malfunction.'

Between the trees and eroded rock outcroppings it looked to Leia like an impossible place for a ship the size of the *Wild Karrde* to land. But Karrde and his crew had clearly pulled this trick before, and with a last-second sputter of precision-aimed turbolaser fire they created just enough of a gap to put down into.

'Now what?' Dankin asked as Karrde cycled back the repulsorlifts.

Karrde looked at Leia, raised an eyebrow in question. 'I'm going in,' Leia told him, the vision of Luke and Mara in danger hovering before her eyes. 'You don't have to come along.'

'The Councilor and I will go look for her friends,' Karrde answered Dankin, unstrapping and getting to his feet. 'Ghent, you'll try to convince the garrison that we don't need any assistance.'

'What about me?' Dankin asked.

Karrde smiled tightly. 'You'll stay ready in case they don't believe him. Come on, Councilor.'

The Noghri who'd returned their signal was nowhere in sight as they stepped out on to the *Wild Karrde*'s ramp. 'Where is he?' Karrde asked, looking around.

'Waiting,' Mobvekhar said, putting a hand to the side of his mouth and giving a complex whistle. An answering whistle came, shifted into a complex warble. 'Our identity is confirmed,' he said. 'He bids us come quickly. The others are no more than a quarter hour ahead.'

A quarter hour. Leia stared out at the starlit darkness of the mountain. Too late to warn them, but maybe not too late to help. 'Come on – we're wasting time,' she said.

'Just a minute,' Karrrde said, looking past her shoulder. 'We have to wait for – ah.'

Leia turned. Coming down the corridor toward them from the aft section of the ship was a middle-aged man with a pair of long-legged quadruped animals in tow. 'Here you go, Capt',' the man said, holding out the leashes.

'Thank you, Chin,' Karrde said, taking them as he squatted down to scratch both animals breifly behind the ears. 'I don't believe you've met my pet vornskrs, Councilor. This one's named Drang; the somewhat more aloof one there is Sturm. On Myrkr they use the Force to hunt their prey. Here, they're going to use it to find Mara. Right?'

The vornskrs made a strange sound, rather like a cackling

purr. 'Good,' Karrde said, straightening up again. 'I believe we're ready now, Councilor. Shall we go?'

CHAPTER 25

The alarms were still hooting in the distance as Han carefully leaned one eye around the corner. According to the floor plans Artoo had pulled up, this should be the major outer defense monitor station in this sector of the garrison. There were likely to be guards, and those guards were likely to be alert.

He was right on both counts. Five meters away down the entry corridor, flanking a heavy blast door, stood a pair of stormtroopers. And they were alert enough to notice the skulking stranger looking at them and to snap their blaster rifles up into firing position.

The smart thing to do – the thing any reasonably nonsuicidal person would do – would be to duck back behind the corner before the shooting started. Instead, Han gripped the corner with his free hand, using the leverage to throw himself completely across the entry corridor. He made it to the other side millimeters ahead of the tracking blaster bolts, flattening himself against the wall as the rapid fire blew out chunks of paneling metal behind him.

They were still firing as Chewbacca leaned around the corner Han had just left and ended the discussion with two quick bowcaster shots.

'Good job, Chewie,' Han grunted, throwing a quick look behind him and then slipping back around the corner. The stormtroopers were out of the fight, all right, leaving nothing in their way but a massive metal door.

Which, like the stormtroopers themselves, was no big deal. At least, not for them. 'Ready?' he asked, dropping into a half-crouch at one side of the door and raising his blaster. There would be another pair of guards inside.

'Ready,' Luke confirmed. There was the *snap-hiss* of the

kid's lightsaber, and the brilliant green blade whipped past Han's head to slice horizontally through the heavy metal of the blast door. Somewhere along the way it caught the internal release mechanism, and as Luke finished the cut the top part of the door shot up along its track into the ceiling.

From the way the stormtroopers were facing the door, it was clear they'd heard the short fight outside. It was also clear that they hadn't expected anyone to be coming through this soon. Han shot one of them as he tried to bring his blaster rifle to bear; Luke lunged half over the bottom part of the door, lightsaber swinging, and took out the other.

The group of Imperials manning their sensor consoles weren't expecting company, either. They were fumbling for sidearms and scrambling for cover as Han and Chewbacca took them out. A dozen shots after that, the room had been reduced to a smoldering collection of junk.

'That ought to do it,' Han decided. 'Better get lost before the reinforcements get here.'

But between the riot down at the main entrance and the wandering band of Myneyrshi, Imperial response time was down. The three intruders made it back along the corridor to the emergency stairway and three levels down to the pump room where they'd left the others.

Two of the Noghri were standing silent guard just inside the door as Han keyed it open. 'Any trouble?' Lando called from somewhere in the tangle of pipes that seemed to fill two thirds of the room.

'Not really,' Han said as Chewbacca closed and locked the door behind them. 'Wouldn't want to try it again, though.'

Lando grunted. 'I don't think you'll have to. They should be adequately convinced that there's a major aerial attack on the way.'

'Let's hope so,' Han said, stepping around to where Lando was fiddling with an archaic-looking control board. Artoo was plugged into a computer socket on the side of the board, while Threepio hovered off to the side like a nervous mother bird. 'Vintage stuff, huh?'

'You've got that,' Lando agreed. 'I think the Emperor must

have just picked up the cloning complex and dropped it in here whole.'

Artoo gibbered indignantly. 'Right – including the programming,' Lando said dryly. 'I know a little about this stuff, Han, but not enough to do any permanent damage. I think we're going to have to use the explosives.'

'Fine with me,' Han said. He would have hated lugging them all the way across Wayland for nothing, anyway. 'Where's Mara?'

'Out there,' Lando said, nodding toward another door half hidden by the pipes. 'In the main room.'

'Let's check it out, Luke,' Han said. He didn't like the idea of Mara wandering around alone in this place. 'Chewie, stay here with Lando. See if there's anything worth blowing up.'

Crossing to the door, he keyed it open. Beyond was a wide circular walkway running around the inside of what seemed to be a huge natural cavern. Directly ahead, framed against a massive equipment column that extended downward from the ceiling through the center of the cavern, Mara was standing at the walkway's railing. 'This the place?' he asked her, glancing around as he started toward her. About twenty other doors opened up onto the walkway at more or less regular intervals, and there were four retractable bridges extending out to a work platform encircling the central equipment column. Aside from a couple of their Noghri skulking around doing guard duty there was no-one else in sight.

But there were sounds. A muted hum of machinery and voices was coming from somewhere, punctuated by the faint clicks of relays and a strange rhythmic pulsing or whooshing sound. Like the whole cavern was breathing . . .

'It's the place,' Mara confirmed, her voice sounding strange. Maybe she thought it sounded like breathing, too. 'Come and see.'

Han threw a glance at Luke, and together they stepped to Mara's side and looked down over the railing.

And it was, indeed, the place.

The cavern was huge, extending downward at least ten

stories below their walkway. It was laid out like a sport arena, with each level being a kind of circular balcony running around the inside of the cavern. Each balcony was a little wider than the one above it, extending further into the center of the cavern and making for a smaller hole around the big equipment column. There were pipes everywhere: huge ones coming off the ducts of the central column, smaller ones running around the edges of each of the balconies, and little ones feeding off them into the neatly arranged metal circles that filled the balconies and main floor.

Thousands of little circles. Each one the top cover plate of a Spaarti cloning cylinder.

Beside Han, Luke made a strange sound in the back of his throat. 'It's hard to believe,' he said, sounding about halfway between awestruck and dumbfounded.

'Believe it,' Han advised him grimly, pulling out his macrobinoculars and focusing them on the main floor below. The ductwork blocked a lot of the view, but he could catch glimpses of men in medtech and guard uniforms scurrying around. They were on some of the balconies, too. 'They're stirred up like a rats' nest down there,' he said. 'Stormtroopers on the main floor and everything.'

He threw a sideways look at Mara. Her expression was tight as she stared down at the cloning tanks, with the haunted look of someone gazing back into the past. 'Bring back memories?' he asked.

'Yes,' she said mechanically. She stood there a moment longer, then slowly straightened up. 'But we can't allow it to stand.'

'Glad you agree,' Han said, studying her face. She looked and sounded OK now, but there was a lot of stuff going on under the surface. *Hold it together, kid*, he told her silently. *Just a little longer, OK?* 'That column in the middle looks like our best shot. You know anything about it?'

She looked across the cavern. 'Not really.' She hesitated. 'But there might be another way. The Emperor wasn't one for leaving things behind for other people to use. Not if he could help it.'

Han threw a glance at Luke. 'You mean this whole place might have a self-destruct?'

'It's possible,' she said, that haunted look back in her eyes again. 'If so, the control will be up in the throne room. I could go and take a look.'

'I don't know,' Han said, looking down into the cloning cavern. It was an awfully big place for them to take on with a single sack of explosives – he'd give her that much. A destruct switch would simplify things a lot. But the idea of Mara and her memories up there in the Emperor's throne room didn't sound so good, either. 'Thanks, but I don't think any of us ought to go wandering around this place alone.'

'I'll go with her,' Luke volunteered. 'She's right – it's worth checking out.'

'It'll be safe enough,' Mara added. 'There's a service-droid turbolift along the walkway that'll get us most of the way there. Most of the Imperials' attention should be focused on the riot at the entrance, anyway.'

Han grimaced. 'All right, get going,' he growled. 'Don't forget to let us know before you pull the switch, OK?'

'We won't,' Luke assured him with a tight grin. 'Come on, Mara.'

They headed down the walkway. 'Where are they going?' Lando asked from behind Han.

'Emperor's throne room,' Han said. 'She thinks he might have put a self-destruct switch up there. You find anything?'

'Artoo's finally got a connection into the main computer,' Lando told him. 'He's looking for schematics of that thing.' He gestured toward the central column.

'We can't wait,' Han decided, turning back as Chewbacca emerged from the pump room with their bag of explosives over one shoulder. 'Chewie, you and Lando take one of those bridges across and get busy.'

'Right,' Lando said, taking a cautious look over the railing. 'What about you?'

'I'm going to go lock us in,' Han told him, pointing to the other doors opening out onto the walkway. 'You – Noghri – come here.'

The two Noghri who'd been standing guard moved silently to him as Lando and Chewbacca headed toward the nearest bridge. 'Your command, Han clan Solo?' one of them asked.

'You – stay here,' he told the nearest one. 'Watch for trouble. You—' He pointed to the other. 'Help me seal off those doors. One good blaster shot into each control box ought to do it. I'll go this way; you go the other.'

He was about two thirds of the way around his side of the walkway when he heard something over the eerie mechanical breathing sounds of the cavern below him. Looking back, he saw Threepio calling and beckoning to him from the pump room door. 'Great,' he muttered. Leave it to Threepio, and sooner or later he'd make a mess of it. Finishing the door he was on, he turned and hurried back.

'Captain Solo!' Threepio gushed in relief as Han came up to him. 'Thank the Maker. Artoo says—'

'What are you trying to do?' Han snapped. 'Bring the whole garrison down on us?'

'Of course not, sir. But Artoo says—'

'You want to talk to me, you come out and find me. Right?'

'Yes, sir. But Artoo says—'

'If you don't know where to look, you use your comlink,' Han said, jabbing a finger at the little cylinder the droid was clutching. 'That's why you've got one. You don't just shout around. You got that?'

'Yes, sir,' Threepio said, his mechanical patience sounding more than a little strained. 'May I continue?'

Han sighed. So much for the lecture. He'd do better talking to a bantha. 'Yeah, what is it?'

'It's about Master Luke,' Threepio said. 'I overheard one of the Noghri say that he and Mara Jade were on their way to the Emperor's throne room.'

'Yeah. So?'

'Well, sir, in the course of his inquiries Artoo has just learned that the Jedi Master Joruus C'baoth is imprisoned in that area.'

Han stared at him. 'What do you mean, that area? Isn't he in the detention center?'

'No, sir,' Threepio said. 'As I said—'

'Why didn't you say so?' Han demanded, yanking out his comlink and thumbing it on.

And just as fast thumbing it off. 'The comlinks appear to be inoperable,' Threepio said primly. 'I discovered that when I attempted to contact you.'

'Great,' Han snarled, the burst of jamming static still echoing in his ears as he looked around. Luke and Mara, walking right into C'baoth's arms. And no way to warn them.

No way except one. 'Keep Artoo busy looking for those schematics,' he told Threepio, shoving the comlink back into his belt. 'While he's at it, tell him to see if he can find out where the jamming is coming from. If he can, send a couple of the Noghri to try and get rid of it. Then get out to that work platform and tell Chewie and Lando where I've gone.'

'Yes, sir,' Threepio said, sounding a little surprised by the flurry of orders and command authority. 'Pardon me, sir, but where *will* you have gone?'

'Where do you think?' Han retorted over his shoulders as he started down the walkway. It never failed, he thought sourly. One way or the other, no matter where they were or what they were doing, somehow he always wound up chasing off after Luke.

And it was starting to look more and more like a good thing he'd come along.

'All right, *Garret's Gold*, hatchways here are sealed,' the controller's voice said. 'Stand by to receive outbound course data.'

'Acknowledged, Control,' Aves said, easing the *Etherway* back from the docking arm and starting a leisurely turn. They were ready here; and from the looks of things, so was everyone else.

'There he is,' Gillespee muttered, pointing out the viewport. 'Right on schedule.'

'You sure that's Mazzic?' Aves asked, peering out at the ship.

'Pretty sure,' Gillespee said. 'Want me to try giving him a call?'

Aves shrugged, looking around the shipyards. They'd set up the rest of the group with a good encrypt code, but it wouldn't be a smart idea to tempt trouble by using it before they had to. 'Let's hold off a minute,' he told Gillespee. 'Wait until we've got something to talk about.'

The words were barely out of his mouth when the whole thing went straight to hell.

'Star Destroyers!' Faughn barked from the comm console. 'Coming in from lightspeed.'

'Vectors?' Gillespee snapped.

'Don't bother,' Aves told him, a cold knife twisting in his gut. He could see the Star Destroyers ahead, all right, appearing out of hyperspace at the edge of the shipyards. And the Dreadnaughts, and the Lancer Frigates, and the Strike Cruisers, and the TIE squadrons. A complete assault fleet, and then some.

And practically every fighting ship of Karrde's smuggler confederation was here. Right in the middle of it.

'So it *was* a trap,' Gillespee said, his voice icy calm.

'I guess so,' Aves said, staring out at the armada still moving into formation. A formation that seemed wrong, somehow.

'Aves, Gillespee, this is Mazzic,' the other smuggler's voice came over the comm. 'Looks like we've been sold out after all. I'm not going to surrender. How about you?'

'I think they deserve to lose at least a couple of Star Destroyers for this,' Gillespee agreed.

'That was my idea,' Mazzic said. 'Too bad Karrde isn't here to see us go out in a blaze of glory.'

He paused, and Aves could feel Gillespee's and Faughn's eyes on him. They would, he knew, go to their deaths believing Karrde had betrayed them. All of them would. 'I'm with you, too,' he told the others quietly. 'If you want, Mazzic, you can have command.'

'Thanks,' Mazzic said. 'I was going to take it anyway. Stand by: we might as well deliver our first punch together.'

Aves took one last look at the armada . . . and suddenly he had it. 'Hold it,' he snapped. 'Mazzic – everyone – hold it. That assault force isn't here for us.'

'What are you talking about?' Gillespee demanded.

'Those Interdictor Cruisers out there,' Aves said. 'Out past that Star Destroyer group – see them? Look at their positioning.'

There was a moment of silence. Mazzic got it first. 'That's not an enclosure configuration,' he said.

'You're right, it's not,' Gillespee agreed. 'Look – you can see a second group of them farther back.'

'It's an entrapment configuration,' Mazzic said, sounding like he didn't believe his own words. 'They're setting up to pull someone out of hyperspace. And then keep him here long enough to pound him.'

Aves looked at Gillespee, found him looking back. 'No,' Gillespee breathed. 'You don't suppose . . . ? I thought they were supposed to be hitting Tangrene.'

'So did I,' Aves told him grimly, the twisting knife back in his gut. 'I guess we were wrong.'

'Or else Thrawn is.' Gillespee looked out at the armada and shook his head. 'No. Probably not.'

'All right, let's not panic,' Mazzic said. 'If the New Republic comes, it just means that much more to occupy the Imperials' attention. Let's stay on schedule and see what happens.'

'Right,' Aves sighed. Square in the middle of an Imperial base during a New Republic attack. Terrific.

'Tell you something, Aves,' Gillespee commented. 'If we get out of this, I'm going to go have some words with your boss.'

'No argument.' Aves looked out at Thrawn's armada. 'Matter of fact, I think maybe I'll go with you.'

Carefully, Mara eased her head out of the emergency stairway and took a look into the corridor beyond. The caution was wasted; this level was as deserted as the three below it had been. 'All clear,' she murmured, stepping out into the corridor.

'No guards here, either?' Skywalker asked, looking around as he joined her.

'No point to it,' she told him. 'Except for the throne room and the royal chambers, there was never much of anything on these top levels.'

'I guess there still isn't. Where's this private turbolift?'

'To the right and around that corner,' she said, pointing with her blaster.

More from habit than any real need, she tried to keep her footsteps quiet as she led the way down the corridor. She reached the cross corridor and turned into it.

There, ten meters dead ahead, two stormtroopers stood flanking the turbolift door, their blaster rifles already lifting to track toward her.

Half a step into the corridor, all her momentum going the wrong direction, there was nowhere for Mara to go but down. She dived for the deck, firing toward them as she fell. One of the stormtroopers toppled back as a burst of flame erupted in his chest armor. The second rifle swung toward her face—

And jerked reflexively away as Skywalker's lightsaber came spinning down the corridor toward him.

It didn't do any real damage, of course – at that distance, and without the Force, Skywalker wasn't that good a shot. But it did a fine job of distracting the stormtrooper, and that was all Mara needed. Even as the Imperial ducked away from the whirling blade, she caught him with two clean shots. He hit the deck and stayed there.

'I guess they don't want anyone going in there,' Skywalker said, coming up beside her.

'I guess not,' Mara agreed, ignoring the hand he offered and getting up on her own. 'Come on.'

The turbolift car had been locked at this level, but it took Mara only a minute to release it. There were only four stops listed: the one they were on, the emergency shuttle hangar, the royal chambers, and the throne room itself. She keyed for the last, and the door slid shut behind them. The trip upward was a short one, and a few seconds later the door on the opposite side of the car slid open. Bracing herself, Mara stepped out.

Into the Emperor's throne room . . . and into a flood of memories.

It was all here, just as she remembered it. The muted sidelights and brooding darkness the Emperor had found so conducive to meditation and thought. The raised section of floor at the far end of the chamber, allowing him to look down from his throne as visitors climbed the staircase into his presence. Viewscreens on the walls on either side of the throne, darkened now, which had enabled him to keep track of the details of his domain.

And for an overview of that domain . . .

She turned to her left, gazing over the railing of the walkway into the huge open space that faced the throne. Floating there in the darkness, a blaze of light twenty meters across, was the galaxy.

Not the standard galaxy hologram any school or shipping business might own. Not even the more precise versions that could be found only in the war rooms of select sector military headquarters. This hologram was sculpted in exquisite and absolutely unique detail, with a single accurately positioned spot of light for each of the galaxy's hundred billion stars. Political regions were delineated by subtle encirclements of color: the Core systems, the Outer Rim Territories, Wild Space, the Unknown Regions. From his throne the Emperor could manipulate the image, highlighting a chosen sector, locating a single system, or tracking a military campaign.

It was as much a work of art as it was a tool. Grand Admiral Thrawn would love it.

And with that thought, the memories of the past faded reluctantly into the realities of the present. Thrawn was in command now, a man who wanted to re-create the Empire in his own image. Wanted it badly enough to unleash a new round of Clone Wars if that would gain it for him.

She took a deep breath. 'All right,' she said. The words echoed around the chamber, pushing the memories still further away. 'If it's here, it'll be built into the throne.'

With an obvious effort, Skywalker pulled his gaze away from the hologram galaxy. 'Let's take a look.'

They headed down the ten-meter walkway that led from the turbolift into the main part of the throne room, walking beneath the overhead catwalk that ran across the front edge of the hologram pit and between the raised guard platforms flanking the stairway. Mara glanced at the platforms as she and Skywalker walked up the steps to the upper level, remembering the red-cloaked Imperial guards who had once stood there in silent watchfulness. Beneath the upper-level floor, visible between the steps as they climbed, the Emperor's monitor and control area was dark and silent. Aside from the galaxy hologram, all of the systems up here appeared to have been shut down.

They reached the top of the steps and headed across toward the throne itself, turned away from them toward the polished rock wall behind it. Mara was looking at it, wondering why the Emperor had left it facing away from his galaxy, when it began to turn around.

She grabbed Skywalker's arm, snapping her blaster up to point at the throne. The massive chair completed its turn—

'So at last you have come to me,' Joruus C'baoth said gravely, gazing out at them from the depths of the throne. 'I knew you would. Together we will teach the galaxy what it means to serve the Jedi.'

CHAPTER 26

'I knew you would be coming to me tonight,' C'baoth said, rising slowly from the throne to face them. 'From the moment you left Coruscant, I knew you would come. That was why I set this night for the people of my city to attack my oppressors.'

'That wasn't necessary,' Luke told him, taking an involuntary step backward as the memories of those near-disastrous days on Jomark came rushing back to him. C'baoth had tried there to subtly corrupt him to the dark side . . . and when he'd failed at that, he'd tried to kill Luke and Mara both.

But he wouldn't be trying that again. Not here. Not without the Force.

'Of course it was necessary,' C'baoth said. 'You needed a distraction to gain entrance to my prison. And they, like all lesser beings, needed purpose. What better purpose could they have than the honor of dying in the service of the Jedi?'

Beside him, Mara muttered something. 'I think you have that backwards,' Luke said. 'The Jedi were the guardians of peace. The servants of the Old Republic, not its masters.'

'Which is why they and the Old Republic failed, Jedi Skywalker,' C'baoth said, jabbing a finger toward him in emphasis. 'Why they failed, and why they died.'

'The Old Republic survived a thousand generations,' Mara put in. 'That doesn't sound like failure to me.'

'Perhaps not,' C'baoth said with obvious disdain. 'You are young, and do not yet see clearly.'

'And you do, of course?'

C'baoth smiled at her. 'Oh, yes, my young apprentice,' he said softly. 'I do indeed. As will you.'

'Don't count on it,' Mara growled. 'We aren't here to get you out.'

'The Force does not rely on what you think are your goals,' C'baoth said. 'Nor do the true masters of the Force. Whether you knew it or not, you came here at my summons.'

'You just go ahead and believe that,' Mara said, motioning to the side with her blaster. 'Move over there.'

'Of course, my young apprentice.' C'baoth took three steps in the indicated direction. 'She has great strength of will, Jedi Skywalker,' he added to Luke as Mara moved warily over to the throne and crouched down to examine the armrest control boards. 'She will be a great power in the galaxy which we shall build.'

'No,' Luke said, shaking his head. This was, perhaps, his last chance to bring the insane Jedi back. To save him, as he had saved Vader aboard the second Death Star. 'You aren't in any shape to build anything, Master C'baoth. You're not well. But I can help you if you'll let me.'

C'baoth's face darkened. 'How dare you say such things?' he demanded. 'How dare you even *think* such blasphemy about the great Jedi Master C'baoth?'

'But that's just it,' Luke said gently. 'You're not the Jedi Master C'baoth. Not the original one, anyway. The proof is there in the *Katana*'s records. Jorus C'baoth died a long time ago during the Outbound Flight Project.'

'Yet I am here.'

'Yes,' Luke nodded. '*You* are. But not Jorus C'baoth. You see, you're his clone.'

C'baoth's whole body went rigid. 'No,' he said. 'No. That can't be.'

Luke shook his head. 'There's no other explanation. Surely that thought has occurred to you before.'

C'baoth took a long, shuddering breath . . . and then, abruptly, he threw his head back and laughed.

'Watch him,' Mara snapped, eyeing the old man warily over the throne's armrest. 'He pulled this same stunt on Jomark, remember?'

'It's all right,' Luke said. 'He can't hurt us.'

'Ah, Skywalker, Skywalker,' C'baoth said, shaking his head. 'You too? Grand Admiral Thrawn, the New Republic, and now you. What is this sudden fascination with clones and cloning?'

He barked another laugh; and then, without warning, turned deadly serious. 'He does not understand, Jedi Skywalker,' he said earnestly. 'Not Grand Admiral Thrawn – not any of them. The true power of the Jedi is not in these simple tricks of matter and energy. The true might of the Jedi is that we alone of all those in the galaxy have the power to grow beyond ourselves. To extend ourselves into all the reaches of the universe.'

Luke glanced at Mara, got a shrug and puzzled look in return. 'We don't understand, either,' he told C'baoth. 'What do you mean?'

C'baoth took a step toward him. 'I have done it, Jedi

Skywalker,' he whispered, his eyes glittering in the dim light. 'With General Covell. What even the Emperor never did. I took his mind in my hands and altered it. Re-formed it and rebuilt it into my own image.'

Luke felt a cold shiver run through him. 'What do you mean, rebuilt it?'

C'baoth nodded, a secret sort of smile playing around his lips. 'Yes – rebuilt it. And that was only the start. Beneath us, down in the depths of the mountain, the future army of the Jedi even now stands in readiness to serve us. What I did with General Covell I will do again, and again, and again. Because what Grand Admiral Thrawn has never realized is that the army he thinks he is creating for himself he is instead creating for me.'

And suddenly Luke understood. The clones growing down in that cavern weren't just physically identical to their original templet. Their minds were identical, too, or close enough to be only minor variations of the same pattern. If C'baoth could learn how to break the mind of any one of them, he could do the same to all the clones in that group.

Luke looked at Mara again. She understood, too. 'You still think he can be saved?' she demanded grimly.

'I need no-one to save me, Mara Jade,' C'baoth told her. 'Tell me, do you really believe I would simply stand by and allow Grand Admiral Thrawn to imprison me this way?'

'I didn't think he'd asked your permission,' Mara bit out, stepping away from the throne. 'There's nothing here for us, Skywalker. Let's get out of here.'

'I did not grant you permission to leave,' C'baoth said, his voice suddenly loud and regal. He raised his hand, and Luke saw that he was holding a small cylinder. 'And you shall not.'

Mara gestured with her blaster. 'You're not going to stop us with *that*,' she said with thinly veiled contempt. 'A remote activator has to have something to activate.'

'And so it does,' C'baoth said, smiling thinly. 'I had my soldiers prepare it for me. Before I sent them outside the mountain with the weapons and orders for my people.'

'Sure.' Mara took a step back toward the stairs, throwing

a wary glance at the ceiling above her as her left hand found the guardrail that separated the raised section of the throne room from the lower level. 'We'll take your word for it.'

C'baoth shook his head. 'You won't have to,' he said softly, pressing the switch. In the back of Luke's mind, something distant and very alien seemed to shriek in agony—

And suddenly, impossibly, he felt a surge of awareness and strength fill him. As if he were waking up from a deep sleep, or stepping from a dark room into the light.

The Force was again with him.

'Mara!' he snapped. But it was too late. Mara's blaster had already wrenched itself from her grip and been flung back across the room; and even as Luke leaped toward her C'baoth's outstretched hand erupted into a brilliant blaze of blue-white lightning.

The blast caught Mara square in the chest, throwing her backward to slam into the guardrail behind her. 'Stop it!' Luke shouted, getting in front of her and igniting his lightsaber. C'baoth ignored him, firing a second burst. Luke caught most of it on his lightsaber blade, grimacing as the part he missed jolted through his muscles. C'baoth fired a third burst, and a fourth, and a fifth—

And then, abruptly, he lowered his hands. 'You will not presume to give me commands, Jedi Skywalker,' he said, his voice strangely petulant. 'I am the master. You are the servant.'

'I'm not your servant,' Luke told him, stepping back and throwing a quick look at Mara. She was still pretty much on her feet, clutching the guardrail for support. Her eyes were open but not fully aware, her breath making little moaning sounds as she exhaled between clenched teeth. Laying his free hand on her shoulder, wincing at the stink of ozone, Luke began a quick probe of her injuries.

'You are indeed my servant,' C'baoth said, the earlier petulance replaced now by a sort of haughty grandeur. 'As is she. Leave her alone, Jedi Skywalker. She required a lesson, and she has now learned it.'

Luke didn't answer. None of her burns seemed too bad, but

her muscles were still twitching uncontrollably. Reaching out with the Force, he tried to draw away some of the pain.

'I said leave her alone,' C'baoth repeated, his voice echoing eerily across the throne room. 'Her life is not in danger. Save your strength rather for the trial that awaits you.' Dramatically, he lifted a hand and pointed.

Luke turned to look. There, silhouetted against the shimmering galaxy holo, stood a figure dressed in what looked like the same brown robe C'baoth was wearing. A figure that seemed somehow familiar . . .

'There is no choice, my young Jedi,' C'baoth said, his voice almost gentle now. 'Don't you understand? You must serve me, or we will not be able to save the galaxy from itself. You must therefore face death and emerge at my side . . . or you must die that another may take your place.' He lifted his eyes to the figure and beckoned. 'Come,' he called. 'And face your destiny.'

The figure moved forward toward the stairs, unhooking a lightsaber from his belt as he came. With the blaze of light from the hologram behind him, the figure's face was still impossible to make out.

Luke stepped away from Mara, a strange and unpleasant buzzing pressure beginning to form against his mind. There was something disturbingly familiar about this confrontation. As if he were about to face someone or something he'd faced once before . . .

Abruptly, the memory clicked. Dagobah – his Jedi training – the dark side cave Yoda had sent him into. His brief dreamlike battle with a vision of Darth Vader . . .

Luke caught his breath, a horrible suspicion squeezing his heart. But no – the silent figure approaching him wasn't tall enough to be Vader. But then who . . . ?

And then the figure stepped into the light . . . and, too late, Luke remembered how that dream battle in the dark side cave had ended. Vader's mask had shattered, and the face behind it had been Luke's own.

As was the face that gazed emotionlessly up at him now. Luke felt himself moving back from the steps, his mind frozen with shock and the buzzing pressure growing against it. 'Yes, Jedi Skywalker,' C'baoth said quietly from behind him. 'He is you. Luuke Skywalker, created from the hand you left behind in the Cloud City on Bespin. Wielding the lightsaber you lost there.'

Luke glanced at the weapon in the clone's hands. It was his, all right. The lightsaber Obi-wan had told him his father had left for him. 'Why?' he managed.

'To bring you to true understanding,' C'baoth said gravely. 'And because your destiny must be fulfilled. One way or another, you must serve me.'

Luke threw a quick glance at him. C'baoth was watching him, his eyes glowing with anticipation. And with madness.

And in that moment, the clone Luuke struck.

He leaped to the top of the stairway, igniting his lightsaber and slashing the blue-white blade viciously toward Luke's chest. Luke jumped to the side, whipping his own weapon up to block the attack. The blades came together with an impact that threw him off balance and nearly tore the lightsaber from his grip. The clone Luuke jumped after him, lightsaber already swinging to the attack; reaching out to the Force, Luke threw himself backwards, flipping over the guardrail and on to one of the raised guard platforms rising from the lower part of the throne room floor. He needed time to think and plan, and to find a way past the distraction of the buzzing in his mind.

But the clone Luuke wasn't going to give him that time. Stepping to the guardrail, he hurled his lightsaber downward at the base of the platform Luke was standing on. It wasn't a clean hit – the blade probably sliced through only half of the base – but it was enough to throw the platform into a sudden tilt. Reaching out again to the Force, Luke did another backflip, trying to reach the overhead catwalk that spanned the throne room five meters behind him.

But the distance was too great, or else his mind too distracted by the buzzing to properly draw on the Force. The back of his knee hit the edge of the catwalk, and instead of landing on his feet he flipped over to slam into it on his back.

'I did not wish to do this to you, Jedi Skywalker,' C'baoth's voice called out. 'I do not wish it still. Join me – let me teach you. Together we can save the galaxy from the lesser peoples who would destroy it.'

'No,' Luke said hoarsely, grabbing a support strut and pulling himself up as he fought to catch his breath. The clone Luuke had retrieved his lightsaber now, and was starting down the stairs toward him.

The clone. *His* clone. Was that what was causing this strange pressure in his mind? The close presence of an exact duplicate that was itself drawing on the Force?

He didn't know, any more than he knew what C'baoth's purpose was in throwing the two of them together. Obi-wan and Master Yoda had both warned him that killing in anger or hatred would lead toward the dark side. Would killing a clone duplicate of himself do the same thing?

Or had C'baoth meant something entirely different? Had he meant that killing his own clone would drive Luke insane?

Either way, it wasn't something Luke was anxious to find out firsthand. And it occurred to him that he really didn't have to. He could drop off the far side of the catwalk, get to the turbolift he and Mara had come up on, and escape.

Leaving Mara here to face C'baoth alone.

He raised his eyes. Mara was still leaning against the guardrail. Possibly not fully conscious. Certainly in no shape to travel.

Setting his teeth together, Luke pulled himself to his feet. Mara had asked him – begged him – to kill her rather than leave her in C'baoth's hands. The least he could do was to stay with her to the end.

Whether it was her end . . . or his.

The explosion drifted up from the cavern below like a distant thunderclap, clearly audible and yet curiously dampened. 'You hear that, Chewie?' Lando asked, leaning back to throw a cautious look over the edge of their work platform. 'You suppose something down there blew up?'

Chewbacca, his hands full of cables and leads as he dug in and around the support lattice of the equipment column, growled a correction: it hadn't been one large explosion, but many simultaneous small ones. Small blasting disks, or something of equally low power. 'You sure?' Lando asked uneasily, peering at the cloning tanks on the balcony one level beneath where they were working. This didn't sound like any normal malfunction.

He stiffened. Thin wisps of smoke could be seen now, rising lazily into the air above the nutrient pipes feeding into the tops of the cloning tanks. A *lot* of wisps of smoke, and they seemed to be rising in a reasonably regular pattern. As if something in each cluster of Spaarti cylinders had blown up . . .

There was the muffled clink of metal on metal behind him. Lando twisted around, to find Threepio stepping gingerly from the bridge onto the work platform, his head tilted to look down into the cavern. 'Is that smoke?' the droid asked, sounding like he wasn't sure he really wanted to know.

'Looks like smoke to me,' Lando agreed. 'What are you doing here?'

'Ah . . .' Resolutely, the droid looked away from whatever was happening below. 'Artoo has found the schematics for that equipment column,' he said, offering Lando a data card. 'He suggests that the negative flow coupler on the main power line might be worth investigating.'

'We'll keep that in mind,' Lando said, sliding the data card into his data pad and throwing a quick look over the platform railing as he handed the data pad to Chewbacca. He and the Wookiee weren't all that visible against the drab colors of the equipment column and the rocky cavern ceiling two meters above them, but Threepio would stand out like a lump of gold on a mud flat. 'Now get out of here before someone spots you.'

'Oh,' Threepio said, stiffening a little more than usual. 'Yes, of course. Also, Artoo has located the source of the comlink jamming in this vicinity. Captain Solo requested that if we found that—'

'Right,' Lando interrupted him. Was that someone moving behind one of the banks of Spaarti cylinders on the next level down? 'I remember. You and Artoo go ahead. And take the Noghri with you.'

The droid seemed taken aback. 'Artoo and me? But sir—'

And with a sound like a spitting tauntaun, a brilliant ripple of blue flashed upward from the cloning balcony below.

'Stun blast!' Lando barked, dropping flat on the work platform and feeling the heavy thud as Chewbacca landed beside him. A second stun blast rippled out, ricocheting off the column above his head as he yanked out his blaster. 'Threepio, get out of here.'

The droid didn't need any encouragement. 'Yes, sir,' he called over his shoulder, already scuttling away down the bridge.

Chewbacca growled a question. 'Over there somewhere,' Lando told him, gesturing with his blaster. 'Watch it, though, they're bound to have more moving in.'

A third stun blast slammed uselessly into the underside of the work platform, and this time Lando spotted the soldier skulking behind one of the cloning cylinders. He fired twice, dropping the Imperial to the floor and making a mess of the cloning cylinder itself. Behind him, another blue ripple sizzled by overhead, followed a split second later by the heavy bark of Chewbacca's bowcaster.

Lando grinned tightly to himself. They were in trouble, but not nearly as much as they could have been. As long as they were sitting up next to all this critical equipment, the Imperials didn't dare use anything stronger than stun settings on them. But at the same time, the Imperials themselves had absolutely no cover down there on the balconies except the cloning tanks. Which meant all they really could do was stay there, probably not bothering their targets any, and get themselves and a lot of valuable equipment blown to bits.

Or else they could simply come one level up and blast away at them from an angle where the heavy metal of the work platform wouldn't keep getting in their way.

From the other side of the equipment column, Chewbacca rumbled: the Imperials were pulling back. 'Probably coming up here,' Lando agreed, glancing around their level at the doors lining the outer walkway. They looked pretty strong, probably only a step or two down from warship-type blast doors. If Han and the Noghri had done a good job of sealing them off, they ought to hold off even a determined group of stormtroopers for a while.

Except for the door to the pump room that Artoo had been working in. Han would have left that one open for them to get out through.

Lando grimaced; but there was nothing for it. Bracing his gun hand against the bottom section of the railing, he took careful aim at the door's control box and fired. The box cover flashed and crumpled, and for a couple of seconds he could see a faint sputtering of sparks through the smoke.

And that was that. The Imperials were locked out. And he and Chewbacca were locked in.

Keeping low, he crept around to the other side of the column. Chewbacca was already back at work, his grease-slicked hands digging back through the cables and pipes, the data pad on the floor by his feet. 'Making any progress?' Lando asked.

Chewbacca growled, tapping at the data pad awkwardly with one foot, and Lando craned his neck to look. It was a schematic of a section of the power cable, showing a coupling with eight leads coming off it.

And just above the coupling, clearly marked, a positive flow regulator. 'Uh-*huh*,' Lando said, a not entirely pleasant sensation running through him. 'You're not by any chance thinking of running that into the negative flow coupler Threepio mentioned, are you?'

In answer, the Wookiee withdrew his hand from the tangle of cables, pulling the partially disconnected negative flow coupler with it. 'Wait a minute,' Lando said, eyeing the coupler warily. He'd heard stories about what happened when you ran a negative flow coupler into a positive flow detonator, and using a positive flow regulator instead of a detonator didn't sound a lot safer. 'What exactly is this supposed to do?'

The Wookiee told him. He'd been right: using a regulator

wasn't any safer. In fact, it was a whole lot more dangerous. 'Let's not go overboard on this, Chewie,' he warned. 'We came here to destroy the cloning cylinders, not bring the whole storehouse down on top of us.'

Chewbacca rumbled insistently. 'All right, fine, we'll keep it in reserve,' Lando sighed.

The Wookiee grunted agreement and got back to work. Grimacing, Lando laid his blaster down and pulled two charges out of their explosives bag. He might as well keep himself busy while he tried to figure out how they were going to get out through locked blast doors and a corridor full of stormtroopers.

And if they wound up falling back on Chewbacca's power core arhythmic resonance scheme . . . well, in that case, getting out of here would probably become an academic question anyway.

Prying open a gap in the power cables with one hand, he got to work.

The timing counter buzzed its five-second warning, and Wedge took a deep breath. This was it. He reached for the hyperspace levers—

And abruptly, the mottled sky of hyperspace faded into starlines and into stars. Around him, the rest of Rogue Squadron flashed into view, still in formation; ahead, the distinctive light patterns and layout of a shipyard could be seen.

They'd arrived at the Bilbringi shipyards. Only they'd arrived too far out. Which could only mean—

'Battle alert!' Rogue Two snapped. 'TIE interceptors coming in – bearing two-nine-three mark twenty.'

'All ships – emergency combat status,' Admiral Ackbar's gravelly voice cut in on the comm. 'Defensive configuration: Starfighter Command to screen positions. It appears to be a trap.'

'Sure does,' Wedge muttered to himself, pulling hard to portside and risking a quick look at his displays. Sure enough, there were the Interdictor Cruisers that had brought them out of hyperspace, staying well back from the massive fleets that were beginning to jockey for battle position. And judging from the way they'd been deployed, the New Republic fleet wasn't going to be jumping to lightspeed anytime soon.

And then the TIE interceptors were on them, and there was no time left to wonder why their carefully planned surprise attack had failed before it had even begun. For the moment the only question was that of survival, one ship and one engagement at a time.

The stealthy footsteps came around the corner ten meters away and continued toward him; and Han, pressed painfully back into the slightly recessed doorway that was the only cover for those same ten meters, abandoned the faint hope that his pursuers would miss him and prepared for the inevitable firefight.

They *should* have turned off. In fact, by all rights they shouldn't have been up here at all. From the snatches of status reports he'd been able to catch while passing by deserted checkpoints, it sounded like everyone who could carry a blaster was supposed to be twenty levels down fighting the natives who were running loose through the garrison. These upper levels didn't seem to even be occupied, and there sure wasn't anything up here except maybe C'baoth that needed any protection.

The footsteps were getting closer. It would be just his luck, Han thought sourly, to run into a couple of deserters looking for a place to hide.

And then, maybe five meters away, the footsteps abruptly stopped . . . and in the sudden silence he heard a stifled gasp.

He'd been spotted.

Han didn't hesitate. Pushing hard off the door behind him, he leaped across the corridor, trying to duplicate that trick down at the defense station, or at least do the best he could without Chewbacca here to back him up. There were fewer of them out there than he'd expected, and further to the side than he expected, and he lost a vital half-second as his blaster tracked toward them—

'Han!' Leia shouted. 'Don't shoot!'

The sheer surprise of it caught Han's timing straight across the knees, and he slammed rather ingloriously into the wall on the opposite side of the corridor. It was Leia, all right. Even more surprising, Talon Karrde was with her, along with those two vornskr pets of his. 'What in blazes are you doing here?' he demanded.

'Luke's in trouble,' Leia said breathlessly, rushing forward and giving him a quick, tense hug. 'He's ahead somewhere—'

'Whoa, sweetheart,' Han assured her, hanging on to her arm as she tried to pull away. 'It's OK – we knew the ysalamiri were here going in.'

Leia shook her head. 'That's just it: they're not. The Force is back. Just before you jumped out of cover.'

Han swore under his breath. 'C'baoth,' he muttered. 'Has to be him.'

'Yes,' Leia said, shivering. 'It is.'

Han threw a look at Karrde. 'I was hired to destroy the Emperor's storehouse,' the smuggler said evenly. 'I brought Sturm and Drang along to help us find Mara.'

Han glanced at the vornskrs. 'You have anyone else with you?' he asked Leia.

She shook her head. 'We ran into a squad of troops three levels down moving this way. Our two Noghri stayed behind to hold them off.'

He looked at Karrde. 'How about your people?'

'They're all in the *Wild Karrde*,' he said. 'Guarding our exit, should we have the chance to use it.'

Han grunted. 'Then I guess it's just us,' he said, shifting his grip on Leia's arm and heading down the corridor. 'Come on. They're up in the throne room – I know the way.'

And as they ran, he tried not to think about the last time he'd faced a Dark Jedi. In Lando's Cloud City on Bespin, when Vader had tortured him and then had him frozen in carbonite.

Somehow, from what Luke had told him, he didn't expect C'baoth to be even that civilized.

CHAPTER 27

The lightsabers flashed, blue-white blade against green-white blade, sizzling where they struck each other, slashing through metal and cable where they hit anything else. Gripping the guardrail with both hands, fighting against the turmoil roiling through her own mind, Mara watched in helpless fascination as the battle raged across the throne room floor. It was like a twisted inversion of the last horrifying vision the Emperor had given her at the instant of his destruction nearly six years ago.

Except that this time it wasn't the Emperor who was facing death. It was Skywalker.

And it was no vision. It was real.

'Watch them closely, Mara Jade,' C'baoth said from where he stood at the top of the steps, his voice hard yet strangely wistful. 'Unless you bow willingly to my authority, you will someday face this same battle.'

Mara threw a sideways look at him. C'baoth was watching this duel he'd orchestrated with a fascination that bordered on the grisly. She'd called it, all right, back when she'd first met him on Jomark. The work he'd done for Thrawn had given him a taste of power; and like the Emperor before him, that taste had not been enough.

But unlike the Emperor, he was not going to be content merely with the control of worlds and armies. His would be a more personal form of empire: minds re-formed and rebuilt into his own conception of what a mind should be.

Which meant that Mara had been right on the other count, too. C'baoth was thoroughly insane.

'It is not insanity to offer the richness of my glory to others,' C'baoth murmured. 'It is a gift which many would die for.'

'You're giving Skywalker a good shot at that part, anyway,' Mara bit out, shaking her head to try and clear it. Between her own memories, an echo of the strange buzzing pressure

397

she was picking up from Skywalker's mind, and C'baoth's overbearing presence two meters away, trying to hang on to a line of thought was like trying to fly an airspeeder in a winter windstorm.

But there was a mental pattern the Emperor had taught her long ago, a pattern for those times when he'd wanted his instructions hidden even from Vader. If she could just clear her mind enough to get it in place—

Through the turmoil came a sudden jolt of pain. 'Do not attempt to hide your thoughts from me, Mara Jade,' C'baoth admonished her sharply. 'You are mine now. It is not right for an apprentice to hide her thoughts from her master.'

'So I'm already your apprentice, huh?' Mara growled, gritting her teeth against the pain and making another try at the pattern. This time, she made it. 'I thought I had at least until I'd knelt at your feet.'

'You mock my vision,' C'baoth said, his voice darkly petulant. 'But you *shall* kneel before me.'

'Just like Skywalker will, right? Assuming he lives through this?'

'He will be mine,' C'baoth agreed, quietly confident. 'As will his sister and her children.'

'And then together you'll heal the galaxy,' Mara said, watching his face and listening to the turmoil in her mind. Yes; the barrier seemed to be keeping C'baoth back. Now if she could just hold on to that privacy a little longer . . .

'You disappoint me, Mara Jade,' C'baoth said, shaking his head. 'Do you truly believe I need to hear your thoughts in order to read your heart? Like the lesser peoples of the galaxy, you seek my destruction. A foolish notion. Did the Emperor teach you nothing about our destiny?'

'He didn't do a good job of reading his own, I know that much,' Mara retorted, listening to her heart thudding as she watched C'baoth. If that erratic mind of his decided she was a genuine threat and launched another of those lightning bolt attacks . . .

C'baoth smiled, holding his arms out to the sides. 'Do you

feel the need to measure your strength against mine, Mara Jade? Come, then, and do so.'

For a pair of heartbeats she eyed him, almost tempted to try. He looked so old and helpless; and she had her mental barrier and some of the best unarmed combat training the Empire at its height could provide. It would take just a few seconds . . .

She took a deep breath and lowered her eyes. No; not now. Not like this. Not with these pressures and distractions spinning through her mind. She'd never make it. 'You kill me now and I won't be able to kneel for you,' she muttered, letting her shoulders slump in an attitude of defeat.

'Very good,' C'baoth purred. 'You have wisdom of a sort, after all. Watch, then, and learn.'

Mara turned back to the guardrail. But not to watch the lightsaber duel. Somewhere down there was the blaster C'baoth had torn from her grip when he did whatever it was he'd done to the mountain's ysalamiri and gotten to the Force again. If she could find it before C'baoth realized that she hadn't really given up . . .

Across the floor, Skywalker leaped up again to the catwalk. The clone was ready for the move, hurling his lightsaber upward right behind him. The blue-white blade missed Skywalker by a hair, slicing instead most of the way through the catwalk floor and one of the support struts holding it to the ceiling. With a tooth-jarring shriek, the strained metal twisted under Skywalker's weight, dumping him back off.

He hit the floor more or less on his feet, dropping down to land on one knee. His hand reached out, and the lightsaber that had been falling toward the clone suddenly changed direction. It arced toward Skywalker's hand—

And stopped dead in midair. Skywalker strained, the muscles of his hand tightening visibly as his mind stretched out. 'Not that way, Jedi Skywalker,' C'baoth said reprovingly; and Mara glanced over to see that his hand, too, was stretched out toward the errant lightsaber. The clone, for his part, was just standing there in his brown robe, as if he knew that C'baoth would be on his side in this battle.

Maybe he did. Maybe there was nothing left in that body but an extension of C'baoth's own mind.

'This duel must be to the death,' C'baoth continued. 'It must be weapon against weapon, mind against mind, soul against soul. Anything less will not bring you to the knowledge you must have if you are to properly serve me.'

Skywalker was good, all right. With the strange buzzing pressure in his mind he must have known he couldn't match C'baoth strength for strength. Mara felt the subtle change in his concentration; and suddenly he swung his own lightsaber over his shoulder, the green-white blade scything toward a point midway along the other ligthsaber handle.

But if C'baoth wouldn't let Skywalker disarm his opponent, he wouldn't let him destroy the weapon, either. Even as the blade sliced downward, a small object shot out of the shadows to Skywalker's right, slamming into his shoulder and deflecting his arm just far enough for his blade to sweep through empty air. An instant later the old Jedi had torn the clone's lightsaber from Skywalker's mental grip, sending it back across the room to its owner. The clone raised it to en guard position; wearily, Skywalker got to his feet and prepared to continue the battle.

But for the moment Mara wasn't interested in the lightsabers. Lying on the floor, maybe two meters back from Skywalker's feet, was the object C'baoth had thrown at him.

Mara's blaster.

She looked sideways at C'baoth, wondering if he was watching her. He wasn't. In fact, he wasn't looking at much of anything. His eyes were unfocused, staring across the throne room, a strangely childlike smile on his face. 'She has come,' he said, his voice almost inaudible over the clash of the lightsabers below. 'Just as I knew she would.' Abruptly, he looked at Mara. 'She is here, Mara Jade,' he said, pointing dramatically toward the turbolift she and Skywalker had come up.

Frowning, not sure she should take her eyes off him, Mara turned her head to look. The turbolift door slid open and Solo stepped out, his blaster ready. And right behind him—

Mara caught her breath, her whole body going tense. It was Leia Organa Solo, holding a blaster in one hand and her lightsaber in the other. And behind her, his pet vornskrs in front of him on leashes—

It was Karrde.

Organa Solo? And *Karrde*?

'Leia – Han – go back,' Skywalker called to them over the clash of the lightsabers as the newcomers moved along the walkway past the galaxy hologram and on into the main part of the throne room. 'It's too danger—'

'Welcome, my new apprentice!' C'baoth shouted joyfully, his voice drowning out Skywalker's as it echoed grandly in the open space. 'Come to me, Leia Organa Solo. I will teach you the true ways of the Force.'

Solo had a different sort of lesson in mind. He reached the end of the walkway, sighted along the barrel of his blaster, and fired.

But even wallowing in self-delusion, a Jedi of C'baoth's power couldn't be taken out that easily. In a blur of motion, Mara's blaster leaped upward from the floor into the path of the shot, its grip shattering into a shower of sparks as Solo's shot expended its energy there. The second shot was likewise blocked; the third caught the blaster's power pack, turning the weapon into a spectacular fireball. The blaster was torn from Solo's grip before he could fire a fourth.

And C'baoth went berserk.

He screamed, a horrible shriek of rage and betrayal that seemed like it would set the air on fire. Mara jerked back as the piercing sound cut through her ears—

And an instant later nearly fell over the guardrail as the Force equivalent of the scream slammed into her.

It was like nothing she'd ever experienced before; not from Vader, not from the Emperor himself. The utter, animal ferocity – the total loss of every shred of self-control – it was like standing alone in the middle of a sudden violent storm. Wave after wave of fury swept over her, ripping through the mental barrier she'd created and battering her mind with a numbing combination of hatred and pain. Dimly, she saw

Skywalker and Organa Solo staggering under the assault; heard Karrde's vornskrs' howling in pain of their own.

And from C'baoth's outstretched hands erupted a blaze of lightning.

Mara winced in sympathetic pain as Solo was thrown backwards into the guardrail at the front of the hologram pit. Through the crackle of the lightning she heard Organa Solo shout her husband's name and jump to his side, dropping her blaster and igniting her lightsaber just in time to catch the third blast of lightning on the green-white blade. Abruptly, C'baoth shifted his aim upward to the damaged catwalk hanging precariously over their heads. The lightning flashed again—

And with a *crack* of exploding metal the center of the catwalk split apart. Pivoting on its last remaining support strut, it toppled ponderously downward toward Organa Solo.

She saw it coming, or maybe Skywalker's training had taught her how to use the Force to anticipate danger. As the heavy metal swung down on her, she slashed upward with her lightsaber, cutting through the catwalk far enough to the side that the main part missed her and Solo as it swung past to crash into the floor in front of Karrde and the vornskrs. But there was no time for her to get out from under the end she had cut off. It caught her across her head and shoulder, knocking the lightsaber from her hand and hammering her to the floor beside Solo.

'Leia!' Skywalker shouted, throwing an anguished glance at his sister. Suddenly the debilitating buzzing in his mind seemed to be forgotten as his fighting abruptly shifted from groggy defense to furious attack. The clone fell back before the onslaught, barely managing to block Skywalker's blows. He jumped up on to the stairway, hastily backed two steps further up toward C'baoth as Skywalker charged after him, then leaped over on to the remaining guard platform. For a second Mara thought Skywalker was going to pursue him up there, or else cut through the platform base and bring him down.

He didn't do either. Standing halfway up the stairs, a sheen

402

of sweat glistening on his face, he gazed up at C'baoth with an expression that sent a shiver down Mara's back.

'Do you also seek to destroy me, Jedi Skywalker?' C'baoth said, his voice quietly deadly. 'For such thoughts are foolish. I could crush you like a small insect beneath my heel.'

'Perhaps,' Skywalker said, breathing heavily. 'But if you do, you'll never have the chance to control my mind.'

C'baoth studied him. 'What do you want?'

Skywalker jerked his head back toward his sister and Solo. 'Let them leave. All of them. Now.' His eyes flicked to Mara. 'Mara, too.'

'And if I do?'

A muscle in Skywalker's cheek twitched. His finger moved, and with a sputtering hiss his lightsaber blade disappeared. 'Let them go,' he said quietly, 'and I'll stay.'

From somewhere nearby a dull thudding noise began, adding an irregular pulsebeat to the eerie breathing sounds whispering through the cloning cavern. A blaster rifle pounding against heavy metal, Lando decided, giving the doors around the walkway a quick look. So far they all seemed secure, but he knew that wouldn't last. The stormtroopers out there weren't firing at the doors just for target practice, and there was bound to be a bag of shaped explosives on their way.

From the other side of the equipment column, Chewbacca rumbled a warning. 'I *am* keeping my head down,' Lando assured him, peering into the gap between two large ducts at the maze of multicolored wiring and piping beyond. Now, where was that repulsor pump connection again . . . ?

He had located the spot and was reaching in with the charge when the callbeep from his comlink unexpectedly went off, echoed a fraction of a second later from Chewbacca's comlink. Frowning, half expecting it to be some hotshot Imperial tech who'd found his channel, he pulled it out. 'Calrissian,' he said.

'Ah – General Calrissian,' Threepio's precise voice came back. 'I see Artoo has been successful in eliminating the jamming. Surprising, actually, given all the trouble which we've been required to—'

'Tell him good job,' Lando cut him off. Now was decidedly not the time for a pleasant little chat with Threepio. 'Was there anything else?'

'Ah, yes, sir, there is,' the droid said. 'The Noghri instructed me to ask whether you wish us to return to assist you.'

There was another thud, a louder one this time. 'I wish you could,' Lando sighed. 'But you'd never make it back in time.' The thud came again, and this time he distinctly saw the door opposite their bridge shake with the impact. 'We'll just have to get out of here by ourselves.'

From the other side of the work platform, Chewbacca rumbled his less-than-enthusiastic opinion of that. 'But if Chewbacca wishes us to return—'

'You won't get here in time,' Lando told him firmly. 'Tell the Noghri if they want to be useful they should head up to the throne room and give Han a hand.'

'It's too late for that,' a new voice put in, almost too quiet to hear.

Lando frowned at the comlink. 'Han?'

'No, it's Talon Karrde,' the other identified himself. 'I came in with Councilor Organa Solo. We're up in the throne room—'

'*Leia's* here?' Lando asked. 'What in—?'

'Shut up and listen,' Karrde cut him off. 'That Jedi Master of Luke's – Joruus C'baoth – is up here, too. He's taken out Solo and Organa Solo both, and has Skywalker fighting what looks to be a clone of himself. He's not paying any attention to me at the moment – there's some kind of face-off going on up there. But he would the minute I tried anything.'

'I thought Luke said the Force was being blocked.'

'It was. Somehow, C'baoth got it back. Are you down with the cloning tanks?'

'We're above them, yes. Why?'

'Organa Solo suggested earlier that there should be a large number of ysalamiri scattered around that area,' Karrde said. 'If you can pull a few of them off their nutrient frames and get them up here, we might have a chance of stopping him.'

Chewbacca growled mournfully, and Lando felt his lip twist

404

as he nodded agreement. So that was what all those blasting disk explosions had been about. 'It's too late for that, too,' he told Karrde. 'C'baoth's already had them all killed.'

For a long moment the comlink was silent. 'I see,' Karrde said at last. 'Well, that explains that. Any suggestions?'

Lando hesitated. 'Not really,' he said. 'If we come up with anything, we'll let you know.'

'Thank you,' Karrde said, a little too dryly. 'I'll be waiting.' There was a click as he left the channel. 'Threepio, you still there?' Lando asked.

'Yes, sir,' the droid answered.

'Get Artoo back on the computer,' Lando told him. 'Have him do whatever he can to shift troops away from that air intake we came in through. Then you and the Noghri start heading that way.'

'We're leaving, sir?' Threepio asked, sounding astonished.

'That's right,' Lando told him. 'And Chewie and I will be right behind you, so you'd better move fast if you don't want to get stepped on. Better alert the two Noghri that Luke sent with that Myneyrshi bunch, too. Got all that?'

'Yes, sir,' Threepio said hesitantly. 'What about Master Luke and the others?'

'Leave that to me,' Lando told him. 'Get busy.'

'Yes, sir,' Threepio said again. Another click, and he was gone.

There was a moment of silence. Chewbacca broke it with the obvious question. 'I don't think we've got a choice anymore,' Lando told him grimly. 'The way Luke and Mara talk about him, C'baoth's at least as dangerous as the Emperor was. Maybe even more so. We've got to try to take out the whole storehouse and hope we get him along with it.'

Chewbacca growled an objection. 'We can't,' Lando shook his head. 'At least not until it's set and running. We warn anyone up there now and C'baoth will know all about it. Might have time to get it stopped.'

There was another muffled blast from the door. 'Come on, let's get this done,' Lando said, picking up the last of his explosives. With luck, they would have time to rig

Chewbacca's arhythmic resonance gimmick before the storm-troopers got in. With a little more luck, the two of them might make it out of the cavern alive.

And with still more, they might be able to find a way to alert Han and the others before the whole storehouse blew up beneath them.

For a long moment the throne room was silent. Mara stared at Skywalker, wondering if he understood what he was saying. To offer to voluntarily stay here with C'baoth . . .

His gaze flicked sideways again to meet hers, and even through the buzzing in his mind she could feel his private dread. He knew what he was saying, all right. And he meant it. If C'baoth accepted his offer, he would go willingly with the insane Jedi. Sacrificing himself to save his friends.

Including the woman who'd once promised to kill him.

She turned away, suddenly unable to watch. Her eyes found Karrde, half hidden behind the wreckage of the catwalk as he knelt between his two vornskrs. Stroking them, talking quietly to them – probably calming them down after that Force-driven tantrum of C'baoth's. She peered at the animals, but they didn't seem to be hurt.

Her head movement must have caught Karrde's eye. He looked up at her, his face expressionless. Still patting the vornskrs, he tilted his head fractionally toward Solo and Organa Solo. Frowning, Mara followed his gaze—

And froze. Beside the section of catwalk wreckage still half covering his wife, Solo was moving. Slowly, a couple of centimeters at a time, he was creeping across the floor.

Toward the blaster Organa Solo had dropped.

'You ask too much, Skywalker,' C'baoth warned softly. 'Mara Jade will be mine. Must be mine. It is the destiny demanded of her by the Force. Not even you may trifle with that.'

'Right,' Mara put in, looking back at C'baoth and putting all the sarcasm into her voice as she could manage. Whatever the risks to herself, she had to draw as much of C'baoth's attention away from the other end of the throne room as she could. 'I still have to kneel at his feet, remember?'

'You insult me, Mara Jade,' C'baoth said, turning an evil smile on her. 'Do you really believe me so easy to mislead?' Still watching her, he crooked a finger—

And as Solo's hand stretched out toward it, the blaster twitched another half meter out of his reach.

From the guard platform came a subtle change in hum. 'Skywalker – look out!' Mara snapped.

Skywalker spun around, lightsaber igniting again and swinging up into defense. The clone, his wind or his courage back, was already halfway through his leap, his lightsaber slicing downward. The two blades met with a crash and an impact that drove Skywalker backward to the edge of the stairway. He took one step more, fought for balance, then dropped off to the floor below.

Mara threw a quick look at Solo as the clone charged over the edge in pursuit. If the clone really was an extension of C'baoth's mind . . .

But no. Even as Solo tried again for the blaster it again slid away from him. Whatever effort C'baoth was expending on the lightsaber duel, he clearly still had enough concentration left to toy with his prisoners.

'You see, Mara Jade?' C'baoth asked quietly. His fury had passed, the brief flicker of fun as he toyed with his prisoners had passed, and now it was time to return to the important business of building his Empire. 'It is inevitable. I will rule . . . and along with Skywalker and his sister, you will serve at my side. And we shall be great together.'

Abruptly, he took a long step back from the guardrail on the other side of the stairway. Just in time; an instant later Skywalker was back, backflipping up from the lower throne room floor. He landed with his back to Mara, floundering a moment as he fought to recover his balance. There was another flash of light, blue-white this time, as the clone leaped up over the guardrail in pursuit, swinging his lightsaber in vicious horizontal arcs to guard against attack. Skywalker moved backward out of his way; glancing past him, Mara saw C'baoth take a hasty backward step of his own. The clone hit the floor and charged, lightsaber still slashing toward Skywalker in wide horizontal arcs. Skywalker continued to give way, apparently unaware that he was backing toward the solid rock wall.

Against which he would be trapped.

They passed by . . . and Mara looked over to find C'baoth once again gazing at her. 'As I said, Mara Jade,' he said. 'Inevitable. And with you and Skywalker beside me, the lesser peoples of the galaxy will flock to us like leaves in the wind. Their hearts and their souls will be ours.'

He looked across the room and beckoned. Still crouching behind the catwalk wreckage, Karrde jerked in surprise as his blaster rose from his holster and shot through the air toward C'baoth. Halfway there it was joined by Organa Solo's dropped lightsaber and the blaster Solo was still doggedly trying to chase down. 'As will their insignificant weapons,' C'baoth added. Holding a negligent hand out to receive them, he turned his eyes back to the duel about to play itself to its conclusion.

It was the chance Mara had been waiting for. Possibly the last chance she would ever have. Reaching through the chaos surrounding her mind, she stretched out to the Force, focusing her eyes and mind on the weapons flying across the room toward C'baoth's hand. She felt his inattentive control snap—

And Organa Solo's lightsaber arced away from the blasters to land firmly in her hand.

C'baoth spun back to face her, the blasters falling with a clatter on to the stairway. 'No!' he screamed, his face twisted horribly with fear, confusion, and dread. Mara felt his sudden frantic tug fumbling at the lightsaber; but it, too, was twisted with confusion and dread, and this time he didn't have surprise on his side. Given time, he would recover from the shock, but Mara had no intention of giving him that time. Igniting the lightsaber, she charged.

The clone must have heard her coming, of course; the distinctive sound of her lightsaber made that inevitable. But with Skywalker backed up against the wall, the temptation to finish off one opponent first was too great to resist. He swung one last time, his lightsaber slashing into the wall as Skywalker ducked low beneath the blade—

And with a brilliant flash of shattered electronics, the wall exploded outward, over Skywalker's head and directly into the clone's face.

Skywalker hadn't been backing into a wall after all. He'd been backing into one of the throne room's viewscreens.

The clone shrieked – the first sound Mara could remember hearing him make – as he staggered backward. He spun toward the sound of her lightsaber, his face twisted with anger and fear, his eyes still dazzled. He raised his lightsaber to attack—

YOU WILL KILL LUKE SKYWALKER.

She ducked beneath the slashing blade, gazing into his face. Skywalker's face. The face that had haunted her nightmares for nearly six years. The face the Emperor had ordered her to destroy.

YOU WILL KILL LUKE SKYWALKER.

And for the first time since she'd found Skywalker and his crippled X-wing floating in deep space, she let herself give in to the voice swirling through her mind. With all her strength, she swung her lightsaber and cut him down.

The clone crumpled, his lightsaber clattering to the floor beside him.

Mara gazed down at him . . . and as she took a ragged breath, the voice in the back of her mind fell silent.

It was done. She had fulfilled the Emperor's last command.

And she was finally free.

CHAPTER 28

'That appears to be all of them, Captain,' Thrawn said, gazing out the bridge viewport at the Rebel warships spread out along the edges of the Interdictor Cruisers' gravity cones. 'Instruct the *Constrainer* and *Sentinel* to secure from entrapment duty and return to their positions in the demarcation line. All warships: prepare to engage the enemy.'

'Yes, sir,' Pellaeon said, shaking his head in silent wonder as he keyed in the orders. Once again, against overwhelming evidence to the contrary, the Grand Admiral had proved himself right. The Rebel assault fleet was here.

And probably wondering at this very moment what had gone wrong with their clever little scheme. 'It occurs to me, Admiral, that we might not want to destroy all of them,' he suggested. 'Someone should be allowed to return to Coruscant to tell them how badly they were outsmarted.'

'I agree, Captain,' Thrawn said. 'Though I doubt that will be their interpretation. More likely they'll conclude instead that they were betrayed.'

'Probably,' Pellaeon agreed, throwing a quick look around the bridge. He'd thought he'd heard a faint sound just then, something like an overstressed bearing or someone rumbling in the back of his throat. He listened closely, but the sound wasn't repeated. 'Though that would work equally well to our advantage.'

'Indeed,' Thrawn said. 'Shall we designate Admiral Ackbar's Star Cruiser for messenger duty?'

Pellaeon smiled tightly. Ackbar. Who'd just barely survived Councilor Borsk Fey'lya's previous accusations of incompetence and treason over the operation at the Sluis Van shipyards. This time, he wouldn't be so lucky. 'A nice touch, Admiral,' he said.

'Thank you, Captain.'

Pellaeon glanced up at Rukh, standing silent guard behind Thrawn's chair, and wondered if the Noghri appreciated the irony of it all. Given the species' lack of sophistication, probably not.

Ahead, space was filling with flashes of laser fire as the opposing starfighter squadrons began to engage. Settling himself comfortably in his chair, Pellaeon glanced over his displays and prepared his mind for battle. For battle, and for victory.

*   *   *

'Watch it, Rogue Leader, you've picked up a couple of tails,' the voice of Rogue Two came in Wedge's ear. 'Rogue Six?'

'Right with you, Rogue Two,' the other confirmed. 'Double-chop on three. One, two—'

Bracing himself, Wedge threw his X-wing into a wild scissors roll. The two TIE fighters, trying to match his maneuver while at the same time not overshooting him, probably never even saw the other two X-wings drop into position behind them. Two messy explosions later, Wedge was clear. 'Thanks,' he said.

'No problem. What now?'

'I don't know,' he admitted, taking a quick look at the battle raging around them. So far, Admiral Ackbar was still holding his Star Cruisers together in combat formation. But the way the periphery support ships were being hammered by the Imperials, the whole thing could dissolve into the mass confusion of a brawl at any minute. In which event, the starfighter squadrons would be basically on their own, hitting wherever and whatever they could.

Which they were for all practical purposes doing now anyway. The trick would be to find something really effective to hit . . .

Rogue Two must have followed the same reasoning. 'You know, Rogue Leader, it occurs to me that those Imperials wouldn't have so many ships available to pound us with if they had to protect their shipyard at the same time.'

Wedge craned his neck to look at the blaze of lights off in the near distance. Silhouetted against them, he could make out the dark, brooding outlines of at least four Golan II battle stations. 'Agreed,' he said. 'But I think it would take more than an attack by even the legendary Rogue Squadron to make them that nervous—'

'Commander Antilles, this is Fleet Central Communications,' a brisk voice cut in. 'I have a signal coded urgent coming in for you under a New Republic diplomatic encrypt. Do you want to bother with it?'

Wedge blinked. A diplomatic encrypt? Way out here? 'I suppose so. Sure, put it through.'

'Yes, sir.' There was a click—

'Hello, Antilles,' a vaguely familiar voice said dryly in his ear. 'Nice to see you again.'

'The feeling's mutual, I'm sure,' Wedge said, frowning. 'Who *is* this?'

'Oh, come now,' the other chided. 'Have you forgotten already those wonderful times we spent together outside the Mumbri Storve cantina?'

The Mumbri Storve—? *'Aves?'*

'Hey, very good,' Aves said. 'Your memory's getting better.'

'You people are starting to be hard to forget,' Wedge told him. 'Where are you?'

'Right smack in the middle of that big blaze of Imperial lights off on your flank,' Aves said, his voice turning a little grim. 'I wish you'd told me you were hitting this place instead of Tangrene like we thought.'

'I wish you'd told *me* what that little job of yours was all about,' Wedge countered. 'Did a good job of fooling each other, didn't we?'

'Sure did. Fooled everybody except the Grand Admiral.'

'Tell me about it. So is this just a social call, or what?'

'It could be,' Aves said. 'Or it couldn't. See, in about ninety seconds some of us are going to make a grab for the CGT array we came here to get. After that, it's a quick goodbye and we punch our way out.'

Punching their way out from an Imperial shipyard. And he made it sound so easy, too. 'Good luck.'

'Thanks. The reason I mention it is that it doesn't matter much to us which direction we pick to punch through. Thought it might make a difference to you.'

Wedge felt a tight smile tugging at his lip. 'It might, at that,' he said. 'Like, say, if you were to come out near those Golan Twos out there. Maybe hitting them a little from behind on the way?'

'Looks like a good route to me,' Aves agreed. ''Course, It'll get nasty outside the perimeter – all those ships and things taking potshots and all. I don't suppose you could find a way to give us a friendly escort from that point on?'

Wedge looked over at the lights, thinking it over. It could work, all right. If Aves' people were able to knock out even one of those Golan IIs, it would open up the shipyard to a New Republic incursion. Unless the Imperials were willing to sacrifice it, they would have to shift some of their battle force over there to close the puncture and chase down any ships that had gotten in.

And from the smugglers' point of view, having an influx of New Republic warships to sneak through on their way out would give them better cover than they would get anywhere else along the perimeter. All in all, a pretty fair exchange. 'You've got a deal,' he told Aves. 'Give me a couple of minutes and I'll get that escort arranged.'

'A *friendly* escort, don't forget,' Aves warned. 'If you know what I mean.'

'I know exactly what you mean,' Wedge assured him. The traditional Mon Calamari loathing for smugglers and smuggling was the stuff of wardroom legend, and Wedge didn't want to get caught in the middle of that any more than Aves did. Probably why the smuggler had come to him instead of offering his assistance to Ackbar and the fleet commanders directly. 'Don't worry, I've got it covered.'

'OK. Whoops – there goes the first charge. See you.'

The comm clicked off. 'We're going in?' Rogue Eleven asked.

'We're going in,' Wedge confirmed, bringing his X-wing around in a tight starboard turn. 'Rogue Two, give Command a quick update and tell them we need some support. Don't mention Aves by name – just tell them we're coordinating with an independent resistance group inside the shipyards.'

'Got it, Rogue Leader.'

'What if Ackbar doesn't want to risk it?' Rogue Seven put in.

Wedge looked out at the lights of the shipyard. So once again, as it had so many times before, it was all going to come down to a matter of trust. Trust in a farm kid, fresh off a backward desert world, to lead him in an attack on the first Death Star. Trust in a former high-stakes gambler, who might or might not have had any real combat experience, to lead him in an attack on the second Death Star. And now, trust in a smuggler who might just as easily betray him for the right price. 'It doesn't matter,' he said. 'With or without support, we're going in.'

Mara's lightsaber flashed, slicing viciously through the clone Luuke. The clone fell, its lightsaber clattering to the floor, and lay still.

And suddenly, the buzzing pressure in Luke's mind was gone.

He rose to his feet in front of the still sparking viewscreen he'd lured the clone to, taking what felt like the first clean breath he'd had in hours. The ordeal was finally over. 'Thank you,' he said quietly to Mara.

She took a step back from the dead clone. 'No problem. Brain all clear now?'

So she'd been able to sense the buzzing in his mind. He'd wondered about that. 'Yes,' he nodded, taking another wonderfully clean breath. 'How about yours?'

She threw him a look that was half amused, half ironic. But for the first time since they'd met he could see that the pain and hatred were gone from her eyes. 'I did what he wanted me to,' she said. 'It's over.'

Luke looked back across the throne room. Karrde had tied the vornskrs' leashes to the collapsed catwalk and was picking his way carefully across the wreckage. Han, on his feet now, was helping a still groggy Leia out from under the section that had fallen on her. 'Leia?' Luke called. 'You all right?'

'I'm fine,' Leia called back. 'Just a little banged up. Let's get out of here, all right?'

Luke turned back to C'baoth. The old Jedi was staring down at the dead clone, his hands working at his sides, his eyes furious and lost and insane. 'Yes,' he agreed. 'Come on, Mara.'

'Go ahead,' Mara said. 'I'll be with you in a minute.'

Luke eyed her. 'What are you going to do?'

'What do you think?' she retorted. 'I'm going to finish the job. Like I should have done on Jomark.'

Slowly, C'baoth raised his eyes to her. 'You will die for this, Mara Jade,' he said, his quiet voice more chilling than any outburst of rage could have been. 'Slowly, and in great pain.' Taking a deep breath, curling his hands into fists in front of his chest, he closed his eyes.

'We'll see about that,' Mara muttered. Raising her lightsaber, she started toward him.

It began as a distant rumble, more felt than really heard. Luke looked around the room, senses tingling with a premonition of danger. But he could see nothing out of place. The sound grew louder, deeper—

And with a thunderous explosion, the sections of throne room ceiling directly above him and Mara suddenly collapsed in a downpour of gravel-sized rocks.

'Look out!' Luke shouted, throwing his arms up to protect his head and trying to leap out of the way. But the center of the rockfall moved with him. He tried again, this time nearly losing his balance as his foot caught in a pile of stones already ankle deep. Too numerous and too small for him to get a grip on through the Force, they kept coming, pummeling against him with bruising impact. Through the dust swirling around him, he saw Mara floundering under a deluge of her own, trying to guard her head with one arm as she slashed vainly at the falling stones with her lightsaber. From across the throne room, Luke could hear Han shouting something, and guessed that they, too, were under the same attack.

And standing untouched by the destructive rock storms he'd unleashed, C'baoth lifted his hands high. 'I am the Jedi Master C'baoth!' he shouted, his voice ringing through the throne room and the roar of the rockfalls. 'The Empire – the universe – is mine.'

Luke dropped his lightsaber back into defense position, senses again tingling with danger. But once again, the knowledge did him little good. C'baoth's lightning burst flashed against the lightsaber blade, the impact knocking Luke off balance and dropping him painfully on to his knees in the pile of stones around him. Even as he struggled to get up, one of the falling rocks slammed hard into the side of his head. He staggered, toppling sideways on to one hand. Again the lightning flashed, throwing coronal fire all through the stone pile and sending wave after wave of agony through him. The lightsaber was plucked from his fingers; dimly he saw it fly over the railing toward the far end of the throne room.

'Stop it,' Mara screamed. Through the haze of pain, Luke saw that she was standing up to her knees in stones, her lightsaber slashing uselessly through the mound as if trying to sweep them away. 'If you're going to kill us, just do it.'

'Patience, my future apprentice,' C'baoth said . . . and squinting through the stones and dust, Luke saw the other's dreamy smile. 'You cannot die yet. Not until I have taken you down to the Grand Admiral's cloning chamber.'

Beneath her rockfall, Mara jerked, her sense flashing with sudden horror. 'What?'

'For I have foreseen that Mara Jade will kneel before me,' C'baoth reminded her. 'One Mara Jade . . . or another.'

'That's it,' Lando said, tapping the activation switch on the last charge. 'Give it a kick and let's get out of here.'

From around the central column Chewbacca growled acknowledgement. Picking up his blaster, Lando stood up, giving each of the doors around the outer walkway a quick look. So far, so good. If they could keep the stormtroopers out for just two more minutes, long enough for Chewbacca and him to get off this work platform and out to the walkway . . .

Chewbacca rumbled a warning. Listening closely, Lando could hear the faint rising-pitch hum of an extremely unhappy negative flow coupler. 'Great, Chewie,' he said. 'Let's go.' He stepped out on to the end of the bridge—

And straight ahead of him, the door opposite the bridge blew up.

'Watch it!' Lando barked, dropping flat on his stomach on the bridge and pouring blaster fire into the cloud of dust and debris expanding out from where the door had been. Already, the sizzling blue ripples of stun fire were starting to erupt from the doorway in their general direction. Behind him, the roar of Chewbacca's bowcaster was answering. So much for those last two minutes.

And with his face pressed as close to the metal-mesh floor as he could get it, Lando found himself looking at the bridge. At the bridge, and the thin but sturdy guardrails running along both sides of it . . .

It was crazy. But that didn't mean it wouldn't work.

'Chewie, get over here,' he called, rolling halfway over and throwing a quick look up at the bridge controls set into the top of the work platform guardrail. Extension control . . . there. Retraction control – emergency stop control—

The bridge shook as Chewbacca landed with a thud on the bridge beside him. 'Keep them busy,' Lando told him. Gauging the distance, he lunged upward, jabbing the retraction control and the emergency stop in quick succession. The bridge lurched out from the work platform and stopped, just far enough for its locking bars to disengage.

Chewbacca rumbled a question as the bridge bobbed gently with the strain of their weight. 'You'll see,' Lando told him. From both sides came flashes of light as two more doors disintegrated. 'Just hang on to the guardrail supports and keep firing. Here we go.' Getting a firm grip himself, he aimed carefully and opened fire.

But not at the stormtroopers now charging out onto the circular walkway. His shots were directed instead at the far end of the bridge, throwing out clouds of sparks as they vaporized sections of the mesh flooring and dug chunks out of the structural support bars beneath. The bridge lurched, bobbing even harder now, as Lando continued to hammer away at its structural integrity. Beside him, Chewbacca rumbled a savage Wookiee phrase that Lando had never heard him use before—

And with a horrible shriek of strained metal, the bridge suddenly gave way. Connected to the walkway only by the still-intact guardrails, it pivoted, ponderously downward. Lando gripped the guardrail tightly as their horizontal position changed rapidly toward a vertical one—

And with a crash that nearly jarred him loose, the bridge slammed up against the guardrail of the cloning balcony three levels down.

'This is our stop,' Lando said. 'Come on.' Jamming his blaster awkwardly into its holster, he swung himself around the steeply angled bridge guardrail to drop on to the cloning balcony floor. Chewbacca, with his natural arboreal skills, was there a good three seconds ahead of him.

They were halfway to the balcony's exit door, dodging between the rows of Spaarti cylinders, when the column behind them blew up.

The charges went first, blowing sections of cable and pipework in a series of dazzling fireballs all around the column's perimeter. An evil-looking cloud of smoke and dust and flash-vaporized nutrient liquids swirled into the air, obscuring the view; from all sides, multicolored fluids began spraying out. The work platform they'd been standing on a minute earlier broke free of its supports and slid roughly down the column, tearing and damaging more equipment as it fell. From inside the cloud came a sputtering of shorted power lines and secondary explosions, each one adding to the rain of debris.

And with a horrible creaking of strained and shattered supports, the external layers of the column began to peel away and fall almost leisurely outward.

Over the din, Chewbacca roared a warning. 'Me, neither,' Lando shouted back. 'Let's get out of here.'

Ten seconds later, bursting past the single token guard who'd been left on this level's exit door, they were out. They were two corridors away when they felt the distant vibration as the column crashed to the cloning cavern floor.

'OK,' Lando panted, pausing and glancing both ways as they reached a cross corridor. Artoo must have done a good job with those troop reassignments; the whole area seemed deserted. 'Exit's that direction,' he told Chewbacca, pulling out his comlink. 'We'll call the others and get out of here.' He keyed for Han—

And jerked back as the comlink erupted with a loud crackling noise. 'Han?' he called.

'Lando?' Han's voice came back, almost inaudible over the noise.

'Right,' Lando confirmed. 'What's happening up there?'

'This crazy Jedi's dropping the roof in on us,' Han shouted. 'Leia and me have a little cover, but he's got Luke and Mara out in the open. Where are you?'

'Down near the cloning cavern,' Lando gritted. If that arhythmic resonance thing of Chewbacca's worked, one of the mountain's reactors would already be starting to flicker with instabilities. If they didn't get out of the mountain before it blew . . . 'You want us to come up and help?'

'Don't bother,' Karrde's voice cut in grimly. 'There's already a large pile of stone in front of the turbolift. Looks like we're here for the duration.'

Chewbacca snarled, his voice filled with frustration. 'Forget it, Chewie, there's nothing you could do anyway,' Han told him. 'We've still got Luke and Mara – maybe they can stop him.'

'What if they can't?' Lando demanded, stomach twisting inside him. 'Look, you haven't got much time – we think we've got an arhythmic resonance going in the power core.'

'Good,' Han said. 'Means C'baoth won't get out either.'

'Han—'

'Go on, get out of here,' Han cut him off. 'Chewie, it's been great; but if we don't make it, someone beside Winter's going to have to take care of Jacen and Jaina. You got that?'

'The *Wild Karrde*'s waiting where you came in,' Karrde added. 'They'll be expecting you.'

'Right,' Lando said, gritting his teeth. 'Good luck.'

He keyed off and jammed the comlink back in his belt. Han was right, there wasn't anything they could do against C'baoth from down here. But with the *Wild Karrde*'s turbolasers and Artoo's set of floor plans . . . 'Come on, Chewie,' he said, turning toward their exit and breaking into a run. 'It's not over yet.'

'Perhaps it is for the best,' C'baoth murmured, gazing at Luke sadly as he stepped toward him. Blinking the dust away from his eyes, Luke looked up at the old Jedi, trying to force back the agony still throbbing through him.

The agony, and the looming sense of defeat. Kneeling on the floor, encased in stones to above his waist with more still falling on him, facing an insane Jedi Master who wanted to kill him . . .

No. *A Jedi must act when he is calm. At peace with the Force.* 'Master C'baoth, listen to me,' he said. 'You're not well. I know that. But I can help you.'

A dozen expressions flicked across C'baoth's face, as if he were trying various emotions on for size. 'Can you, now,' he said, settling on wry amusement. 'And why should you do that for me?'

'Because you need it,' Luke said. 'And because we need you. You have a vast store of experience and power that you could use for the good of the New Republic.'

C'baoth snorted. 'The Jedi Master Joruus C'baoth does not serve lesser peoples, Jedi Skywalker.'

'Why not? All the great Jedi Masters of the Old Republic did.'

'And that was their failing,' C'baoth said, jabbing a finger at Luke. 'That was why the lesser people rose up and killed them.'

'But they didn't—'

'Enough!' C'baoth thundered. 'It doesn't matter what you think the lesser peoples need from me. *I* am the one who will decide that. They will accept my rule, or they will die.' His eyes flashed. 'You had that choice, Jedi Skywalker. And more – you could have ruled beside me. Instead, you chose death.'

A drop of sweat or blood trickled down the side of Luke's face. 'What about Mara?'

C'baoth shook his head. 'Mara Jade is no longer any concern of yours,' he said. 'I will deal with her later.'

'No,' Mara snapped. 'You will deal with me *now*.'

Luke looked over at her. The stones were still raining down above her head; but to his astonishment, the knee-high pile of rock that had been trapping her in place was gone. And now he saw why: those lightsaber slashes she'd been making earlier hadn't been the useless sweeping motions that he'd assumed. Instead, she'd been slicing huge gashes in the floor, releasing the stones to drain through to the monitor area below.

Raising her lightsaber, she charged.

C'baoth swung around to face her, his face contorted with rage. 'No!' he screamed; and again the blue-white lightning crackled from his fingertips. Mara caught the burst on her lightsaber, her mad rush faltering as coronal fire burned all around her. C'baoth fired again and again, backing toward the throne and the solid wall behind it. Doggedly, Mara kept coming.

Abruptly, the rockfall over her head ceased. From the edge of the pile that had half buried Luke, stones began flying toward C'baoth. Curving around behind him, they shot straight into Mara's face. She staggered backward, squeezing her eyes shut against the hailstorm and throwing up her right elbow to try to block them away.

Setting his teeth, Luke tried to heave away the stones weighing him down. He couldn't leave Mara to fight alone. But it was no use; his muscles were still too weakened from C'baoth's last attack. He tried again anyway, ignoring the fresh pain the effort sent through him. He looked at Mara—

And saw her face suddenly change. He frowned; and then he heard it too. Leia's voice, speaking in his mind—

Keep your eyes closed, Mara, and listen to my voice. I can see; I'll guide you.

'No!' C'baoth screamed again. 'No! She is mine!'

Luke looked over at the other end of the throne room, wondering how C'baoth would lash out at Leia in retaliation. But there was nothing. Even the stones had stopped falling on the section of catwalk they were all huddled beneath. Perhaps the long battle had finally begun to drain C'baoth's strength, and he could no longer risk splitting his attention. Beyond the catwalk, lying half buried in the pile of stone that now blocked the turbolift door, Luke spotted the metallic glint of his lightsaber. If he could call it to him, and regain enough strength to join Mara's battle . . .

And then, another motion caught his eye. Tied to the

catwalk to one side, untouched by the rockfall that had attacked their owner, Karrde's pet vornskrs were tugging at their leashes.

Straining toward Mara. And toward C'baoth.

A wild vornskr had nearly killed Mara during their trek through the Myrkr forest. It seemed only fitting, somehow, for these two to help save her. The lightsaber stirred under Luke's call, igniting as his mind found the control. It rolled off the rock pile, the brilliant green blade throwing sparks from the stones as it bounced across them. Luke strained, and the weapon lifted into the air and flew toward him.

And as it reached the ruined catwalk, he let the blade dip to slice neatly through the vornskrs' leashes.

C'baoth saw them coming, of course. His back nearly to the throne room wall now, he shifted his aim, sending a burst of lightning toward the charging predators as they came up over the stairway. One of them howled and fell to the floor, skidding across the scattered stones; the other staggered but kept coming.

The distraction was all the opening Mara needed. She leaped forward against the rocks still pummeling against her face, covering the last remaining distance between her and C'baoth; and as he brought his hands desperately back toward her, she dropped onto her knees in front of him and stabbed viciously upward with her lightsaber. With a last, mournful scream, C'baoth crumpled—

And as it had with the Emperor aboard the Death Star, the dark side energy within him burst out in a violent explosion of blue fire.

Luke was ready. Throwing every last bit of strength into the effort, he caught Mara in a solid Force grip, pulling her back away from that burst of energy as fast as he could. He felt the wave-front slam into him; felt the slight easing of stress as Leia's strength joined his effort.

And then, suddenly, it was all over.

For a long minute he lay still, gasping for air, fighting against the unconsciousness threatening to roll over him.

Dimly, he felt the stones being pushed away from around him. 'Are you all right, Luke?' Leia asked.

He forced open his eyes. Dust-covered and bruised, she didn't look much better than he felt. 'I'm fine,' he told her, pushing against the remaining stones and getting his feet under him. 'How about the others?'

'They're not too bad,' she said, catching his arm to help steady him. 'But Han's going to need medical treatment – he's got some bad burns.'

'So does Mara,' Karrde said grimly, coming up the steps holding an unconscious Mara in his arms. 'We have to get her to the *Wild Karrde* as quickly as possible.'

'So give them a call,' Han said. He was kneeling over the dead Luuke clone, gazing down at him. 'Tell them to come pick us up.'

'Pick us up where?' Karrde frowned.

Han pointed toward the spot where C'baoth had died. 'Right there.'

Luke turned and looked. The massive detonation of dark side energy had made a shambles of that end of the throne room. The walls and ceiling were blackened and cratered; the metal of the floor where C'baoth had stood was buckled and half melted; the throne itself had been ripped away and was lying smoldering a meter from its base.

And behind it, through a jagged crack in the rear wall, he could see the bright twinkle of a single star.

'Right,' Luke said, taking a deep breath. 'Leia?'

'I see it,' she nodded, handing him his lightsaber and igniting hers. 'Let's get busy.'

The two Rebel Assault Frigates broke to either side of the beleaguered Golan II, delivering massive broadsides as they veered off. A section of the battle station flared and went dark; and against its darkened bulk another wave of Rebel starfighters could be seen slipping past into the shipyards beyond.

And Pellaeon was no longer smiling.

'Don't panic, Captain,' Thrawn said. But he, too, was

starting to sound grim. 'We're not defeated yet. Not by a long shot.'

Pellaeon's board pinged. He looked at it – 'Sir, we have a priority message coming in from Wayland,' he told Thrawn, his stomach twisting with a sudden horrible premonition. Wayland – the cloning facility—

'Read it, Captain,' Thrawn said, his voice deadly quiet.

'Decrypt is coming in now, sir,' Pellaeon said, tapping the board impatiently as the message slowly began to come up. It was exactly as he'd feared. 'The mountain is under attack, sir,' he told Thrawn. 'Two different forces of natives, plus some Rebel saboteurs—' He broke off, frowning in disbelief. 'And a group of Noghri—'

He never got to read any more of the report. Abruptly, a gray-skinned hand slashed out of nowhere, catching him across the throat.

He gagged, falling limply in his chair, his whole body instantly paralyzed. 'For the treachery of the Empire against the Noghri people,' Rukh's voice said quietly from beside him as he gasped for breath. 'We were betrayed. We have been revenged.'

There was a whisper of movement, and he was gone. Still gasping, struggling against the inertia of his stunned muscles, Pellaeon fought to get a hand up to his command board. With one final effort he made it, trying twice before he was able to hit the emergency alert.

And as the wailing of the alarm cut through the noise of a Star Destroyer at battle, he finally managed to turn his head.

Thrawn was sitting upright in his chair, his face strangely calm. In the middle of his chest, a dark red stain was spreading across the spotless white of his Grand Admiral's uniform. Glittering in the center of the stain was the tip of Rukh's assassin's knife.

Thrawn caught his eye; and to Pellaeon's astonishment, the Grand Admiral smiled. 'But,' he whispered, 'it was so artistically done.'

The smile faded. The glow in his eyes did likewise . . . and Thrawn, the last Grand Admiral, was gone.

'Captain Pellaeon?' the comm officer called urgently as the medic team arrived – too late – to the Grand Admiral's chair. 'The *Nemesis* and *Stormhawk* are requesting orders. What shall I tell them?'

Pellaeon looked up at the viewports. At the chaos that had erupted behind the defenses of the supposedly secure shipyards; at the unexpected need to split his forces to its defense; at the Rebel fleet taking full advantage of the diversion. In the blink of an eye, the universe had suddenly turned against them.

Thrawn could still have pulled an Imperial victory out of it. But he, Pellaeon, was not Thrawn.

'Signal to all ships,' he rasped. The words ached in his throat, in a way that had nothing to do with the throbbing pain of Rukh's treacherous attack. 'Prepare to retreat.'

CHAPTER 29

The sun had set beneath a thin layer of western clouds, and the colors of the evening sky were beginning to fade into the encroaching darkness of Coruscant night. Leaning on the chest-high wrought-stone railing at the edge of the Palace roof, listening to the breezes whispering by her ears, Mara gazed out at the lights and vehicles of the Imperial City below. Buzzing with activity, there was still something strangely peaceful about it.

Or maybe the peace was in her. Either way, it made for a nice change.

Twenty meters behind her, the door out onto the roof opened. She stretched out with the Force; but she knew who it had to be. And she was right. 'Mara?' Luke called softly.

'Over here,' she called back, grimacing out at the city below. From his sense she could tell he was here for her answer.

So much for inner peace.

'Quite a view, isn't it?' Luke commented, coming up beside her and gazing out over the city. 'Must bring back memories for you.'

She threw him a patient look. 'Translation: How am I feeling about the homecoming this time. You know, Skywalker – just between us – you're pretty pathetic when you try to be devious. If I were you, I'd give it up and just stick with that straight-out farm boy honesty.'

'Sorry,' he said. 'Too much time spent around Han, I guess.'

'And Karrde and me, I suppose?'

'You want a straight-out farm boy honest answer to that?' She threw him a crooked smile. 'I'm sorry I even brought it up.'

Luke smiled back, then turned serious again. 'So how *are* you feeling?'

Mara looked back out at the lights. 'Strange,' she told him. 'It's sort of like coming home . . . only it isn't. I've never really stood here and just *looked* at the city like this. The only times I was ever up here were to watch for a certain airspeeder to arrive or to keep an eye on some particular building or something like that. Business for the Emperor. I don't think he ever saw the Imperial City as people and lights – to him it was just power and opportunities.'

'Probably how he saw everything,' Luke agreed. 'And speaking about opportunities . . . ?'

Mara grimaced. She'd been right: he was here for her answer. 'The whole thing's ridiculous,' she said. 'You know it, and I know it.'

'Karrde doesn't think so.'

'Karrde's even a worse idealist than you are sometimes,' she shot back. 'In the first place, he's never going to be able to hold this smuggler coalition of his together.'

'Maybe not,' Luke said. 'But think of the possibilities if he can. There are a lot of contacts and information sources out there in the fringe that the New Republc doesn't have any access to at all.'

'So what do you need information sources for?' Mara countered. 'Thrawn's dead, his cloning center is a shambles, and the Empire's in retreat again. You've won.'

'We won at Endor, too,' Luke pointed out. 'That didn't stop us from years of so-called mopping-up action. There's still a lot of work yet to be done.'

'It still doesn't make any sense to put me in the middle of it,' Mara argued. 'If you want a liaison between you and the smugglers, why don't you get Karrde to do it?'

'Because Karrde's a smuggler. You were just a smuggler's assistant.'

She snorted. 'Big difference.'

'To some people, it is,' Luke said. 'This whole negotiation process is running as much on appearance and image as it is on reality. Anyway, Karrde's already said he won't do it. Now that those vornskrs of his have recovered, he wants to get back out to his people.'

Mara shook her head. 'I'm not a politician,' she insisted. 'Not a diplomat, either.'

'But you're someone both sides are willing to trust,' Luke said. 'That's what's important here.'

Mara made a face. 'You don't know these people, Sky-walker. Trust me – Chewbacca and the guys you're sending out to transplant the Noghri to their new world are going to have a lot more fun.'

He touched her hand. 'You can do it, Mara. I know you can.'

She sighed. 'I have to think about it.'

'That's all right,' he said. 'Just come on downstairs when-ever you're ready.'

'Sure.' She threw a sideways look at him. 'Was there something else?'

He smiled. 'You're getting good at that.'

'Your fault for teaching me too well. Come on, what is it?'

'Just this.' Reaching into his tunic, he pulled out a lightsaber.

'What's this?' Mara asked, frowning.

'It's my old lightsaber,' Luke told her quietly. 'The one I lost at Cloud City, and nearly got killed with at Wayland.' He held it out. 'I'd like you to have it.'

She looked up at him, startled. 'Me? Why?'

He shrugged self-consciously. 'Lots of reasons. Because you earned it. Because you're on your way to becoming a Jedi and you'll need it. Mostly, though, because I want you to have it.'

Slowly, almost reluctantly, she took the weapon. 'Thank you.'

'You're welcome.' He touched her hand again. 'I'll be in the conference room with the others. Come on down when you've decided.'

He turned and walked away across the Palace roof. Mara turned to gaze out at the lights of the city again, the cool metal of the lightsaber pressed against her hand. Luke's lightsaber. Probably one of his last links to the past . . . and he was giving it away.

Was there a message in that for her? Probably. Like she'd said, subtlety wasn't one of Luke's strong points. But if that was why he'd done it, he'd been wasting his time. Her last link with the past had been broken in the Mount Tantiss throne room.

Her past was over. It was time to get on with the future. And the New Republic was that future. Whether she liked it or not.

Behind her, she heard Luke open the roof door. 'Hang on a minute,' she called after him. 'I'll come with you.'

THE END

STAR WARS Volume 1: Heir To The Empire
by Timothy Zahn

The Adventure Continues!

A long time ago in a galaxy far, far away . . .

It is a time of renewal, five years after the destruction of the Death Star and the defeat of Darth Vadar and the Empire.

But with the war seemingly won, strains are now beginning to show in the rebel alliance. New challenges to galactic peace have arisen, and Luke Skywalker hears a voice from his past, a voice with a warning.

Beware the Dark Side . . .

Heir To The Empire is the first volume in the authorized sequel to the most popular series in movie history.

A Bantam Paperback
0 553 40471 7

STAR WARS Volume 2: Dark Force Rising
by Timothy Zahn

Dark Force Rising moves with the speed of light across a dazzling landscape of galactic proportions, from world to world, from adventure to adventure, as Good and Evil clash across the vastness of space 'a long time ago, in a galaxy far, far away . . .'

Five years after the *Return of the Jedi*, the fragile Republic that was born with the defeat of Darth Vadar, the Emperor, and the infamous *Death Star* stands threatened from within and without. The dying Empire's most cunning and ruthless warlord – Grand Admiral Thrawn – has taken command of the remnants of the Imperial fleet and launched a massive campaign aimed at the Republic's destruction. With the aid of unimaginable weapons Thrawn plans to overwhelm the New Republic, and impose his iron rule throughout the Galaxy.

Meanwhile, dissension and personal ambition threaten to tear the Republic apart. As Princess Leia – pregnant with Jedi twins – risks her life to bring a proud and lethal alien race into alliance with the Republic, Han and Lando Calrissian race against time to find proof of treason inside the highest Republic Council.

But most dangerous of all is a new Dark Jedi, risen from the ashes of a shrouded past, consumed by bitterness, and thoroughly, utterly insane . . .

A Bantam Paperback
0 553 40442 5

FORWARD THE FOUNDATION
by Isaac Asimov

For more than forty years, Isaac Asimov thrilled millions of readers with his bestselling *Foundation* series, a spellbinding tale of the future that spans thousands of years and dozens of worlds. Completed just weeks before his death in April 1992, *Forward the Foundation* is the seventh and concluding volume of his masterwork, which was awarded a Hugo for the 'Best All-Time Science Fiction Series'.

In the earlier *Foundation* novels, Hari Seldon, the guiding genius of the Foundation, was a figure of history. By going back to the great mathematician's life, in *Forward the Foundation*, Asimov fills in the remaining gaps in his epic story. Asimov acknowledged that he always regarded Seldon as his *alter ego*, and this novel is all the more poignant for the fact that he himself died only weeks after writing about Seldon's death.

A resounding *tour de force*, *Forward the Foundation* offers the dramatic climax to the Foundation series, and perhaps the greatest moment in science fiction to date.

A Bantam Paperback
0 553 40488 1

A SELECTION OF SCIENCE FICTION AND
FANTASY TITLES FROM BANTAM BOOKS

THE PRICES SHOWN BELOW WERE CORRECT AT THE TIME OF GOING TO PRESS.
HOWEVER TRANSWORLD PUBLISHERS RESERVE THE RIGHT TO SHOW NEW
RETAIL PRICES ON COVERS WHICH MAY DIFFER FROM THOSE PREVIOUSLY
ADVERTISED IN THE TEXT OR ELSEWHERE.

☐ 40068 1	AZAZEL	*Issac Asimov*	£3.99
☐ 40488 1	FORWARD THE FOUNDATION	*Issac Asimov*	£4.99
☐ 40069 X	NEMESIS	*Issac Asimov*	£4.99
☐ 29138 6	STAR TREK 1	*James Blish*	£3.99
☐ 29139 4	STAR TREK 2	*James Blish*	£3.99
☐ 29140 8	STAR TREK 3	*James Blish*	£3.99
☐ 17452 5	UPLIFT WAR	*David Brin*	£3.99
☐ 17162 3	SUNDIVER	*David Brin*	£3.99
☐ 17452 5	STARTIDE RISING	*David Brin*	£3.99
☐ 17184 4	THE PRACTICE EFFECT	*David Brin*	£3.99
☐ 40317 6	ÆSTIVAL TIDE	*Elizabeth Hand*	£4.99
☐ 40317 6	WINTERLONG	*Elizabeth Hand*	£4.99
☐ 17351 0	STAINLESS STEEL RAT GETS DRAFTED	*Harry Harrison*	£2.99
☐ 17396 0	STAINLESS STEEL RAT SAVES THE WORLD	*Harry Harrison*	£2.50
☐ 40371 0	KING OF MORNING, QUEEN OF DAY	*Ian McDonald*	£4.99
☐ 40274 9	STAR OF THE GUARDIANS Book 1: The Lost King	*Margaret Weis*	£4.99
☐ 40275 7	STAR OF THE GUARDIANS Book 2: The King's Test	*Margaret Weis*	£4.99
☐ 40276 5	STAR OF THE GUARDIANS Book 3: King's Sacrifice	*Margaret Weis*	£4.99
☐ 17586 6	FORGING THE DARKSWORD	*Margaret Weis & Tracy Hickman*	£3.99
☐ 17535 1	DOOM OF THE DARKSWORD	*Margaret Weis & Tracy Hickman*	£3.50
☐ 17536 X	TRIUMPH OF THE DARKSWORD	*Margaret Weis & Tracy Hickman*	£3.99
☐ 40265 X	DEATH GATE CYCLE 1: Dragon Wing	*Margaret Weis & Tracy Hickman*	£4.99
☐ 40266 8	DEATH GATE CYCLE 2: Elven Star	*Margaret Weis & Tracy Hickman*	£4.99
☐ 40375 3	DEATH GATE CYCLE 3: Fire Sea	*Margaret Weis & Tracy Hickman*	£4.99
☐ 40376 1	DEATH GATE CYCLE 4: Serpent Mage	*Margaret Weis & Tracy Hickman*	£4.99
☐ 40377 X	DEATH GATE CYCLE 5: The Hand of Chaos	*Margaret Weis & Tracy Hickman*	£4.99
☐ 17684 6	ROSE OF THE PROPHET 1: The Will of the Wanderer	*Margaret Weis & Tracy Hickman*	£3.99
☐ 40045 2	ROSE OF THE PROPHET 2: Paladin of the Night	*Margaret Weis & Tracy Hickman*	£3.99
☐ 40177 7	ROSE OF THE PROPHET 3: The Prophet of Akhran	*Margaret Weis & Tracy Hickman*	£4.50
☐ 40471 7	STAR WARS 1: Heir to the Empire	*Timothy Zhan*	£3.99
☐ 40442 5	STAR WARS 2: Dark Force Rising	*Timothy Zhan*	£3.99

All Corgi/Bantam Books are available at your bookshop or newsagent, or can be ordered from the
following address:
Transworld Publishers Ltd, Cash Sales Department,
P.O. Box 11, Falmouth, Cornwall TR10 9EN

Please send a cheque or postal order (no currency) and allow £1.00 for postage and packing for the
first book plus 30p for each subsequent book ordered to a maximum charge of £3.00 if ordering seven
or more books.

Overseas customers, including Eire, please allow £2.00 for postage and packing for the first book,
£1.00 for the second book, and an additional 50p for each subsequent title ordered.

NAME (Block Letters)..

ADDRESS ....

....